Praise for

𝔄 Quest for God and Spices

"Opulent in historical detail and charming in its roster of characters, both authentic and imagined, Dean Cycon's *A Quest for God and Spices* is a grand historical joyride through the medieval world. Savor seafood pies in the merchant halls of Genoa, eavesdrop on the chambers of the Vatican as a pope obsesses over a new crusade. Risk the perilous trade routes from the west of Europe deep into Byzantium. Follow secret maps, while navigating dangerous intrigues and dodging assassins—all on a quest for material and spiritual riches."

—David R. Gillham, *New York Times* bestselling author of *City of Women*

"Dean Cycon transports readers to the intricate world of medieval Europe, weaving a tale rich with intrigue, politics, and the intoxicating lure of the spice trade. This historical novel unveils a hidden tapestry of history, from the shadowy corridors of Vatican power to the bustling markets between Genoa and Constantinople. With vivid detail and masterful storytelling, Cycon immerses readers in a journey where the stakes are as high as the rewards and every alliance is a gamble."

—Randy Susan Meyers, international bestselling author of *The Many Mothers of Ivy Puddingstone*

"A philosophical novel that touches on early medieval politics and theology and the clash of cultures during a turbulent time in Europe. A fascinating cast of characters from all walks of life and a vivid depiction of daily life, along with a journey that takes us from Genoa to Rome and all the way to Constantinople. I highly recommend it."

—Marina Pacheco, bestselling author of the Medieval Mysteries of Galen series

"*A Quest for God and Spices* establishes Dean Cycon at the head of this country's finest writers of historical fiction. With a meticulous eye that captures the feel of time long past and the places that live now only in memory, Cycon's work elevates the genre to a height rarely reached."

—Greg Fields, author of *The Bright Freight of Memory*, 2024 PEN/Faulkner Literary Award nominee

"Dean Cycon has served up a feast for his readers. They will relish the rich historical details, finely wrought characters, and driving plot on this epic journey from Genoa to Constantinople and beyond."

—Christopher Ives, professor of religious studies, Stonehill College

"This is a book to get lost in. In *A Quest for God and Spices*, Dean Cycon has created an immersive experience, bringing the reader into the vividly rendered world he creates. With an unerring eye, he brings the reader into a lush, harsh, and always beautifully rendered world of intrigue, trade, and shifting alliances. At its core, the book explores the complex and very well- observed relationship between a man grasping at heaven and another grasping at earth. With the characters of Mauro and Nicolo, Cycon interweaves Apollonian and Dionysian themes in ways that surprise and delight. A wonderfully textured work that explores grand philosophical questions while at the same time delighting the reader in the granular twists and turns of lust, greed, and ribald adventure. Cycon's love of the period and his research shines through in every scene and brings to life the twelfth century, from Italy to Egypt, in a way that is immediate and immersive. His characters are sharp-witted, sharp-tongued, and beautifully delineated. Cycon's prose is wonderfully calibrated, suffused with masterful control of dialogue, action, and characterization.

—Alfredo Botello, author of *180 Days* and *Spin Cycle: Notes from a Reluctant Caregiver*

EDITORIAL PRAISE FOR

A Quest for God and Spices

"A captivating adventure filled with both danger and astute theological inquiry. Two unlikely candidates are sent on a dangerous mission by the pope to Constantinople at the dawn of the thirteenth century. In this historically rigorous and dramatically absorbing tale, Brother Mauro, the quintessential intellectual, turns out to be surprisingly resourceful, and Nicolo, for all his worldly intelligence, callowly gullible. The author's writing is consistently clear . . . and the plot is gripping and brimming with suspense.

—*Kirkus Reviews*

"FIVE STARS. A wonderfully well-written historical novel that captures the era perfectly. I highly recommend this novel and its follow-up, *The Emerald Scepter* to all readers, especially history buffs."

—*Readers' Favorite*

"RECOMMENDED . . . compelling and captivating. The writing is polished and professional, and Cycon has done the necessary research to bring these exotic locations and cultures alive with vivid sights and scents. Both the main characters are likable and flawed . . . The book also has a wide variety of secondary characters with their own interesting stories and personalities."

—*The US Review of Books*

"A vibrant travelogue conjuring the rich complexities of the medieval world at the dawn of the thirteenth century . . . an immersive, illuminating pleasure."

—*BookLife Reviews*

ALSO BY DEAN CYCON

A Quest for God and Spices
by Dean Cycon

© Copyright 2025 Dean Cycon

ISBN 979-8-88824-515-6

All rights reserved. No part of this publication may be reproduced, stored in a retrieval system, or transmitted in any form or by any means—electronic, mechanical, photocopy, recording, or any other—except for brief quotations in printed reviews, without the prior written permission of the author.

This is a work of fiction. All the characters in this book are fictitious, and any resemblance to actual persons, living or dead, is purely coincidental. The names, incidents, dialogue, and opinions expressed are products of the author's imagination and are not to be construed as real.

Published by

◣köehlerbooks™

3705 Shore Drive
Virginia Beach, VA 23455
800-435-4811
www.koehlerbooks.com

A QUEST FOR GOD AND SPICES

THE EMISSARIES
BOOK ONE

DEAN CYCON

VIRGINIA BEACH
CAPE CHARLES

Hominibus semper inviso servatore fidem, Sive deus sive minor animo, sive lucida lucro. Raro tamen salvator exit, et in pulverem somnia resolvuntur. Ergo imperia fata.

(Men have forever put their faith in the savior unseen, be it a god, lesser spirit, or shiny lucre. Yet the savior rarely comes forth, and the dreams of men crumble into dust. Thus, the fate of empires.)

—Attributed to Pliny the Elder

CHAPTER 1

GENOA

"YOU DID WELL this year, Ludovici," Nicolo said, looking at his friend's list of purchases from the Great Fair at Troyes. Spanish linens, English woolens, and a few minor French trade goods. Profitable, Nicolo thought, but nothing exciting. "When you pay back the loan and share out the profits from the commendare your pocket should jingle with coins. The women will hear you coming before they smell you, if you are lucky."

Nicolo and his friends wedged themselves around one of the few rough wooden tables in the widow Balena's house, gorging on seafood pie and the excellent ale she prepared from her dead husband's secret recipe (a pinch of cinnamon and coriander in the mash). Like many a sailor's or merchant's widow in Genoa, the widow Balena kept afloat by opening her home for cheap dinners several nights each week. The precious spices she brewed into the ale were hard to come by and cost the widow dearly. Still, the unique taste of her brew drew men like bees to the nectar of the rock roses and peonies that dotted the walls and roadsides of the city. It was a good investment. This evening so many of Genoa's merchants had come to celebrate their successes at the Great Fair that her larger storeroom could hold no more. Tomorrow would be the Day of Settlement, when these young men would pay back the moneys or goods advanced for their ventures—tonight all they wanted to do was tell improbable tales of their travels and trades, drink, and spend.

The silver deniers, livres, and copper groats clinked in Balena's apron as she plunked two more ales on the table in front of Nicolo. It didn't matter that the widow couldn't read the different languages inscribed on the coins. Silver was silver and copper was copper. The noise from the rowdy crowd of brash young merchants hurt her ears, but a successful fair meant coins in everybody's purse, and a wonderful assortment of utensils, cheeses, wines, sugar, oils, and more from the homes, farms, and workshops of Europe to grace the lives of the Genoese. Nicolo scanned the room with pride. He knew that these men kept the blessed wheel of trade—the lifeblood of Genoa—turning and turning.

Ludovici took back the list of purchases, folded it carefully, and tucked it inside his worn brown velvet vest. He gave Nicolo a conspiratorial wink. "I am not going to pay my loan back just yet. I hear the cardinal is going to convince the pope to annul all loans from the Jews. I will wait and see what happens. Maybe I won't have to pay the money back at all." He made a motion to smooth his nascent mustache and sat back with a triumphant grin.

Nicolo frowned. "You are going to swindle your Jewish neighbors who loaned you the money for the Great Fair? Even if the church gives you an excuse, that wouldn't be right."

Ludovici ran his fingers through his greasy hair and squirmed in his seat. "Well, I always abide by the rules of the church. Sometimes it makes life hard, sometimes it helps." He took a sip of ale. "Anyway, my House is even smaller than yours, Nicolo diCarlo. Unless we figure out how to make more money, we will always be in the shadows of those damned great merchant families of our sweet Genoa. You and I both dream of having our own *fondaco* someday. Imagine, a warehouse right on the wharf! That would show them who we are, right?"

Nicolo laughed and saluted Ludovici with his mug. "It's true, my friend. Then I will sleep in a real bed, not atop a crate of spades from Milan covered by English wool. But no more fairs for me! I will make my fortune in the Syrian trade. Soon I will be taking those French, English, and Genoese goods to the crusader kingdoms of Antioch, Tripoli, and Tyre, or maybe to our trading settlements throughout the Muslim lands from Cairo to Aleppo. I want to travel and get lost in the souks and bazaars, maybe meet a dark beauty, eh?"

"Hah! If wishes were fishes, you would never be hungry, Nicolo. Antonio does all the Syrian trade for your family. You will spend your life in French taverns or maybe English brothels if you're lucky. You better accept it, Nicolo. We are the youngest. Our older brothers get all the glory."

Nicolo steamed inside. He had always been in the shadow of his taller, handsomer big brother. Their father, Marcus, relied on Antonio for everything it seemed, and Nicolo felt like all that was left for him were the crumbs and the clean-up. Their mother had been taken when Nicolo was very young by what the priests had called a "secret disease," which meant anything happening inside a woman that the priests or doctors didn't understand. He didn't remember her, although Marcus often remarked how Nicolo's sweet face and golden hair were so much like hers. Nicolo's father treated his younger son as too tender for this world, lavishing praise and responsibility on Antonio. Nicolo had never been permitted to venture overseas, being limited to the fairs and regional commerce. Even though Nicolo turned profit at the fairs, bringing home goods and coin aplenty, Antonio continually mocked his efforts as "children's trade." Nicolo hated the taunt and felt held back from achieving a name for himself and greater success for the family. He was smart enough. He was better at calculation than his older brother and was learning the new mathematics of the Arabs from his uncle, Benjamin the Jew. But Marcus said he was too impetuous, not ready for the rough and tumble of the Syrian trade.

"That is so, Ludovici, but Antonio is away to Milan and Venice for the new crusade. My father is too old to make the long sea voyages, so I will be the *factore* for our House on the next venture to the Syrian lands." A cloud passed over Nicolo's face. "Unless Antonio returns first."

"Nicolo!" boomed the voice of Petrus, the miller. "Stop your dreaming of whores and treasure. Let us begin the contest! Your nose against our drinks!"

Nicolo shook his head and smiled. "Well, Petrus, if you are willing to buy me drinks all night, who am I to deny you the pleasure?"

A cheer rose through the room. Somebody tied a blindfold tightly around Nicolo's head. He was well-known as a "nose," able to differentiate between the scents of spices and to sniff out whether the bag of grain on offer was near to mold or overly fermented. Even before he wore undergarments, Nicolo had been trained well by Marcus in the nose game.

Petrus quieted the crowd.

"We all know the rules, good Genoese. If Nicolo identifies the spice that is offered, the owner buys him a drink. If Nicolo can't do it, he buys one for the owner."

"Count me out!" cried Barbieri, the knife merchant. "Nicolo's got a snout like a pig for truffles. I'll keep my coin, thank you!" Barbieri was pushed to the back of the crowd amid much laughter and derision.

Nicolo easily identified the proffered thyme, lavender, and rosemary. Those were just local aromatic herbs used to prepare his nose for the more serious challenge of the foreign spices. His head began to swirl through the cinnamon, cassia, and mace, gulping down his winnings every time. He hesitated when a cloth full of peppercorns passed beneath his nose. He took several short breaths in and out, sensing the different textures and qualities of the sample. There was something off about this one. It was too sharp and grassy for pepper. Antonio used to trick Nicolo like this, his cruel humor actually improving Nicolo's nose. Had Antonio been trying to help prepare him or just mock his younger brother?

"This should be pepper, precious pepper—but it is not! These berries are made of oil, common mustard, and clay. Whoever bought these was tricked by the French bastard who rolled and sold them. Maybe you can pass them off to a Pisan or Corsican if you are lucky!"

Even the widow Balena howled as the merchant owner was pounded with fists and derided for his stupidity. Nicolo took off the blindfold and raised his hand to quiet the crowd.

"Poor Carlo. For your loss I will buy your drink tonight."

More cheers, a short fistfight in the back of the room, a broken stool. Nicolo noticed Balena gritting her teeth, probably thinking about the cost of the stool. *Surely it's a small price for her to pay for tonight's enrichment.*

As the fight broke up, Nicolo's friends broke out into a popular new song.

And the Genoese are so many,
They travel the world so fair
That wherever they travel and abide
They make a new Genoa there!

After identifying saffron, cumin, peppermint, and coriander and polishing off his winnings, Nicolo could barely keep his head up. But he needed to look strong in front of all his friends, so he raised his empty mug high.

"Let's have a toast!" He grabbed a small sack of spice that had been used in the game and held it aloft. "We know, good Genoese, that pepper, cinnamon, and these other spices have changed the way we eat, the way we smell, even how we preserve our dead. We can no longer live without them. Spices are our source of joy and prosperity." There were many shouts of agreement. "Yet we pay so dearly for these spices. Why? Because the merchants of Venice have a lock on the trade. More and more of our coin goes out of Genoa and into the pockets of the Venetians, while our people struggle to afford their spices." A bottle appeared and someone refilled his mug. "To the day we find the source of these spices and break the backs of the Venetians and their Muslim partners!"

A wild cheer rose as the merchants of Genoa drank deeply.

CHAPTER 2

ROME

LOTARIO DICONTI, POPE INNOCENT III, paced the polished Carrera marble floor of his private suite in the Lateran Palace. He clenched the aging missive from Presbyter John in his delicate hands and wished he could choke the secrets from the enigmatic document.

"I have read this letter a thousand times, Censio. I know Presbyter John is the key to recapturing Jerusalem and regaining the only relic of the True Cross. The last two crusades have failed, and our new crusade is struggling to begin. We will not succeed without his armies. Where is his righteous kingdom? What distances and dangers must be overcome to reach him?" The pope put the letter down and massaged his temples, calming the blinding pain that came on like a thunderbolt and receded quickly. He picked up the manuscript again and shook it angrily. "And where, *where* is William?"

Censio, the pope's private secretary, brought the pope a cup of tea steeped from willow bark. This was the pope's second cup of the early day. Censio was concerned that, while it did seem to soothe the pain, too much of it would cause vomiting, especially for someone as slight and physically frail as this man. He thought about the only relic of the True Cross, at least the only one the church recognized. He knew that Saint Helena, the mother of the emperor Constantine of Byzantium was said to have found the three crosses of Calvary and identified the True Cross by holding it to a dead man and bringing him back to life. She had the True Cross cut into thousands of small pieces that were dispersed all over Europe and the Holy Land. "By now there are enough pieces in the churches of Europe to construct a fully rigged war galley," he muttered to himself.

Censio understood the pope's frustration about William the Physician. Ever since Rome received Presbyter John's letter in 1165 describing his kingdom and pledging his loyalty and massive army to the crusades, successive popes had sought to find the powerful, unknown king in the distant East. None of the many emissaries sent had succeeded in reaching past the Seljuk Turks, who ravaged the lands to the east of Byzantium. None had returned.

"I fear William is lost to us," Censio said in a gentle tone, his low, droning voice a practiced salve for this new pope and for many before him. "It has been three years since he began his emissary."

Lotario sighed. "It is my fear as well. William was not fit for the venture. He was chosen due to friendship and position, not requisite skill. This has always been the problem with the emissaries."

A TIMID COUGH interrupted the pope's pacing. Lotario turned to see a recently appointed page, trembling with fear. "Your Holiness, it is time to meet with Cardinal Orsini regarding the new candidates."

Lotario pressed his temples again. The headaches came on whenever he had to meet with Cardinal Orsini. *Orsini is emblematic of the rot within the church that must be exorcised.* There was a lingering culture of privilege and corruption among the cardinals, the bishops, and their subalterns, although there were no longer orgies, murders, and licentious abuses of every kind within the Vatican itself. These poisons seeped out into the monasteries and the local pulpits, many of which had become the repositories of second sons, idiots, and ne'er-do-wells who used the church to pad their purses and their beds. Ordinary people, who sought God's protection and love in this dark world, were losing faith in the church as God's manifest presence, turning to a host of bizarre and heretical cults throughout Europe.

Lotario sighed. *A cleansing is needed, and I will be its agent.*

Censio helped Lotario cover his white linen tunic with a full-length red and white robe that symbolized purity and supremacy. He replaced the red *zucchetto* skull cap that he and all the cardinals wore with a white one reserved for the pope alone. The pope wanted to use everything he could think of to project his authority to the cardinal. Yet Orsini was clever and hard to defeat. When both men were apostolic secretaries, before Orsini was elevated to cardinal by Pope Clement III ten years earlier, they had played chess together regularly. It was Orsini who had brought the new chess pieces from the Persians styled after kings, queens, knights, and bishops to replace the old clay discs with ancient Roman markings. Orsini was always two steps ahead of Lotario or coming from behind with surprising and often foolhardy ferocity. He would have made a brilliant general, but he had chosen the accumulation of power within the church instead. Lotario had to admit the cardinal's tactical skills and raw intelligence were truly useful. Orsini himself had authored the College of Cardinals' new plan to send out two emissaries instead of one to search for Presbyter John. *What was his real motive in this? Could selfish interest ever be in true service? Did it matter so long as the plan worked, Christendom was united and purified, and Jerusalem was regained?* Even as pope, Lotario found himself at a loss to understand the mysterious ways of the Lord and the unfathomable minds of his fellow men.

※

"It is always such an honor to be in your presence, Your Holiness." Cardinal Orsini stood and bowed as the pope entered the great hall. The tapestries cascading down the high walls from the gilded moldings celebrated the glory and power of the office of pope. Angels trumpeting hosannas on the vaulted ceiling reminded Lotario of his position as the holy intermediary on earth. Still, in this sacred place, the pope struggled to fight back the feeling he was being mocked by the cleric before him. There was nothing in the cardinal's demeanor to suggest this, but Lotario knew Orsini well and had seen his unctuousness and humility mask sinister intent. Where the pope wore robes of spiritual authority, the cardinal was bedecked in fine silk and ornate jewelry that signaled power in this world. Orsini was a large man, a foot taller than the slight pope.

Lotario noticed the cardinal had grown quite fleshy in recent years. Certainly that came with age and the inactivity of high church office. But Lotario suspected it was also the result of Orsini's known habit of excessive drink and rumored dalliances with children—including, if the whispers were true, with Orsini's own illegitimate daughter, Lucretia. However, his personal life did not prevent him from rising through the ranks of the church. Whether due to patronage or blackmail, he had forged a large following within the church hierarchy. And how did the cardinal amass such great wealth? Behind the tapestries, the walls of the Vatican contained many secrets even the pope could not pry open.

Orsini looked into the steely gray eyes of the pope. The cardinal had been furious, of course, when the College of Cardinals had chosen Lotario instead of him as the new pope. He thought he had bought, cajoled, and arranged sufficient support to ensure his own ascension. Although the majority protested to him privately afterward that they had voted for Orsini, he was certain several were lying—he just didn't know which ones. The white smoke that rose from the College's inner sanctum and hailed the selection had spoken no names. *Cowards find such courage behind a secret ballot*, Orsini thought as he sized up the pope. But no matter, Orsini was a gracious loser. In fact, he realized he could exercise his power more effectively in the shadow of the pope. He had more freedom as a cardinal anyway. No papal guards with their prying eyes and wagging tongues to interfere with his private pleasures. *And now this opportunity to serve both Church and self so handily.*

"Your report, Cardinal Orsini," Lotario said abruptly.

Orsini noted the ice in Lotario's words. *He always was a snarling pup*, Orsini thought. *Yet I can forgive his insolence as long as I get what I want.*

"Lotario, I . . ."

"Cardinal Orsini! I absolutely insist you address me with the proper honorific. You must show respect for this office."

Orsini was delighted by the pope's reaction but adopted a repentant tone. "I am sorry, Your Holiness. It is difficult to change the habits of familiarity and friendship of so many years. Please forgive me."

"Continue," gritted the pope.

"Your Grace, I believe we have found the perfect emissaries. Two men whose abilities are wonderfully complementary. A combination of immense learning and practical skill." Orsini thought of William the Physician, a learned and likable fellow who had likely been robbed and waylaid before clearing the gates of Rome. He never thought William a wise choice to find Presbyter John, but until now his voice had held no sway in such matters.

"The learned man is Brother Mauro, the teacher of logic and rhetoric at the new university in Bologna. He is well regarded as a theologian and acquainted with the works of the pagan Aristotle who is so relished in Constantinople. While I personally challenge the usefulness of pagan writings, the College of Cardinals is certain this man can represent the true Word of God. He will use his talents to help bring Byzantium back into the fold as well as present our case to Presbyter John."

Lotario was aware of Brother Mauro, the monk who had left the monastery at Livorno several years earlier to teach at the new university. Mauro had been a troublemaker in the eyes of the abbot at Livorno. The monk's required, rote daily recitation of scripture often veered into commentary—a forbidden act. Yet it was precisely this fresh and sober thinking that Lotario applauded. He believed in Scholasticism, the use of logic and reason to support faith and challenge heresy, even though so many in the church fought to prevent independent and evolving thought. Were they trying to keep the faith pure or to maintain control over education and information—and therefore the minds of men? By all accounts, Mauro was incorruptible and devoted to research and teaching. *I cannot find fault with this choice, nor can I fathom the benefit to Orsini. Perhaps I am being overly harsh on the cardinal.*

"A good choice. A very good choice. My congratulations. And the companion?"

Orsini assumed the same blank look he used at chess. *Give nothing away.* "A young merchant from Genoa, quite capable of navigating the laws, customs, and unknown lands through which the emissaries must pass. Your Grace knows his family. The House of diCarlo. Their eldest son has taken the cross and is at this moment on his way to Venice with documents for the doge and to negotiate for the crusade."

"Does the father welcome having both his sons away on crusade?" asked the pope. "Usually a family only sends one son."

"Marcus diCarlo is a pious man, even if he is a Genoese merchant," sniffed the cardinal, pulling a loose gold thread from the piping of his silk sleeve. "Although I do not know him personally, he is well respected for fair dealings and supporting the church in Genoa. And perhaps, if I may hazard an opinion, Your Grace, as the family aspires to a higher position in Genoese society, having two sons in service to your office may be particularly appealing."

I cannot fathom a personal advantage to Orsini here either, thought Lotario. "Very well, let us interview these intrepids as soon as possible."

The cardinal bowed deeply. "Of course, Your Grace. With your mastery of rhetoric and logic, and your university experience, you certainly should examine the monk. As the young merchant is merely his servant and travel guide, I will ensure the lad is suitable and not bother Your Grace with that detail."

The pope thought for a minute. The monk was the critical player here. Lotario really didn't need to talk to the young companion. He came from a good family that had always provided loyal service to the church. "Thank you, Cardinal. That will suffice."

Orsini smiled inwardly. *Checkmate.*

CHAPTER 3

BOLOGNA

EVEN FROM THE street, Father Clement could hear the sonorous voice of Brother Mauro through the broken second-floor window. He pinched his nose against the smell of piss and spoiled food as he entered the dilapidated tradesmen's tavern. The priest hated these assignments for the cardinal, preferring instead the velvet cushion upon which he usually lounged while in his office at the Vatican. Yet, he was the cardinal's main counselor and was trusted to do the most delicate tasks. A small annoyance in return for the comfort and security of his office, and certainly better than being an administrator in the monastery. Clement was also aware that this decrepit wooden building and many others in Bologna were owned by the cardinal himself. The cardinal made a small fortune off the rents as well as a percentage of the rough trade that went on inside.

Father Clement stepped gingerly over the snoring whores, the burly cart drivers, and the foppish university students who lined the dirt floor and the few uneven tables in the place. *How could people waste away their days like this?* He knocked over an empty wooden flagon as he worked his way toward the stairs. The flagon rolled off the table and whacked a sleeping miller on the head.

"Careful, you motherless bastard, or I'll ram your balls down your throat!" snarled the nearly comatose tradesman.

Father Clement scowled at the deadened form yet ignored the complaint as he climbed the stairs in the direction of that familiar, deep voice. He stopped before a door on the second-floor landing, clucking his tongue at the sign on the door: University of Bologna—Logic and Rhetoric Class.

"University," he said dismissively. Clement knew the only true knowledge came from the Good Book, as studied in the monasteries. People did not need to think; they needed to obey. This new "university" movement was an affront to the church and could become dangerous to the social order if it caught on. He could not understand why the pope had supported the creation of this university and the expansion of the one in Paris. Most of the teachers were renegade monks from the monasteries, like Brother Mauro, and most of the so-called students were the wastrel second or third sons of nobility. Let their fathers pay tuition to keep these spoiled young men occupied. Writing skills, rhetoric, and the "natural philosophies" might produce the occasional useful scribe, notary, or counselor for the hinterlands. But these new universities were clearly more valuable for the rent they produced than for any potential contribution to society. *No, he thought, they will never be a serious challenge to the orthodoxy of monastic education.*

Father Clement quietly opened the door and slipped unnoticed onto a splintery wooden bench in the back of the room. Beside him a student dozed beneath the hood of his full black robe. Ahead, ten young men with hoods thrown back and sleeves rolled up sat before an animated, white-bearded monk—Brother Mauro. Clement was shocked by the casual manner of the class. Instead of scribing notes on dark, wax-covered shared tables with a sharpened bone or metal stylus, these students either took no notes at all or else they scribbled them down on their own personal parchments. Students shouted and interrupted Mauro, and the whole group seemed to argue with the master. He cupped his left hand to his ear, trying hard to hear through the cacophony what was going on at the front of the room.

"But what, then, is the true nature and purpose of love?" queried Mauro.

A very young man with a slight blond fuzz on his face ventured tentatively. "The highest purpose of love is to become a philosopher, a lover of wisdom."

"That's because you haven't gotten bedded yet!" cried out an older student to guffaws, hoots, and foot stomping.

Mauro replied quickly. "According to Plato, there are different kinds of love. There is lust, which you, Thomas, seem to embrace. This is common love, based on the body and not the soul. So, are love of God and love of a woman different types of love?"

An overweight student with a face scarred by pox called out passionately. "Lust is not love. Love is found in everything that exists, even in plants and animals. Love is a joining with God."

"Yeah, Gerome," countered another, "you go find your love joining with animals. For me, love is the most powerful gift of God in helping men gain honor. It is what inspires a man to earn the admiration of his fellows, for example by bravery on the battlefield."

Mauro raised both his hands, his eyes shining at the engagement of the students in the debate. "So are love of God and love of a woman different?"

The chubby boy answered quickly. "Yes! If we live for the love of God, we can escape the clutches of women and find wholeness."

"You miss the point of love. It is in the love of a woman where a man becomes whole. He regains the rib God took from him to form woman," stated a lanky, handsome dark-haired young man.

"However, Plato tells us man and woman were originally one doubled body, with faces and limbs turned away from each other. Zeus cut them apart to punish them for trying to climb to his realm. They have sought their missing halves ever since," Mauro noted. "This is why we say we have become whole when we find our true love."

The lanky youth snorted. "He said that to get a laugh. No one can believe such pagan silliness."

"But doesn't it sound to you like Adam losing a rib?"

The room became silent. Mauro sensed he had taken things a little too far in this session. The students needed to think about the nature of love, not fear they were committing heresy by comparing the Bible to pre-Christian works. The monk sat back in his chair and smiled at his students.

"Let me suggest a synthesis of these arguments. Perhaps the nature of love changes with age, just as our bodies do. As above, so below, it is said. In our youth we are prone to lust and to seek pleasures of the flesh. Yet as we age, we seek wisdom and the purity of beauty in all forms." Mauro watched the dawning of understanding in some of his pupil's faces. It felt good. It felt purposeful. "A spirited argument, indeed, my young fellows. Tomorrow, be prepared to switch sides and argue the opposite points. Remember, we are working on the structure of the argument for the moment rather than what is right or what is wrong, per se. Also, we will compare love and true pleasure according to Epicurus. Read his Letter to Herodotus for next class."

The students filed out, slapping each other on the back and laughing raucously. Two of the young men sniggered about the erotic language (as well as the name) of the Roman poet Maximianus that Brother Mauro had read at the beginning of the class. Father Clement shook his head and walked slowly toward Brother Mauro. When the moon-faced monk smiled broadly in welcome, Father Clement gave a brusque nod in return. *Maximianus, indeed,* he steamed. He was disgusted with what Brother Mauro was doing, teaching these boys about Plato and of all people, Epicurus. But Father Clement was here for the church and tried to keep his personal feelings in check.

"Epicurus? He was a debaucher who took pleasure in gluttony and bestiality."

Mauro chuckled gently. "Actually, those things are merely what his enemies said about him. How often men with good minds are attacked with untruths to diminish their influence."

"Socrates, yes, I know. Don't try to charm me into heresy

with your pagan friends. And how can you have these young men knowingly argue points that are not true? Why do you repeat your error of veering from truth into speculation? That is exactly what got you dismissed from the monastery. Have you learned nothing? Do you wish to guide these young men astray?"

Brother Mauro showed a wan smile. "Oh, Clement, I do them no harm. The Lord gave us free will and good minds to struggle toward the truth. Syllogisms, harangues, apothegms, and epigrams, the devices of reason and rhetoric, have the power to sharpen the mind for this blessed pursuit. Truth will always win out, don't you agree?"

Father Clement was befuddled by the terms Mauro used. *He is trying to confuse me, as he did at the monastery.* "Don't be so clever with me, Mauro. You allow these stallions too much rein. Once the bonds of respect and obedience are broken, they are difficult if not impossible to repair. You of all people should know this, as your disobedience caused your fall from grace at the monastery. Be careful how far you go with this." *The cardinal is wise to get rid of this man*, thought Father Clement. *It is easier to snuff out a candle than to smother a brush fire.* He smoothed his black velvet cassock with his long, bony fingers. "In any event, the cardinal has convinced His Holiness you are the right man for a sensitive diplomatic task."

"Me?" said the startled monk. "I am no diplomat. And I was not aware the cardinal held such a high opinion of me. What, may I inquire, is the nature of this sensitive diplomatic task?"

Clement bristled. "I am not authorized to discuss that with you. Pack your bag, leave immediately for Rome, and present yourself to His Holiness. I will say this much: you will be headed to Constantinople thereafter."

"An audience with the pope himself! How wonderful! And the great Constantinople! But what of my classes? We have several upcoming lectures remaining on the works of Pliny the Elder."

Father Clement winced at the name. Another heretic. "I am certain the tavern keeper will keep your—what do you call them?—*scolari*, your 'scholars' occupied. Perhaps Father Raulf from the monastery can come down and continue your good works."

"Raulf is a boring, half-deaf lump with eternal gas. I doubt my scholars would accept him."

"Accept him?" quizzed Father Clement.

"Yes, in our university it is the students who choose the master. They select him and negotiate his compensation per class."

"What a curious structure your university has. I, for one, do not think teaching should be a popularity contest or a business negotiation. There are simple and straightforward truths that book no argument, that merely must be recited and memorized as we do in the monasteries." The priest turned at the sound of laughter from the tavern below. He gave the monk a cold look. "Those scholars of yours are lucky to make it up the stairs, given the worldly temptations that lay below."

Mauro chuckled. "True enough, attendance is a trial by fire, but we have full classes. The students are sincere in their search for knowledge. Frankly, I am more concerned with them on their way out of the class than in."

"You may find this discussion humorous, Mauro," Father Clement hissed, "but I am not here to debate the merits of your classes or your university. I am here to deliver a command from His Holiness, and you would do well to get your affairs in order and get packing. Find some other miscreant from your university to teach your classes."

※

Mauro entered his cramped room above the glassblower's workshop, blinking repeatedly and waving his hands to disperse the acrid fumes that rose through the floorboards. His mind reeled with the possibilities of his new assignment. He was being called upon to use his talents as a rhetorician to resolve some papal dispute, that much seemed logical. But of what nature? That would have to wait. In the meantime, he needed to place his precious manuscripts in the care of the university. He went to his small writing desk and searched for a parchment. In his poverty, he usually scraped off the correspondence he received and reused the parchment. A cheap vellum of deerskin was all he possessed at the moment, so full of hair it could have been a vest. Its condition made writing nearly impossible. He took out his sharpening stone and scraped the hairs off the parchment, causing some small tears in the material. With the parchment sufficiently smooth, Mauro took out a quill pen and an inkpot. He wrote down the names of all the manuscripts he would be leaving behind, along with general instructions for the remainder of the course. He wondered how long he would be gone from his old friends Aristotle, Plato, Cicero, and the others. They were his daily companions, his joy, and his solace in this mad world. They allowed him a chance to dig beneath the surface of what was accepted, to see for himself what God had planted in the minds of the ancients and to bring forth that knowledge once more. It was not that Mauro doubted the veracity of the Holy Book—oh no, God was the center of his universe. It was just that he was so . . . curious about things in this world and not of it.

Mauro had been in the monastery since childhood and had known no life beyond textual study. He had made it his life's work to translate the ancients from Greek into Latin. *Translatio*, as it was called, bordered on heresy to the more conservative churchmen, as it brought forth writings considered pagan and forbidden by the very nature of their pre-Christian heritage. There were so few pagan manuscripts left since the darkness had descended upon the Holy Roman Empire over the ages. Some remained in monastic libraries, crumbling and forbidden. Some were in the private libraries of noble houses, ignored and unknown. What great storehouses of wisdom were out there if only Mauro could find them? Perhaps in Constantinople? He had heard the Byzantines had a love of knowledge and much translation was being done there. And their understandings of doctrine were so different from Rome's. Mauro would finally have an opportunity to share opinions and knowledge with other scholars and seekers.

Brother Mauro had also been working for years on his own *Summa Theologia*, a text that took the major questions of faith, lined up the arguments on all sides of each question and came up with reasoned answers. It was a daring piece of writing that he kept locked in a small wooden box under his straw mattress, but Mauro felt called to the work. What a different path he had taken from Clement since their days together at the monastery. Clement seemed to care nothing about the search for deep truth, appearing to thrive instead on proximity to power and blind adherence to the rules and dogma of the day.

Mauro reflected on his life at the monastery. Each day was spent in the drafty, damp *scriptorium*. He would stomp his feet and hug himself to keep warm as he pushed through the rote recitation and strict copying of texts, no variation or opining permitted. Yet Mauro knew there was always subtle rebellion in the monastery. He would often find small notes in the margins of copied texts, such as "Finished, Thank God, on the fourth of May in the year of our Lord 1165" or "Whoever reads this note, may he be blessed with wine and women, as I was not." Truly, the copying was drudgery, almost a punishment for being in the monastery. But the sonorous chanting of the Latin words during recitation often caused Mauro to float out of his body. And he *saw*, he actually *saw and felt* the meaning of those words. He couldn't stop himself from expounding, from sharing their beauty and profundity. The abbot, of course, didn't approve of that one bit, nor did Father Clement, who had the pleasure of rapping Mauro's knuckles to bring him back from his swoon. But if the monastery got in the way of Mauro's search for meaning, then he had to leave the monastery. His dismissal had not caused him grief. Rather it felt like a gift of freedom, regardless of how Clement and the other monks interpreted his departure. He felt his true religious life began when he had walked out of the isolated monastery and toward Livorno, one of a new breed of homeless, itinerant monks roaming the countryside, educating the people. It was his fortune to be overheard one rainy afternoon sermonizing under a tree in Bologna by the rector of this new institution, the university. Mauro was offered a job, subject to student approval, teaching logic and rhetorical skills, and sharing his learning, research, and insights in the classroom.

Mauro's research also introduced him to the most intelligent and interesting people, fellow seekers of ancient, long-buried knowledge. There was much translation being done in Al-Andalus, as Muslim-conquered Iberia was called, but to engage with Muslim translators of pagan writings was both heresy and political suicide. He had heard of Avicenna, a renowned Muslim doctor and translator, but could not find his works and didn't dare keep copies anyway. Mauro did happen upon the works of a man called Maimonides, a Jewish physician living in Cairo, who had translated and written so much of the ancients and had published his own philosophical musings as well. Mauro was dazzled by Maimonides's philosophies, seamlessly yet systematically comparing and blending Muslim, Jewish, and Christian themes. Maimonides also sought to find the political and cultural context of doctrine, including the Ten Commandments. This was a new and bold approach, heretical in the eyes of most churchmen.

Yet it was the Maimonides's sources that made Mauro long for travel. He cited Aristotelian works on astrology, mathematics, and magic. He revealed Greek texts on theurgy—the use of ritual and talismans to invoke the divine to intercede in one's life. Mauro noted (but dared not speak) how similar these practices were in substance, certainly not in form, to the growing acceptance within the church of petition, prayer, and devotional practices to seek divine intervention. He thought of transubstantiation, for example, where the wine used in communion turned into the actual blood of Christ. Although this belief had been around since the time of Bishop Cyprian seven hundred years earlier and was widely practiced, it was not official Church doctrine. Mauro longed to be in those great libraries and monasteries of the known world where ancient texts were freely available for study and translation. He imagined himself in heated debate with Maimonides and others, all searching to deepen man's understanding of God and the meaning of life.

Mauro suddenly realized he was absolutely unaware of the nature of this papal mission. What exactly was he being called upon to do? Would he stay in Constantinople? Was he to venture to other lands within the Byzantine Empire? Would he be sent to Cairo, where he could meet and debate Maimonides? Mauro reveled in the mystery and became increasingly excited as he put away his writing materials. He would go by road from Bologna to Genoa. Afterward, the road to Rome was too dangerous to travel on foot and the distances between safe lodgings too great. He would have to travel from Genoa to Rome by boat. That thought made him shudder. He did not like the sea. It was too vast to comprehend. The darkness beneath the ever-moving surface made Mauro lose his reason. The sea was like the heavenly realms in its unknowable endlessness, but it seemed a place of darkness, not of light. Mauro sat down on his coarse hay bedding and took a deep breath. He let go of his fear of the sea as he thought, *I am going to Rome.*

CHAPTER 4

GENOA

AS HE STEPPED back to let his visitors enter, Marcus diCarlo tried not to look worried. *No good could come of a visit from representatives of both the law and the church*, Marcus thought. He led the men to his sitting room, a small area situated to keep prying eyes from seeing the contents of his storeroom. He knew he should have offered ale to the men, but Marcus sensed that this was not a social call. The priest's black cassock and pale skin gave him the aura of a prophet of doom, and the lawyer's black outfit reinforced the message. Marcus thought irrelevantly for a moment about the contrast in the cost between the velvet cassock and one of wool but brought himself back to the moment. *All right then, let them have at me.*

Father Clement surveyed the meager trade articles in Marcus's house, those he could see, anyway. Functional articles like spades, brooms, and bolts of rough wool cluttered the anteroom. *Either the diCarlos only deal in minor goods or they put these here to obscure the more valuable materials in their warehouse.* The priest made a mental note to find out. The diCarlo family had always been useful to the church, acting as a go-between for the commercial endeavors of local churchmen and even the cardinal himself. These families, like all merchants, were merely tools for the church to accomplish its earthlier goals. He smiled warmly at the merchant. "Marcus, I am sure that you know Albertus Augeri, the lawyer and notary. I have asked him to accompany me in discussing a most delicate matter."

Marcus knew of the notary. These men kept official ledgers of all commercial transactions in Genoa. Although a handshake had always been sufficient to consummate a deal among the merchants of Genoa, somehow this class of men had managed to insinuate themselves into the very fabric of daily commerce. These days no deal was valid unless it had been entered into a notary's ledger, even if it was nothing more than a two-sentence notation regarding a minor loan or advance. Marcus was unsure whether this represented progress toward a more efficient commercial system or the calculated triumph of a group of greedy, yet clever and well-connected men. But this man was also a lawyer, an advocate. *What is he doing here with the priest?*

Father Clement continued. "Marcus, I am terribly sorry to hear of the loss of the *San Giorgio*. All that cargo." He let out a practiced sigh. "And of course those poor souls on board. Tragic. So many Genoese lost their investments in that piracy, including, as you certainly know, the office of the cardinal himself, as well as many of the local clergy here."

"Yes, Father, it was a tragedy. We don't yet know for sure if it was the Pisans or those damnable Corsican pirates, the *corsairs*, but the cargo and the crew were totally lost."

"Well, yes, and that brings us to the sad business of reparations."

Marcus thumped his hand to his chest. "Excuse me?"

Father Clement looked mildly surprised. "Why Marcus, it was your House that chartered the vessel and your House that created the consortium of investors for the venture. You bear responsibility for the loss and must repay the investors in full according to the law."

The blood drained from Marcus's face. Repayment of the entire investment would more than break his House. That meant the rest of his life in debtor's prison and his sons on their own. Now he understood why the lawyer was here. But he knew that he was not liable, he knew the maritime law of Genoa.

He took a deep breath before replying. "I am afraid I don't understand your position, Father. We all signed onto a *societas maris*. It was a standard maritime trade contract. Everyone was responsible for their own investment in case of a loss."

"Quite true," interjected the lawyer Augeri in a voice edged with the tension that precedes combat. "Yet as agent, the responsibility for loss was completely yours in the case of . . . negligence."

Marcus's eyes widened. "Negligence! It was piracy! I couldn't have expected an act of piracy almost within sight of our harbor. This is insanity! There was no negligence here."

Father Clement looked sad. "Oh, Marcus, I wish it were so. But you should have foreseen the possibility of the attack. After all, Genoa is in a constant state of hostility with Pisa and Corsica as well. And apparently your captain was sailing too close to the shore, thereby inviting attack."

"Indeed, it would have been prudent to divide such a valuable shipment among two or three ships to minimize the risk of loss," intoned the notary. "Of course, you took the risk to get your cargo to port before any others, seeking to get the best prices. You put your commercial gain above the best interests of the investors."

"Certainly you can argue the case before the Commune Council of Genoa, but I doubt you will find a sympathetic ear," the priest interjected.

Marcus felt the room closing in around him. He knew the council was made up of members of the Great Houses of Genoa and there were few who would support a small House against the financial interests of the cardinal and the clergy. They might even enjoy giving Marcus his comeuppance for daring to aspire to their status.

Sensing Marcus's despair, Father Clement knew it was time to go in for the kill.

"There, there, Marcus, don't be so defensive. You have long been a friend of the church and there is a way to resolve this . . . difficulty. His

Holiness is sending a deputation to Constantinople to help bring the errant Byzantines back to the church. The chosen emissary is a wise and learned monk, but he does not have the experience of the road. His Holiness desires him a companion. He specifically mentioned your son."

"But Antonio is already away to Florence, Milan, and Venice on behalf of the crusade . . ."

"Not Antonio, Marcus. Your younger son, Nicolo."

"Nicolo? He's a smart young man, but he hasn't traveled much beyond the fairs. Besides, I have already given a son to the crusades. With Nicolo gone I will have no one here to help me."

Father Clement gave a serpentine smile. "Of course, you have sacrificed much for the crusade, and it has been noted. Antonio will be rewarded upon his return with a notary's office here in Genoa or in Rome, as you like. That will guarantee your House access to many contracts and opportunities with the church. Nicolo's mission will not be long, nor will it be dangerous, unless you count the boredom of having to listen to theological debates. And it is well-known in Genoa that your youngest is somewhat . . . less than responsible. I believe supervised travel with a more mature man of the cloth will do the boy some good, and I am sure you agree."

"If I may, Father," interjected the notary, "let me get to the point, as there is a much sweeter honey in the pot. If Nicolo serves the emissary honorably on this important mission, the cardinal has declared that you will be absolved of any wrongdoing or negligence regarding the loss of the *San Giorgio*. A fair trade, if I do say so myself."

Father Clement put his claw-like hand on Marcus's sleeve and led him to a corner of the room, turning his back to the notary. "Look, Marcus," he whispered, "this is a good deal for you. I lost a considerable amount of money on that voyage, as did many of the clergy in Genoa and most of your friendly whores, as well. Yet we are all willing to forgive, at least the clergy are, if you will support this mission to Constantinople. Have your son ready to proceed to Rome immediately for the monk's papal audience. There is nothing in this but good for the House of diCarlo and for all of Christendom."

Marcus quickly calculated the gains and the losses of this potential venture. He didn't care about the cardinal's and the priests' losses. They knew the risks they were taking. He was pained by the loss of life and the loss of the investments of his friends, the local sailors, and the town whores. Marcus made a mental calculation of their losses to see what, if anything, he might be able to pay back. Genoa was a small, close-knit community. Marcus did not want to chance losing the trust and friendship of the working people of the waterfront. And what of Nicolo? The fairs were over and there was little to do immediately. Nicolo did have a habit of getting into trouble when he wasn't kept busy. The boy was smart enough and could use the travel. He would have the chance to use his new mathematics skills in the markets of Constantinople, maybe find some interesting trade goods there. How long could this Church business last? Five or six months? By that time, Antonio would be back, and his House would be readying trade missions for the following spring. And it was critical to avoid any liability for the piracy loss. It was trumped up, but it would cost a lot to fight and there was no guarantee of justice with high churchmen involved. Marcus made up his mind. He turned back to the notary with a forced, ingratiating smile.

"Of course the House of diCarlo will accept this honor. Nicolo will be ready to begin his service tomorrow. I trust there will be a full agreement in the notarial records?"

"Of course," replied the priest, visibly relieved. "Oh, and one other thing before we go. You would be well advised to keep your distance from Benjamin the Jew. The winds of change are blowing, and I wouldn't want to see you hurt by that association."

Marcus was startled. "Benjamin is a distant relative on my wife's side. He is an honorable man who teaches Nicolo the new mathematics of the Arabs. It is a harmless pursuit but one that may be very useful in business in the future. Besides, I thought His Holiness was ordering greater protection for the Jews."

"Indeed he is. But His Holiness is also considering negating all debts from Christians to Jews, as they are contrary to scripture."

Marcus was astounded to hear this from Father Clement. Marcus knew the priest had taken short-term loans from local Jews. He probably borrowed money to invest in the *San Giorgio* venture. "Contrary to scripture? How is that?"

Clement raised himself up to his full height and adopted a stentorian, pious tone. "In accordance with long-standing Church law, based on the Prophet Ezekiel and Saint Luke, interest charged on a loan is forbidden, it is *turpe lucrum*—filthy gain. We know that all loans from Jews carry interest. Thus, the debts are usurious and forbidden." He looked to the notary for confirmation before continuing. "We know that your House receives, how shall I call them, *advances* from Benjamin, which are nothing but loans with interest disguised as investments. Don't protest, Marcus, this is not unknown in Genoa. I am just cautioning you for the good of your House to be careful with this relationship."

Marcus held back his anger. *Damned holy hypocrite.* Marcus was well aware that although Christians were barred from lending to one another, there was a loophole for Jews lending to Christians. That was in Deuteronomy, plain as day. He knew that everybody doing business in Genoa, including the cardinal himself, had taken loans from Benjamin and the few remaining Jews in the city. He also knew from Benjamin that this was a well-known pattern among the church and the nobility. Borrow a lot of money from the Jews and then claim the loans weren't valid under Church law. This was usually the precursor to expelling the Jews and confiscating their property. But there were very few Jews left in Genoa after the last expulsion a decade ago. *The cardinal must be trying to wring out every coin he can before making some change to the law of Jews that'll benefit him and his cronies. Well, that is their cross to bear, as they say, not mine. Time to kiss the priest's boney ass again, for the sake of the family.*

"I greatly appreciate your sage advice and will certainly keep Nicolo away from those people."

NICOLO AWOKE TO a hammering inside his head, slowly realizing that his father was pounding on the door of his "room"— the small warehouse in the back of the house where he slept, guarding some of the trade goods at the same time. The young man slid off the wool seconds (the shavings of some English sheep's ass, complete with flecks of dried dung, but still more comfortable than straw) that topped the packing crate he used for a bed. He stubbed his toe on a Milanese shovel and banged his head on a hanging Florentine chamber pot as he made his way to the bolted door.

"Coming, Father!" he mumbled. Nicolo splashed water on his face from a Venetian silver goblet he kept near the bed, shook the cobwebs from his head and opened the door. There stood Marcus, his face a thundercloud of anger. Nicolo panicked. "I am sorry I came home so late, Father. We were celebrating our success at the fair and it got a little out of control. I didn't lose any of our funds this time, I swear it!"

Marcus couldn't hold onto his anger in the face of Nicolo's ridiculous appearance and penitence. He shook his head and sighed. "Forget about last night, my son. This new day brings more than enough troubles of its own." Marcus explained the visit from Father Clement.

"This sounds like a good deal, Father. We will be off the hook for the sinking of the *San Giorgio,* and I can travel and look for trades for our House." *And,* Nicolo thought, *I get to escape Genoa for Rome and Constantinople. I can make my own name, have my own adventures, and come back a rich man! That will show Antonio who I really am!* He looked his father in the eye imploringly. "Please Father, I can do this. I will bring riches and fame to the House. I will make us the richest House in all of Genoa, I—"

"I have already agreed to it, my son. But control yourself. It is that impetuousness that always gets you into trouble. You have so many skills, my son. The new math, your knowledge of the values in trade—and that nose of yours!" Marco pinched Nicolo's nose. "Keep it safe and don't put it where it doesn't belong." He put his hands on his son's unshaven but soft cheeks. "All I want is for you to come home alive and to do the House honor. Our reward will be a notary's position for your older brother when he returns from the business of the crusade. Isn't that wonderful? When Antonio is set up in Rome, you will have ample opportunity to make your mark here."

Nicolo choked back his anger. *Why am I always in the shadow of Antonio? I am cleverer than he is. I know the new mathematics. Just because he was born first? But I am going to Constantinople. The greatest trading port in the world. I can make a fortune there in a fortnight.*

Marcus put his hand on his youngest son's shoulder. "I know what you are thinking. My young stallion is champing at his bit again. That is a good thing, but you must wait your turn." He smiled fondly at Nicolo. "You know, I was the youngest son in my family too. The older boys were groomed for the notaries or other positions at court. I was always angry about that growing up. But they also had the responsibility of supporting the entire family. Be thankful that weight will never rest upon your shoulders. We youngest were always to be merchants, make some money, support ourselves, and generally stay out of trouble. If you play your cards right, Nicolo, we will all get what we want. Now go to your Uncle Benjamin's house, thank him for your lessons, and say goodbye. We need to put a little distance between us and your uncle for the moment. Then go to the docks and arrange passage on the next galley southward. You are going to Rome."

As Nicolo headed toward the door Marcus added, "And get your hair cut before you leave, short and clean like your brother's. That shaggy mane of yours will make you look unprofessional in front of the important people you will meet in Rome."

NICOLO'S MIND RACED through a thousand possibilities as he walked the streets of Genoa toward the ghetto, where the remaining Jews lived. The term was currently in vogue to describe Jewish sections of towns. It had originated in Venice, Uncle Benjamin said, where the Jews were isolated on a small island, or gheti, in the coarse Venetian dialect. It was also a dark play on words, as the verb ghettar meant to throw out or cast away. Nicolo had heard the term used commonly now for any Jewish quarter throughout the trading realms. He walked up the broad Via della Magdalena, with the sun shining on his face and glistening off the granite underfoot. He passed the workmen placing the last stones in the new Cathedral of San Lorenzo. He stopped and looked up. It was the tallest church in Genoa by far, a testament to the increased riches of the booming Genoese trading houses. The outer walls of the church were built of alternating layers of white and black marble. The door frames and lintels were cut from a green stone imported from far down the coast. He spied his friend Robert, the mason, on a scaffold nearby.

"Hey, Robert! What news?"

His friend stopped troweling, looked down, and brightened. "Ah, Nicolo! Wonderful news! We are going to receive a very special relic to christen the church, a relic from Rome itself!"

"And what piece of a miracle will that be, my friend?"

"The basin that held the head of John the Baptist! Can you imagine! And from France a silver reliquary arm containing the hair of the Virgin Mary herself!"

Nicolo contained a chuckle. He thought this relic business was outrageous. There were four basins that once held the head of John the Baptist (and even one actual head) for sale at the Troyes fair alone this year. *Either there were a lot of fakes, or the Sainted John washed his hair often*, he mused to himself. "A miracle for us all!" he shouted back to his friend as he moved on. *There does seem to be quite a market for relics,* he thought. *Maybe I should keep my eyes open for a bargain or two in Constantinople.* Nicolo wondered how men could be so easily fooled by a replica of something that is supposed to be sacred, or by something that never existed. But if the counterfeit could evoke such a powerful response—bringing people to tears and wails and getting them to throw some of their few coins in the collection box—did it matter if it was real or not? What is a market, after all, but the creation and satisfaction of a craving?

Yes, Nicolo concluded, he would be doing a great service to the religious among them by supplying Genoa with bogus but authentic-looking relics. He also considered how lucky he was to live in Genoa, a city controlled by hardheaded men of commerce, not superstitious religious fools like Robert. And yet religion was big business in Genoa. It was not that the Genoese themselves were so pious. Rather, a new economy was developing to service the thousands of religious pilgrims on their way from Europe north of Genoa to the Holy Land. Pilgrims loved churches and relics, so churches and relics they got. They needed accommodation, so new buildings like the *ospitale* had sprung up to house them. And of course, where there were travelers there were prostitutes. Genoa always had a thriving rough trade. After all, it was a major seaport, and whores and sailors kept each other afloat. But the boom in pilgrims had brought an explosion in the sex trade. In spite of the church's very explicit prohibition on prostitution, the ever-practical Genoese recognized the inevitability and perhaps necessity of the trade and chose to formally embrace it. Prostitutes were registered, regulated, and taxed. Most were assigned to special houses and strictly limited to certain areas of the city. Of course, those houses could not be located anywhere near the courtyards of the Great Houses, even though their sons were among the most regular of customers. Instead, they were set up down by the docks, where the transient clients tended to be. Thus was the sex trade made safer for the women and their clients, and the commune profited by the steady tax revenues it produced.

As he walked further up the hill toward the ghetto, Nicolo could see the twin watchtowers that marked the great gate of Porta Soprana in the new stone wall that protected Genoa from marauders in the hills to the east. Travelers by land from Milan or Florence were at constant risk of attack by feuding armies, German mercenaries, or knife-wielding rogues. He could see the richly garbed guardsmen peering out of the two tall towers that rose from Porta Soprana, but they looked west toward the sea, not east toward the hills. Even though the wall was recently built, it had become something of an honor for the sons of the Great Houses to stand guard over the town instead of paid watchmen. Nicolo knew that the real motive was that the "guards" could look out to sea from that high point and spot ships approaching Genoa on the slate gray Ligurian sea before others knew of their presence. Then these noble guardsmen would desert their posts in the towers and share the news with their families, guaranteeing that their houses would be the first to profit from the goods contained aboard those vessels. The wall served another purpose, Nicolo reflected. The price of housing inside Genoa was climbing higher every year, yet it was possible to build a house outside the wall for little or nothing if you were willing to take the risk. Many of the minor merchant houses, like that upstart Columbus family, had begun building just beyond the gate. Nicolo scoffed at the idea of that small trading family ever amounting to anything as he approached the house of his uncle.

THE FEW REMAINING Jewish families in Genoa lived in an unremarkable area. The wooden houses were small and the windows smaller, the latter a protective measure against hooligans who attacked the houses every Easter in drunken retribution for the murder of their Lord. The new pope had forbidden such attacks, but they happened every year anyway. The entrance to the ghetto used to be guarded by a watchman, who questioned anyone going in or out about their business, and a heavy chain was strung across the narrow alley leading to the quarter at night to keep out marauding horsemen. But as most of the Jews had left Genoa, the town fathers decided to spare the expense of security. The guard post was deserted, and the chain was sold to a visiting French ship owner.

Inside Benjamin's house, a small group of Jews gathered to share news of the latest disaster to befall their community. One family was considering returning to France, even though six years earlier King Phillip had expelled them, confiscated their vineyards and property, and reneged on all loan obligations. Jean Strauss, the father of this family, noted the irony of returning.

"King Phillip and his corrupt administrators so mismanaged the property they looted from us that now the good king wants us back. He wants us to manage our old vineyards for him and produce the revenues he so sorely needs for his crusades! Can you believe the arrogance? Yet where else can we go? It is clear that we can't stay here much longer. That damned cardinal is poisoning the new pope's mind against us. So far, the pope has been generous. After all, he prohibited people from beating us with clubs on our holy days, and outlawed digging up our corpses and holding them for ransom, didn't he? And yet, and yet, how long until he bends to the will of the cardinal and all those who profit by our persecution? Some of the towns are beginning to force our kin to wear the yellow cloth, just like the Mohammedans do to the Christians when they retake lands from the Latin kingdoms."

An older, red-haired man spoke. "Ahh, they made us wear the yellow cloth in England, too, but it was easy enough to buy an exemption from the local priests. And we only had to wear it in the town we lived in—we could take it off when we traveled. It's just another way to squeeze a few coins out of us, that's all."

"I am certain that this is just a passing phase," said Benjamin in a soothing tone. "In a few years all of these leaders will come to their senses, realize our importance to their communities, and all will be well."

"Well, we aren't going to wait for the Messiah, Benjamin. We are headed north, to the German lands. Jews have never been persecuted there and the princes are calling for Jews to come and settle," said another man, a glassblower from Milan.

"Not quite true," replied Strauss. "The walled cities are safe enough, but the ignorant and superstitious people in the countryside rise up and kill us whenever there is a rumor or tragedy. A child goes missing or dies from some ailment—we are to blame. A church is robbed of its golden chalice—we melted it down and sold it. Things get bad for us every time a madman or a false preacher happens by."

Another of the French Jews, Eliezer the leatherworker, shook his head in agreement. "These Christians have no sense of their own history. The old Roman emperors used to blame them for floods, fires, and even the silence of their temple oracles. You'd think they'd have more sympathy, but now it's their turn to blame us for all their misfortunes."

"The crusades make it worse," added Simon, a middle-aged rabbi who had come to Genoa from the kingdom of Hungary. "It is not safe to live anywhere that is on the crusader's path to the Holy Land. The knights and their followers slaughter our brothers and sisters each time they pass through. They say they are cleansing the path to Jerusalem. Some of the churchmen urge the pilgrims to kill Jews and be forgiven their sins as they embark on the crusade. Sure, a few bishops try to protect our congregations, but many of the local clergy participate in the carnage and grab the dead's possessions in the name of their parish. Now this new pope is calling for another crusade, since King Richard the Lionheart failed to take back Jerusalem. Pilgrims and camp followers are already flocking through Genoa. How long will it be before they smite us right here, even in the face of the pope's protection?"

Benjamin sighed. "The history of violence against us is true enough, but the madness and slaughter of the crusades has largely died down. The first crusade was an unruly one. It was disorganized and brutal. The violence has dropped considerably since the priest

Bernard of Clairvaux published his pastoral letters forbidding harm to Jews during crusade."

Simon shook his head wearily. "Do I need to remind you of the crusader Emiho of Leiningen, who slaughtered a thousand of our flock in Mainze and a thousand more on his rampage through Hungary before the king stopped him? There has always been hatred, jealousy, and violence toward us, but these crusades offer the steppe-wolves an excuse for wholesale slaughter."

Eliezer offered hopefully "Yes, but sometimes the crusaders and even the priests can be bribed to leave us alone. Here in Genoa, men rule for commerce not religion, and don't want their comfort disturbed. They have been good to us."

"For now," observed Simon dryly. "Yet I have heard that the cardinal is trying to get the pope to revoke the ban on usury. The rulers will have no use for us if that happens. They will be able to get loans from their own people. Once our value to them is gone, we will be left to the mobs and torn to pieces." He noticed Benjamin looking doubtful. "You have become wealthy and comfortable, Benjamin. You think like a Christian because you live like a Christian. You think you are safe, but you are not. Wealth invites envy, envy invites intolerance and hatred. We know where that leads. Don't forget the lessons of our history among the Christians. A conflagration is always just a spark away."

"And you, my cousin, have become too cynical. You spy a murderer in the eye of every Christian. Not all Christians are that way, not even the majority. We have done well here in the company of good people. We are safe and won't be leaving."

Simon scratched his bearded chin and scowled. "We are always under threat. There is only one small group in all of Christendom who can count on being left alone. The pope's Jews."

Eliezer cocked his head. "I don't know that expression."

Simon continued wearily. "Eliezer, don't you know that the pope allows a small number of Jewish families to live in the shadow of the Vatican walls? They are under the protection of his office. The church believes that the ultimate punishment for the nonsense that we murdered our rabbi, their Lord Jesus, would be to keep some of us alive to witness the coming of the Messiah. The surviving Jews would go to Hell in eternal agony after that, and a Jewless paradise on earth would arrive. So there you have it, prisoners awaiting the ultimate torture."

Eliezer was aghast. "That's ridiculous!"

"Of course it is," Simon said with resignation, "but they believe it nonetheless." He looked slowly around the room at this misbegotten gathering. He saw men who looked so different from each other, yet in the eyes of the Gentiles were all the same. Some he had known a lifetime; others had recently come into the community in Genoa. He knew that he would never see most of them again after they dispersed. Any thoughts of safety for his wandering people were illusory. "And we, my friends, are not even the pope's Jews."

Nicolo knocked four times, paused, and knocked twice, the agreed-upon signal. The scarred, windowless door opened slowly, revealing a stunning young woman of eighteen, with raven black hair and twinkling blue eyes.

"Welcome cousin!" cried Esther. She turned toward the darkened room, "Father, it's Nicolo!"

Benjamin got out of his chair and walked up to Nicolo, embracing him and shepherding him into the main room of his house. He closed the inner door to keep his other guests hidden. "What a wonderful surprise, Nicolo, but what are you doing here today? Your lesson isn't until the morrow."

Nicolo explained about Father Clement's visit, all the while casting furtive glances at his comely cousin. They had grown up together and had run freely through the town as children. Of course, that had stopped when Esther came of age, but they held a deep affection for each other. Esther was Nicolo's tutor and adviser in all things woman.

Since they were so close, she spoke freely and bluntly, arming Nicolo for the struggles ahead. At the same time, she pounded into him the need to be respectful and keep his cleverness and charms at the ready, not to squander them every chance he got. Nicolo took her advice seriously, refraining from too much whoring with his friends. When the time came, he would be a gallant and a charmer.

Nicolo also learned how to be a good loser from Esther, who was even better at the Arab mathematics than he was. Uncle Benjamin would often pit them against each other to see who could tally sums or solve mathematical riddles faster. Usually Esther won, sometimes distracting Nicolo's attention by mischievously brushing a hand against his leg during the calculations. Nicolo was willing to pay the price for those precious moments. Also, since a woman's rights to own property and engage in commerce for her own account were secure in the laws of Genoa, even for the Jews, Esther had made a small fortune investing in various trade ventures. Jews could not be members of most guilds, but they could back them financially, and Esther was particularly adept at spotting the trends in fashionable clothing and beating other merchants to the marketplace. She even invested in the Syrian trade, purchasing bolts of silk and gold thread. Nicolo was certain she'd had cargo on the *San Giorgio*, but was too polite to ask, especially in front of her father.

BENJAMIN PONDERED NICOLO'S words. He knew Nicolo was ready to go out into the world, and this was an amazing opportunity. At the same time, he knew that there were many other young men in Genoa who could serve the theologian on his trip to Constantinople, and the family had already committed one son to take the cross. So why Nicolo? Unless there was some danger of the lad not returning. The church wouldn't want to waste the life of the son of a Great House. No, something else was happening. He spoke evenly to Nicolo.

"Nicolo, you are a gifted lad. You know trade well and you know the new mathematics better than anyone in Genoa." He ignored the flash of anger in his daughter's eyes. "But you are not yet wise to the ways of the church or the nobility. My advice is to be humble, act the part of the servant to this theologian, and keep your eyes open for opportunities. But never, never, trust anyone you don't know or reveal anything about yourself unless necessary. Information is power, my nephew. Gather it but don't share it. And whatever you do," he said, turning toward Esther with a smile, "don't let yourself be swept away by a woman. They can be your best allies or your fiercest enemies. They are often used by their fathers or lords to pry information out of foolish young men. Be on your guard."

Nicolo laughed. "I have been schooled by the best, Uncle Benjamin. No skirt will be pulled over my eyes unless I want it to be." He could not see Esther's blush in the darkened room.

"You should also know, Nicolo, that wherever you go along the trade routes from Rome to Constantinople and even beyond, there will be a family of Jewish traders you can count on for information and even for help. These good people have had to rely upon their wits to keep them alive throughout these troubled lands. They and we are always strangers at the whim of the powerful and a step away from the mob. To ensure their survival they have become very sharp in knowing which way the winds blow; the winds of commerce to feed their families, of course, but more importantly, the winds of changing circumstance. You know what I mean, Nicolo. Wherever there is a plague it is blamed on the Jews. Wherever there is a scandal or business misfortune the guilty party, usually a powerful man, accuses the local Jews of perfidy. Many common people believe this nonsense and take perverse pleasure in tormenting their Jewish neighbors. That is why Jews seem so wily and clever. We have learned hard lessons in survival in a hostile world. We can offer wise counsel. Don't be afraid to call on one of us, Nicolo. You are family."

Esther walked Nicolo to the door as her father returned to the men in the rear of the house. As they brushed arms in the narrow hallway, Nicolo was entranced by the light scent of some unknown oil that Esther had dabbed behind her ears. She had become something of an alchemist of late, mixing essential oils to produce these intoxicating fragrances. Nicolo was aware that she had created a market selling small vials of her preparations to other merchants' daughters, and Genoa had become more delightful for it. Of course, she couldn't join the perfumers' guild. Not because she was a Jewess, per se, but because she couldn't swear the required Christian oath on their patron saint, Mary Magdalene, chosen because she had anointed the feet of Jesus with fragrant oils. Esther looked up at her handsome cousin, her eyes clouded by a deep sadness. Nicolo raised an eyebrow and gave her a cocky grin.

"What's the matter, sweet cousin? Jealous that I am going on a great adventure? Don't worry, I will be back in no time—and as a rich man."

Of course she envied Nicolo. He could travel alone anywhere he wanted, buy and sell anything at all. Even though in Genoa she had more freedom than women in France and elsewhere—especially Jewish women—Esther was painfully aware of the limits on her opportunities. She did the best she could with what she was allowed, but she dreamed of what she could do if she had Nicolo's unappreciated freedoms. But that was not what troubled her. She shook her head slowly. "Oh, Nicolo, I don't care where you go or how rich you become. I just don't know if we will be here when you return."

"What are you talking about?" He pushed back the lock of hair that had fallen before her eyes. Those beautiful eyes swam in liquid blue pools.

"Father says there is trouble brewing. Most of the other families are thinking of leaving Genoa soon."

Nicolo had never thought about being without Esther. His heart began to ache. Was it the magic of her unfamiliar and maddeningly alluring scent that caused Nicolo to open up to a tenderness he had never experienced, or was he finally acknowledging the depth of his lifelong feelings for Esther? He took her hand and squeezed it gently, holding it for a hundred swirling revolutions of the sun and moon before speaking. "Beloved cousin, there is nothing that will keep us apart. Wherever I go, I will return to you. Wherever you are, I will find you."

※

AFTER LEAVING BENJAMIN'S house, Nicolo went down the hill to the port. The sights, sounds, and smells of busy Genoa ultimately taking his mind away from his cousin. He passed the many wooden and brick warehouses belonging to the Great Houses, trying to decide which one would belong to his family after his successful venture to Constantinople. The families had taken to calling the warehouses "fondacci," a word Antonio said came from the Arabic funduq. Nicolo thought it arrogant to adopt the foreign word, especially from the Muslims, and that the families were just trying to rub their worldliness into the faces of the lesser houses. He walked down side streets such as Sail Alley and Rope Way, named after the rows of workshops belonging to the tradesmen who supplied the Genoese merchant galleys with the ropes, chains, barrels, nails, sails, oars, and a hundred other necessities for a successful voyage. Sinewy, sweaty men at hot forges grunted in recognition as he passed. Dogs yowled as hot sparks shot out from the forges before the hiss of water cooled the glowing iron of newly hammered barrel hoops. The low hum of the rope-winding devices provided a constant background for the euphony of Genoa's burgeoning maritime manufacture. Nicolo knew so many of the young men who apprenticed in these workshops that it took most of the afternoon to get to the docks. He stopped briefly at the corner of Cooper Alley and Love Way, where he shared pleasantries with a few of the blurry-eyed ladies of the morning shift, who leaned languidly against the stone warehouse walls. He could linger without cost in the scent of the crushed flowers and oils they rubbed around their necks and between their enticing breasts. Were these Esther's concoctions or had imitators found a new audience among these women? He broke free from the last conversation with Rosalaura (as well as the hand she slipped down his pants) and walked out of the alleys and into the graying afternoon. Relics and whores, he mused. Business is booming in Genoa!

Nicolo marveled at the forest of masts that greeted him. He thrilled at the confusion of shouted commands and ribald comments, the squeal of ungreased blocks raising cargo, and the tatting of hammers that rent the tangy air of the harbor. Genoa had become the greatest power in the Mediterranean. The clumsy, almost square buses carried tons of grains up and down the coast. Flat-bottomed scows took enormous granite pieces and giant logs to the builders of churches and plazas throughout the northern shores of the Mediterranean. Its galleys were huge and swift, the largest carrying over a hundred rowers and soldiers. The Genoese were such formidable sailors that they had even been chosen by Emperor Charlemagne long ago to do the impossible—to transport an elephant from North Africa to Rome on the deck of a galley. Nicolo ached to ride those galleys into the future and onto distant shores.

The early fathers of modern Genoa had turned a deep, natural cove surrounded by an arching peninsula into a protected and fortified harbor. The *molos*, as the earthen and stone wharves were called, were already two hundred years old when Nicolo was born. They and their protective walls and towers had been built largely of ballast bricks from ships returning to Genoa without large cargoes and chinked with waste scraps of Carrera marble from the building trades. The marble and bricks had the odd habit of releasing reddish liquid when it rained. It was said they cried tears of blood to remind mariners of family and friends taken by the sea. *They cried this day for the men of the San Giorgio,* Nicolo thought solemnly. *Good men sacrificed for the glory of Genoa, their deaths a willing butcher's bill paid for a chance at fortune. How much am I prepared to pay for that chance?*

Nicolo strolled down the wharf imitating a sailor's gait and whistling a popular tune. He was careful not to slip on a slime-covered dock plank and look the fool as he approached Captain Marcelo, an old family friend and one of the best captains in the fleet. The captain was overseeing the loading of massive hewn timbers and granite onto a long, flat-bottomed scow. The captain gripped Nicolo's hand with bone-crushing strength, his smile creasing a face more weathered and worn than the parchment chart of the Ligurian coast the mariner carried aboard.

"We are shipping this stuff to Bonifacio on the isle of Corsica. We took that port last month and need to expand the wharves. I must speak with your brother about building supplies, contracting more craftsmen, and arranging a grain shipment from Malaga to Bonifacio soon."

Always Antonio. "My brother is away arranging supplies for the crusade, but I will be happy to get these contracts set up for you," Nicolo said brightly.

The old captain frowned and fished a splinter from a gnarled finger with his teeth. "You? You're just a guppy. Well, maybe I need to talk to the Columbus family. They're always hungry for the work."

"No, please," Nicolo urged. "Let me get my father to speak to you today. You know my family will do the job well and at a fair price."

Captain Marcelo relented, his smile revealing how he enjoyed the stricken look on Nicolo's face. "Well, all right then. I'll have a word with your father."

Nicolo then described his need for a swift passage to Rome. When the captain demurred that there was no room on the next ship as it was filled with pilgrims on their way to Rome and then on to the crusade, Nicolo confided that he was on a mission for the pope himself. Captain Marcelo looked at Nicolo skeptically, scratching his grizzled chin.

"His Holiness himself, y'say? Well, maybe we can squeeze one more pilgrim in the hold. After all, it is only a three-day voyage—if the winds are fair and the Pisans stay in port."

Nicolo thanked the captain profusely and headed back toward his home.

※

Marcelo thought about finding out what this secret mission was, if in fact it was anything at all. He knew Nicolo, like most young men of Genoa, was full of himself, full of tales, and as fickle as the winds off Porto Venere, but the captain never missed an opportunity to put a coin or two in his sea chest. Behind him, old Giulio spat loudly as he coiled the bitter end of a dock line.

"Why were you teasing that boy? You know you were going to talk to Marcus about the provisions today."

Captain Marcelo grunted. "The boy is puffed up like a French pastry and he's as green as goose shit. He needs a little seasoning before he can become a decent trader for his House. He's got to learn how to react to uncertainty." He shook his head and stared hard at the crew loading the granite. "These young fancies don't understand how much their fathers struggled to build their houses. They've grown up with too much privilege and see the world through the bottom of a flagon. Old Marcus won't live forever. This boy's got to earn his sea legs before he can stand on his own. He's got a long way to go before he can match that older brother of his."

※

Not far from the docks, Brother Mauro sat on the second-floor balcony of the Ospitale of San Giovani de Pré. The hospital was a business idea borne of the need to house and feed the hundreds of pilgrims who passed through Genoa on their way to the various crusades. Instead of having to beg on the streets for lodging in stables, churches, or private homes, pilgrims could come to the hospital and be guaranteed food and lodging at a reasonable price—safe from the pickpockets, whores, and toughs who preyed upon the pilgrims in every town they passed through. The first floor of the hospital held the beds and dining area for the pilgrims. The second was for the many pilgrims who became ill along the way. This floor had a roof but no walls, as it was believed that the sea breeze would blow away the afflictions of the stricken travelers. Mauro took a deep breath of the briny sea air, becoming lost in thoughts of using his rhetorical skills to help return the errant Byzantines to the true church.

Mauro looked out over the masts into the gray sea that seemed to merge with the distant horizon. He had never been at sea and reflected on the immensity of it and the terror it held for him. He tried to calm himself by thinking of all the positive connotations of water in the faith. *Christ was baptized in the River Jordan. Moses floated down the River Nile to escape death at the hands of the Egyptians. The Waters of Life meant sustenance and redemption. Amos said that divine justice shall flow like a river.* His inclination toward rhetoric challenged that comfort. *Ah, but those were all fresh waters. Salt water is the realm of Satan and monsters. The sea represents temptation and the dark fate of those who succumb to the desires of the world. Fresh water is life affirming—salt water is life taking.* Mauro sank into misery. He sought to comfort himself for the morrow's voyage with the words of the Psalms:

If I take the wings of the morning and dwell in the uttermost parts of the sea

Even there your hand shall lead me, and your right hand shall hold me.

THE EARLY MORNING sky was gray and full of menace as one hundred pilgrims boarded the galley *Minervi*. All but two scurried safely across the wobbly boarding plank, while the crew laughingly fished the others out of the harbor. They all wore the rough, brown wool robes and loose head coverings of pilgrimage, made shabby by weeks on the road, and each clutched a small sack that contained a few copper coins, a wooden spoon, and for a lucky few, an extra shirt. The galley was short, at forty feet long, and squat, designed to be jammed with trade goods and passengers for brief coastal runs. A large boom was secured to the single mast, allowing a huge, ungainly sail to be raised by four crewmen hauling on the coarse, bristly manila halyards. Although the large sail made for greater speed, it also made for exaggerated roll, pitch, and yaw—and very queasy stomachs. Nicolo arrived late in the boarding and had to squeeze between two fat pilgrims blubbering prayers of protection in some Northern dialect while gripping each other's hands tightly. He looked back at the raised poop deck to see Captain Fiori smiling and shaking his head. Fiori was the same age as Nicolo and had grown up on the galleys. Nicolo tried to move back toward the stern but was too engulfed in the sweat and prayers of the pious to make any sternway. Mauro looked back at the captain, as well, wondering fearfully if the man was an angel who would deliver him safely on his first sea voyage, or was he Charon, ferrying these poor souls across the River Styx to their eternal damnation. At the captain's command the twenty rowers began to pull, taking the *Minervi* away from the dock and out of the harbor. Nicolo noticed how quickly the rank human and tidal smells of the harbor were replaced by the sweet, salty air of the open sea.

<hr>

MARCUS LEANED AGAINST the molo with his arms crossed, watching the *Minervi* cast off with a mixture of feelings. Both of his sons were gone, and he was alone for the first time in his life. Antonio, as always, was forging ahead on a well-paid and portentous trip. Nicolo was off to . . . where? He thought about how different his sons were. Antonio was serious and straightforward. Marcus knew that Antonio looked askance at Nicolo, disapproving of the younger brother's flippant and casual attitude toward life. Antonio was hard on Nicolo. Was it out of love and protectiveness, or insensitivity? Marcus couldn't tell. He wished his sons could be less combative and competitive with each other. After all, besides Marcus they were all each other had in this world. He tried to raise his sons equally, but their demands were so different. Antonio seemed to thrive on responsibility, so Marcus gave him more and more. Nicolo didn't seem interested in making money or improving his lot; he just enjoyed taverns, a little trade, and the occasional tart, so Marcus didn't treat him as seriously. Marcus felt a twinge in his heart. Were his sons different because of who they were or because of how he had treated them? He was doing the best he could to raise his sons without a mother. If Nicolo needed more, he would have to find it out in the world. With a start, he realized it was time for Nicolo to leave Genoa after all. As the monotonous chant of the *Minervi*'s rowers and the splash of syncopated oars faded away, Marcus silently wished his youngest son luck, God's speed, and a safe return. He knew he would not come back the same man.

※

THE WIND WAS steady and strong from the northwest. If it held there would be one tack all the way from Genoa to Rome, and the rowers would have no work to do until the port of Civitavecchia was hailed. A flock of black-hooded gulls cawed ceaselessly as they followed the galley, seeming to mimic and mock the pilgrims. Captain Fiori looked up at the gulls and back over his shoulder at the brooding clouds beginning to scud across the sky from the western horizon. A steady passage, for sure, he thought, but a wet one. Fiori's family had been seafarers forever. His uncles built these coastal galleys south of Genoa in Vernazza, on the Cinque Terre. He and his four brothers were the captains who guided the vessels in the trade. Lately, more and more of their business came from ferrying pilgrims to Rome and beyond. There were so many, in fact, that the family had set up a regular schedule of departures, something unheard of on the docks of Genoa until now. It was boring but steady and remunerative work.

Mauro's fear of the sea was quickly forgotten, replaced by a deep, green queasiness he had never known. The monk held onto the rail, trying to stay upright as the tiny galley rolled from side to side. He felt the runny eggs he had for breakfast at the hospital sliding around in his belly—and they wanted to escape. It didn't help that pilgrims on both sides of him were puking into the sea. Finally, he cried, "Mother of God!" and belched out a torrent of yoke and slime.

One of the crewmen shouted out mercilessly. "Look! A holy man! See how he casts his bread upon the waters!" Some of the other sailors laughed. The black-hooded gulls screamed and dove into the sea, snapping at the floating remnants of Mauro's misery. The captain just sighed. He was used to pilgrims throwing up all over his galley.

Nicolo looked at the burly, graying monk who let out that plaintive plea and pinched his nose. He had his sea legs and no tolerance for those who didn't. He looked back at Captain Fiori who beckoned him to the poop, shouting "Clear away all! Let that man through!"

On the small poop, Nicolo stood next to the steersman, who maneuvered a large oar to keep the galley from yawing in the following sea. Captain Fiori clasped his hand on Nicolo's shoulder and gave him a wry smile.

"The word on the dock was that you are going to Rome to take holy orders." Pleased by Nicolo's shocked look, Fiori continued. "Now, now don't be upset. Lots of youngest sons take the orders. After all, Antonio can handle the House of diCarlo, so you are free to follow God's path. Besides, you will have more chances to pry open the local locks as a priest than you ever had in Genoa." Fiori laughed and Nicolo realized he was playing him. Fiori then quizzed him on his venture, but Nicolo only replied vaguely that he was going to Rome to meet with some new trading partners. Captain Fiori changed tack, realizing that Nicolo wasn't going to budge. He talked about the recent port captures and the continuing maritime wars with Pisa, Amalfi, and occasionally Sicily.

"With any luck, we will have Pera and half the old Byzantine territories on the mainland soon."

Nicolo said he was more interested in trade than conquest, which made Captain Fiori snort with derision. "If we don't control the seas, you can't trade. By the end of this day we will be sailing past the flotsam of the *San Giorgio* most likely. There's your trade without power, Nicolo. We need colonies, ports, and control over the seas to keep Genoa strong. That is the basis of trade. Only from there can you merchants come in and trade in peace."

"I see your point, Fiori, but we are at peace with many of the Arab lands. They need our commerce, we need theirs. Ever since trade has strengthened between Genoa and Egypt and Syria there have been no attacks by Muslim pirates on our shipping. If we build strong trade networks, there will be no war and no need to control their lands or they ours. So here we are, at peace with the infidels and at war with all the other Christian lands between here and the Syrian coast."

"Well, maybe you are right, but try telling that to the Venetians. They used to be a pissant little colony and now they are our fiercest competitors for trade and control of the sea. The old doge is a scheming bastard who is only interested in loot. I know Antonio is headed to Venice right now. He will be lucky if he doesn't wind up with a knife in his back instead of a contract in his hand." Fiori noticed the pained look on Nicolo's face and quickly added "Nah, your brother is a smart fellow. He won't let himself be ambushed or tricked in Venice. He'll be fine."

Nicolo didn't want to argue with his friend. He was worried about Antonio, much to his surprise. He also saw Fiori's point about conflict with the Venetians. Nicolo had only traded in the safe places to the north of Genoa, long established territories with well-regulated commerce and patrolled roads. No, it was different out on the open sea and beyond. He thanked Captain Fiori for the insight.

The seas flattened overnight, and the wind steadied. They sighted no other sails. Stomachs calmed and nerves were soothed. At noon on the second day it began to rain. It was a drizzle at first but quickly turned into a downpour. The galley was an open vessel, except for the small cuddies under the poop and the bow. Those places were reserved for delicate cargo and the officers. Nicolo was invited by Captain Fiori to sit under the poop deck during the worst of the rains.

Mauro sat stoically on the deck, his thick woolen robe getting heavier by the hour. He tried to pass the time talking to some of the pilgrims, but most of them were illiterate and had nothing to say beyond platitudinous repetitions of what some country monk had told them. Instead, he used the time to recall the philosophies of Plato. He thought of the Allegory of the Cave, where Socrates tells of man's ignorance, confusing the shadows cast by a fire on a cave wall with reality. Knowledge allowed men to break the chains that bound them in the half-light of the cave and emerge into the sunlight. Alas, most men would run back into the cave, seeking the comfort of the known. Was ignorance bliss, or was the pain and hard work needed to become liberated from ignorance worth the journey? He lined up the arguments, pro and con, in his mind. He may have mumbled his points and counterpoints, because when he came out of his reverie most pilgrims had moved as far away from him as the crowded and salt-sprayed slippery deck would allow. The rain relented on the dawn of the third day, replaced by a broiling sun. The crew and passengers were dry and content by the time the galley reached the approach to Civitavecchia harbor.

CHAPTER 5

ROME

PAOLO, THE PAPAL tailor, held up the mirror and held his breath. He silently prayed to Homobonus, the recently venerated saint of tailors, that the pope would approve of his new red velvet hat. It was taller than that of any previous pontiff for whom Paolo had worked. At the pope's direction, Paolo had placed two jeweled tiaras on the conical hat instead of the traditional single tiara. He suspected that this short pope wanted the new hat to enhance both his physical stature and his temporal authority. After all, this man had been pope for just over a year and had already wrested control of the church away from the now dead German who called himself Henry VI, the Holy Roman emperor—as if there was any empire left from those glorious days of Paolo's Roman ancestors. Since the German had been poisoned in Sicily the year before, there were only a bunch of squabbling kingdoms and treacherous nobles vying for the crown. Indeed, the pope had just created for himself the title of vicar of Christ to show that he was equal to kings in this world and superior in the next. *Yes*, Paolo concluded, *my tall, jeweled hat is perfect for the head of our new pope.* But these thoughts were not the province of a mere tailor. Paolo was just happy, no, *blessed* to have the work. He had four daughters to feed—and to hide from that lascivious cardinal and the visiting high churchmen who sought his services while in Rome. Paolo knew he had to keep his fingers busy, his eyes open, and his mouth shut.

The pope turned from the hand mirror and walked to one of the long, gilded mirrors that graced the walls of his private chamber. He stood up straight and struck a pose of authority. "This is a masterpiece, Paolo. Such fine velvet and regal jewels must have cost you considerable coin."

"The price of wool for the velvet is higher than last year to be sure, Your Holiness. There is a shortage of first quality wool from the English flocks." The tailor cursed the fickle weather in those bleak lands. "And, in truth, high quality silk has gone up in price as well, although I cannot explain why. Good silk is one of the Venetian monopolies. The Venetians obtain their silks from the Muslims, who get them from God knows where in the strange East, where the finest silks are produced. Pardon my language, Your Holiness. And the dyeing, plus the difficult weaving of the silk with wool to make the velvet!" the tailor blurted. "The dyeing guild, the weavers' guild, and the raw silk and wool merchants each demand payment up front," he lamented as he thought, *while I have to wait forever to be paid.* He had taken out a very large loan from Moses, his old friend and moneylender, to purchase the jeweled tiaras. *Almost a year's earnings! Well, at least under this good pope I no longer have to give ten percent of my fee secretly to the apostolic secretary.*

The pope smiled. He took off the hat, inspected the fine stitchery, and passed it back to Paolo. He rubbed his temples gently.

Paolo panicked. "Is it too tight, Your Holiness? I can repair it within the hour." The tailor worked his fingers together nervously, as if he were still sewing the hat.

"No, Paolo," the pope said gently. "It is perfect. There is much that weighs heavily upon my head. Your exquisite work only lightens the load. Thank you, you may go."

Immensely relieved, Paolo cradled the hat as he bowed and

backed out of the room. After the polished double doors closed, he walked quickly down the marble corridor, thinking about the first tiara hat he had made for Pope Alexander III twenty years earlier. That pope couldn't pay the Vatican bills, so he pledged the hat to some merchants in Rome for twelve thousand florins. The merchants allowed the pope to wear the hat on special feast days, but it had to be returned each time until it was redeemed four years later. *Disgraceful!* Paolo wondered again how long it would take for him to get paid. He left the building with his head swirling about money, the changing times, and his daughters.

Lotario moved to the balcony of his suite, followed by Censio. He listened to the incessant pings and thwacks of the hammers of stonemasons repairing the massive Leonine Walls, the forty-foot-high surrounds topped with archers' towers that had protected the papal court for almost four hundred years. He turned toward the shouts of the foreman overseeing the construction of the new Vatican buildings.

"Lift together! Together, you pitiful worms! Be thankful you can touch the stones that will bring glory to us all! Together, I said!" The foreman cursed at the unfortunate, unskilled pilgrims in their gray-hooded frocks who volunteered their labors for the sake of the church. Although they were mostly strong, if simple, farmers, their grunts of effort and pain showed they were not accustomed to hefting such large granite blocks.

"How fitting," Lotario mused, "that the new seat of our authority is being built with stones from the crumbling remains of the pagan Emperor Nero's vile circus. Perhaps those very slabs were drenched with the blood of the martyred Apostle Peter."

Censio shrugged. After forty years in service to the Vatican, there was little that surprised or enlightened him. "Isn't that always the way of succession, Your Holiness? The new power builds its temples on the sepulchres of the old. All our great churches are built atop the crypts of Romans, Greeks, Celts, and other nonbelievers. Mosques become churches and churches become mosques as control of cities and towns in the Holy Lands change time and again."

The pope lifted an eyebrow. "I don't know what I value more, Censio, your wisdom or your cynicism." Lotario turned to observe the construction of the expanded administration, a great library, and a new armory for the growing Papal Guard. "Stone by stone we are rebuilding the church itself." The pope let his gaze go to the south, as if he could see all the way to the Holy Land. "Our future depends upon Jerusalem, Censio. It is a mirror unto our souls. God has taken away our sacred jewel because of our sins, our loss of piety, just as my predecessor Gregory predicted a dozen years ago." Jerusalem had surrendered to the Muslim raider Saladin later in the same year as Gregory's encyclical, *Audita Tremendi*. "And what of the progress of our new crusade?"

"I must confess it has been difficult, Your Holiness," Censio reported. "Fewer princes and kings are willing to take the cross, even though doing so cleanses their sins, suspends their debts, and protects their lands while on the sacred mission. But your new strategy of looking past the kings to the nobility is bearing fruit. We have word from Champagne that a dozen powerful French nobles are meeting to consider taking the cross," he said. *While their kings avoid their duty or pay the church handsomely for exemptions.*

The pope had already sent emissaries throughout the Christian realm to secure troops, money, and supplies for the crusade. He had even sent that Genoese merchant to the detestable doge of Venice to negotiate for ships and horses to ferry the crusaders to the Holy Land. The new strategy of going from Venice and Constantinople by ship to the Latin kingdoms closest to Jerusalem was proving quicker than the long land route, yet it relied on the doge for successful execution. *I am embracing the Devil in this, but Jerusalem must be regained.*

Cleanse and reunite the church, join the crusade with the massive forces of Presbyter John from the distant East, and Jerusalem and the True Cross will be restored. Lotario rubbed his temples again. *And perhaps then my headaches will go away.*

⚜

THE PORT WAS fifty miles away from Rome, yet it was the great city's main outlet to the sea. Like so much of that scarred land, Civitavecchia had been under the control of the Byzantines as the northernmost extension of their power, of the Saracens who sacked Rome, and of various counts and monasteries over time. It was now part of the prefect of Vico, although there was some talk of making it part of the church's lands. It was a thriving hub of trade, diplomacy, and treachery. Mauro gathered his belongings and trudged off the *Minervi* and onto land. He and many of the pilgrims began lurching and swaying down the road, their unsure legs trying to regain the land. Mauro walked toward Trefontane, an ancient monastic complex with vast landholdings and secular power halfway between the port and the great city. Of course, the monastery's position was helped by the law requiring all grain grown in the prefect to be milled at the monastery. If a farmer was unable to pay for the milling, the abbot could seize his lands, and often did. The monastery had been destroyed and rebuilt several times over the centuries, but only seemed to come back stronger, like some stubborn weed. It had been sacked by its own monks and all the treasures stolen, yet still managed to have a marvelous amount of silver and gold, fabulous statuary, and reliquary. The real fame of the monastery, however, was in its amazing medicinal herb garden. The monks at Trefontane were known for their uncanny ability to prepare poultices and medicines to treat the ill. Mauro knew that if these same skills were possessed by a woman instead of a monk, she might be stoned or burned as a witch by the locals. He was aware that much of the medical knowledge at Trefontane was obtained through the great works of the Arab doctor Avicenna, which had come to the monastery from Sicilian traders and through monks passing by from Al-Andalus. The church formally rejected these writings as heretical and had strictly forbidden the practice of medicine by clergy as a violation of God's design. Yet, as a practical matter, the writings were very useful in the understanding and treatment of illness, and the new pope seemed more open to understanding how people could be cured of illnesses than previous popes. After an introduction and a tour of the medicinal garden, the abbot asked Mauro to translate a difficult passage from a Greek manuscript in the library that was beyond the skill of any of the resident monks. In return, the abbot allowed Mauro to spend the night in the library, reading their banned copy of Avicenna.

Nicolo spent the first night in port on board the galley, drinking a tart, acidic Sicilian wine with Fiori and his officers. In the morning he began the long walk over sunbaked roads to Rome, knowing he would need to stay at a tavern along the way. This close to Rome the roads were pretty safe, but Nicolo didn't want to take any chances. He carried a small knife under his loose-fitting tunic. He felt certain he could defend himself against a loaf of bread or a breast of chicken, but he had never used it against another man and hoped he never would.

On the second night he stopped at a small inn. He opened the door to a fetid, steamy, packed house. Fresh mutton was on offer and the ale, the sailors told him, was particularly good. Nicolo ordered a plate but found the mutton exceptionally bland. He realized that an inn that catered to passing travelers wouldn't waste coins to add expensive cinnamon, pepper, or other spices to this meal. If he ever sold spices, he would lower the cost. Then more innkeepers and ordinary people would buy them. He could make up the lost profit in volume. But that wouldn't happen while the Venetians controlled the spice trade. By the time the spices arrived in Genoa they were so expensive that the most people could afford was a single nutmeg, a spoonful of pepper or cloves. *What did they cost at the source?* he wondered. *Where is the source?*

Rough looking tradesmen played dice at the next table. The dicemakers' guild had strict rules against fraudulent dice, so the sharpers had to pay dearly to get them. In the dull light of the tavern, dice trickery abounded. Nicolo jumped every time the tradesmen slammed the dice down, and constantly put his hand under his tunic to ensure his knife was still in place. The mule driver seated next to him pushed over to create more distance, thinking that Nicolo was fiddling with his manhood under the table. With the clearer view of the room this afforded, Nicolo noticed the bearded older monk from the galley sitting at the far end of the room. Nicolo ignored him, even though he was the only familiar face in the inn. The fire was warm, and the ale drawn from the large oak barrels by the well-endowed serving wenches ran thick and creamy. After several pots, Nicolo was feeling quite content. Just as he began to doze, the door crashed open and a huge, armored knight ranged into the room. He wore a full metal basinet with eye holes on his head. A chainmail breastplate adorned his front. His large hands were covered in gauntlets with white crosses painted on the cuffs. All his armor was battered and dented, as if the knight had rolled down a mountain—or suffered from years of combat. Nicolo had never seen a fully suited knight, even though his family had sold hundreds of greaves and cuisses for protecting the legs and vambraces for the arms to passing crusaders and local nobles who wanted to act the part. The knight was encircled around his neck and waist by a heavy chain that dragged behind him like a bridal train for the damned. The metal-covered giant shouted for ale, but it was obvious to Nicolo that he had already found a large quantity elsewhere. He lumbered to the tap, lifted the faceguard on his basinet, and quaffed down a big wooden flagon without a breath. The knight staggered upright, smacked his lips, and turned to survey the room. When he saw Mauro in his brown woolen frock, his eyes went large and he shouted out, "There's one of them bastards!" He charged toward the terrified monk, knocking over three benches of diners and a serving wench, splattering the room with mutton and ale. As the inn erupted in curses and fistfights, the knight grabbed Mauro by the scruff of his neck and dragged him out the door. The owner slammed the door behind them and pleaded with his guests to end the melee. Most of the patrons laughed and turned back to their meals or dice. Nicolo hesitated for a moment, not wanting to get involved with something in a strange land. He didn't know the giant knight or the monk. But the monk had been in Genoa and on the galley. He was an older man. What could he have done to offend the knight? Nicolo rushed out the door in time to see the knight lift the monk high off the ground and roar that he was going to kill him. The knight was so huge and completely covered in that hard armor—what could Nicolo do? He noticed that while the knight's knees were protected by poleyns, the back of his knees were not armored, to allow forward bending. He lunged toward the knight and slammed into the exposed back of his knees. The knight toppled and landed on his stomach, the monk rolling away. Before he could get up, Nicolo sat squarely between his shoulders. The combined weight of the armor and the young man pinned the knight to the ground. The giant bellowed over and over to be released, eventually quieting down and beginning to weep. The monk crawled over, and he and Nicolo exchanged glances, nodding in agreement on the next step. They rolled the knight over and sat him up. The knight came face to face with Mauro.

"Please forgive me, brother," the knight began to plead through his tears. "I have had too much drink and have allowed my sorrows and anger to overcome my senses."

Nicolo stepped back from the knight. "Why did you attack this poor monk? Has he ever done anything to you?"

"It is because of monks that I wear this heavy chain and cannot take off my armor. I can't get up without help. Assist me to stand and let's go back into the tavern. I will tell you my tale." Nicolo was suspicious, but Mauro spoke with amazing compassion.

"Poor knight, we will help you. You must have been done a terrible wrong to end up like this. Even though I am a monk, I have also suffered abuse at the hands of my fellows. We are your friends now, unburden yourself to us."

Back in the tavern the knight rolled up the chain and placed it on the table in front of him. He refused Nicolo's entreaty to have another drink, asking for water instead. After a long draft, he began.

"I was a farmer in France. I was always big and strong, so when the lord of our manor wanted to buy his way out of the crusades, he told me to go in his stead. He kitted me out in fine armor, knighted me, and I took the cross. My lord said that taking the cross guaranteed that my lands would be safe from seizure or judgment while I was on the holy mission. I left my farm in the care of my wife and young children, along with my younger brother. It took two years of hard fighting around Damascus for me to see the pointlessness of it. Most of the knights at that point were more interested in loot and rape than in the glory of God. We slaughtered their people, including the women and children. They did the same to ours. So when my time was up, I decided to return home, as was my right. It took another year to get there, as there were few ship owners willing to take former crusaders back across the sea without charge. But I had no money and no choice. I took jobs guarding other men's property, avenging wrongs, serving alongside the huge Germans and Norsemen in the Varangian Guard of the emperor of Byzantium. Finally, I was able to reach my beloved France and find my way home.

"When I got to my farm, I found that my wife, my children, and my little brother were dead, murdered by monks who had left the Cistercian monastery nearby and wanted our land. It didn't matter to them that I had taken the cross or that it was my land by right of inheritance. They wanted it and they took it. They filled in my fishpond. They plowed under my fields of oats and barley that we made into bread for sale to the townspeople and to fill our winter larder. They planted wheat everywhere instead, so that they could mill it at the monastery and sell it to the nobles. When they heard that I had returned, the cowardly bastards fled back to the monastery."

Mauro felt sick at the tale. He knew his brother monks could be petty and might steal small objects or coins from the monastery. He was aware that Clement had absconded with the commissions the monastery received from nobles for copying manuscripts. But he never imagined that monks—or anyone else—could be capable of such heinous acts under the mantle of the church. The knight wiped his nose on his mailed hand and continued.

"When I found out the truth, I went to the monastery and confronted the abbot. He told me that the murderers were not really monks, but a new order called 'lay brothers.' The Cistercians had created these lay brothers to do their manual labor since the monks were not allowed to have servants. Seems most of these lay brothers were thugs and petty thieves who couldn't find honest work elsewhere. I swore to the abbot that I would kill him and every monk in the place if he didn't turn over the men who had murdered my family and stolen my soil. They held out for forty days, but I never gave up my vigil outside the gates of the monastery. Finally, I made a deal with the abbot. An ecclesiastic court would hold its trial. The lay brothers would be found innocent and released. That way they could be kicked out of the monastery without the abbot feeling he had blood on his hands. He would turn them out and turn the other cheek, provided I did not kill them on the grounds of the monastery. Then I could reclaim my rights to the land. After I killed the lay brothers, I went before the ecclesiastic court with two witnesses who testified that the men had accidentally run into my sword while I was practicing. The abbot pronounced the agreed-upon sentence. I was absolved of murder but had to do a heavy penance. I was to carry these chains of guilt all the way to the holy lands and back, never taking them off. I have been to the Latin kingdom of Antioch and now am on my way home. When I return, I must climb the one-hundred-and-twenty-six steps of Roc Amadour to the Chapel of Our Lady on my knees to receive prayers of purification. Then my chains will be removed."

Mauro asked permission to say a blessing over the knight, which he accepted, and Nicolo brushed off his armor and bought him a hot meal. The three men shared a small room at the inn, with the knight sleeping propped up against the wall so that the two travelers could share the one straw bed. They were all so exhausted from the travel and the ordeal of the night that they fell asleep without saying a word to each other. In the morning they parted company with the knight, who picked up his chains and lumbered and clanked slowly north toward home.

Nicolo asked where the monk was going and realized that he did not know his name.

"I am Mauro, a teacher at the University of Bologna. I am on my way to Rome to study at the Vatican libraries."

"And I am Nicolo of House diCarlo in Genoa. I am on a mission—" Nicolo stopped himself. He really needed to control his need for recognition. This was supposed to be a secret mission and here he was, blabbering about it to the first person he met—and a monk at that! He quickly recovered ". . . a trade mission for my father."

"Shall we walk to Rome together, my young friend and rescuer?" asked Mauro sweetly. "It is only a half day away and I would greatly enjoy your company." They walked the road together, sharing pleasantries and thoughts. The casual chatter made the day go by quickly. Soon the hills of Rome and many of the shining marble buildings of the Eternal City came into view. Bronze bells of varied timbre began to toll from a dozen church towers. Mauro felt as if angels were welcoming him with sweet song.

"Oh! It is so magnificent!" Mauro gasped and fell to his knees. "I have never seen Rome before!"

What a country fool, thought Nicolo, *he'll probably read his manuscripts, go back to Bologna, and never leave his cloister again.*

THE MEN SAID their goodbyes at the first crossroad in Rome. Mauro headed toward the easily recognizable Vatican compound and Nicolo toward the commercial district. The younger man had been given the address of a local tailor named Paolo with whom he could stay during his time in Rome. Paolo apparently did some work for the cardinal and the pope, and his house was considered an inconspicuous place for Nicolo to lodge. That suited Nicolo, who liked to talk to tradesmen about the latest happenings in their guilds.

The young merchant walked through different neighborhoods, each filled with the penned animals, small forges, or vats of dyes of their trades. The slaughterhouses were the furthest away—and for good reasons. The bellowing of animals being slaughtered mixed with the smells of manure and fear were almost too much for Nicolo to bear. He put his sleeve over his nose and hurried on to the tanning district. Once again, the acrid odors of the acid baths used to cure and soften the hides tore at his nose and made his eyes tear. Nicolo ran past the pack of barking dogs that seemed to guard the hides encrusted with their dung and hung out to soften. He entered the dyeing neighborhood and joined the throng of people stepping gingerly around the rivulets of woad and madder dyes that created the blues and reds and meandered through the muddy lanes. He didn't want to arrive at his host's house with one brown and one red shoe. The hooded guildsmen nodded as Nicolo passed, but never ceased stirring their huge vats that bubbled over wood fires. Nicolo mused that they looked like warlocks creating mayhem and spells in their brews, but the dyed crucifixes hung to dry across the openings of some of the vat sheds dispelled the notion. As he entered the weaving and tailoring districts, he heard the clacks of looms and the sound of children laughing and singing from the second floors as they spent the day and night spinning and weaving the dyed wools. *It is good that little children are engaged so industriously all day to keep them out of trouble*, he thought.

Nicolo found Paolo's house on a cobblestone side street of the Via Condolezza. He was surprised that a mere tailor could have a two-story house, with a beautifully carved wooden door and large glass windows. He rapped on the door using the bronze knocker cleverly shaped like a large thimble. A young man more or less Nicolo's age answered. A red woolen tunic was draped over his arm and his mouth was full of pins. Nicolo introduced himself, holding out a letter of introduction from Father Clement. Nicolo could see an older, balding man approaching from behind the young man.

"You must be Nicolo," the older man stated, holding the letter close to his face and reading it quickly. "I am Paolo. Please come in." The door behind Nicolo closed and the younger man disappeared. Paolo told Nicolo that the other man was his apprentice, Rico. "He has three more years to serve before he can swear his oath on the relic of Saint Homobonus to become a guild member." Paolo rattled off the requirements for membership, interspersed with complaints about Rico's sloppy cuttings and the cost of wasted materials. But the stoop-shouldered tailor did note that having an apprentice allowed him to cut back his workday from fourteen to twelve hours. Nicolo noticed four young, pretty women stealing glances at him around the door frame into the parlor. Paolo didn't stop talking but followed Nicolo's gaze. The tailor realized that once again a man had come into his house who might lust after his daughters, and he determined to keep Nicolo out of the family living quarters during the short time he would be a guest. He also thought to tell his wife to set a separate wine cup for the guest instead of allowing him to use the communal table cup, as was customary. This should be a subtle but clear signal to the young man to keep his distance from the girls at the other end of the table.

NICOLO'S HEAD WAS still smarting from the syrupy Portuguese wine from Oporto at Paolo's the night before when he entered the papal compound. He barely took note of the Papal Guard in their finery or the hundreds of monks, priests, high clergy, workmen, and petitioners who swarmed the grounds chattering and chanting, praying, and pontificating. He was directed immediately to the cardinal's office, where he was offered, and could not refuse, yet more wine. Nicolo breathed in the bouquet, sniffed a hint of cardamom, and wondered where the wine was from. The priests in Genoa lived simple lives, although they could purchase goods and participate in ventures. But in Rome, it seemed, the clergy lived lavishly.

※

WITH FATHER CLEMENT away on business it fell to Father Franco to rouse the cardinal from his morning repose. Franco had only been in Rome for eight months in the position of assistant to Father Clement. He loved his work calculating taxes and tithes owed the church, as those moneys allowed the Holy See to grow and pursue its good works. Other aspects of his work were less satisfying. He approached the bedchamber meekly, listening for sounds that would indicate the cardinal was up and about. He winced when he pressed his ear to the door. Beyond he could hear the giggles and laughter of the children. He knocked discreetly, then more insistently. The noises subsided.

"Enter!" boomed the cardinal's stern voice. Franco took a deep breath and turned the handle. He stepped tentatively into the bedchamber to see the cardinal still in bed, reading some manuscript. He was swathed in a huge white comforter. To Franco, he seemed the embodiment of Saint Peter, judging the young cleric from atop a fluffy cloud. The cardinal put the manuscript aside nonchalantly. "What is it, Franco?"

"Your morning meeting with the young merchant of Genoa, your Grace." Franco kept his eyes down but tried not to look uncomfortable.

The key to success at the Vatican, Father Clement had advised him, was to be discreet without appearing judgmental or self-conscious. "Shall I prepare your robes?" Franco tried not to notice the squirming lumps on either side of the cardinal.

"No thank you, Franco." With that the cardinal dismissed the visibly distressed young priest. *Mewling cream-faced weakling.*

※

AFTER THE DOOR closed the cardinal grabbed the two lumps. "I have you now!" he shouted to squeals of delight. "All right children, you may come out." Two blond heads popped from under the quilt and snuggled into the cardinal's arms. "You must get dressed and prepare for your lessons." He squeezed them affectionately.

He loved his children more than he loved the church itself. He watched the twins scurry from the bed and out through the door at the back of his bedchamber. His heart ached as he considered for the thousandth time how he could not embrace them in public. The cardinal was the child of a clerical marriage, from the time before the Lateran Council had forbidden the practice. The Byzantine church still allowed priests to marry, and many priests in Rome had children. He clenched his teeth at the hypocrisy of his brethren. *Why should I be denied love and comfort in this life? Why must I denounce the passion of my parents or the fruits of my torrid affair with a noblewoman? Why must my life be dictated by some foolish decision made by dried-up old men before I was born? Yet this is the path I have chosen.* But Orsini did love the church. He was angry at men, not at God.

※

CARDINAL ORSINI HIMSELF opened his inner sanctum door and beckoned Nicolo to enter. He made his guest comfortable with soft bread and a hard, pungent cheese as he sat next to him on a velvet cushion. The cardinal seemed to be sizing up the young merchant, and Nicolo made sure he kept his eyes slightly downward in respect and supplication before this powerful man.

"I can see that you are a smart lad, and you come well recommended from our friends in Genoa for this mission. Do you know why you are here?" quizzed the cardinal gently.

Nicolo looked up into hard blue eyes. He felt like a piece of meat before a baited bear. "I was told I would be accompanying a noted theologian on a mission to Constantinople. I would be his servant and companion. I know nothing more."

Cardinal Orsini thought for a moment before replying. "It is true, Nicolo. The Holy Father and I believe that your presence will help our good brother to navigate the highways and waterways to Constantinople. He is a very learned man, but as with most such fellows, may lack the . . . how shall I say . . . *worldly* experience of a traveled merchant such as yourself."

Nicolo puffed up at the flattery. This man knew his worth. Maybe these high churchmen weren't so bad after all, at least not this one. With a benefactor such as the cardinal, Nicolo's path and future prosperity could be assured.

He smoothed his finest blue velvet vest and smiled. "Thank you, Cardinal Orsini. I do not consider myself as experienced as my father or brother, but I have traveled, I have negotiated the roads and the taverns and made good account of myself. I am at the church's service." Then he quickly added, "And, of course, at your service."

Orsini beamed at the young man. "Then let me share a confidence, Nicolo." The cardinal went on to describe the larger mission beyond laying the groundwork for uniting the church and Byzantium again. As he described the letter from Presbyter John, the earlier attempts to reach him, and the potential of a united Christendom regaining Jerusalem, the young merchant's eyes widened.

What a grand adventure! What a chance to make a name for myself, Nicolo thought.

Orsini studied Nicolo. *It is time to test the lad.* The cardinal called for wine to be served and waited for the young man to drink. "I understand you are fluent in the Arab mathematics?"

Nicolo drained his cup and replied. "Yes, Your Grace. My father thought that it would become the way we do all calculations in the future. It is faster and easier to do sums and calculate percentages and fractions than our current system of numerals from the Roman times."

"How so?"

"The Arab mathematics uses separate symbols for the numerals one through nine and uses a symbol called 'zero' to represent, well, nothing, or to be a placeholder for larger numbers. Once you learn this system, our Roman numerals seem clumsy and slow to manipulate. I think merchants using the Arab system have an advantage over our traders."

"Well, Nicolo, commercial advantage is always to be desired." *This young pup does like to bark, but let's see if he can bite.* "If this new system is as good as you say, shall we test it?"

Nicolo smiled broadly. "As you wish, Your Grace. I can write out the sums or do the calculations in my head."

The cardinal called for Father Vitale, the secretary of the exchequer. The old priest shortly entered, huffing from the exertion of carrying his ever-present counting table. The surface of the small wooden table was scored with grooves from left to right. The grooves were marked I, X, C, and M, representing the Roman counters for ones, tens, hundreds, and thousands. Father Vitale dumped a bag of clay counting pieces the size of grapes onto the table. He arranged the pieces along the bottom of the table, his hands splayed above in readiness. He turned and smiled fiercely at Nicolo.

"Father Vitale is in charge of the papal accounts. He is the fastest calculator in the Vatican. Let us begin with an easy problem." Father Vitale's body was rigid with tension. Nicolo sat straight in his chair, his hands folded in his lap. Orsini leaned forward and picked up the wine bottle. "What is the sum of twenty-three bottles of wine and fifty-eight bottles?" Father Vitale scrambled to lay two pieces in the

X groove and three in the I groove. Before he could finish placing a counter between the X groove and the C groove representing fifty, and one between the I and X grooves to represent five, Nicolo spoke up casually.

"Eighty-one."

The secretary looked up from his counting table in surprise. "That is witchery! It is not possible to do sums so rapidly!"

The cardinal looked at Nicolo and raised an eyebrow. "Is this witchery, Nicolo?"

The young man's eyes widened with fear. "No, Your Grace, no! It is simply a different set of symbols that are easier to manipulate. Anyone can learn them—even Father Vitale."

Orsini's eyes burned into Nicolo's. "Yet nobody in Rome knows this math. I have heard that you learned it from . . . a Jew."

Nicolo was unsure how to react. He recalled his father's warning to distance himself from Uncle Benjamin, so his first thought was to deny or downplay the association. Yet he was certain that the cardinal already knew about Uncle Benjamin. The man was powerful and very dangerous. *If I deny and he already knows, I am shown to be a liar and not worthy of his trust. Yet if I acknowledge my uncle as a Jew, I will tarnish myself in his eyes. Why are these churchmen so hateful toward the Jews?* Nicolo knew that the Jews in the Syrian lands paid their *jizya*, the head tax, and were left to go about their business. The Arabs even classified the Jews and the Christians as the same, the People of the Book. But this was Rome, and there obviously was no comradery with the Jews here. He needed to be honest with the cardinal, at least to a point.

"The Jews in Genoa are merchants in the Syrian trade, Your Grace. I have been told that for centuries they have lived and worked peacefully in those lands and have acquired much valuable knowledge, including the Arab mathematics. They know where and how to buy small lots of spices and other goods and how to get around the Venetians. In Genoa they share their knowledge freely, perhaps as a means of gaining favor and trust."

This young man is wiser than his years, thought the cardinal, *and clever with a turn of phrase. He is trying to please me yet not give away his true feelings.* "Yes, but can you ever truly trust a Jew, Nicolo?" he asked, leaning slightly toward Nicolo. *I know he is upset by the question but let us see how he answers.*

Nicolo felt that the cardinal was baiting him, digging into his personal life. He definitely knew about Uncle Benjamin. Maybe he even knew about Nicolo's feelings for Esther. He had to control himself. He could not let his eyes, his voice, even his breathing betray him. The cardinal was staring right through Nicolo's eyes into his soul. *I must not let him in!*

"I am not that experienced in these matters, Your Grace. The few Jews I have met in Genoa seem like anyone else. They love their families, they want to make money, and they honor their commitments. They have taught me a skill that can help my House to grow. That is all I know."

He is clever. He is telling me the truth without telling me the whole truth. He will be very useful. "Fair enough, Nicolo. But simple sums cannot show us much. Let us turn to more difficult calculations." The cardinal made Nicolo and the secretary perform subtraction, multiplication, and even the sharing out of a voyage's profits. Nicolo required a quill and ink for the more complex transactions, but in each case he easily arrived at the correct answer ahead of the increasingly befuddled secretary. The cardinal eventually dismissed Father Vitale, who shook his head and grumbled something about Jews and Arabs and their accursed calculations as he packed his counters.

"Zero? What is a zero?" Vitale muttered. "That 'nothing' the boy touts is the realm of Satan. The Lord of Darkness and the Jewish magic helped him confuse me and slow my counting." He left the room in a cloud of anger.

The cardinal congratulated Nicolo on his knowledge of the Arab mathematics and his speed and accuracy. The young man cast a radiant smile toward the cleric. Sensing his opening, Orsini made his move.

"Yet there is more in this journey than keeping our good brother out of trouble as he does the work of the Lord, my young friend. All along the route to Constantinople, to the Muslim lands and beyond, are trade opportunities that a merchant can only dream of. The steel of Damascus, the silks of Persia . . . and the spices, the source of the spices. The man who finds the source of the spices can free us all from those damnable Venetians. He would become the wealthiest man on this earth. Does that appeal to you? Would you want to bring such glory and riches upon the House of diCarlo? Of course you would—and you can! The strength of Christendom lies not only in its spiritual purity but also its manifest power on earth. Just as a man needs to eat to be strong for battle, so must the church have material sustenance to maintain its mission, to educate and care for the people, to battle heretics and infidels. Wealth and holiness are not opposed to each other, Nicolo. Yes, the things of this world can lead to evil temptation, but they can also be used for good. You can have it all, Nicolo, if you work with me to bring riches back to the church while you help our good brother to mend and strengthen our Christian mission."

Between the wine, the compliments, and the promise of adventure, Nicolo's head was swirling. This was more than he had ever imagined! But he knew he had to be a merchant, not a star-struck boy. He took a deep breath and spoke to the cardinal in a voice that barely betrayed the quiver.

"Your Grace, I am honored to be chosen for this mission, and I certainly accept. Shall we call in a papal secretary to notarize the transaction?"

Cardinal Orsini nearly exploded. *The gall of this young pup!* Yet he admired his spunk. The cardinal never lost the serene expression he had displayed throughout the interview. "Ordinarily yes, my boy, but this mission is so secret that only His Holiness and I are heir to it. The monk's search for knowledge in Constantinople will be public, but your search for Presbyter John will not. If the Muslims learn of this, you will be executed, most slowly and painfully, as a spy. Nor can we afford information about your deeper commercial mission to get out. If the Byzantines or the Venetians hear of it, you will be knifed in the back. No word, no documents, just an agreement between you as representative of the House of diCarlo, and I, and of course His Holiness, on behalf of the church. No one else must know, not your father, not the good monk. The stakes are life and death—yours, in fact."

A shudder ran up Nicolo's spine. This was no romp at the fair or at the brothel. *Life or death—mine. So be it. I will never have another chance like this.* He pressed on. "Of course I understand the seriousness of this, Cardinal Orsini. At the same time, I need assurances that if anything happens to me during or after the mission, my family's interests in whatever I have accomplished will be protected."

"An astute observation, Nicolo. The Holy Father and I had discussed this very thing. The church is prepared to offer your House the exclusive right to import any goods that you find that are not already well-known nor readily available in Rome or Genoa. If you find the source of our beloved spices, or at least can get past the Venetians and release us from their death grip, your House shall be the exclusive spice importer."

Nicolo was swept away by the grandness of it. He envisioned the new *fondaco* right on the wharf, the large house on the hill, the finest silk garments. He saw Antonio humbly bowing when he entered Nicolo's grand office. All he had to do was make it back alive. His reverie was interrupted by the cardinal's deep voice.

"You will be supplied with silver for the voyage to Constantinople, and you will be in charge of the finances for both of you. From what I have seen of your mathematical skills, you should have no trouble keeping count of your expenses." Orsini gave Nicolo a stern look. "I need not remind you, young man, that the funds belong to the church. They are not to be used for your personal investments. Do I make myself clear?"

Nicolo's throat went dry. "Of course, Your Grace. The church funds are only for our sustenance, nothing more. I will ensure that I have my own funds for trading."

"Good. You will be given notes to carry to Constantinople, to be redeemed at offices of the Knights Templar. They have developed a new system of money trade that does not require you to carry many coins."

Nicolo was about to tell the cardinal that he was well aware of that system, that it had been devised and used by Jewish merchants around the known world for centuries. Yet he held his tongue and let the cardinal continue.

"Beyond our lands and the Latin kingdoms, you will have to make your own way and take employment or trade to keep yourself in coin. Of course, the good monk will be a traveling seeker of wisdom. You will be his nephew and companion. I am certain that you are clever enough to take advantage of opportunities to support and even enrich yourself along the way." *Now to ensnare this young hare in his own greed.* "Furthermore, Presbyter John has stated in his letter that the emissary who reaches his court will be free to partake of all the pleasures of his kingdom and will leave laden with treasure. That means all the jewels that are found in such abundance in his rivers—emeralds, sapphires, topazes, onyxes, and more! He also tells us that pepper grows in his lands. Where pepper grows the other spices must grow as well. Do you understand? Find the lands of Presbyter John and you find the source of the spices."

BROTHER MAURO LODGED at the residence for visiting priests within the Vatican compound. He was free to wander the grounds and visit the libraries, where priests and monks from throughout Europe sat poring through mountains of manuscripts scattered across long wooden tables. The walls were lined from floor to ceiling with more tomes, volumes bound in leather or sheaves loosely assembled and tied with blue strings. He imagined spending the rest of his life in this place, studying, translating, and writing reflective analyses. Above the shelving were paintings of angels and scenes from the Holy Book, statues of saints and reliquaries containing holy objects. He stood there in awe, taking in the sounds of the library. Amid the coughing of the priests, shuffling of the manuscripts and scribbling of silver writing nibs, Mauro could detect a low whisper. He didn't think anything of it for a while, until he realized that the sound was not coming from the earnest priests at the tables. He followed the whispers around the large tables, right up to the shelves. It is the manuscripts. They are whispering, he realized. Mauro strained closer to the parchments. He walked along the shelves, fingering the aged documents. He heard ancient Greek, Latin—and was that Aramaic, the language of the Apostles? He heard arguments, pleas, emotional and rational imprecations. So many competing voices through the ages. What is the Truth? How can we know? Am I rising to understanding or falling into confusion? As he swooned with bliss and deep thought, Mauro tripped over a priest's outstretched leg and scattered withered vellum pages across the floor. The priest howled in pain and cursed the monk in French. The librarian rushed over to the commotion, rapped Mauro hard on the head with a cane, and sent him out of the library. As he rubbed his aching head and felt the bump rising on his shaved pate, Mauro walked toward the great cathedral of Saint Peter. He lingered before the colonnaded, arched atrium called "the Garden of Paradise" that fronted the massive basilica where the founder of the church had been martyred, crucified, and buried over a thousand years earlier. He knew that a simple church had once been erected over the tomb, followed by a greater church and then this magnificent basilica. Mauro longed to enter the cathedral and be near the remains of Saint Peter. He wanted to pray where so many great saints, popes, and high churchmen had prayed before. He felt certain that Plato was right, that the stones absorbed the prayers and created an opening to the divine, and those who prayed basking in that power would elevate their souls. But that exquisite experience would have to wait. It was time for his audience with Pope Innocent III.

Brother Mauro stood before the Lateran Palace, gathering his courage to enter.

"Excuse me, Father, excuse me, Your Grace!"

Mauro looked down to see a small boy, no more than five or six, pulling at his robe. The boy was poorly dressed, shoeless, and dirty, but smiled upward with a mouth of small, discolored teeth. He held a leather box in his outstretched hands. The box was wrapped with a chain and a lock, with a slit in the top. Mauro recognized it immediately as a donation box from a small church. He smiled back at the child.

"I am not a father, nor Your Grace, my child. I am but a poor monk. How may I be of service to you?"

The boy looked at Mauro imploringly, his eyes welling with tears. "Please, good monk, I am raising donations for the crusade. I live at the abbot's orphanage up the street and many of us boys will be going with the knights and pilgrims to the Holy Land. We are called by Our Lord to begin a children's crusade! Please, good monk, please share a coin or two so that I might have food and clothing to touch the sacred sands of the Holy Land."

Mauro was moved by the sincerity and passion of the child. He saw in the boy the same longing for communion with God that he had experienced when he entered the monastery at Livorno. He had been about the same age as this child, and just as poor and disheveled. He reached into his small leather purse and pulled out a copper groat.

"This is not a worthy amount, child, but it is much of what I have. Go with God on your journey. Be safe and be caring to those around you." He put the coin into the box. The child's lips quivered as he clutched the box to his breast.

"You are good and kind, sir. May you be blessed in all of your days." The boy's face shined beatifically, and he raced away. Mauro watched him leave the papal compound and turned back to the palace. He took a deep breath, called upon all the saints to calm him and clear his mind, and entered the building.

※

As THE CHILD turned the corner beyond the compound he was grabbed roughly by the neck and dragged into the shadows of the nearby alley. A short, burly man yanked the box from his hands.

"Let's see what you got so far today, Stephen," he said casually. He took a key off his belt and clicked the lock on the chain. He opened the box and took out the copper groat. He bit it, squinted at it, and placed it in his own leather pouch. "Good lad. Not a fortune, to be sure, but enough for a drink for me and some soup and bread for you tonight." He tousled the boy's head softly. "There are lots of good folks who will be happy to help send you to Jerusalem on the Lord's work if that's what you tell 'em, Stephen. Lord knows they'd only give you a good smack if you told 'em you wanted their coin to buy some food for yourself or drink for your old uncle." He paused to pick a nit from the boy's hair. "Let it be a lesson, boy. Few people care about you in this world, so you have to make them think they are doing something for themselves or for the Good Lord. That's what the churchmen do and look how fat most of them are. Now get back out there and see what else you can earn this fine morning. And may God bless you."

※

MAURO SAT IN the anteroom, enjoying the faint aroma of incense that permeated the well-appointed room. He looked down at his poor woolen robe and ragged sandals. They were in such sharp contrast to the wealth and the glory all around him. How could he stand before the pope, himself, dressed as a pauper? Mauro felt very self-conscious and struggled to remember that he was a mere monk who searched for truth in the writings of others, not a saint or great man of this world. He calmed himself by recalling the words of Saint Peter:

Your beauty should not come from outward adornment, such as elaborate hairstyles and the wearing of gold jewelry or fine clothes. Rather, it should be that of your inner self, the unfading beauty of a gentle and quiet spirit, which is of great worth in God's sight.

The papal guards on each side of the big doors at the end of the room snapped to attention as the entrance to the inner sanctum opened. Mauro rose to his feet shakily and responded to the invitation of the papal secretary to enter. Pope Innocent III looked up from his writing desk. Mauro's bowels nearly gave way as he stood eye to eye with God's representative on earth. The pope's eyes were a steel gray, like a morning sky that would soon be pierced by shafts of sunlight, opening straight to heaven.

Lotario saw the stricken look on Mauro's face and smiled. "Please, good Brother Mauro, come and sit by me. You needn't be so nervous. We are both men of the cloth and men of learning. I welcome you to the Holy See."

Mauro was relieved but still in awe of the man and the office he held. "Thank you, Your Holiness. I am so honored to be invited to Rome. Please ask anything of me that I might serve the church."

The pope looked at Mauro's simple clothing and his earnest expression. He contrasted that with the cardinal's daily dress of gilded crosses, rings, and jewels. *Who is the better man?*

"I have heard that you are quite interested in the teachings of the pagan Greeks and early Romans, and that you have been translating texts that not everyone in the church approves of."

Mauro panicked. *Am I to be punished for heresy?* He looked down and stuttered "I only search for knowledge to deepen my faith and provide arguments that strengthen the faith of others."

Lotario smiled more broadly. "That is precisely why you are here, good monk. I was a master at the University of Paris before I came to Rome, and although I studied law, not natural philosophies, I am familiar with Scholasticism. Don't look so worried, Brother Mauro, in this office you are free to speak your mind. A deep inquiry into how men understand God is an honored journey here. It is mostly in the fields and towns that men fear thought, as I am certain you know. But let me ask you a specific question. I am considering banning one of Aristotle's works, *Metaphysics*. It is a recent translation that directly contradicts major teachings of the faith. For example, Aristotle wrote of a hierarchy of gods. One above all others, yes, but not all-powerful and who cannot control the daily activities and choices of men. Those were the domain of the lesser gods." The pope sat back and looked inquiringly at Mauro. "As you can see, Aristotle drifts off into serious error that cannot be tolerated. The College of Cardinals are firmly united in the opinion that even the slightest exposure to errant thinking can confuse people and lead them astray. What is your view?"

Mauro was surprised. He had begun to fear that he was there to be excoriated for his behavior and maybe thrown out of the church. He stroked his bushy gray beard nervously and pursed his lips. He began to push up his sleeves to his elbows as he always did before a debate but quickly stopped as he was so self-conscious in the presence of the pope. "As a logician I have to say that Aristotle constructed reasonable arguments, but, of course, Aristotle was a human and humans err. I don't believe thought per se should be prohibited. A strong mind supplements faith and promotes firm argument against those who are in error or those who may be wavering. I find so much in my own translations of Aristotle that supports the faith. I believe it would be unfortunate to limit access to his writings."

The pope smiled. "Yes, tell me of your translations. I have heard that you do not do proper word-for-word translation, but rather imbue the words with nuance and meaning different from what is prescribed in the monasteries. What guides you in this?"

"Your Holiness, when I read the words of the ancients, I feel a connection that goes past my eyes and my brain and seems to reach down into my very soul. I have no other way of describing it. The words are not just words. Rather, they evoke passages from our Holy Book or touch my own life as if I were a mere vessel, a continuum of some sort. The translation just pours out of me."

The pope pondered Mauro's words, noticing the longing on the monk's face. "That is both logical and beautiful, Brother Mauro. Of the five highest ideals of our beliefs, only faith, hope, and charity are original. Wisdom and justice come to us from Plato. Of course, you have never lived in ancient Greece or Rome, so it is not possible for you to understand the context within which the pagans wrote. Can any translation truly capture the original meaning of a text? I often wonder about this myself."

"If I may, Your Holiness, I am not certain it is even necessary to do so. If the ancients wrote of the human condition, there must be parts of the writing that are particular to their time and place. But we are all men living with the same struggles and hopes, I believe. So even if the translation isn't exactly as the author intended, it still might have value to us."

"Do your explorations of the pagan writings ever call your faith into question?"

"No, Your Holiness. They only challenge me to examine our own texts more closely for the right argument, and to go deeper into my own love for God for strength and support."

"Your talent with reasoned argument will serve us well in the struggle for the heart of the church. We need to bring the Byzantines back to the righteous path. This is more urgent since the seizure of Jerusalem, and the continuing threat of a Muslim invasion of the neighboring Latin kingdoms and of Constantinople itself. We need to unite Christendom to regain Jerusalem and to repel the infidels."

"I am deeply honored by the faith you have in me, Your Holiness. I do understand the Byzantine arguments. But I am no diplomat. I wouldn't have any idea about negotiating a treaty or anything else. I am merely a scholar."

"Do not be concerned with those details, Brother Mauro. They will be handled by our legates, secretaries, and notaries once you have done your work. Your sole task will be to use all of your knowledge, wisdom, and skills to meet with sympathetic clergy and men of influence in Constantinople and support them to make the case for reunification. I believe there is some sympathy for our great mission. Alas, it has been difficult to get a clear picture from the reports sent by our legates. Once you meet with them you will have a better sense of the way forward in Constantinople. But once that is accomplished, an ever-greater challenge lies ahead." The pope described the search for Presbyter John and the need to join forces with that devout and powerful sovereign to push back the Muslim advances. He gave Mauro a copy of the letter from Presbyter John, urging him to study it carefully.

"The letter is written in the ornate language of sovereigns, thus much of it will make no sense to you. Most importantly, it states Presbyter John's desire to take his armies to the Holy Land and wage war against the enemies of our Lord. I want you to discern the sovereign's current commitment to our faith, as there has been no contact with him for thirty-five years, and to prepare arguments to ensure that he comes under our banner." The pope warned Mauro of the fate of William the Physician and other emissaries. "The letter only gives the vaguest of references to where the kingdom of Presbyter John can be found. Yet I am confident that with the services and good counsel of your traveling companion, the likelihood of finding the kingdom is great. You will meet this man after our audience is completed."

The pope stood up and walked to the window. He seemed to be considering something for a long while before he turned to Mauro and spoke again. "Let me share with you another aspect of your mission, which will add enormously to the ability of the Holy Church to thrive in the times ahead. You will be passing through many lands. Christian lands, Muslim lands, and lands still in the darkness of pagan thought. I want you to learn as much as you can about the beliefs and philosophies of the peoples you encounter in your search to find Presbyter John. It is important for us to know and understand these errant ways so that they may be conquered by the Word or by the sword. You will be the truest of pilgrims in holy service."

Mauro was surprised and overjoyed. He felt comfortable arguing the positions of the church in the face of the Byzantine errors. But to travel and study other faiths? He was being given permission by the pope himself to inquire, to study, and to learn. It was a freedom unheard of in the monasteries. But he needed to be clear about this, as such inquiry could border on heresy.

"Your Holiness, please help me to understand. In my inquiry, will I have permission to read the writings of the pagans and of other faiths?"

"Yes, Brother Mauro, precisely. I wish you to explore monasteries and libraries. Find manuscripts that document pagan and other beliefs. Read them, translate them, and engage in debates with men of other faiths, if you would. I know that your love of God is strong and that your constant inquiry is only to deepen both your knowledge and love, although you may experience doubt or confusion at times. I trust you to drink from many wells but not quench your thirst for knowing God from anything but the true fount."

Mauro immediately thought of his *Summa Theologia*. Could he expand it to incorporate the beliefs of other religions and beliefs? If so, it would be a masterpiece worthy of Maimonides himself. His reverie was stopped by the stern words of the pope.

"But I must caution you, Brother Mauro. Once you leave the Byzantine lands you will be nothing more than a humble servant of God, wandering the known world in search of truth. You can only reveal your ultimate mission when you come face-to-face with Presbyter John."

A gentle knock interrupted the conversation. The doors opened and Cardinal Orsini entered the room, followed by the same young merchant who had saved Mauro's life.

The monk beamed joyfully at the reunion. Nicolo smiled broadly, hiding the wince of disappointment at having to travel the world with a country monk.

THE NEXT MORNING, Censio led Mauro and Nicolo through the largest library and into the scriptorium, where scribes, illustrators and binders worked away copying texts. The room reminded Mauro of the monastery at Livorno. He felt his knuckles throb in memory of the beatings administered by Clement. They passed on to a large, damp room beneath the library and were introduced to Archbishop Theodorus, the archivist of the collection of correspondences and personal papers of the popes known as the Secret Archives. Unlike the great library above, the Secret Archives could only be accessed by permission of the pope. Massive mounds of parchments lay scattered in no apparent order across the dimly lit, unadorned room. Theodorus seemed embarrassed by the arrival of visitors. He squinted at Mauro through bushy white eyebrows.

"I apologize for the disarray here. I am the first person to be charged with organizing the papal documents and correspondence. When a pope dies, all his writings and letters are collected here. This room has been more a mausoleum than an archive, but I am here to remedy that. I am afraid I have inherited quite a mess." He scuttled about, pushing piles of parchments and bound volumes out of the way to create a path to the only table in the dimly lit room. When the men were seated, he unbent his back with a grimace. "I understand you are here to learn about Presbyter John. I am afraid there is little documentation of the sovereign beyond the letter and a few comments by the chroniclers. Yet do not despair. I am something of a living archive for Presbyter John's relationship to the Holy See." He leaned back in his hard, wooden chair and closed his eyes, calling up long-filed memories from the archive of his mind. "I was a boy of fifteen and a page here in the Vatican when a Syrian Archbishop—Hugh of Jabala, I believe—first announced the existence of Presbyter John. Ha! That was well over fifty years ago, yet I remember it as if it were yesterday. I was so impressed with his swarthy complexion, silk robes, and jeweled turban. I had never seen a Syrian before. Hugh and his retinue seemed like exotic characters from a fabled past. Hugh had come at the behest of Raymond, the prince of Antioch to seek help fighting off the Seljuk Turks, who had captured Edessa and were descending upon Antioch. Hugh told the story of an eastern Christian King John, whose large army had defeated the brother kings of Persia and Medes in a great battle at Ecbatana, near Edessa. Then King John set off for Jerusalem but could not cross the Tigris River because it was too deep and wide. He went north to wait for the river to freeze but after a year returned to his kingdom in the East. That is why Hugh wanted help, because the eastern king called John had gone away and the Latin kingdoms were not powerful enough to hold back the Muslims much longer. That was the beginning of the Second Crusade. I remember how exciting it was to hear that report as a boy."

"What happened then? Did the king ever come back?" Nicolo asked.

The old librarian shook his head. "No. Nothing was heard from the king for another twenty years. Then his letter appeared in 1165. It was addressed to the Byzantine Emperor Emanuel and also to the Holy Roman emperor. A copy was sent to the Vatican. That is what you have in your hands," he said, pointing at the parchment Mauro was holding. "It is at once a strange and wondrous letter. The king calls himself Presbyter, or Priest. I think that shows his humility and obedience to God, even as a sovereign. According to the letter, his is a large kingdom, comprised of seventy-two tributary kingdoms encompassing the Three Indias."

"Three Indias?" Nicolo shook his head. "I have never heard of them. Where are they?"

"They are far beyond the Syrian lands. To the north, they circumscribe the great deserts and mountains of Sind. To the east, the lands of Hind. And to the south they include the lands and islands of Zanzi." Theodorus looked at Nicolo and Mauro, noting their blank stares. "These lands are no longer known to us. They belong to Islam and pagan rulers. Presbyter John must be very powerful to survive being surrounded by so many enemies of the Lord."

Nicolo was fascinated. "Hind? Sind? Zanzi? How can it be I have never heard of these lands? I am a merchant, and I know all the lands of the world."

Theodorus smiled and patted Nicolo on the shoulder. "The knowledge of these lands was taken from us five hundred years ago. Our ancient forebearers, the Greeks and the Romans, traded with all of the Indias. They traveled on roads and sailed on seas we no longer know. I believe that when the Goths and Saracens overran Rome and so much of Europe and the dark times came, we lost our collective memory of the world. We huddled together fearing the darkness and the unknown and took comfort in the Good Book. But as with all things on this earth, control and corruption followed and knowledge beyond our faith was forbidden. We may have gained eternal sanctuary, but we lost our way in this world. Then the trade routes to the Far East were absorbed under the mantle of Islam, so we ceased receiving information beyond Constantinople. We have lost all the knowledge and wisdom gained by our ancestors. It is so strange. The ancient Greeks and Romans knew more about our world a millennium ago than we do now. That knowledge is only now being revived, as you know, Brother Mauro." He looked at the monk wistfully. "How I envy you the chance to go to Constantinople. Ahh, to be able to speak freely with scholars and men of faith who see the world and Christianity from different perspectives. And to have access to all those pagan works without fear of retribution by conservative churchmen! It is ironic that the light brought to the world by the church is so often used to suppress people's search for understanding."

Mauro hadn't thought about the larger context of his quest for knowledge. He began to appreciate anew how blessed he was to be given permission to reach back in time and help ward off the darkness that had descended upon Europe and Christianity. Nicolo was captivated by the thought of lands beyond Europe and the Syrian territories unknown to other Europeans. What treasures might he find? What rewards and adventures awaited him in the land of Presbyter John?

※

DURING THE NEXT few weeks, Mauro and Nicolo met with the pope, the cardinal, apostolic secretaries, or diplomats on a daily basis. They pored over the letter from Presbyter John along with Theodorus and the papal cosmographers, searching for clues to the whereabouts of the kingdom. However, there was little beyond general descriptions of great sandy seas, grand mountain ranges, and rivers that flowed from Paradise or dried up one day each week, leaving precious gems on the shore. Of course, everyone knew of the Tower of Babel, which according to the letter was within the sovereign's realm, but nobody knew where it might be. Even the names of the subject peoples in the kingdom of Presbyter John were odd and unknown. The letter stated that seventy-two provinces or minor kingdoms paid homage to Presbyter John, but the only cities mentioned were Samarkand and Susa, places unknown to the cosmographers. It was written that the patriarch of Saint Thomas the Apostle dined often with the sovereign, but as that patriarchy was of the Assyrian Church, little was known of it in Rome. It was understood that Saint Thomas traveled to the Indias to preach the Gospel, but none of the experts knew where he had gone, what he had accomplished, and where exactly the Indias were.

Nicolo was often bored at these meetings. His mind wandered off into foreign lands, calculating the values of different currencies, deciding what goods to buy in the exotic marketplaces. Each day the men were told to spend an hour or two together, so they could get to know each other better and pull off their mummer's play about being related. A Vatican notary counseled the men to learn about each other's families and create a familial connection that would be beyond reproach or suspicion as they traveled. After a week the notary quizzed the men together about their families, satisfied that the fanciful common link was through Nicolo's mother and Mauro's sister, who were cousins. As the men practiced reciting their family connections they corrected each other with gusto. The notary observed that they were both a bit headstrong and rebellious, which could be seen as a family trait. The papal diplomats had advised Mauro to treat the younger man with kindness and guidance. They said he was like a young colt who must be reined in from time to time, but also given his head so as not to break his spirit. The merchant was to treat the monk with deference yet familiarity. Nicolo had no trouble being respectful to the older man but found himself thinking what an unworldly fellow Mauro was. He began to consider him as a slightly befuddled uncle, which added a certain compassion and caring to his demeanor whenever he spoke to Mauro. The monk, for his part, saw in Nicolo that same free thinking and energetic mind that he enjoyed with the best of his *scolari* in Bologna, but it was clear that the young man did not think of the profound matters of our place under heaven. Mauro thought that was a shame, yet he soon gave up trying to engage Nicolo in these subjects, enjoying his company as a nephew and companion instead.

After these meetings, Mauro quickly retreated to the libraries to take advantage of the great collections before departing. He met several more times with Theodorus to try and understand the obscure religious references in Presbyter John's letter and to enjoy the old archivist's perspective and breadth of knowledge. Theodorus confided to Mauro that there were many ancient texts, most declared heretical and forbidden, that told of Saint Thomas's travels in the Indias and even mentioned the names of the kings he had converted, such as Gondophares. The saint had traveled the great coasts of the Indias on hot and troubled seas, establishing churches along the way. But none of those texts could be found in the libraries of the Vatican, and the locations of the kingdom of Gondophares and the apostle's churches were not known.

Nicolo wandered the markets and the different guild neighborhoods each day, learning what was on offer at what price and making an occasional drinking companion. He met the son of one of the diplomats in the papal court, a young Pisan merchant named Fibonacci, who had grown up in the Syrian lands and was an expert in the Arab mathematics. The two drank wine and calculated sums together, the slower buying a drink for the faster. Nicolo tried to teach Fibonacci how to differentiate between certain spices by smell, but Fibonacci had a head for numbers, not a nose for scents. Nicolo told Fibonacci about the French fairs, and the Pisan gave Nicolo insight into trading in Constantinople and the Syrian lands. Fibonacci also taught Nicolo some choice words in Arabic, which he said would impress the people he met along the way even if he learned no more than what Fibonacci taught him. He told Nicolo that the most important lesson was that even though the Arabs were decent people, they were hard bargainers and expected hard bargaining in return.

"In Byzantium you are expected to respond with half of what the offering price is, but if you ever go to the Syrian lands you must start at only one-quarter of the price. Also, be wary of dealing with the first merchant you meet in a marketplace. You can always come back to that first merchant, but don't let him sell you anything at first nor let him guide you to others. He will grab onto you and almost claim you as property, getting angry at other merchants who try to deal with you."

They shared notes on currencies, of gold and silver and copper, and how to detect false coin. Fibonacci taught Nicolo how to spot a silver coin that was so debased that it turned copper reddish when rubbed hard. He said that the coin "blushed with shame" when discovered. He described the rates of customs duties to be paid for exporting goods from Egypt, Syrian lands, and crusader kingdoms. Fibonacci's friendship and the dinners at the tailor's house helped the days go by until the pope told Nicolo and Mauro that it was time to begin their embassy.

Their final meeting with the pope and the cardinal was privat;

not even the apostolic secretaries were allowed in the room. The pope reminded the men of the serious and dangerous nature of their mission. No one had ever reached the kingdom of Presbyter John and returned to Rome. The cardinal reiterated the need for strict secrecy, looking long and hard at Nicolo in particular. They reviewed for the thousandth time who their trusted contacts were in Constantinople and how to retrieve funds from the Templars when needed. Just before the meeting adjourned, the pope told Mauro that he had another important mission for him. They were to stop in the kingdom of Sicily, which was on the sea route to Constantinople.

"Sicily is a cauldron; it always has been. The kingdom consists of the main island of Sicily and several large colonies on the mainland. The island was under Muslim control for four hundred years. It is very close across the sea to the Syrian lands. Sicily was brought back to the fold by the Normans less than one hundred years ago. The mountainous center of the island remains populated by infidels, yet Sicily is a tolerant place, where people of many faiths live and trade in peace. With the death of Emperor Henry VI, the crown passed to his child, Frederick, with the emperor's wife, Constance, acting as regent. Constance made Frederick my ward to protect the child from sharing the fate of so many of Sicily's rulers before him. Constance died last year after she renounced Frederick's claim to the Holy Roman Empire while keeping the crown of Sicily. Markward of Anweiler, the military marshal to the late Henry, now claims to be regent to the young king, but really desires to rule in his own name. Markward is a brutal man who wants to reincorporate the kingdom of Sicily into the Holy Roman Empire. He has already taken the kingdom's province of Calabria on the mainland as well as invaded the kingdom of Naples, and now seeks to control the island of Sicily itself. He has also made an unholy alliance with the Muslim community on Sicily, which seeks to reestablish control of the center of the island as an independent emirate."

Mauro was bewildered. "But Your Holiness, I know nothing of

kings and crowns. I am at a loss for how I can be of service to the church there."

The pope realized he had overwhelmed the monk. "I am sorry, you do not need to know all of this. The young King Frederick is still my ward. I wish for you to become a temporary tutor to the boy. He is only five years old but is extraordinarily bright and eager to learn. He displays a capacity for learning far beyond his years. It is important that his questioning mind is introduced to logic if he is to grow to be a good ruler and deepen his faith and obedience to the church. You will not be there long, but you will excite the boy's mind and give him direction until we can arrange a permanent tutor. I have in mind Censio, my private secretary, whom you have met, yet his duties are not done here."

Mauro still looked ill at ease, so the pope continued. "Here is a letter of introduction to the abbot who resides at the monastery San Giovanni of the Hermits. You and Nicolo will stay with the abbot. He is a powerful and knowledgeable man. Most important, he is the confessor to the king, so you will have immediate and private access to young Frederick. San Giovanni is a simple place. It has no library to speak of, but its cloister was built over an old mosque, as were so many of the great churches of Sicily. A marvelous garden of exotic and aromatic plants surrounds the cloister. I think you will experience deep meditation and prayer among the orange trees, jasmine, and roses there. Sicily will also give you your first look into the world of the Byzantines. Their beautiful mosaics adorn almost every church and many of the churchmen understand Byzantine dogma and thought. It is quite an exquisite place, and you will enjoy your time there. But I strongly advise you two to keep close. The alleys of Palermo, the royal seat, are full of intrigue and sharp knives. They call them *stiletti*, and they have only one purpose."

The pope then blessed and dismissed the men. Mauro returned to the priests' quarters in silence. The monk spent the night on his knees in prayer and meditation, pleading for guidance and strength for the mission to come.

Nicolo's final supper with Paolo's family was a subdued affair. The tailor's four daughters looked longingly down the table toward their handsome and interesting guest. Paolo sat like a stone wall between the girls and the object of their attention. He had to admit that Nicolo had been polite and appropriate throughout his stay, but at the same time he couldn't wait for his young guest to leave. He didn't like the air of intrigue around the young merchant and longed to restore his quiet family routine. After the family retired to their private quarters, Rico asked Nicolo to help him pack up and carry some boxes out to a waiting cart and horse. The boxes were full of masks that Paolo and Rico had been making for several weeks, in anticipation of some private ball. As they packed the boxes Nicolo marveled at the masks. They would cover the eyes, forehead, and nose of the wearer with beautiful displays of feathers, jewels, and velvets. Each mask seemed to be the essence of an animal or bird or perhaps some spirit. Nicolo found them fascinating and sometimes frightening. He asked Rico where the ball was and who was hosting the party.

"Some of the powerful and wealthy men in Rome put on masked balls like this for visiting nobles or other out-of-town guests. Paolo always makes the masks and makes good coin doing it. I deliver the masks or costumes to the back of the hall. Sometimes I sneak in to eat something or look at the women. They are always so beautiful and seem so available—or at least I wish they were." He sighed. "Hey, Nicolo, why don't you help me deliver these masks? You can get a peek at the women and maybe even grab a drink. It is your last night here and we can celebrate together."

Nicolo had spent the last three days sitting in meetings with the cardinal and Brother Mauro learning the names of churchmen and politicians in Constantinople, followed by those long, restrained dinners with Paolo and his increasingly provocative daughters. His sole nightly social exchange had been the occasional stolen glance at one of the daughters as he passed a plate of pork or turnips. If the plate lingered too long in the passing, Paolo would cough forcefully, eliciting giggles from the girls and a smirk from Rico. Paolo was acutely aware of Nicolo's stiff posture across the table as he charmed his daughters with tales of travel, but the tailor didn't notice the young merchant's stiffness below the table each night. Nicolo ached for a good time and agreed to go with the apprentice.

The cart lurched down the rutted street with the young men jostling on the rough wooden driver's bench. Rico barely used his knotted rope on the ancient, decrepit mule, which seemed to know the streets well. They were soon lost in laughter, making fun of Paolo's propriety and guessing which daughter would be the first with child. The apprentice also made oblique references to Juliana, confiding that his ass had been squeezed more than once by Paolo's wife as she passed by his cutting station.

"She also gets excited whenever she beats me for a cutting error," he confided.

After a winding trip through the back streets, the cart stopped before the rear entryway to a large compound. The young men hustled their boxes in through the portcullis and were ushered into the back of the main house by an elderly stern-faced man.

"You are late, Rico," the man intoned. "Get these boxes into the main room, set the masks up along the dining table, and leave before the guests arrive. You can stop by the kitchen and have a cup of wine for your services."

Rico and Nicolo made several trips back and forth, stealing cups of wine in each direction. They laid out all the masks as they were told. Horses, pigs, falcons, goats, and dozens of creatures real and fanciful stared up at Nicolo from the table through eyeless sockets. As they turned to leave, Rico grabbed Nicolo's arm.

"Hey, Nicolo, let's have some fun. Grab a mask and we can hide in the alcove. After the guests arrive we can join the party for a bit.

With the music and the dancing nobody will notice us. I do it all the time and never get caught. We can have a few drinks and look at the fancy women. You will love how they smell of flowers and ripe fruit."

It was too much for Nicolo to refuse. An escapade on his last night with wine and high-born women? The men chuckled and grabbed masks. They left them in the alcove and headed down to the kitchen for more wine. The old servant was not to be seen, so Nicolo and Rico ran back to the alcove instead of out the back door. They waited for what seemed to be an eternity as people started to come in. First the servants brought in the food, large platters of fruit, flagons of wine, and baskets of breads. Next came musicians, setting up their lyres, flutes, and drums. The men huddled in the small alcove wearing their masks. They had to turn away several times from servants, pretending to be guests engaged in conversation. Over time the room filled. Nicolo could smell the perfumes, closing his eyes and guessing at the scents. He saw men dressed in long robes and masks, totally cloaking the wearers in anonymity and mystery. Other men wore velvet tunics and the puffed sleeves that were so recently popular. The women wore tightly fitted corsets, cut enticingly low in the front and tied with leather straps in the front and on the sides. Nicolo noticed that the men were freely touching the women's bare arms, their hair, and occasionally a breast.

"Nicolo, it is time to join the party," urged Rico in an urgent whisper. "We can only stay for a moment, so we don't get caught." He immediately walked out of the alcove, leaving Nicolo alone. Nicolo looked around the room. He walked inconspicuously to the table with the wine flagons, poured himself a cup, and drank slowly. He took a second cup and a third, until he felt a warm glow in his chest and a liquid courage pulsing through his body. He wondered who these people were. Merchants, no doubt, as they were free with their laughter and their guttural conversation. Some nobles, as well, cupping breasts freely now and swirling to the music. But all were masked. He spied a young woman nearby, surrounded by other women but no men. *She must be really highborn. Nobody would try to lay a hand on her even with a mask on*, he thought. She had long blond hair made up in a tumble of ringlets that cascaded over her right shoulder, leaving her bare left shoulder gleaming in the candlelight. Nicolo wondered if she had oiled her body to produce that sheen. He was so drawn to her that he didn't realize he was walking her way until he was stopped cold by a look and a provocative smile. The young woman took a step toward Nicolo and her entourage melted away. Her mask was a bird of prey, but even the sharp beak and fierce eyebrow feathers could not hide her lovely blue gray eyes. *Such powerful eyes*, Nicolo thought, *at once familiar and frightening, yet I can't break away from them.* He walked up to her as if in a trance and took her outstretched hands. They turned in circles to the music, the perfume surrounding Nicolo as they swirled. *Peach, sweet ripe peach. No, too light, must be summer melon.*

"You are not from here," she spoke in a low, husky voice. "Are you from the North with those golden curls on your head?" Her voice robbed him of any will as the room faded away.

"I am only here for tonight. On the morrow I must leave on a long voyage."

She smiled under the mask. Her teeth were so white, her lips full and naturally red. "Then let this night be a memorable one. Put your arms around me and dance." She drew him closer. The scent reached out and enveloped Nicolo like a physical force. He felt her hands glide down his back, and her left hand discover his right hip and the front of his thigh. Soon his hands were all over her body and hers everywhere on his as the music pulsed louder and more urgently. Nicolo looked over her shoulder as they turned, seeing men and women embracing and fondling everywhere. They coupled in pairs and even in groups, the laughter blurring with the moans and sighs. This was not the style of dance he had learned in Genoa.

"Tell me your name," Nicolo gasped. "I must know, who are you?"

She laughed. "There are no names here tonight. There are no

titles, no sirs, no madams. We are all here for flesh and sweat, nothing more." She embraced Nicolo tightly, pressing her full body against his. "Soon the King of the Night will arrive, and we will all make love in his presence. If you can spend your seed more than three times you will receive a red scarf or another token of the king's favor." A bolt of fear shot through Nicolo, and he held her at arm's length.

"The King of the Night? Is this some ritual of Satan?"

She laughed again and soothed his brow with a small, soft hand. "No, my feverish boy, this is a masquerade ball. We do this every month. It allows the good sisters to quench their thirst, while the fathers purge themselves of vile humors, confess, and return to their offices."

Nicolo was stunned. "You mean all these men are priests? The women are nuns? You are a nun?"

"Don't be so alarmed, sweet country pumpkin, they are all men and women with desires of the flesh like you and me. But do not fear for your soul: I am not a sister. I am the daughter of the king, and you will be my prince this night." A loud commotion from the anteroom drew everyone's attention. "Ah, here comes my father now."

Nicolo turned around to see a man in a red robe and stag mask being carried into the room on the shoulders of laughing men. They were shouting "Hail the king! The King of the Night!" The rest of the crowd took up the chant. As the King of the Night was being escorted around the large room, he passed close enough for Nicolo to get a better look. He was a very large man, and even under the mask, Nicolo could see his fleshy jowls. It was the cardinal. Nicolo turned away quickly. He didn't want the cardinal to see him at this debauchery. But what was the cardinal doing here, and apparently in charge of all this? Nicolo suddenly realized he had been snared in a situation with the cardinal that he didn't understand. He wanted to flee, but the cardinal's daughter (could that be?) held his arm tightly.

"My love of the night, I need to relieve myself after all this wine," he pleaded.

She looked at him skeptically, then grabbed him between the legs and spoke with a flash of anger. "That hardness doesn't feel like it needs to piss. Are you already after another woman? Do you prefer a sister?"

"No, my golden-haired angel. I just need a moment. I will return straight to your arms. You are more of a woman than I could ever have dreamed possible. Get us more wine and I will return soon."

She released her claw-like grip slowly. "I will be right here waiting for you. God help you if you linger. Tell me your name so that I can have you unmanned if you do not come back to me."

"No names, no titles, my love. I am here to open your gates of heaven, no more." Nicolo broke away and fled to the kitchen. He stopped once safely inside and thought about his predicament. This was a strange turn of events. The cardinal was now his patron, his path to riches for himself and his family, but he was also a . . . what? Nicolo's mind raced, but he quickly came to a resolution. *If I can find the kingdom of Presbyter John and the source of the spices, the cardinal will make me the richest man in Genoa. What do I care if he is the King of the Night or the Prince of Darkness himself?* He looked around to make sure no one was watching and bolted out the back door toward the gate he had entered earlier. Rico sat in the cart, looking anxious.

"Nicolo, where the hell have you been? We could have gotten caught in there."

"Why the hell didn't you tell me these were all priests and nuns?"

Rico was perplexed. He pointed to the vine-covered wall. "But Nicolo, the sign next to the entrance says, 'Convent of Santa Clara.' What did you expect?" He saw the confused look on Nicolo's face. "Relax, my friend, this is Rome, the Eternal City of sin. Everybody had a good time tonight. The churchmen and the nuns had their fun. We ate and drank our fill. Even Paolo made good money on those masks. What's the problem with that?" Rico flicked the knotted rope at the mule, and the cart clattered into the night.

CHAPTER 6

SICILY

AFTER A WEEK of easy sailing, the *Minervi* approached La Cala, the deep harbor at Palermo. Nicolo had spent the voyage on the poop deck, pretending not to know the older monk seated in the waist. But Captain Fiori had a sharp weather eye. He noticed how the monk smiled up at Nicolo every day and seemed crestfallen when the young merchant didn't respond. Something was going on here. After he ordered the sails struck and furled and the oars shifted to take the *Minervi* into the quay, he joined Nicolo at the rail. The men stared up the grand valley beyond the city, enjoying the golden glow of the morning sun shining upon thousands of fruiting lemon and orange trees.

"It is a beautiful sight, eh? They call it *Conca d'Oro*, the Golden Valley." Nicolo smiled and nodded in agreement. Fiori continued. "My friend, I feel you are keeping a secret from me. You and that monk have something going on. He has been mooning at you ever since Rome. Are you sure you didn't take secret orders in Rome? Spill your guts, Nicolo. We are coming to a dangerous place at a dangerous time."

Nicolo winced. "Ah, Fiori, you are too smart for me by half. Listen, my friend, from here on I have to pretend that old monk is my uncle, and that I am here as his companion so that he doesn't get waylaid as he goes from monastery to monastery. Please don't press me for more than that."

Fiori thought about it. He had grown up with Nicolo and knew him to be clever and ambitious. What was he doing in Sicily with the old monk? He knew the monk was no relative of Nicolo's. But a friend is a friend, and Fiori would keep Nicolo's confidence, for a price anyway. He placed his hand firmly on Nicolo's shoulder.

"Hey, my old friend, you can trust me. But there must be something in this for you, no, for your family, for your father to let you out of his sight while Antonio is away. I will keep my mouth shut, but I want in on it, whatever it is. Our families have always helped each other, right?"

Nicolo trusted Fiori, but he knew that a Genoese's confidence would be secured more firmly with a little sweetening of commerce. "Look, Fiori, here's the thing. The monk is a friend of my mother's brother, so it is not difficult for me to think of him as my uncle. He is on his way to Constantinople to study. I am just helping him get around without getting lost. In return my father told me to keep a weather eye out for a good deal. I was hoping to find a good cargo here to send back to Genoa. If nothing comes up, I will carry on to Constantinople. But if there are some useful goods to be had, maybe I will stay for a while. If you have space in your hold on the return to Genoa, maybe you can transport something back for me. I will give you the exclusive right to ship our goods on this trip. But I need to keep it quiet. If the word gets out here, any Pisan or Venetian could have my throat cut. Are you in?"

Fiori's eyes sparkled. "Sure, Nicolo, that's what friends are for. My silence for an exclusive agreement . . . and twenty percent of the value of the cargo."

"You take no risk, Fiori! Take the goods back for the cost of the space on board. It shouldn't matter to you if I am transporting gold or pig shit."

"Five percent is for the space. That's pretty standard these days, even for pig shit. And ten percent for my silence."

"Five and five," Nicolo countered.

"Agreed," beamed Fiori, "and it better not be pig shit. I could only sell that to the widow Balena for her pies." The two shook hands. "But now that we are partners, I need to share something important. Nicolo, I shouldn't be telling you this, but it could save the life of your uncle and maybe yours too. There is word on the docks of Genoa that most of the fleet is being chartered by some general who served under the old emperor. His name is Markward, and he is a real shitbag. He wants the crown of Sicily for himself and has gathered five thousand German troops to invade this island in another month or so."

"Really? Why would the commune agree to transport those German troops again? The emperor never paid for all that the last time they invaded Sicily."

"Yeah, it seems like throwing good money after bad. Sometimes you must invest more to prop up a bad deal in hopes that it will come through. If Markward succeeds, he will pay off the earlier debt with the riches he sacks from Sicily. There is a lot of gold here, especially in the churches. Also, it is better for us to get those damned German beasts away from our own shores, lest Markward desires our sweet Genoa instead of this island that smells of fish and Syrian curry. Whatever you and your monk must do here, you better finish it up and get out before Markward arrives. I am sailing north in ten days, so make your score quickly. And stop mooning over the beauty of the valley. You ought to know by now that you can't trust beauty. It is often a mask for betrayal."

THE DOCKS OF La Cala were humming with activity. Ships from Constantinople, Venice, the Syrian lands, even far away France were moored in the harbor, waiting to unload their varied cargoes. Barefoot crewmen wearing the motley caps and clothing of a dozen nations hefted bales of fabric, rolled barrels of oils, and wheeled barrows of fish up and down the docks. Alfonzo, the master of the *Minervi*, shook hands with the customs inspector of the port.

"Greetings, Alfonzo, what have you on board? Another herd of pilgrims? More meat for the butchers of Jerusalem?"

"Yes, Rodrigo, but they pay their passage and don't spoil like that piss-wine you sold us on our last voyage."

The customs inspector feigned indignation. "Alfonzo! You know that I am not a merchant. I did not vouch for the cargo. I only made introductions. It was your responsibility, not mine, to ensure the quality of the goods."

"Ahhh, never mind. We sold it to some fishermen in Porto Venere. We didn't make the profit that we should have, but we didn't lose any coin either. They needed it for their celebration of *La Virgin Bianca*, as they call our Mother Mary. Anyway, you may be interested in a few of those pilgrims. You see that young dandy over there with the old monk? That boy is the youngest son of Marcus diCarlo of Genoa. He is supposed to be the companion of the monk, his uncle, but I heard him talking to the captain about some deal to fill *Minervi*'s holds on the return voyage."

"Thank you, Alfonzo. Count Eugenio will be interested in this. He would want to know if there is a new trader in port so he can whet his greedy beak anew. Why don't you visit my cousin's tavern later and have a drink on my account."

"Three would be better after that long trip, and the information is certainly worth that." He smiled through broken teeth at the customs inspector. "Don't you agree?"

"Definitely worth two, I stand corrected. Now be on your way before my men take a closer look at those barrels of iron nails your crew is unloading. They roll easily for such a heavy cargo."

When Alfonzo took his leave, the customs inspector called over one of the dock workers. The man was slight of build and had a limp. He was not much of a lumper, as the cargo movers were called, but he did have his uses.

"Mahmoud, I want you to follow those two over there—don't stare at them, you idiot! See what they are up to and let the count know what you find out, with my compliments. They are headed toward the market. Keep your distance, ask anybody they speak to what they are about, and don't steal anything this time. I can't protect you anymore and you will be even more useless with only one hand."

"Of course, my master," replied Mahmoud unctuously. As he bowed and retreated, he muttered under his breath. "And as soon as the emirate is restored, yours will be the first throat I cut."

※

The port was much bigger than Genoa's and Nicolo couldn't identify some of the ships' pennants. In fact, Palermo was the wealthiest Mediterranean seaport besides Constantinople. He was enthralled by the variety of goods on the dock as well as the many shades of skin of the sailors and dock workers. Although he was used to seeing red, blond, and dark hair from the various Europeans who frequented the fairs, he had never seen Syrians or Nubians before. What a marvelous world we live in, he thought as he ogled at the array of humanity on the docks. I have so much to see and experience yet. Mauro tugged at Nicolo's tunic and implored him to move on. They needed to get to the abbey. One of *Minervi*'s crewmen told them that the shortest way to the abbey was through the Ballarò, the Arab market that stretched to the south and east of the port.

As they entered the labyrinth of alleys and passageways, they were assaulted by smells both familiar and foreign. Hawkers pleaded with them to look at their wares, with no obligation to buy. Metalwares, leather goods, and small buckets edged from the stalls out into the alleyways, making fast passage impossible. The shouting, squawking, tumult, and hubbub excited Nicolo. Although the massive confusion of sounds and sights went far beyond the organized markets at the Troyes fair, it was sweet and harmonious to the young Genoese.

Mauro was uncomfortable with the crush of humanity and the babel of guttural and harsh languages. He clung to Nicolo's arm. They were engulfed by carts and stands selling fish and sea creatures that Nicolo had never seen before. At one stand Mauro gasped and shouted, "The Leviathan!" as they stood before a fish bigger than either of them. The Arab trader laughed and told them that it was a tuna, the largest fish in the sea, and that they weighed as much as five hundred pounds. Their steaks were blood red and tastier than any beef, but they were best eaten fresh and were not exported. The tuna could not be cured and preserved, unlike the sardinellas, anchovies, and mackerel that were salted and barreled. Nicolo bought some clams for the abbot and they moved on. Mauro grew increasingly uneasy as Nicolo stopped to talk to every trader about prices, credit, shipping, and other things totally alien to the monk. The young merchant succeeded in impressing some of the traders by demonstrating his knowledge of their math, and in turn they offered him the "local price" for their goods. Short of coin and wary of the monk's presence while he contemplated purchases, Nicolo begged off, promising to come back the next day. Mauro pleaded with Nicolo to get going as the sinking sun seemed to set fire to the tops of buildings that leaned in over the market alleys. Nicolo finally relented and the travelers strode on toward the abbey. In their wake, Mahmoud stopped to question each merchant they had spoken to, gathering bits of information to share with the count.

<hr />

"He knows the Arab math?" Eugenio sat back in his leather chair and thought about that. None of the northern merchants and few of the Genoese, Pisans, or others who spent time in the Syrian lands could use the system. This foretold a change in commerce, he thought. Eugenio's mother was Sicilian, but his father was Greek. Having spent his life in polyglot Sicily, Eugenio knew that as long as people couldn't or wouldn't speak to each other, they needed intermediaries. His strength had always been as the go-between who profited from (and often created) misunderstanding. Was this young man a potential ally or foe? Was he the harbinger of changing fortune for Eugenio? At fifty-five years of age, he was getting too old for intrigue, and his gout was getting worse. He needed to get to the bottom of this immediately. The count gave Mahmoud a silver denier and thanked him in Arabic, asking him to keep his eyes on the merchant when he returned to the Ballarò or the docks of La Cala. He decided to meet the young man himself. He summoned Gabriella. Shortly, a striking, dark-haired young woman entered the study. She curtsied deeply, her thick curls tumbling over the creamy, olive skin of her right shoulder.

"My dear niece, I would like you to go to the Ballarò tomorrow when Cora goes to buy food. There is a special young man from the North I would like you to meet. Please invite him to join us for our evening meal. Wear something lovely that shows off your exquisite neck and shoulders, perhaps the green silk dress I gave you for your birthday. I am sure he will not refuse."

The girl shrugged and sighed. "As you wish, Uncle. Shall I be the bait that hooks the fish? Will you club him when we haul him into the boat?"

Eugenio laughed. "Your wit is as sharp as your mother's. Yes, lure him alongside, but have no fear. I only wish to learn what he is about. I think we will both find him fascinating."

MAURO LOOKED UP as the men approached San Giovanni of the Hermits. He had never seen a church building such as this. Five ocher-colored domes sat atop the austere, squat monastery, and the windows were narrow, tall, and arched at the top. At the entryway he asked to see the abbot, giving the letter of introduction to the old priest who greeted them. The priest led them through the small church, which was decorated with richly detailed wall mosaics and a tiled floor. There were no depictions of holy scenes, as in the churches of Bologna and Rome, only intricate swirling and geometric patterns. The old priest noticed Mauro's wonder at the designs and explained that the monastery had originally been a mosque, and in the Muslim faith there could be no depictions of their prophet or any heavenly messengers. The patterns were meant to provide worshippers with nonhuman imagery to contemplate to bring them to a higher plane.

"They do have a way of calming the mind when one sits here in contemplation. Yet, to us, they are beautiful works of art, nothing more." He also pointed out how the domes sat on squat, square buildings in the monastery compound. "The square below and the round above, that is how both the Muslims and the Byzantines symbolize the relationship of earth and heaven."

The priest led the men to the cloister, where the abbot sat reading on the stone bench by the well. He reviewed the papal document and looked hard at Mauro and Nicolo. He was a short, stocky man. A thick mat of gray hair covered his head like a warrior's helmet. After what seemed to Mauro an eternity, the abbot relaxed.

"I see our Holy Father has tasked you with tutoring the young king during your brief stay. That is good. He is an intelligent child whose mind takes to knowledge as a Sicilian sponge draws water. Your presence will delight him, as he is surrounded all day by grasping, greedy relatives and courtiers. But he is the king here in Sicily and by blood of the Holy Roman Empire, although his mother renounced that title on his behalf. While the last several kings of Sicily have met with tragic ends through poison, torture, and even castration, I believe that young Frederick will persevere. I will bring you to him tomorrow and we shall see how he takes to his new tutor. You may stay in the priory. We are not a rich church, and we offer no comforts here. But we have a powerful place in the kingdom and are relied upon by both the king and His Holiness. That requires balancing the needs of the soul with the challenges of the court." The abbot pushed the sleeves of his black robe up to his elbows and lowered his voice. "That balance is under immense threat from within and without. The Holy

Roman emperor never looked kindly upon losing the kingdom of Sicily, especially to the influence of our Holy Father. The time to shape the boy's mind is short. No matter who controls the armies that occupy this scarred island, the king's allegiance must always be to the church."

"Kings and armies, the hunger for power. I am afraid I do not understand any of this. It seems as if the world is falling apart," Mauro sighed.

The old abbot smiled. "It always is, good Brother. Alliances shift, power changes hands, men send other men to do evil to each other. Does anything really change? When I read about the lives of the ancient Greeks or our Roman forbearers five hundred or even a thousand years ago, it seems as if it could be today. I wonder if people will say the same five hundred years hence. Yet what is constant and what must remain constant? Our faith. Our belief that our Church has the right of it, and that we must remain a source of light and of God's manifest presence forever." The abbot sighed wearily and took in a deep breath of the scent of orange blossoms growing outside the cloister. Nicolo didn't hear the abbot's words, as he was lost in the hint of jasmine from the clusters of small white flowers in the nearby trees. He was always amazed at the lightness and purity of a scent in nature, before it was pressed and distilled into an essential oil.

"I see you are headed to Constantinople. I understand that the Holy Father wishes to reunite Rome and Byzantium, but I am afraid our Christian faith is fragmented and torn asunder in many other places, as well. In the Syrian lands, where our faith has its roots, there are many churches. The Assyrian Church, the Nestorians, the Church of the East, the Yazidis. Each is ancient and has its own understanding of the fundamentals of Christian belief. Even beyond, I have heard stories of wandering monks, such as Saint Thomas, who have taken the Word of God into distant heathen realms and flourished. Will Jerusalem be returned if only Rome and Byzantium come together, or will that require the stitching together of all the lost fragments of Christ's vision for humanity? Who can say?"

As they settled onto their hay mattresses that night, Nicolo told Mauro that he wanted to spend the new day back in the Ballarò. He said he'd found all the different food from the sea, tools, and woven clothing fascinating. After all, he said, there is nothing for him to do here at the abbey, and he played no part in tutoring the young king. Mauro agreed that it would be good to keep his mind occupied and said that they would see each other again at supper.

After hard millet bread and a thick pea soup in the morning, Nicolo wandered back to the Ballarò. He played three sponge sellers off each other and came away with a deal that, even accounting for Fiori's cut, would bring a nice profit in Genoa. Next, he moved on to the dried fish merchants. He stood next to an older woman who haggled for salted sardinellas while her companion, a striking dark-haired young woman, waited patiently. Nicolo smiled at the younger woman, and they began to converse. Her name was Gabriella, and she had eyes as black and fiery as her hair. She was impressed with Nicolo's skill at negotiating with "the Moors" as she called the Arab traders and told Nicolo that her uncle, Count Eugenio, would enjoy meeting him. When her kitchen servant, Cora, finished buying the salted fish, Gabriella invited Nicolo to dine with her family that evening. She laughed when she learned that Nicolo was staying at San Giovanni monastery, arching one eyebrow and delivering a sly smile.

"You don't strike me as a pious man. Are you here to take vows of celibacy?"

Nicolo flushed. "Of course not! I am merely accompanying my uncle, a learned monk, as he travels to Constantinople for study. I am an independent merchant. I represent my House in Genoa." Nicolo realized that he was almost babbling. He needed to control himself and not be so swept away by this dark beauty.

"We shall send a man to fetch you from your prayers this

afternoon. My uncle is very interested in commerce. Perhaps he can help you find a bargain." She moved closer and whispered. "You may find something here that is very different from what you are used to in Genoa."

Nicolo walked away smiling, his mind on those shoulders and that neck.

Mauro accompanied the abbot to the royal palace to conduct mass for the king and his courtiers. They walked into the Palatine Chapel built by the Norman King Roger fifty years earlier. Mauro stood with his mouth agape at the exquisite Byzantine mosaics that adorned the walls, granite columns, floor, and ceiling. Depictions of Christ, Mary, many saints, and angels much larger than life stared down at the monk. The porphyry, malachite and gold, rich colors and detailed imagery filled every inch of the chapel. In the presence of such majesty, Mauro wondered why the Muslims forbade images. They meant so much to him, making all the figures of Christianity real and accessible in the moment. He was led to a seat in the back of the chapel, while the abbot walked to the chapel altar and ministered to the young king and his retinue.

When the mass was over, the king was led out a side door into an adjoining garden and the abbot returned to Mauro. The abbot smiled as he noticed the tears in the monk's eyes. He put his hand on Mauro's shoulder and led him into the garden. It was as if he had stumbled into Eden. The gardens were extensive and luxuriant. A riot of plants flourished around artificial ponds, fountains, and waterfalls. The abbot explained that the palace and the garden originally belonged to the former emir and that many of the plants had been brought from the Syrian lands.

King Frederick II was a slight boy of five, yet he looked directly into Mauro's face with a surprising maturity. His reddish-blond hair told of his German heritage, but he was already fluent in his mother tongue, Latin, Arabic, and the common tongue of Sicily. Mauro was struck by the raw intelligence in his face and found himself eager to engage the young sovereign. When the abbot introduced Mauro to the king as his new visiting tutor the boy cried out in delight.

"We must begin immediately! What shall we do first? Shall we talk about law? How does logic apply to law?"

The abbot chuckled and bowed to the king. "Your Majesty's eagerness to learn is well-known throughout the kingdom and even in Rome. Our good Brother Mauro will spend each afternoon with you discussing your questions and so much more."

"I want to begin now!" the king exclaimed. "Tell me something. Here in Sicily, there are Muslims, Christians, and Jews. Each group has their own laws, and we are supposed to allow each to apply them to their own community. Why shouldn't there be one law for everybody?"

The abbot grinned when he saw Mauro's stricken expression.

"Your Highness, our good Brother Mauro has just arrived. He doesn't have experience in the ways of our kingdom. Our Sicily has always been a land of many peoples. In that way it is very different from other lands. As you know, good King Roger created that rule so that the communities could regulate themselves according to their own customs, to keep harmony in the kingdom. If there is a problem between communities, the case is brought to the Crown for resolution. This system of justice has worked well for over a hundred years. Yet it depends on the king being a fair and just ruler."

The king crossed his arms on his chest and crunched his face into a stubborn visage.

"How can I be fair and just when the way we find the truth is so stupid? If two men come to me with a problem, I am supposed to order them to suffer an ordeal to find out who is telling the truth. How does putting a man's head in a bucket of water or his feet in a fire or forcing two men to fight find the truth?"

Mauro stepped forward. "If I may, Your Highness, I completely agree with you. Pain and torture do not ensure truthfulness, nor does strength of arms ensure that justice will prevail. How would you wish to see the truth come out in such a situation?"

"I should ask them questions. I should listen to each man and decide for myself who is telling the truth and what is fair. I am the king."

"There was once a man named Plato, and he thought as you do. Yet he wanted to make sure that a king was wise so that he would always be fair and just. Shall we meet tomorrow and talk about Plato? There are other learned men who have thought about how a wise ruler can make good decisions. We can talk about them too."

The young king smiled up at the older monk. "Yes, I would like that."

When Mauro returned to the priory that afternoon, he found Nicolo putting on a good tunic of light blue linen.

"Good day, Nicolo. I don't think it is necessary for you to dress for supper in such a fashion."

Nicolo explained that he had been invited to sup with a count and his family. Mauro felt left out, but Nicolo explained that the talk would all be of commerce. "However, if this count is a learned man, perhaps he has a library. If so, I will ask if you can visit one of these days." That seemed to satisfy the monk, so Nicolo finished his dressing and went out of the monastery to wait in the waning sunlight for the count's man.

Within a short time a slightly bent man leading a donkey appeared. He introduced himself as Mahmoud, a servant of Count Eugenio. Nicolo stated that he thought he had seen Mahmoud at the dock when *Minervi* had berthed. The man replied easily that he was there to oversee the landing of some wine from a French ship, although he preferred the strong native wine of Sicily to that dry Galician stuff. Nicolo commented that he looked forward to trying the Sicilian wine tonight. Mahmoud smiled and said that the count was known for his generosity, and that Nicolo would have more than his fill. Nicolo mounted the donkey, and Mahmoud led his charge through the streets of Palermo toward the count's villa. They passed through La Kalsa, the ancient Arab section of town. Nicolo noticed that the architecture of this area was different from that surrounding the abbey. Mahmoud said that in his lifetime, the Norman rulers had torn down much of Arabic Palermo, building grand churches, cathedrals, mansions, bridges, and other structures in a style that seemed out of place.

"But, of course," he quickly added, "that is the right of the conqueror, isn't it? Everyone who comes to Sicily leaves his mark."

They passed the Church of the Magione, originally built for the Cistercians less than a decade earlier. Nicolo heard the clanging of swords, a coarse tongue, and laughter from the small cloister that abutted the church. Mahmoud explained that the church had been taken away from the order by the old emperor just before he died and given to the Teutonic Order of Knights as their headquarters after they had crushed a local uprising against the emperor. That growling, guttural tongue was German, and Mahmoud shared his opinion that they were uncouth and dangerous men who upset the delicate balance of cultures that had been the hallmark of Sicily forever. Nicolo remembered Fiori's comments about Markward and his German army massing to invade the island but said nothing to Mahmoud. The donkey clattered across the Admiral's Bridge that spanned the slow flowing Oreto River. Young boys cast nets from the bridge and hauled up sardines while others raised crab pots from the brackish river. In another fifteen minutes they entered a spectacular area of palm groves and bubbling pools. Nicolo was amazed to see peacocks for the first time in his life, just wandering the groves. Mahmoud saw the wonder on the young man's face.

"We are now in *jah'nat al-ard*, the terrestrial paradise. It has been corrupted by the Sicilians to Genoard, but it is still beautiful." Nicolo gasped as one of the big male peacocks spread his tail plumage. Mahmoud looked again at Nicolo's finery. "The male makes a great show, strutting about with his tail spread out. He does not have to be a great fighter or leader to impress the female. He only has to display his beautiful feathers. Who is the bigger fool; the foppish male or the female who chooses him?"

Just beyond Genoard they approached La Ziza, the home of Count Eugenio. Mahmoud explained that the name meant "splendor" in Sicilian Arabic, and that the mansion had once been the summer home of the emir and then King William III.

"He was the last of the Norman rulers. He died three years ago when Emperor Henry sent those German knights in. He was blinded and castrated. Then they sent him to the mainland or killed him. Nobody knows for certain."

"And that is when Count Eugenio became the owner of this mansion?" asked Nicolo tentatively.

Mahmoud stopped the donkey and looked back toward Nicolo with a smile. "Payment for services rendered."

The men entered La Ziza through its massive entryway, which looked to Nicolo as if it had been made for a giant. The main hall occupied the entire center of the first floor. Mahmoud told Nicolo that there were corridors and rooms off each part of the main hall, "the public rooms," and that the family of the count lived on the upper two floors. The floor was made of marble, interlaced with gold and silver mathematics designs, as were the walls. They passed the huge fountain in the middle of the main hall and started up the broad granite stairway. A servant greeted them at the top of the stairs and Mahmoud retreated, leaving Nicolo to follow the new man. Nicolo was led into a small study with a large sword hanging over the mantle of the fireplace. It had a beautifully jeweled hilt and a wide blade with symbols and characters that Nicolo did not recognize. The walls were lined with small statues, mounted animal heads, and odd-looking weapons and tools.

"I see you find my collection interesting." Nicolo turned to see a man roughly the age of his father enter the study. He wore a red cloak over his shoulders in the style of royalty and a green velvet tunic beneath. The man had rings on each of his fingers, alternating between gold and silver. His hair was salt and pepper, as was his closely cropped beard. His left leg was swaddled in bandages, and he favored the leg as he approached Nicolo. Count Eugenio introduced himself and described some of the items on the walls.

"The sword is the fabled Excalibur. It was given to one of our Sicilian kings by Richard the Lionheart on his way to the last crusade. He probably should have kept it since he wasn't able to retake Jerusalem and then was taken hostage on his return home. It was given to me by King William before he was . . . dethroned."

Nicolo couldn't tell if the slight smile was for the sword or for the dispatching of the king. *No matter*, he thought, *if this count believes that sword is Excalibur, I can make a fortune in old armor if I say it came from some great knight. This man is disturbing, but that niece of his is worth the visit.*

"This is a fascinating collection, Count Eugenio, but I must confess that I do not know what some of these things are for."

The count brightened. "Ahh, most of these are Arabic torture devices left from the emirate. They are called "Truth Seekers." This one squeezes the thumb until it bursts, and that one does the same to more delicate parts of a man's body. Oh, don't look so nervous, my young friend—they are here to remind me of the savagery of the past rulers of this island and how enlightened we have become." Nicolo looked relieved. Eugenio changed the subject. "But let us move to the dining hall. We have prepared a wonderful array of local foods for you to try, as well as some of the best wines in Sicily. I am very eager to talk trade with you and see if there is anything I can do to make your stay in Palermo profitable."

"Thank you, Count Eugenio. I am really here to ensure that my uncle, a learned monk, makes it safely to Constantinople. Of course, as a merchant I cannot help but be amazed by the many goods so new and exciting to me. I must say that I am looking at sending a few things back to my House in Genoa to support this expensive voyage with my uncle, and perhaps a more long-term arrangement could be had that would be beneficial to both Genoese and Sicilians."

"Then you have come to the right house, Nicolo, as I am a trader myself. I can assure you of good prices and high quality for anything that might interest you. It would serve you to have someone looking out for your interests, as between the devious Arabs, the scheming locals, and the random Pisans, Venetians, and French who work the port, it can be hard to deal fairly. Actually, you are here at an auspicious time. Many of the Venetian traders have been recalled to provision the crusades, so there are a lot of opportunities to be had. You know when the buyers are fewer, the prices must fall, eh? But let us eat and drink, there will be plenty of time to talk trade."

Nicolo was torn between the count's offer, which could certainly make his life easier, and Fibonnacci's warning not to be ensnared by the first merchant he met who offered to be the intermediary for all Nicolo's trade. He needed to be careful not to commit himself. He felt cocky. He knew how to navigate traders and would not let himself be bullied or even gently led where he didn't want to go.

They sat at a beautiful marble table. It was a solid piece almost twenty feet long. Count Eugenio commented that it came from a quarry in Syracusa hundreds of years ago, when slaves worked the face of the quarry with hand tools.

"Can you imagine the months of backbreaking work that went into cutting and smoothing this piece?" the count said as he glided his hands over the surface of the table. I admire the skill of the artisans who made this table, but I do not envy their hard work. Trade is a much more suitable occupation, wouldn't you agree?" Before Nicolo could respond, the count looked past him and beamed.

"Ahh, and here is my lovely niece, Gabriella, whom you met in the Ballarò. She is my only heir and the beloved of my life. Isn't she the most exquisite creature, Nicolo?"

Nicolo turned and nearly choked on the grape in his mouth.

Gabriella looked radiant in a green satin (or was it silk?) dress embroidered in gold thread that fell off her shoulders and dipped low between her breasts. Nicolo wondered how it was held up; she just seemed to float inside it. She wore gilt slippers. Her elegant hands were covered with designs in henna. He had never seen a Christian woman adorned with such Syrian influences. The combination of her physical beauty and her exotic dress disoriented Nicolo. He caught himself as he stared speechless and stuttered a greeting. Gabriella smiled shyly . . . or did she mock him gently? Nicolo was already so confused and taken by her presence that he thought it best to bow and stay there until she was seated across the table from him.

Nicolo began to relax as the kitchen servant Cora brought out food and as the wine began to flow. He devoured the skewers of fish with cinnamon and ginger but struggled through the meatballs cooked in vinegar. Count Eugenio was describing the different wines on the table, which came from this or that valley. Nicolo sampled several but had trouble concentrating. He kept peeking over to those breasts and that neck—*how could a neck be so captivating? It was just a stretch of skin no different from an arm or a leg.* Yet to Nicolo it was a soft and slightly pulsing organ. He had to stroke it, to kiss it.

"I said, Nicolo, which of the wines do you prefer? I will make you a gift of a few bottles to take back to your monastery."

Nicolo startled and grabbed the first bottle within reach. "I am not certain, Count Eugenio. They are all delightful. But this one had a certain essence that captured me."

Gabriella covered her mouth with a linen serviette and muffled a laugh. "You have quite a mouth for wine, sir. That bottle is vinegar. Perhaps you meant this one." She handed Nicolo another bottle. He sniffed it to hide his embarrassment, agreeing that was the one he meant.

Eugenio smiled at Nicolo. "Don't be concerned, Nicolo. The necks look much the same, don't they?"

Did he mean the vinegar or was he chastising me for staring at his niece?

"I see you have chosen a mascalese from the slopes of Mungibeddu volcano, or Mount Etna as you call it. It is a dark and smoldering wine, surprisingly earthy. It has much in common with my lovely niece, wouldn't you agree?"

Nicolo tried to have more self-control for the remainder of the meal. He managed to talk coherently about his travels to France, his brother's work procuring material for the crusade, and his uncle's desire to study in the libraries of Constantinople. Eugenio told Nicolo that he had a wonderful library right here at La Ziza, largely inherited from the former king, and that his uncle could come and peruse his collection at his leisure. He could even have one of the volumes as a gift, as the library had so many. Nicolo was delighted to have something to offer Mauro, as he was having such a good time while the monk sat nursemaid to the child king. He thanked Eugenio for his kindness. After a few more bottles of wine and a course of roast capon with grape sauce, the count yawned and stretched.

"Well, my young friend, I must retire soon. But I do want to show you one other treasure before you leave." He called for a servant and ordered him to bring in the "globe." Nicolo was not sure what the word meant. Two servants returned carrying a round silver object as wide and as heavy as the widow Balena's rear end.

"This is a depiction of the entire world, engraved on this sphere of two hundred pounds of pure silver by a very learned Arab cosmographer, Al-Idrisi. The Arabs know more about the world than we do and jealously guard their trade routes to the south and especially to the east. Al-Idrisi spent many years in Sicily at the behest of King Roger drawing maps of the known world and writing manuscripts detailing trade routes. He created a masterpiece, *Nuzhat al-Mushtaq*, or 'The Delight of He Who Desires to Journey through the Climates' that holds much of this knowledge. I have a Latin copy of the book, which we call *The Book of Roger*, in my library. The cosmographer made this 'globe' for King Roger, and I have been blessed to become its new owner."

"But it is round. I thought the world was shaped like a discus." Nicolo was intrigued by the globe. He also wondered how he could see that book. It might lead to the realm of Presbyter John.

"No, the Arabs have known for centuries that the world is round, or more precisely the shape of a woman's breast, and the Romans knew it before them. I don't know why the church and the philosophers resist this knowledge, but the Arabs are happy to keep us in the dark. Look, here is Europe and here is Constantinople, and here are the Syrian lands. You can see the rivers and the mountains etched into the globe. Is it not a most beautiful thing?"

Nicolo put his finger on the globe, tracing the flow of rivers through Europe and looking at the shape of the lands in the southern latitudes. "I have no knowledge of any lands other than Europe. But look how there are lands beyond Constantinople. So many mountains and rivers. Where do they lead? What kind of peoples live there? What do they eat and wear and trade?" Nicolo was so excited as his entire world was opened by this round silver object. "And look far to the east, could that be the land of Presbyter John?" It came out before Nicolo could stop himself.

Count Eugenio looked at Nicolo curiously.

"Presbyter John? What do you know of that far away king?" *Only courtiers and priests talked of Presbyter John. Why would a young merchant know or care about this?*

"I have only heard stories that far to the East there is a kingdom of great wealth and power. My father told me stories about Presbyter John when I was a child. I hadn't thought of him for years, but seeing this globe made me remember the stories." Nicolo tried to keep a blank expression on his face. He couldn't let the count or anyone else know about this. How could he be so stupid and brash? Too much wine.

The count told the servant to remove the globe, stating it was time to end the dinner, as his gout was acting up. He asked Gabriella to walk Nicolo to the main door, where Mahmoud would be waiting to take him and his wine bottles back to the monastery in safety. The count graciously excused himself, and Nicolo felt that his gaffe had not caused a problem.

Gabriella took Nicolo's arm as she glided down the stairway. All thoughts of the globe and Presbyter John were washed away by her perfume. Cinnamon? *If only I could get closer to that neck and get lost in the fragrance and softness.* She bade him good night with a gentle squeeze of his arm and a smile that to Nicolo was more than a polite gesture. She said that she looked forward to seeing Nicolo again, perhaps when he returned with his uncle to look at the library. Or perhaps at the Ballarò. Nicolo could barely control his excitement at the thought of spending more time, maybe intimate time, with this amazing woman. She was so beautiful and so clever. She reminded Nicolo of Uncle Benjamin's daughter, but he hoped that she was more available.

He rode the donkey back to the monastery, dreaming that each jolt and lurch of the animal's back was another thrust on top of Gabriella. Mahmoud complimented Nicolo on how at ease he seemed atop the beast. He had never seen anybody smile while riding a donkey.

※

GABRIELLA STOOD NEXT to Count Eugenio as Cora applied a salve of crushed autumn crocus to his swollen left foot. "Rich food, excessive wine drinking, and too many strawberries. Uncle, you are doing everything you can to kill yourself."

Eugenio waved Cora away. "Go back to the kitchen, Cora, and bring me more wine. This bottle's nearly empty. Gabriella and I must think. The young man has given us a clue, now we need to find out what he is about. More wine?"

Gabriella shook her head. "I think best with a clear head, Uncle."

"Well, I don't. Why would a merchant like Marcus diCarlo send away his second son when his eldest is already away for the crusade? Why would a young merchant of Genoa know anything about

Presbyter John? He stared at the globe even harder than he stared at your breasts. We must have him back with his uncle. We will maneuver for you to be alone with him. Use your many charms to get him to talk. Young men love to impress beautiful women with how important, worldly, and manly they are. Be in awe of him and I am certain that all will be revealed."

"And then? Will he end up in the river as food for the crabs?"

"That depends on what he is doing." Eugenio noticed a slightly pained look on Gabriella's face come and go like a shadow. "Do not fear for the boy, my dear. If he has nothing to offer, he will be on his way. If he is a threat in some manner to me or any of my clients . . . that will be another matter."

Gabriella took a breath and asked the count the question that always lingered around their conversations. "And if I pry the pearl from the oyster and you get the prize you seek, will you abide by your word to me?"

Count Eugenio looked perplexed for a moment, then smiled warmly at Gabriella. "Yes, my dear. This will be the crown on your head. You will have what you seek."

"A promise? No more evasion?"

The count feigned deep hurt. "How can you doubt me so? Yes, my niece. If you get him to tell you what they are about, and it has meaning to me, I will grant your wish."

<hr>

NICOLO TOSSED AND turned on the straw mattress that night, his mind unable to quiet his body's urges. Eventually, his grunts and breathing woke up Mauro. The monk sat up and rubbed his face hard with his two hands.

"Oh, you have returned from your dinner. Did you enjoy yourself?"

Nicolo told Mauro about Count Eugenio's offer for Mauro to visit his library and about the globe and *The Book of Roger*. "When you visit Count Eugenio's library you must look for *The Book of Roger*. It contains a map of parts of the world we don't know about. It could be the way to Presbyter John. You should steal the book."

Mauro was shocked. "I can't do that! It would be a sin!"

"But he probably stole it when the last king was murdered. He has no more right to it than we do. You could steal it, and we could return it to King Frederick when we were done looking at it. Or you could just borrow it without telling the count."

Mauro was adamant. He was a scholar, a man of God, not some petty thief.

Nicolo was undeterred by Mauro's protests. "How about this: You look at the book in the library. You copy down the names of the towns and rivers to the east of Constantinople in another manuscript. Then you ask the count for that manuscript as a gift. He said you could take one as a gift. Take something obscure that would hold no interest to the count. Maybe something religious."

"You think religious texts have no value?"

"No, no that is not what I meant. It is just that Count Eugenio does not strike me as a philosopher or a man much concerned with his soul. Of all the books in his library he probably would be least interested in a religious book. But of course you would, so it makes sense to ask for one."

Mauro calmed down and considered Nicolo's logic. If most of these volumes were stolen anyway, Count Eugenio had no real claim on them. If the books never left the library and were under the guardianship of a man who did not seem to care what they contained and was willing to give one away, Mauro would be doing a service to the church to bring one out of there. If he gave it to the abbey after using it to smuggle the information out, then all would be well. *Besides*, Mauro thought, *who knows what wonderful volumes there might be? Yes, I should do this.*

Nicolo was pleased with his plan, and pleased at how easily he could get the older monk to agree. He sent a note to the count requesting a dinner the coming Sunday. He would get the information from that book. He dreamed of Gabriella.

※

THE YOUNG MERCHANT spent the week visiting warehouses and shops in Palermo at the suggestion of Count Eugene, who was to get 5 percent of the value of whatever cargo came through his contacts. Nicolo knew he could get better deals without an intermediary, but he also didn't have much time left in Sicily and certainly not enough time to cultivate trade relationships. The count did have a good sense of what would sell in Genoa. Nicolo bought several loads of turmeric, pepper, and cassia, and ten butts of red wine. He was excited to find gum Arabic on offer, which Mauro had told him was important in the preparation of ink and pigments for holy manuscripts. He took a chance on a cask of dried galangal, which many people believed helped older men maintain sexual arousal. This should appeal to the dried-up old men of the Great Houses of Genoa, he thought with a malicious grin.

By Friday morning Nicolo realized that he did not have the money to buy all the goods he had agreed to purchase. His advance from the cardinal and the small amount he had from his family were insufficient. He decided to visit the Knights Templar and receive an advance as per the cardinal's instructions. He gulped down the *meusa* that was offered at the monastery. The thick bread stuffed with boiled cattle spleen and chopped lung was filling and certainly appropriate for priests who had taken vows of poverty, but Nicolo had developed a taste for Cora's exquisite cooking and Gabriella's company. He gathered up his receipts and his parchment from the cardinal and walked to the Templar's quarters in a large house on a hill overlooking the harbor. He was challenged at the door by a huge man wearing a black tunic with a red cross on the front and a black mantle over his shoulders. He directed Nicolo to enter the hall, where three knights sat around a small table throwing dice. Unlike the sergeant at the door, these men wore white surcoats with red crosses on front and back. Nicolo approached the group and handed them the cardinal's letter.

"What's this?" growled a bearded knight as he reviewed the cardinal's instructions. "This letter is meant for our brothers in Constantinople. It says so right here. See? You can't redeem this here." Nicolo explained that he had bought many goods for resale in Genoa and that the church would be receiving its share as agreed upon by the cardinal. He needed the advance here in Sicily. "That may be so, my young friend, but we are the bankers of the church, and we must abide by the rules of our order. This letter says that you are to receive advances for expenses. It doesn't say anything about cargoes or goods for resale. It sounds to me like you are trying to cheat the church. We should probably arrest you and take those goods in the name of the church." Seeing the fear on Nicolo's face, the knight relented. "Ah, you're lucky we're in the middle of this game. I don't want to stop now while I'm winning to take you to the cells. Look, you can only redeem this in Constantinople and only for expenses of your travels." The knight saw Nicolo relax. *Another arrogant young trader, only interested in his own gain*, he thought. "There is nothing we can do, but I might have a way to help you out."

"Please, sir, anything."

"A bunch of Jews live just south of the city. They have lenders there. I don't know if they will help you or not, or what price you may have to pay, but it's worth a chance. Now leave us to our duties." The knight turned his back to Nicolo as the other two snickered and shook their heads. Nicolo could hear the laughter and the dice rolling again as he left the building.

※

IT WAS WELL past midday when Nicolo reached the outskirts of Palermo. He asked many people where he could find the Jewish quarter and who might be a lender there. Finally, he reached the home of Isaac ben Yiju. The old Jew who answered the door was guarded when Nicolo asked if he was a lender. But after Nicolo explained his situation, ben Yiju begrudgingly let him in. He cleared some books off a chair in his front parlor and asked Nicolo to sit.

"So, you have overcommitted yourself on this cargo and need help. Why should I help you? I don't know you or your family in Genoa. How can I be certain I will ever see my money again?" Nicolo told him about Uncle Benjamin and his family connection to the Jewish community of Genoa. The old man glared at Nicolo.

"Oh! So you think all Jews know each other and have some sort of secret bond? Do you know that most of us in Sicily were forced to come here by King Roger fifty years ago? He kidnapped our families in Tunis during that crusade and brought us here to be his lenders and go-betweens for the Syrian lands. Some of us have prospered and some have starved. What irony! Saladin takes Jerusalem and lets Jews come and go freely. Roger takes Tunis and kidnaps Jews to Sicily and won't let us leave. We were better off under the Muslims than under these Christians." He shook his head and continued. "Anyway, we have no connection with the Jews in Genoa or in France or elsewhere in Europe. We don't speak the same language. We don't wear the same clothes or eat the same food. Yes, we pray the same prayers in the ancient tongue, but prayers aren't commerce. Don't expect special treatment from us because you have some distant Jewish relative. If that were the case, we would have to loan money to every Christian who lives, since Jesus was a Jew in his lifetime." The old man took several deep breaths to calm himself. Nicolo felt awkward.

"I am truly sorry, sir. I really don't know much about Jews beyond what my uncle and his family have taught me. Jews have always been kind and fair to our family in Genoa. I am not asking for special treatment. I just want to borrow money for this cargo shipment guaranteed by the goods, just like anybody else. I realize that you don't know me or my family, but I beg you to help me out. This is my first purchase on my own. I need to show my father I can do this, that I am ready to trade and help support my family. Please."

Ben Yiju saw the despair in Nicolo's face. *This world is nothing but pain*, he thought. *This young man is sincere, and he did not come here to insult me; he is truly seeking my help. This is more than a trade deal; this is about his maturing into a man. That I can support.* He looked out the window and saw the sun dropping behind the neighboring rooftops. *The Sabbath is approaching. Let this be the last mitzvah I perform this week. The Good Lord knows I need all the points I can get in this world.*

"Well, let's see how much you have bought and who you owe commissions and how much you will need," the old man grumbled. "If you made some good deals that will turn a profit in Genoa, perhaps we can take a chance on you." Nicolo nearly leaped from his seat with excitement and started to rattle off cargoes and prices. "Wait, wait, slow down. We need to document everything. If we are going to help you it must be at your risk, not ours. Show me all your receipts and notes."

Nicolo took out all of his documentation. Ben Yiju looked everything over carefully and grunted. "Huh, you paid too much for most of this, but that is to be expected when you are new in port. As soon as you landed the word got around. The oarsman tells the tavernkeeper. Someone at the tavern overhears them. The customs inspector grills the crew and passes the information along. Within a day the prices shoot up ten percent to cover the informant's fees and to grab a few more coins from your shiny new purse." He laughed hoarsely and shook his head. "'Hey, there's a young trader in town and he doesn't know that a Sicilian cane of cloth is only eight palms long and a Genoese cane is nine palms.' So, they sell you a cane of linen and short you eleven percent of the material."

Nicolo's face reddened. He knew that he was woefully underprepared for this venture. Everything in Sicily was so different from the situation in Troyes. At the fairs you went from booth to booth making deals and collecting slips of parchment. Then you took the parchment to the Office of the Garbler, who weighed out casks and barrels before they were filled to ensure the proper weight was included in your purchase. Fair officials checked the final quality of goods before shipment. Payment went through the exchequers, not directly to the merchant. That way the differences in weights between Genoa and London or Paris and values of coinage could be harmonized. A merchant paid with golden crowns that were worth the same throughout the fair or paid with drafts drawn on some agreed-upon lender. Here in Sicily everything was just merchant to merchant. There was nobody to watch over the transaction and guarantee that the olive oil purchased was the same as delivered dockside, or that the barrels of gum Arabic he bought were not full of tree sap. He bought two barrels of murex shells that Paolo the tailor had told him were essential for dyeing leather purple and were very difficult to find and gave the seller three golden crowns. In return he received a handful of coins, among them ten Castilian maravedis, a Turkish sultani, and a Venetian ounce of silver. Nicolo knew that a Venetian ounce weighed 460 grains, yet a Genoese ounce weighed only 405 grains, a Castilian pound was 7085 grains, but the Genoese equivalent was only 5528 grains. He had never traded maravedis or sultanis and had no way of judging their value without a set of scales or a Garbler. He didn't have the experience of his father or his brother, so he had accepted at its face that the deal was fairly done. He knew that he did this out of embarrassment, to look competent to the other traders, but now he felt a total fool. His friends in Genoa, his father, and half the whores on Love Way knew more about these things than he did.

The old man saw the defeat on Nicolo's face.

"Ahh, don't feel bad, young man. This is standard trade practice in this wicked place. You can't avoid it until you have more trading under your belt, so you'll just have to build the losses into your ultimate sale price. Consider it the cost of your education. From now on, don't let these merchants pressure you into making a deal before you have made your calculations. Take the time to learn the differences in the coins and measures used in different places before you get there or as soon as you arrive. If you can master the Arab math, you can quickly learn the ways of commerce outside of Genoa. And don't think you are the only trader to have his codpiece pulled down in the town square. Even Count Eugenio has been made the fool from time to time." Ben Yiju studied Nicolo's list of purchases again. "But even with your foolishness and inexperience, looking at this stuff I think you can still make a nice profit."

Nicolo took a breath deep into his chest and let go of some of his anxiety. He described the commissions he had promised. Ten percent for Fiori, five percent for Count Eugenio. *The count must have been feeling generous*, Ben Yiju thought, *or else he plans to make his coin off this boy in another way.* Ben Yiju was impressed when Nicolo quickly added up all the cargo costs using the Arab mathematics. He looked at the figures.

"All right then. Your total cost of goods is 15,000 silver deniers and then there is another 2,250 in commissions. You need 17,250 and you have put down 5,000 on the cargo. That leaves 12,250 deniers to pay." He sat back and rubbed his eyes. "In addition, you will have to pay ten percent customs duty on the value of the dry cargo going out of Palermo—such as the linens, rare woods, medicinal plants—that's 1,000, and twelve percent on the fish and foodstuffs, that's 600, and I believe nine percent going into Genoa, for another 1,350. That's an additional 2,950."

"My family will pay the import duties in Genoa, so I won't need the 1,350. That brings the total to . . ." Nicolo scribbled the numbers down. "Thirteen thousand, eight hundred fifty."

The old man considered the youth sitting before him. *He is quick and smart, that's good. He is worth the risk, and who knows? Maybe this will open up more trading opportunities for us in Genoa. Perhaps I can send my nephew out of this accursed land and make a relationship with this young man's Jewish relatives. They owe us a favor now.*

"That's a lot of money to advance a total stranger. We will charge ten percent on that. That's quite a deal as the going rate in Genoa and

Constantinople is twenty percent. I will send one of our young men to pay the commissions and invoices with you, collect the papers, and prepare the documents for customs. They have to be done in a particular way here in Sicily and we don't want to give the customs inspector any opportunity to dip into your purse at the dock. He is good at finding excuses to hold up the vessel and squeeze a small facilitation payment out of cargo owners." He noted the smile and look of relief on Nicolo's face. "But we take no part of your risk. This is a personal loan to you and your family, not a partnership on the sale of the goods. If you lose everything in a storm or a pirate attack, that is your loss, not ours. We will prepare three sets of documents. One we will keep. The second goes with the ship captain for delivery to your family. The third goes to your Uncle Benjamin. He can arrange payment from your family onto the books of some lender in Genoa for further payment to our named agent there. Agreed?"

Nicolo took the proffered hand readily.

Mauro spent the entire day with the king, who took him by the hand to show him wondrous things and peppered him with unending questions. The king's menagerie was filled with exotic animals that were gifts from rulers throughout the known world. Mauro saw an elephant, a tiger, a camel, a giraffe, and so many colorful birds that he clapped his hands in delight, acting more childlike than the king. He felt humbled in the presence of God's wondrous creations. They had a long discussion of how Noah could have carried, cared for, and cleaned up after thousands of such animals in an ark that Frederick calculated was not much bigger than his zoo and gardens.

Frederick took immediately to Mauro's teachings of the art of logical thinking and argument. He interrogated Mauro on whether the Biblical prescription of an eye for an eye was a call for revenge or a limit to the punishment justice required. He asked Mauro many questions about spiritual matters with a scientific sharpness that was unsettling to the monk.

"Brother Mauro, is the soul visible?"

Mauro was perplexed by the question, which he had never considered. "I don't really know, Your Highness. The soul is real, yet it is an immaterial essence."

The king looked disappointed with Mauro's answer. "We shall see for ourselves then."

In the afternoon the king took Mauro into a chamber beneath the palace. They were let into a locked room by armed guards. A huge barrel sat in the middle of the otherwise empty room. The king led Mauro to a ladder and signaled him to climb with him to the top of the closed barrel. Frederick looked into the small hole at the top of the barrel and shouted to the guards below.

"Is he still alive?"

"We believe so, Your Highness, but his moans are coming less frequently. He should be dead by the end of this day.'

"Excellent!" the king cried out. "I want you to stay up here for the rest of the day. When you hear the prisoner's last breath, get close to the hole and watch for the soul escaping." He looked at Mauro with a child's innocence and smiled. "Look how I am using this logic that you taught me! It is so useful. It will help me answer so many questions I have."

Frederick told Mauro of other ideas he had and how logic could help him solve many of life's mysteries. He wanted to know if children raised without the interference of parents would speak the natural language of Adam and Eve. What would happen if he fed one man and starved another and cut open their bowels? Would they digest differently? Mauro was distraught. He had only applied logic and reason to disputations in the monastery or in the university. He had never experienced them in action in the world. Frederick was so curious, yet at the same time he didn't seem to have any control over his wild mind, and as king there were few who would question or try to interfere with his actions. He took his concerns to the abbot, who sighed and took Mauro's hand.

"The young king may not live long, given the impending invasion. We cannot know what God has in store for young Frederick. It is preordained as it is with all of us. Yet you are helping him hone his faculties for the trials ahead. It is all any of us can do."

Mauro realized he could do no more with the boy king on this visit to Sicily. He looked forward to Constantinople, where he would use his logic and rhetoric to advance understanding and bring unification. His skills and hard work would be appreciated by men of learning, not perverted by a royal child.

The abbot reflected how much Brother Mauro seemed the innocent. He was so deeply engaged in the pursuit of truth and spirit, yet he knew so little about the ways of this wicked world. How would he react to the deception and political machinations that swirled beneath the surface—and often above—in Constantinople? Would he rise or be crushed?

※

THE COUNT WAS a charming host at the Sunday supper. He seemed very interested in Mauro's thoughts, so much so that Nicolo could stare at Gabriella's breasts and exchange sly smiles in a most uninhibited manner. Cora started her gastronomic performance with spaghetti al ricci, a pasta with sea urchin favored by Al-Idrisi. The pasta came from the new factory owned by a young Muslim merchant, whose family grew the durum wheat used in the pasta. Her second dish was couscous al pesce, which featured large chunks of swordfish. After the fish and the wine, she brought in a tray of gelatinous sweets she called marzipan, which had recently been created at a convent in Martorana. This was followed by blatantly breast-shaped cakes made in the Monastery of the Virgins of Palermo to honor St. Agatha. Finally, the count ordered a servant to escort Mauro to the library. He begged to be excused, as his gout was flaring again. He asked Gabriella to entertain Nicolo while Mauro enjoyed the library.

Mauro marveled at the ceiling-to-floor shelves of bound books and loose manuscripts in the library. He was left alone by the servant to wander the stacks, picking out a title here and there, reading the Latin and Greek names but realizing he could not translate the Arabic volumes. There were many large manuscripts celebrating the reigns of Sicilian kings and nobility. A series of twenty volumes cataloged the laws and edicts of the kingdom. At random intervals Mauro found the works of Pliny the Elder, Macrobius, and Plato. He stood on a chair and reached for the title *The Book of Roger* but paused when he saw a volume of Xenophon the Athenian next to it. He grabbed the latter volume and took it down. The book was entitled *Cyropaedia*, "The Education of Cyrus." Mauro had heard of this writing. It was an exploration of the education and experiences that forged the life of Cyrus the Great, the Persian king whom Xenophon thought the ideal ruler. Cyrus had united many diverse peoples into one empire. Surely there was much of interest here for the young king of Sicily. He read and read until the Greek letters swirled on the pages before him. His head slowly sank into the volume and he fell asleep contented. He woke after a short time and realized that he needed to look at *The Book of Roger*. He placed *Cyropaedia* onto the large writing desk in the center of the room. He took down *The Book of Roger* and opened it to the map, titled "Tabulae Rogeriana." He had never spent time looking at maps, so it took a while for Mauro to orient himself to the geography. He ultimately found Rome and Sicily. He looked across the Mediterranean Sea and found Jerusalem.

※

GABRIELLA LED NICOLO to the gardens. They walked among the lemon and jasmine trees, the scents making Nicolo swoon. He explained to Gabriella that he was very sensitive to scents, and that he had been trained by his father to differentiate the spices and to tell whether a cargo of fruit was ripe or rotten or whether it contained rat droppings from the hold of a ship.

Gabriella arched a black eyebrow. "I don't believe you, Nicolo." Gabriella took Nicolo's hand and led him beneath a large lemon tree. She turned and leaned against the tree, liberating several small white lemon petals to swirl around and land on her black hair. She looked deep into Nicolo's eyes. "Show me."

Nicolo smiled easily. He slowly approached her neck, sniffing long and deep. "Cinnamon," he whispered. He leaned in closer, his nose grazing her neck from her shoulder to beneath her ear. "And vanilla, rare vanilla from distant Taprobana."

Gabriella squirmed with delight.

"Nicolo, you are truly a master at your craft. But please, I am not experienced in the world of men. My uncle keeps me close to the hearth. I am feeling very flush and need some water. May we go back inside?" Nicolo was shocked at the rebuff. He thought he had her under his spell. This only made her more desirable. He took a deep breath and agreed. They entered the kitchen area on the first floor. As Gabriella sipped water from an earthen jug, Nicolo came up behind her and put his hands on her waist. Gabriella grabbed his hands in hers and wrapped them around her body, just under her breasts. Nicolo could feel her heart racing and breath quickening. "Please, Nicolo, I cannot be so intimate so soon. Let us do something else to take our minds off our bodies. Please."

Well, thought Nicolo, *if I can't explore her body perhaps, I can explore the world.* "Of course, my love. Then will you show me the globe again? It is so interesting to me."

Gabriella looked around nervously. "I don't think my uncle would approve. The globe is his special treasure. He never lets anyone look at it without his permission and his presence."

Nicolo sensed her fear but also her desire to please him.

"It will be our secret, my cinnamon beauty. I just want to see the way to Constantinople and perhaps the Holy Land. It is as if I am seeing the world from the eyes of a bird. I want to experience that one more time." He smiled softly and imploringly at Gabriella. She relented and begged him to follow her silently up the stairs and into the room that held the globe. They took off their leather shoes to muffle the sound of their footsteps and Nicolo noticed that her feet were as perfect as her neck. They entered the room and Gabriella lit a candle, placing it on a small table next to the globe. They leaned in toward the globe together.

"Look, my sweet, here we are in Sicily." Nicolo took her left-hand pointer finger and glided it over the small island. "And here is the Strait of Messina. Follow the coast up to Rome and further north to Genoa." Her finger quivered a bit under his gentle pressure.

"I wish I could see those lands," she sighed. "I wish I could go there with you." She turned toward Nicolo and leaned back against the globe. He leaned against her gently.

"That would be a dream, indeed," he cooed. "For now, though, shall I kiss you in Paris?"

"Yes," she breathed.

He pressed his lips gently against hers. Warm, soft, and moist. "I shall kiss you in Rome and Genoa." He moved down to lightly brush her breasts with his lips. She shuddered and held his shoulders tightly. He continued downward.

"And an expression of love in the Holy Land." Nicolo pressed his face into her gown beneath her waist. It felt hard as metal. He looked up in surprise. Gabriella laughed gently.

"That is your punishment for sacrilege, my wild traveler. I am trapped in this leather girdle and locked away. It is called a 'belt of purity.' My uncle keeps the key hidden somewhere."

Nicolo stood up and pressed himself against her. She pushed him back gently and smiled sadly. "Even that battering ram you have against me cannot break down the gate, I am afraid." Nicolo looked defeated. Gabriella smiled brightly. "But do not despair, Nicolo, I think I can find the key. Come for dinner again tomorrow night and we will see if your siege tactics can succeed. I want to be with you, but we need discretion. My uncle will sleep deeply, especially if he has too much wine. He will always share the last cup, so just keep drinking until he is satiated. Then you will have your reward. Now we must leave this room before the servants see us and tell my uncle. He would be very upset with you and with me if he discovered that I have taken you to see the globe."

Nicolo thought of the torture devices in the other room and felt a twinge in his, *how did the count put it?* delicate parts. He did not want to anger Count Eugenio.

The men rode silently back to the abbey. Mauro was lost in thought about Xenophon. He broke from his reverie and asked his smiling companion what he was thinking about.

"Geography."

IN THEIR ROOM at the abbey, Nicolo quickly asked Mauro about *The Book of Roger*. Had he found it? Did he follow the world eastward from Constantinople? Mauro's face glowed and he looked dreamy.

"Oh, yes, my son. I found so many books, so many manuscripts, it was a heavenly experience." Nicolo pressed him about *The Book of Roger*. "Yes, yes, I found it. It contained a map of the entire world. A wondrous map. I could find the Holy Land. There was Jerusalem. There was the Sea of Galilee. I felt as if I was there . . ." Mauro leaned back on the mattress with a swoon.

"But what about the path to the east of Constantinople, toward the lands of Presbyter John? Did you write the names down? Did you draw the map?"

Mauro looked down at his sandals. "No. I was so blessed to be in the Holy Land that I forgot to look away to the east. I am sorry."

"Brother Mauro, we need that information. I have never heard of anything like that book. Well, we are going back again tomorrow night and this time you must concentrate on your mission. Find a book that you would like as a gift, write down the names of the places to the east of Constantinople and draw a map if there is time and room. You can bring a parchment and a writing quill and tell the count that you want to write the names of the best Christian volumes down for the abbot. Tell him the abbot is very interested in his library."

"I will," Mauro replied meekly.

COUNT EUGENIO PUSHED away the bowl of bread crumbled into a rabbit broth that Cora had prepared for breakfast. He turned to Gabriella, who was toying with her food. "Well? What did you learn from the boy?"

"Nothing, except that he wants what every man wants."

"I could have told you that, my niece. Our time is running out. They will be leaving Sicily soon and I want to know what he is about!"

Gabriella smiled. "Don't choke on your breakfast, dear uncle. We already know that he seeks information on the roads beyond Constantinople and that he has heard of this Presbyter John. There is more he has to tell." She sat back and curled her thick black hair around her left pointer finger, thinking of his touch on the globe. "When I was a child, my brothers taught me how to lure in and hook a fish from the bridge. First, you jiggle the line subtly. Then you set the hook and yank it. He is desperate to touch me. I have him completely under my control. Tonight, after you fall asleep at the table, I will squeeze everything out of him."

Eugenio raised an eyebrow. "Do leave something for the crabs, my dear."

THE COUNT RETIRED after an enormous dinner of eggplants stuffed with ricotta, pine nuts, currants and tomatoes, and half a dozen bottles of hearty Syracusa red wine followed by two of limoncello. He didn't touch the plate of candied cucuzza gourds that Cora had prepared, saying that the dessert was obviously meant for Nicolo, as Eugenio had no energy left for sweet things. Gabriella whispered to Nicolo that the count was making a pun, as cucuzza was also a term of endearment in Palermo, and she glared at Eugenio when Nicolo reached for his wine cup. The count told Mauro to enjoy the library, and to leave the volume he wished to have on the writing desk. His servants would wrap the volume and deliver it on the morrow to Mauro at the monastery. He generously invited the men to return for supper on Sunday, a traditional time for large feasts, when they would celebrate all their mutual good fortune.

Mauro was happily led back to the library to make his list for the abbot and explore the wonderful collection. Once alone he went to the writing desk. Xenophon remained open to the chapter where Cyrus recalls the lessons of Cambyses that those who are attentive to God in good times as well as bad have the right to ask blessings. Mauro started to think about this, but remembered he had a job to do. He took out the quill, ink, and parchment and began to write down some of the religious titles on the shelves. Then he took down *The Book of Roger*, opened to the map and began to write down the strange geography to the east of Constantinople onto the last pages of Xenophon. He had trouble reading the names, as they were either Arabic versions from Al-Idrisi or just so strange to Mauro's tongue. When he finished he placed *The Book of Roger* back on the shelf, congratulating himself on being so clever and thorough. He rubbed his eyes to ease the strain of reading the small letters in the dim light of the library. He then spied another volume, *The Book of Holy Places*, and took it down to peruse at the desk. The author had listed hundreds of Christian holy places around Europe and the Syrian lands, most of which were unknown to Mauro. Each site had a description of the miracle that had occurred there or the holy order that lived there, as well as what indulgences could be purchased. He decided to leave the book on the desk and made a mental note to look at it more closely during his next visit.

※

Gabriella led Nicolo back to the garden, but as soon as the servants left them alone, she spirited him into a back doorway. They walked quietly down a hall and into a small room. There was little in the room besides a large bed. A few small paintings of saints stared sternly from the walls. Gabriella slipped her hand under the pillow and produced a small key.

"I give you the key to heaven" she said in a husky voice. "Take me there now." Nicolo could barely breathe with the rush of excitement. In a brief whirl of time, clothing, and the scent of cinnamon he found himself lying next to Gabriella on the bed. Her dress was gone. She lay there in a silk slip, which she slowly pulled up to reveal the belt of purity. She handed the key to Nicolo and guided his hand toward the small brass lock that held the girdle in place. He hesitated to turn the key. Gabriella laughed quietly. "Don't be so afraid. It does not bring me pain. Pity the poor Arab girls whose fathers put the lock right through their sweet soft lips down there." She squeezed Nicolo's hand. "Now free me," she whispered.

Nicolo turned the key firmly. The lock clicked and Gabriella opened the girdle. Nicolo put his lips on her belly and started to kiss her gently below the navel. He noted a texture and a smell and asked quietly if Gabriella had covered her skin with olive oil. She told him that all their soaps were made with soft olive oil, not that hard beef tallow that was used in the North. Nicolo thought that Esther would like the soap and could turn a profit if he sent her a small cargo. His calculation was interrupted when Gabriella purred that Sicilian olive oil was very powerful.

"No matter how hot the pan gets, it holds its strength and doesn't break down."

They came together with the urgency and insistence of new love, yet with the tenderness and hopefulness of sanctuary. The oil never dissipated. During the second (or was it the third?) delight of wet intimacy Nicolo found himself dreaming in erotic reverie of Esther. He knew he cared about his cousin and was aware of a playful tension when they were together, but he had never fantasized about her like this. Yet with Gabriella he was free to love without the restrictions on him in Genoa. This dark beauty opened up a world where emotions and sex intersected. He had experienced each, but never at the same time. Even Antonio had never experienced that. For the first time he felt equal to, no, *superior* to his brother in something besides mathematics. Esther . . . Gabriella . . . Esther. He was lost in a swirl of faces, black hair, and blue and black eyes. Where was he?

"What did you say?" Gabriella grabbed his shoulders and pushed him up abruptly. "Did you call me by another woman's name? Who is Esther?" She found herself strangely angry. Was it jealousy? She hardly knew this boy and she was doing this to get information, not out of love. Or was she merely upset that this man, any man, would dare to call her by another name during lovemaking.

Nicolo was alarmed but quickly recovered and spoke soothingly. "No, no, my cinnamon girl. There is no other in this bed but you. I said '*esita, esita.*' That means 'slowly, slowly, hesitate a bit' in our Genoese dialect. I only wanted to prolong the moment."

Gabriella looked at him skeptically but remembered her mission and relaxed.

"That is well, my love, because I was going to call for the Truth Seeker if I smelled betrayal." She looked hard at him for a moment and laughed. They tumbled into each other again.

As they lay tangled in sheets and sweat, Gabriella stroked Nicolo's face gently. "You are so amazing to me, Nicolo. Why did heaven drop you in my arms? How did such a brilliant, handsome, and clever merchant prince end up carrying the bags of an old monk? Surely you are doing penitence for some evil deed. Did you steal the family fortune? Sleep with the wife of a nobleman? Tell me everything, Nicolo. I am yours. I am your secret keeper. When I put the belt back on, I will shut away my life and hold your secrets until you and only you return. Tell me."

In the swoon of the night, pumped up by the love and admiration of this incredible woman, Nicolo told his tale. As Gabriella listened, she realized that his life was in serious danger. Markward was coming soon to wrest the kingdom away from the influence of the pope. If she told the count, he might have Nicolo killed to protect his privilege with Markward. She didn't want to be responsible for Nicolo's death, but if she didn't tell Eugenio any of this, it would be she who suffered.

"Nicolo, you know that this is a very dangerous time to be in Sicily. You need to get away as soon as you can."

Nicolo felt the caress on his arm. *She cares about me deeply.* "We will be gone soon enough. I need to finish my business on the docks, see the vessel loaded and spend more time in your arms. I know that Markward is coming and that we should be away before he and his German dogs arrive, but we have time yet. And there are plenty of monks and traders running around Palermo. We are safe as long as nobody knows more about us than that."

※

COUNT EUGENIO WAS in an expansive mood. The representative from the Jews had delivered his commissions on Nicolo's trades. His servant had wrapped and delivered the library book to Mauro at the monastery, assuring the abbot would be kindly disposed toward Eugenio in the struggle to come. And the information about the boy and the monk! This was a valuable cargo, indeed. He had his money and his information. He had no further use for his latest guests. Should he sell them to Markward? Kill them now? Eugenio visualized all the pieces swirling on the board. Oh, he had almost forgotten the emir.

He called for Mahmoud, enjoying a fine fare of Cora's before the man arrived. She had arranged a plate of orange slices, intermixing the dark blood sanguigno with the blond biondo oranges of the island. Eugenio chuckled to think that Cora might be showing her disapproval of his behavior with Gabriella and Nicolo. The woman never spoke without being asked, but she managed to get her point across through her servings at times. Or was this all Eugenio's imagination? He had never thought to ask the kitchen woman, enjoying the food and the mystery instead. What would I do without that food of hers? He laughed out loud when she brought in his morning pupa di cena figure made of sugar. Today it was a penis cut in half. Mahmoud entered and frowned at the plate.

"I have prepared a letter for you to deliver to the emir. It describes a bold plot that could disrupt our wonderful relationship and destroy a large part of the trade here in the future. Take this to him immediately. Tell him that my price for this information is first preference on the coming saffron harvest with exclusive right to sell to European traders in Sicily. He can have the Syrians. The Byzantines are up for grabs. And when you return, I will have a special task for you, the kind you enjoy, that will bring this interesting visit to a close."

Mahmoud left at once, knowing that the donkey ride into the mountains would take the entire day and part of the evening. He did not want to be on the roads after dark, even in his own clan's territory. Whatever this information was, the emir would pay Mahmoud handsomely for being the courier. A good price on the summer wheat crop would do nicely. He could have it milled in Palermo and sell to the foreign traders at a good profit. It was a beautiful day. He rode out of the city and into the Val de Mazara, where the displaced Arab population of Palermo grew the cotton, papyrus, sugarcane, oranges, lemons, and wheat that the kingdom and its trading partners had come to depend upon. The smell of the blossoms and the dry, low hills of the Val de Mazara reminded him of home. He deeply missed his family, the food, and even the bird sounds of Tunis. He was happy to get out of Palermo. Three hundred thousand souls were too many for Mahmoud to tolerate day after day. He was a child of the countryside.

Mahmoud was received warmly at the emir's palace deep within the Val de Mazara. This was in such contrast to the way he was treated in Palermo. Yet Mahmoud knew that he had an important task here keeping the emir informed regarding the politics of Palermo, the traders in port and the shifting alliances between the various tumultuous communities of Sicily. All toward the goal of reconquest—for this he would play the fool to Eugenio, the customs inspector, and so many others. It was his way of jihad, not the glorious great jihad of soul-searching nor even the lesser jihad of standing in a line of battle, but a sacrifice for the struggle nonetheless. He was shown to the great hall, where he sat comfortably on cushions, eating dates and sipping tea as he waited for the emir. He was joined by a thin, muscular young man who played an *oud*, the Arabic stringed instrument that French crusaders had recently brought to Europe under the name *l'oud* and were now calling the "lute." The young man strummed ancient *maqams*, the haunting, repetitive melodies that Mahmoud remembered so well from his childhood. He lay back on the cushions and drifted away to Tunis.

Mahmoud stood and bowed as Emir Muhammad Ibn Abbad entered the room. Mahmoud reflected that since the siege of Palermo one hundred years earlier, the emirate had been abolished by the Norman conquerors. The remaining emirs had died in battle, retired to the mountains, or converted to Christianity like the hated Ibn Hamud, who became part of the Christian nobility. Ibn Abbad was a descendant of Ayyub Ibn Tamid, the Great Unifier of the fragmented Muslim fiefdoms of Sicily. He was the rightful heir to the emirate and was known as the emir even without a country to rule. Mahmoud knew that Ibn Abbad was a true emir, not one of those who had received the title for payment to those corrupt Seljuk princes. Ibn Abbad's lineage was from the West, a Berber, not a Turk from the East. He had led a peaceful life while Muslims in Sicily were under royal protection during the reign of King William. Yet upon William's death the order was lifted, and the community of believers was set upon by the Christians. They survived by segregating themselves in the southwest of the island, with the exception of the merchants and artisans in the Ballarò and the hundreds of Saracen archers in the employ of the crown of Sicily. Mahmoud shook his head slowly at the thought. *From this, our mountain of faith, we have been whittled down to this small valley.*

The emir embraced Mahmoud warmly and asked him to be seated once again. After some respectful pleasantries, the likes of which he never experienced from Eugenio, Mahmoud passed the count's letter to the emir. Ibn Abbad broke the seal and read the contents, pausing several times to digest the news.

"This is very serious," the emir intoned. "We must get this news to Al-Adil immediately. It is too important to keep here. Tarik!" The young man stopped playing the oud and stood up. "Tell our falconer we must send a message to Al-Adil at once. I will prepare it shortly." Tarik bowed then sprinted out of the room. The emir turned back to Mahmoud. He looked at the little man. *And here is our ragtag army—informants, saboteurs, small knives. Not enough to retake Sicily, but sufficient to provide Al-Adil with important information toward the greater goal of cleansing all infidel kingdoms from Syria to Egypt. Then the promised invasion of Sicily.* Would this happen in his lifetime? Was Al-Adil the man to carry the mantle of his brother Saladin onwards? He thought of the irony that his family's Berber heritage would be rescued not by a man of the west, but by Al-Adil, a man from the East—and a Kurd at that! Were they all just grains of sand in a turning hourglass? He sighed and spoke to Mahmoud. "What else did the count tell you?"

"He was thinking of how best to eliminate them, now that he has gotten whatever gain he thought he could. He mentioned turning them over to the Germans when Markward arrives or having them killed and dumped into the Oreto."

The emir sat back on the cushions. "We already have an

arrangement with Markward. We will offer no resistance to his rule if he grants us sovereignty over the interior of the island. That will allow us undisturbed time to strengthen our forces here for the eventual reconquest. These Europeans are so easily convinced that we are weak and ready to make deals with them to save ourselves from their military might." He tapped the letter with his finger. "As for Count Eugenio, he does like to kill. That we cannot allow. We must ensure that these men leave Sicily safely before Markward and his trained beasts land. Their fate is up to Al-Adil. He has ample time to deal with them as he wishes in Constantinople. It is an easy place to die and be forgotten."

NICOLO WATCHED THE crew of the *Minervi* load the casks of dried fish, the sponges, the bolts of fabric, and other cargo into the hold. He noticed Fiori jump over the ship's rail and approach him with a pouch held in his hand.

"I've got the documents, and we will be done loading tonight. Then we sail for Genoa. Nicolo, come with us and get out of here. The next Genoese ships you see will be bristling like a tailor's pin cushion with weapons and Germans. They are shipping out of Naples as we speak and will arrive in a few days."

Nicolo clapped his hand on the captain's shoulder in gratitude.

"Thanks, Fiori, but I need to go with my uncle to Constantinople. I will wait until those Germans disembark and we'll grab the first Genoese ship outbound to Pera or Constantinople."

"You don't get it, Nicolo. All the king's advisers and the pope's followers will be rounded up. The valuable ones will be ransomed and the less fortunate tortured and killed. You can guess where a young merchant and an old monk figure there. Look, I can arrange passage for you and your uncle on a Pisan galley leaving for Constantinople tonight. You will have to play the simpleton with your uncle. Keep your mouth shut and nobody will bother you. If they find out you're a Genoese merchant they'll throw you overboard. We are still at war with Pisa."

"I'll think about it, Fiori. And thanks."

"Well, don't think too hard. Just show up dressed as a pilgrim and take that smart-ass grin off your face. It will all be arranged."

<hr />

Gabriella entered the dining hall dressed in a light blue gown and humming a tune. She was surprised to see Count Eugenio alone at the table in a casual evening robe.

"Uncle, you are not dressed to receive our guests. Are you ill?" Count Eugenio put down the wine goblet and smiled. In his left hand he twirled the little key that Gabriella had returned to him that morning. It sickened her to think he had so much power over her.

"No, my niece. But there has been a change of plans. We will not be joined tonight by Nicolo. Nor Brother Mauro. Instead, you will be having a rendezvous with them on the Admiral's Bridge to tell them something very important."

Gabriella felt a chill. She looked at Eugenio with suspicion. "All right. I will get a cloak and ready myself."

"Actually, my dear, you aren't feeling that well, so you won't be able to meet them."

Gabriella knew Eugenio well enough to understand his meaning. She regretted telling Eugenio anything about Nicolo's mission. She had betrayed the young man's deepest trust, but it was the only way to assure that Eugenio lived up to his agreement. She had to get word to Nicolo not to show up at the bridge. But if she did and Nicolo escaped, what would she have left to bargain with? *Damn Eugenio and his power. Damn Nicolo and his love. Damn all men and their games.*

"As you wish, Uncle," she said with forced gaiety. "I will retire with a headache. Perhaps Cora can bring my supper to my room, and I will have it alone in bed."

"Certainly, child. But I am concerned for your condition. I will have one of the servants stay by your door to ensure you do not catch a night chill."

Gabriella curtsied and left the room, her mind racing ahead to the horrible scene on the bridge. *I must get to the bridge before they do. I must get out of the house. But how?*

※

It was well after dark when she approached the bridge, her features hidden beneath a large shawl. She waited an eternity until she heard the clopping of two donkeys and the voices of men coming from the other side of the bridge. When the men reached the nadir of the bridge, she began to run toward them. Suddenly, four shapes charged out of the darkness from behind the riders. They grabbed the men off the donkeys, and she could hear the cries as the men were repeatedly stabbed. She shrank back into the shadows and watched in horror, knowing there was nothing she could do. The hooded men threw the bodies into the Oreto, the loud splashes the only sound echoing through the night. They turned and ran back toward town. The driver picked up the reins and continued toward her. When he got close, they recognized each other. Mahmoud looked directly at her and shrugged his shoulders.

"Don't be afraid, *habibti*. Tonight we will all get what we want. Those men? They were just two French sailors. Do not feel sorry for them. Sailors will die at sea and drowning is a terrible death. Sometimes they will die in a tavern brawl. It does not matter. Nobody will mourn them, and the count will have his two bodies." He flicked the rein of the lead donkey and walked toward La Ziza.

※

Nicolo and Mauro were enjoying a late-night bowl of hot crab soup with the abbot when Father Gioffri ran into the dining hall. He was grossly fat, and the short run had taken its toll. He bent over and grabbed his chest, breathing heavily.

"At the gate. A woman. Looking for you, Nicolo. Hurry!"

Nicolo dropped his spoon and ran to the gate. It was still locked, and the hooded woman gripped the bars. He knew it was Gabriella. He ran up to her and she pulled her hood back to speak. Nicolo was startled.

"Cora? What are you doing here? Where is Gabriella?" The kitchen woman looked afraid. She grabbed Nicolo's hands through the gate. He thought irrelevantly about her strong grip and the stronger smell of garlic on her breath.

"Nicolo, you must leave Sicily. You must leave tonight!" Her fingers dug into Nicolo's. "Count Eugenio knows why you are here. He arranged to kill you and Brother Mauro tonight but luckily two other men took your place." Cora crossed herself.

Nicolo was stunned. "What? How did the count know about us? Nobody knew . . . except Gabriella." *Could Gabriella have betrayed me? Was I the puppet when I thought I was the puppeteer?* He banged his fist over and over on the wrought iron, moaning and repeating Gabriella's name.

"Nicolo, there is no time for this. You know nothing of the count, of our lives. She did what she had to do. She sent me to warn you. That will have to be good enough for you. I must go back to La Ziza, and you must leave Sicily!" She turned and fled into the darkness.

Nicolo ran back to the dining hall, meeting the monk and the abbot on the way. He told them about Cora's warning. The abbot warned them to hurry. He instructed Father Gioffri to go to the wardrobe and find two monk's robes with cowls to give the men. He wished them luck and ran to the sanctuary. Nicolo and Mauro quickly gathered their belongings. Nicolo made certain that Mauro packed the wrapped book, their key to finding Presbyter John. They threw on the brown monk's robes. Their belts were red, identifying them from a different monastery. No one on the street would associate them with the Hermitage. Clearly, the abbot had dealt with such matters before. They walked rapidly toward the docks, hoping that the Pisan galley was not yet underway. Nicolo silently prayed that one of the yawl boats would be available to take them out to the ship, which was too big to warp to the dock and was anchored farther out.

"I can't believe she would betray me like that. I just can't believe it!" Nicolo muttered as he struggled in the currents of anger and despair.

Mauro wanted to comfort the young man, but he knew that broken hearts were beyond his abilities to repair with psalms and quotes, no matter how powerful. He realized that he knew so little about people, why they did what they did. And he knew nothing of women and love. The world was so much deeper than he knew from his books and manuscripts. He couldn't help King Frederick, and he couldn't help Nicolo. He felt that his time in Sicily had been wasted. All he could offer was that Nicolo didn't know the whole story and perhaps he couldn't judge Gabriella's actions yet.

It did little to stem Nicolo's fury, but when they reached the docks the younger man calmed down. He remembered Fiori's words. He had to play the simpleton and keep his mouth shut. This was a Pisan ship. *From the frying pan into the fire*, he thought miserably. They saw the yawl boat. It was full of pilgrims and sheep. The rowers had just dropped their oars into the harbor. They ran to the bosun, and Mauro asked to be taken out to the vessel. The muscular man looked them over and scowled.

"More pilgrims? Jesus, get in. This is the last boat of the night, and we shove off at dawn. Why the hell we give good cargo space to you lot is beyond me. We need good knights and good swords in the Holy Land, not prayer-spouting dolts, cripples, and spastics."

Once the yawl boat was secured to the galley the passengers and sheep were hauled aboard. A sailor grabbed Nicolo's arm roughly and shoved him forward. "You two can sleep on deck with the sheep, and you can clean up their shit in the morning for good measure." Nicolo began to sweat as he heard the familiar Pisan accent. "Got nothing to say, pilgrim? Well, that's good, 'cause I might have to shove a marlinspike up your ass if you mouth off to me."

Mauro stepped forward. "Excuse me, Captain. My nephew here is a simpleton. He can't speak and he does what he is told without complaint. He has taken vows and will join me in the Holy Land to redeem our souls and recover the True Cross."

The sailor laughed and looked skyward. "Lord, have these people no minds of their own? They are being led to slaughter year after year. Yet they keep coming." He sized up Nicolo. "Well, I'm not the captain and it's a good thing he's an idiot, and a quiet one at that. We'll have lots of work for someone who keeps his mouth shut and follows orders. Maybe by the end of this trip, we'll make him an admiral. Would you like that, boy?" Nicolo smiled simply and bobbed his head. "An idiot, indeed. Well, get to your place over there and bed down for the night."

Nicolo grabbed Mauro's arm and let the monk lead him forward. "Well done," he whispered begrudgingly. Mauro smiled in the darkness. He realized that this was the first compliment he had ever gotten from Nicolo.

⁂

FROM THE THIRD-FLOOR balcony in the early morning light, Gabriella could see the Pisan galley weighing anchor and heading out of the short harbor road. She had prayed all night that the ruse would work. She shuddered at the consequences if it didn't. Count Eugenio came up from behind her, putting his arm around her shoulder.

"It is a sad and beautiful morning, my dear. Mahmoud told me that there was a robbery on the bridge last night. It appears your rendezvous couldn't take place. I am sorry. I know you had affection for the boy."

Gabriella smiled inwardly but held a sad demeanor. She sighed and spoke wistfully. "I did care for the boy and yet I betrayed him. I suppose it doesn't matter anymore." She waited for Count Eugenio to comfort her. She waited and waited, growing angrier as the moments went by. Finally, he cleared his throat and spoke.

"No, it does not matter anymore. But you have done what we agreed upon and I must honor my commitment to you. I hate to lose your mother. Cora was the best cook we have ever had in this household. Your father was foolish to side with King William during the revolt. He lost his head and his property and his precious wife Cora came to me by way of reward. You were fortunate that you were already of age and out of the house or you would have been mine as well." He moved his leg uncomfortably. "Lucky, too, that at this stage of my life I am more interested in food than in flesh." The count looked at Gabriella, but the young woman gave nothing away. "I have your mother's document of manumission signed and in your room. Of course, as a free woman you could choose to stay here. I have many uses for your talents and the rewards will be substantial, my dear niece." He winked at her.

Gabriella held back a shudder of revulsion. She wanted to kick his bad leg and throw him over the balcony. It would look like an accident, but she quickly calculated that the rail was too high for her to lift his saggy flesh. *Another time,* she thought darkly. *Perhaps Cora can prepare a final, special meal for the count.*

"No thank you, my dear uncle. I have had quite enough of Palermo, power, and intrigue. I only wish to take my mother back to Syracusa and live simply." She absently touched her belly. *And someday I may see Nicolo again.* Gabriella gave a last long look toward the harbor. The sails seemed like doves winging their way toward freedom. She wished she could be on one of them, perhaps the one with Nicolo. But that was not her lot. She needed to return home with her mother and try to start their lives again. She had been under the tutelage and control of Count Eugenio for almost three years. She had been used as a lure, as a messenger, and as a sympathetic ear to that disgusting man, as had her mother. And now it was over. Gabriella turned and left the balcony.

Count Eugenio followed her with his eyes. "A pity."

CHAPTER 7

VENICE

ANTONIO LEANED BACK against the bulkhead of the fast, six-oared *traghetto*. All around him these sleek craft skimmed across the surface like so many water spiders, back and forth from the mainland to the cluster of islands known as Venice, La Serenissima. He looked out over the bow to see dozens of vessels plying the lagoon waters, each uniquely designed for its task and the peculiar waterway. The Genoese were excellent open-seas fishermen, and Antonio had seen many different fishing and sailing craft during his sojourns to the Syrian lands. But these Venetians were truly one with the sea. He had never experienced such a range of activity on so many different craft in such a small space. The forward oarsman watched Antonio staring at the vessels and smiled.

"Hey, you like our boats? That prawn-tailed one with the curved, upturned sternposts, that's a *batella*. It carries produce and passengers. And look over there! See the heavy, box-like one with the huge lug sail and oversized rudder? We call that one a *bragozza*. It's a trawler." Antonio was mesmerized as he watched the vessel slowly pull trawl nets through the rich, brackish waters of the lagoon. "We've got the best seafood in the world!" The oarsman laughed and returned to his pull. Antonio looked forward to sampling the treasures of the Venetian lagoon, as well as the opportunities that awaited him on shore.

Antonio's mission to Milan had been so successful that the pope ordered him to Venice immediately. Although his travels from Milan to Venice took him through the beautiful cities of Verona, Brescia, and Padua, Antonio hadn't stopped to admire the views or the women. He could think of nothing but negotiating with the doge himself. Venetians were the acknowledged masters of the bargain, and it would take all of Antonio's skills and charm to squeeze a deal out of these people, especially the old blind doge, Enrico Dandolo. The ninety-four-year-old Dandolo had only been doge for eight years and had already transformed Venice from a merchant republic to a maritime empire. He was a legend throughout the Mediterranean.

"Those little islands look like lumps of dung sticking out of this beautiful sea."

Antonio turned toward the source of the comment and laughter—six French nobles who stood apart from the few other passengers. The French were a motley assortment of battle-hardened knights and more courtly gentlemen. The word on the dock before Antonio boarded was that they had been sent to Venice to plead with the doge to supply ships and crews for their crusader armies. Antonio had heard that the kings of France and England would not commit to the crusade, keeping their vast treasuries intact. The nobles had taken the cross but had no such resources. Thus, beyond outfitting a few hundred knights, they were unable to pay for food, lodging, and transportation for the vast armies of pilgrim warriors amassing under their banners. Usually, crusader armies swarmed like locusts through Europe on their way overland through Byzantium to the holy lands, devouring local crops, confiscating livestock, murdering, and taking the spoils of local Jews on the long march. However, the new strategy was to sail to the holy lands, bypassing the many kingdoms along the way that had to be cajoled or conquered into allowing the armies to pass. This strategy had succeeded under Richard the Lionheart during the last Crusade, but he'd had the treasury of England, swollen by the Saladin Tithe he had imposed on the English to pay for the attempted recapture of Jerusalem. This time the nobles were hoping to gather and stage from Venice, whose wealth might be borrowed in the form of ships and crews.

Antonio spoke passable French, sufficient to trade successfully at the Troyes fair before their father had turned that work over to Nicolo. He even spoke well enough to make sly wordplay with the women in the Troyes taverns. Yet when he'd tried to introduce himself after the men boarded the ferry they acted as if he was speaking some Moorish tongue, completely ignoring him. He had experienced this reaction from time to time in France if he didn't pronounce the language exactly as they did. At first, Antonio thought the French snobbish, yet over time he realized that they simply had a limited ability to understand. In the Syrian lands, any attempt to speak the local language was met with enthusiasm and assistance. In Genoa, a foreigner speaking the language could be understood no matter how badly he butchered the words. The French obviously had limited intelligence. But this was different. They'd understood him perfectly and chose to ignore him. He knew that the nobles felt superior to him, a mere merchant, and it made his blood boil. In Genoa, a man rose through the social ranks on his own merit, not because his mother was fortunate enough to be wedded and bedded by one of the nobility.

Antonio forced those thoughts from his mind, turning instead to the fame and riches that would be his if he succeeded here. He would be rewarded with a notary position in the Vatican itself. That would allow him to steer contracts toward his family and friends, increasing both his family's wealth and position and his personal network of contacts, allies, and business partners. He would finally be able to marry. Who would he choose? Perhaps Gloria, the prettiest of the three daughters of Vecchio, the master shipbuilder of Vernazza. A marriage that combined shipping and commerce would increase the power of his family enormously. What about the fiery Serena from Porto Venere? No other woman had matched him in lust and laughter. No, her father, brothers, and uncles were all pirates, a useful and condoned profession during times of war but perilous during peace—not a good long-term wager. Maybe a pirate's daughter would be more suitable for Nicolo, since his younger brother had no serious prospects anyway. Antonio looked ahead toward the islands of Venice. Perhaps the doge had a beautiful granddaughter (*or great granddaughter—he was so old!*). A merging of Genoa, Venice, and Rome would catapult Antonio into even greater heights of power and wealth. Possibilities awaited as infinite as the horizon beyond those approaching islands. *Lumps of dung, indeed*, he thought. *They are a treasure chest of sparkling jewels.*

The ferry entered the wide, winding waterway known as the Grand Canal that cleaved the main island in two. The low island on the starboard side of the broad canal seemed like an endless pasture, interrupted by the occasional church, monastery, vineyard, or wharf. To port, Antonio saw houses both meager and great built over the mud flats. Antonio's vessel had to wait as huge piles of oak logs from the forests of Veneto floated past, destined to be dragged ashore up ahead. The buildings were set upon dozens of these wooden poles, giving the appearance of a gaggle of washerwomen hiking their skirts to avoid the brackish water. Most were simple wood and brick structures, yet several were being sheathed over in marble, with grand landings being built directly on the canal.

Great wealth is flowing into Venice, he thought admiringly. The shore seemed like an anthill. Hundreds of workers shoveled sand and mud from barges to create new land areas. Clever mechanical contraptions repeatedly banged the hardwood poles deep into the mud, creating the foundations for new buildings. Vessels of every possible description worked the canal. Passenger ferries vied for space with cargo barges and animal-filled scows. Rafts awash to the gunnels with bricks sat anchored beneath new buildings as the workmen used ingenious pulley systems to hoist the bricks fifty feet in the air to create the upper levels. Odd-shaped craft they called *gondolas* carried people back and forth across the waterways. *Where are the bridges? So much activity!* Antonio thought about how far this cluster of mud flats had evolved. Early on, lowly fishermen were the only inhabitants, scraping out a living from an endless series of marshy islets. Their isolation and safety were guaranteed by the impossibility of navigating the lagoon that flowed murkily and treacherously between the mainland and the islands. Only the locals knew where the shifting sandbars, underwater hazards, and the passable channels were. Then the islets became the refuge of mainlanders fleeing the constant invasions by Germanic tribes, such as the Lombards (the "Long Beards"), the Goths, and the Huns. Yet relative peace during the last hundred years had allowed permanent settlement. Over time these industrious peoples, supported by the wealth, manpower, and technologies of the mainland, had filled in so much of the marshland and small inlets that several great islands now stood in their place. Venice looked set to surpass Genoa in wealth and power. It was a good time to make alliances.

Antonio reached down and felt the leather courier's bag he carried. It contained two important papal documents. The first authorized Antonio to negotiate for ships, horses, and men on behalf of the Papal Guard and associated army organized by the church. In this he would be competing with the French nobles for the material of war. He hoped their mutual religious calling would not devolve into a bidding war. The second document demonstrated how much power Venice had developed in its relations with the church, even though Venice was a loyal Catholic realm. Although Christian countries were forbidden to engage in commerce with Muslims since the fall of Jerusalem, the parchment gave official Church sanction to Venice for such trade, except for any items useful in war. This was an acknowledgment of Venice's reliance on its long-term trade with Muslim countries. Wherever a crusader went, a Venetian trader soon followed, offering essential services to the crusaders and building a local trade network for export. These were no mere opportunistic ventures. The Venetians had developed a sophisticated system to ensure their dominance in the Syrian trade. Almost every boy over sixteen was sent to a Venetian trading post for a few years to learn trade, Arabic, and the Arab mathematics. Muslim princes and tribal leaders knew the Venetians and had a level of trust with them that no occasional trader could hope for. The Venetians had a near monopoly on the best goods coming from these lands. The papal document was more significantly an admission of how dependent Europe had become on the Muslim spices and luxury goods that were largely under Venetian control. It was an outrage that Venice demanded this trade exemption as the price of contributing to the crusade. Yet the Venetians were experts in driving a bargain to their benefit. Antonio knew that many high churchmen made good coin off the Syrian trade and not even a crusade would interfere with that. Still, many in the church and the ruling classes of Europe opposed the exemption for Venice out of moral conviction or pure commercial jealousy. He was aware that his life could be in danger if these French emissaries knew what he carried.

The ferry slowed and tied up to a wharf before the only bridge that crossed the Grand Canal. It was a low, wooden structure that sat upon dozens of large wooden casks. Although obviously stable, the bridge bobbed and weaved with the current, the many Venetians crossing in each direction using the same wide-legged crab walk Antonio had seen sailors use on board ships to the Syrian lands. The Frenchmen pushed their way past Antonio to disembark first.

A friendly shout of "Welcome to Venice!" dispersed the cloud of anger that enveloped Antonio. He looked up to see a round, jolly-faced cleric waving him ashore. The man introduced himself as Romundo, but he was more popularly called "Rotundo." As soon as Antonio got off the ferry, he was engulfed in the incredible bustle of what Rotundo called "the Rialto."

"Here is the center of commerce in Venice. These men sitting behind the rows of benches on the right are the *benchieri*, or 'bankers' as we have started to call them. The merchants make their deals and take them to the bankers, who make entries in their ledgers crediting one account and debiting the other account. It is all very smooth and efficient." Antonio stopped near one bench to listen in on a trade. The merchants immediately noticed him and shut up, turning to glare at the Genoese. Rotundo laughed and continued. "The action is concentrated at the Rialto because the doge opened a new mint right over there, so all the transactions are right where the money is. That makes the ultimate settlement and changing of funds simple." The mint was an imposing marble building, guarded by finely dressed soldiers with long halberds or pikes at their sides. Rotundo explained that the doge had devised a common, harmonized coinage to replace the many coins of different weights and purities from so many different countries and regions that made Mediterranean trade difficult and unpredictable. "Even the well-respected Byzantine aspron trachy, made up of thirty percent gold, ten percent copper, and sixty percent silver, has been so manipulated by the venal emperors of Byzantium over the years that instead of four it takes six aspron trachy to make one gold hyperper. Can you imagine?"

Antonio was aware of the situation from his own experience and welcomed a more efficient system of coinage—but did it have to come from the Venetians? He had begun to see the new Venetian high value grosso and the low value bianco show up in far flung ports and bazaars, slowly but surely supplanting the Genoese, Pisan, French, Hungarian, and other coins used in commerce. Merchants trusted the Venetian coins because their purity and value were guaranteed by La Serenissima itself—no other coin had that guarantee. He worried that if the Venetians controlled the coinage, they could manipulate it to their advantage, changing weights and values at will. The coins were not only a means to make the markets more efficient, but the bold imprint of the winged lion of St. Mark and the doge on one side and Jesus Christ on the other made the clear statement that Venice was positioning itself to be the successor to Constantinople and the old Roman Empire.

The men walked down Campo San Bartolomeo, passing stalls and warehouses bulging with exotic merchandise. Clothing of every possible color and texture, jeweled goblets of gold, gleaming silver bits and stirrups, furniture carved from exotic red and black wood, even small marble statuary. Antonio had bought and sold in Tyre, Beirut, and Acre, and knew the breadth of goods available. But he had never seen so much amassed in one place from all those Syrian ports and beyond. Even the meanest stalls contained treasures that matched the best merchandise on offer in Genoa. Intricately tooled leatherware, exotic spices with names that even he had never heard of. Even common wares like amphora, ewers, and craters for storing and decanting oils were decorated with mosaic scenes of whimsy and profundity. *Venice is truly a colossus of trade. I could learn much here*, he mused.

And yet Venice was a fierce competitor to Genoa and would not share her knowledge easily. That was plain from the suspicious stares Antonio received as he passed some of the establishments. Antonio understood that—he would treat a Venetian visitor to Genoa similarly. They passed men in rich robes, turbans, and even random pieces of exotic fabric sewn into the ordinary clothing of less wealthy women. Antonio thought them wondrous. One stall was dedicated to turbans. Antonio had seen many turbans in the Syrian lands and was aware that different colors conveyed different meanings. The stall offered blue for scholars, whose minds were open as wide as the sky, white for saintliness, and black for humility. There were the flat, wrapped turbans of daily life and the green felt cones wrapped with silk brims that were favored by the Turkish wealthy. Even the Jewish turbans of metropolitan Cairo were for sale. Antonio suspected that these turbans did not carry the significance they did in their native lands. They were merely fashionable. Venetians seemed to be obsessed with the culture of the Syrian lands.

"Perhaps it is a deeper sickness or longing in their souls," Rotundo pondered aloud. "They wish to throw off the yoke of

Byzantium, to whom they have so long been tethered. Maybe this is their new identity, their new culture. The Venetians have a new word; they call it 'taste.' If you are wealthy enough to afford spices, your food tastes better, so you are considered to have 'taste.' So it is with all this Arab clothing, furniture, carpets, and more. If you can own them, you have 'taste'."

"'Taste,' what a queer concept," mumbled Antonio.

Rotundo chuckled and slapped Antonio on the shoulder. "You must be hungry after the ferry ride across the lagoon. Come, let me take you to a special place I know that makes the best *vongole* and *gamberi*. I love clams and shrimp, don't you?" He smacked his lips. "Mmm, Venice is a wonderful place to serve God. The food is so plentiful and fresh from the lagoon. I have been posted to France, Iberia, and all over this land, but the food in Venice is the best."

Rotundo led Antonio past the merchants of the Rialto and the Campo, behind the canal-fronting buildings, and down a nearby alley. The power and efficiency of Venice quickly faded in these dirty, muddy back lanes. Dung and mud smeared Antonio's new boots. Scamelors roamed the streets and filthy, scabrous men and women lay in the doorways and alleys amid piles of trash. The men had to avoid human waste thrown from windows and dodge pigs squealing past. Antonio took some comfort in the squalor, as the bowels of Venice appeared as those of any other European city. Obviously not every family drew from the deep well of Venetian wealth.

"I have a feeling you brought me this way for a reason," Antonio remarked to Rotundo.

Rotundo stopped walking and smiled. "Yes, it is easy to become blinded by the things of this world, but as representatives of the church we must always remember the flock we tend. Actually, the Venetians use some of their wealth to support the poor here. They provide food stations to feed those who cannot afford to eat. Ha! The poor here eat better than tradesmen in most places. The Venetians also have homes for the upkeep of poor girls where they are prepared for marriage or the convent. I cannot say whether it is out of Christian piety or a desire to prevent revolt, but it does serve the poor well enough."

Eventually they wound their way through the alleys and out onto a small plaza. They sat and shared wine at a crowded tavern, as Rotundo initiated Antonio into the intricacies of Venetian power. He explained that Venice sat at a critical crossroads between Constantinople and Rome, between the old Christian power and the new. The religious schism between the two was real enough, Rotundo remarked, but underneath laid secular control of trade routes, treasuries, and tribute. Byzantium had historically been the seat of the Roman Empire after Rome had been sacked so long ago. The emperors did not want to give up that mantle, especially not to the German descendants of the Huns and Goths who had sacked Rome, become Christian, and been paid off in titles, land, and power by the church. Venice was staunchly Roman Catholic, yet at the same time it had a long relationship with Orthodox Byzantium and many special trade privileges with that empire. But Byzantium was facing the twilight of a long decline. Its emperors had become erratic and prone to patricide and infanticide in their lust to obtain or retain power. They had authorized the wholesale slaughter of all "Latins" only a decade earlier, and the mobs of Constantinople murdered and raped every Pisan and Genoese woman and child they could find, while torturing and killing almost all of the Roman priests. The Vatican legate himself was murdered and his severed head tied to a stray dog's tail and chased around the Hippodrome. Fortunately, all the Venetians in Constantinople had been exiled or locked up before that, allowing them to escape the slaughter. The Venetians mounted a massive expedition, headed by a younger Enrico Dandolo, to free the Venetians held in the dungeons of Constantinople. Not only was the expedition a failure, but the defeated sailors brought plague back to Venice. The people murdered the doge in anger, but no blame was assigned to Dandolo. It was only in the last year that the new doge had been able to negotiate for the release of the imprisoned

Venetians and the reestablishment of Venetian customs exemptions and other trade privileges with Byzantium.

"The Venetians seem willing to forgive and forget in a most Christian fashion as long as their trade privileges are sanctified," noted Rotundo. "Not so the Byzantines. Even now, the son of the last deposed emperor is wandering around the Veneto, trying to gain support for an attack on Constantinople to regain his crown."

"What a hornet's nest!" cried Antonio.

"Yes, but the Venetians see it as so many chess pieces, all to be moved about with the sole goal of gaining as much commercial power as possible. They know that kings and emperors, even popes, come and go with astonishing regularity, but commerce is like the sea that surrounds Venice—eternal and essential." Rotundo let go a formidable burp. "Do pass me the wine, won't you?"

The men continued on foot, crossing several of the small canals that intersected the island. A few had wooden bridges, but most required a few seconds passage on small ferries in exchange for copper coin. Antonio was amazed at how Venice seemed to live on the water. He watched as an ornate, gilded funereal barge slowly poled past, followed by several simple, black mourners' scows. Finally, they arrived at a large, three-story wooden inn. Before entering, Rotundo took Antonio aside and whispered conspiratorially.

"I have arranged for you to stay on the third floor. The Frenchmen are on the floor below you. If you put your ear to the floor, you may get a French lesson that will serve you well. They may have ignored you on the ferry, but they will sing like birds to you tonight. Relax here for the evening and I will take you to see the doge in the morning." Rotundo noticed the slight twinge of Antonio's eyes when the doge was mentioned. He put his hand on the merchant's shoulder. "Listen, Antonio. The doge is old and blind, but he is as sharp as a Damascus blade. He can smell fear or false flattery easily enough. He respects strength and integrity. Be honest and clear with him and all will go well."

※

THE INNKEEPER USHERED Antonio into the foyer. The Genoese was immediately struck by the lavish decor and opulence of the inn. The wooden floors were covered in exquisite Persian carpets, while the walls were sculpted panels with inlaid marquetry. Glass-fronted cabinets held ceramics and silver objects that Antonio couldn't identify.

Antonio settled into his room and lay back on the large four-poster bed adorned with carvings of lions and fish, pondering the day to come. After an hour he heard muffled voices from the room below. He rolled off the bed and looked at the floor, finding the widest chink between adjacent floorboards. He pressed his ear to the crack.

※

GEOFFROY DE VILLEHARDOUIN sat in the common room waiting for his companions to gather. As marshal of Champagne and the most experienced military campaigner, he was in charge of the delegation. Not that it mattered much. His fellow Frenchmen had their primary allegiances to different nobles, although they were supposedly on a common mission for the crusade. On their travels through Europe to Venice he had gotten to know the strengths and weaknesses of each. He had allowed them their foibles along the way but made it clear that when they arrived before the doge he would be the field marshal once again. There were six of them all told, two representatives each of the three most important nobles of France. He was there on behalf of Thibaut, count of Champagne and Brie, and was accompanied by Miles the Brabant, a young troubadour. Geoffroy figured the count was having a joke at his expense sending the poet, but he actually enjoyed his company and his clever lyrics. Count Baldwin of Flanders had sent Conon of Bethune (another poet!) and the coarse courtier Alard Maquereau. Count Louis of Blois and Chartres sent John of

Friaise, a young nephew with solid military experience, and Walter of Gaudonville, a wounded old soldier who had become seneschal of Blois. As the declining sun found a path along the alleys and through their window, the men came together.

"The doge is still a man of God and will heed the call of the church," stated John emphatically. "We must ensure that our requests are contained in their proper context. He will support the crusade."

"I will sing him a verse of love and devotion to the church," Conon offered. "That will melt his hard heart enough for him to listen to reason."

Alard snorted and shook his head. "I will kiss his ancient blind arse, if that's what it takes. We need those ships and crews."

"You would give away too much, Alard. You are too quick to throw your lord's money around irresponsibly. Remember the cows you bought him as a gift—with his coin? They turned out to be old bulls!" The men laughed at Walter's comment as Alard steamed.

"That may be," the courtier said flatly, "but the doge is a greedy old man, just as these Venetians are a greedy people. If they don't see the advantage to themselves, they will not support us."

"They are no different from us in that, nor different from any man," Conon replied soothingly. "We all seek security and respect but find it in different ways. The knight seeks it in glory for his lord or his lady. The lord seeks it in land and rents. The priest seeks it in our Lord and Savior. Venetians seek security in commerce."

"Spoken like a true poet," Alard grumbled. "You seek it in wine and skirts."

Geoffroy had been listening to this banter for over a month and had had enough. He let out a roar that made Antonio jump off the floor above. "Listen to me! The doge controls all the cards. We need to plead with him as Christians and sweeten the deal with coin and commerce. That will be the winning strategy here. I will introduce us and state our case, and each of you will say something polite and supportive to our cause. We will see how he responds and take it from there. No outbursts, no singing, and no sour looks, no matter what the old doge says." He shot a hard glance at Alard, who put up his open palms in submission. "Each of us carries the *carte blanc*, the signed blank parchments from our lords. We have full authority to consummate the deal in their names and that's what we will do. You all know we can't go back without signed agreements."

"We can't go back anyway since none of us has any coin left," sighed Miles.

"We know that, but the doge doesn't," the marshal observed. "We need to get the old man to loan us some money for ourselves as well as for the ships."

Alard laughed. "Good luck to you, friend. The doge is as tight as a horse's arse in fly season. You'll have to be a damned fine negotiator to get him to build those ships without any money from us and get him to give us an allowance to boot!"

"It's not like we have any choice, Alard," said Conor.

The old marshal stood up and stretched his weary back. "We go from a position of strength, give nothing away to the doge or anyone else. It's all or nothing here, men. Every count and baron from Champagne to Cayeau has taken the cross. Thirty thousand knights, squires, and foot soldiers are assembling. We must make the deal."

※

Rotundo came for Antonio as the sun rose and the Frenchmen were still asleep. They zigzagged through the muddy alleys and across the small bridges until they came to the Grand Canal. There, they boarded a *traghetto* for the row to the landing at Piazza San Marco, the huge, granite paved plaza that was the seat of power in Venice. As they approached the plaza, they passed larger and larger warehouses and palaces. The structures became adorned with ancient Roman columns and statuary. Antonio commented that the Venetians must surely be rapacious, that they must have pillaged every Roman ruin between here and Constantinople to create this ostentatious display.

Rotundo shook his head. "Actually, most of these have been purchased. The doges ordered their diplomats and merchants in distant lands to bring back these stone works. It seems they have sought to recreate the splendor of ancient Rome and lay claim to being its rightful heir." He considered a moment and shrugged. "I do suspect many were stolen." Rotundo altered the subject. "But notice how each building has a similar design. The ground floors have arched passages. These are the warehouse entrances. The boats pull right into the warehouse and offload their cargo away from prying eyes. You wouldn't know it, but behind those warehouse areas are secluded courtyards and hidden gardens. The offices and meeting rooms for the business of the family are on the second floor."

Antonio looked up at the arched and pointed windows and the row of balconies along that floor. The building style was Byzantine or maybe Arabic; Antonio really didn't know the subtle differences in architecture. He noticed that several buildings had beautiful diamond-shaped brickwork while others had that new marble facing. The doorways were crowned with attenuated arches or other decorations. "The third floor," continued Rotundo, "is where the family lives. That is usually where the rarest and most expensive treasures are found." He looked at Antonio, who seemed lost in thought. "Don't you get it? I am talking about their daughters!"

The *traghetto* pulled up to the plaza at a landing before two huge marble columns. At the top of one a bronze winged lion roared out to sea. The other was topped by a statue of Saint Theodore, who Rotundo said was the patron saint of Venice before being displaced by Saint Mark. An old man held sway with a crowd at a gambling table between the two columns. A rotting corpse swung slowly above his head in the light sea breeze, dangling on a rope between the two columns.

"The Republic tried to raise three Roman temple columns twenty years ago," Rotundo explained as Antonio stared fixedly at the swinging corpse. "The first toppled over and sank in the mud. It has never been recovered. The doge put out a call for engineers to figure out how to raise them properly. One man came forward and said if he could do this, his payment should be the right to have a gambling table between the columns for life. He was successful and so was his gambling table. He has lived a long life as well, much to the chagrin of the council. They couldn't go back on their word but couldn't tolerate the crowds around the table all day while a few yards away the council debated great matters of state. So, the council decreed that the spot would also be used for public executions for serious crimes like murder, treason, pedophilia, and pollution of the lagoon, thinking that would keep the crowds away. You can see that it hasn't." Rotundo giggled. "I guess it only sends the message that life is a gamble, eh?"

They walked into the great plaza. Antonio was amazed at the size and magnificence of Piazza San Marco. It was as splendid as any in Rome and far beyond anything in Genoa.

"Two decades ago this plaza was nothing but a muddy field." Rotundo observed. "The former doge, Ziani, wanted to create a monument to Venetian power in the world to rival the plazas of Rome and Constantinople. A thousand workmen drained the mire and laid the granite plaza. It is truly a marvel."

A magnificent church, Basilica San Marco, commanded the far end of the plaza. Its soaring arches were of Byzantine design and covered with sparkling mosaics illustrating biblical scenes. The figures in the mosaics seemed to move in the glisten of the low-angled morning light.

"That is where the body of Saint Mark lies," Rotundo remarked reverently. "It was brought here by two brave Venetian merchants in Alexandria. When they heard that the sultan was going to tear down the church that housed the body of Saint Mark and use the granite to expand his own palace they decided to smuggle the body of the saint to Venice. They put the bones in a barrel and covered it with a layer of pork. The Muslim customs inspectors wouldn't go near the barrel, and they were able to spirit him away successfully. Ever since I learned that I have eaten a good Parma ham with a certain reverence."

A long marble three-storied palace abutted the church, gleaming in the morning sun. Lace-like filigreed marble adorned each of the forty-seven arches that fronted the plaza. The palace was the home of the doge and the administrative chambers of the Great Council and courts of Venice. A huge bell tower stood opposite the doge's palace.

Even at this early hour, the plaza was filled with hawkers and passing tradesmen. Fifty or so older men in purple robes and what appeared to Antonio to be old Romanesque togas were also gathered in front of the palace. Rotundo explained that these were the council members, and their robe and sleeve colors represented their importance in the Venetian governing hierarchy. Antonio looked up and saw an old man in a white robe and cap standing on the second-floor balcony that spanned the length of the doge's palace. He was staring out to sea.

"Is that the doge?" Antonio asked. "He doesn't seem blind. He is looking out at the sea with such purpose."

"It is indeed Enrico Dandolo," agreed Rotundo. "He is totally blind, yet every day he walks out on the balcony and stares at the sea. Nobody knows what he is seeing in his mind, and nobody would dare to ask."

"Has he been blind since birth?"

"No, he lost his sight about twenty years ago. I think he was hit over the head in Constantinople in a fight, although some people believe that the old emperor had ground glass put in his eyes. That is a traditional punishment there, although they do it so frequently it should probably be called a pastime. Whatever happened, he lost his eyes in the service of La Serenissima, and the people love him for that. Let's go into the palace; it is time for you to meet the doge."

Doge Enrico Dandolo stood on the balcony with his face to the sea. He felt the cool breeze on his cheeks and in his blank eyes. He missed being able to observe the sea and the enormous amount of activity on the Grand Canal and beyond. Yet he could feel it and he could hear it. He could tell the weather by the sound of the waves lapping and the boats cracking against the granite bulkhead of the great plaza. He felt the weight of the air as fronts of weather moved in. Dandolo's life was written by the sea. He had been born at the height of a furious and historic storm. The storm surge inundated the ground floors of every building in Venice. He entered this world as the corpses of cattle and the elderly washed onto Piazza San Marco. The sea wanted Enrico Dandolo, but he was not born to be a fisherman. The Dandolos were of patrician stock. Generations of Dandolos had been raised in service to La Serenissima. They had been diplomats and doges, priests and patriarchs, legislators and legates. At the same time, of course, they had always been merchants and traders. By the time he lost his sight, Dandolo had lived a longer and more accomplished life as a diplomat for the Republic than any man alive. He never felt handicapped by the loss. In fact, his blindness served. The word in the warehouses and on the piers was that Dandolo's sight had been lost in a blow to the head in Constantinople, or in the famous glass grinding incident. Dandolo chuckled to himself. He knew neither of those were true. His eyesight had deteriorated over a decade or so and in spite of many doctors' efforts, there was simply nothing he could do about it. He allowed the stories to go on and to grow and change. He was the man who had bravely lost his sight in the service of La Serenissima. As a politician this was a great badge of honor. Why disabuse the people of a heroic legend that served them and him so well?

The world fell away slowly for Dandolo, who became immersed in a realm of shadows, smells, and sounds. It was only after he lost his sight that he began to hear *her*. First a murmur, then a whisper, like the sound of the ocean in a seashell. Initially he thought it was some reaction of his body to the blindness, like hearing the coursing of his blood through his veins. But it grew louder, more insistent. Ultimately the sounds became more distinct, forming words that he could hear and understand. It was the sea. It never troubled Dandolo that he could hear the sea, or that eventually he could even converse with her. Every May, during the Feast of the Annunciation, their relationship was recognized at *La Sensa,* the formal marriage of Venice and the sea that took place out on the lagoon. Each year, they were committed to each other anew before man and God. To Dandolo, this ceremony was not some meaningless pomp and ritual, but the consummation of his deep love for her. He enjoyed their intimacy. He called upon her for counsel and succor. But ultimately, Dandolo thought, it was a sign of his supreme maturation as doge. Venice was La Serenissima. The sea was La Serenissima. The sea and Venice were one. He was the vessel through which the sea manifested her wishes in the lives of men.

The Venetian Trinity. Dandolo smiled at the thought. He took a deep breath of the salty air. His head swirled in the moment. He felt the surge of the sea in his body, his blood flowing with the tide. *Great things are afoot for us, my beloved. Help me to realize our destiny.*

ANTONIO WAS CALLED into the doge's administrative office by an older man wearing a purple robe with black sleeves. He entered to find the doge sitting on a slightly raised dais, putting the old man's head just above Antonio's. The merchant stepped forward and bowed gracefully as he spoke.

"It is an honor to meet you, Your Excellency. I am Antonio diCarlo, representing the Holy See."

A younger man, by the timbre of his voice. His manners are good, Dandolo thought. *I hear sincerity and honesty in his tone. Let's see what he is made of.* "Thank you, young man." He paused and looked as if a sudden thought came to him. "DiCarlo? Isn't that a Genoese name? Are you here representing the Holy Father or your merchant House?"

Antonio remembered Rotundo's advice. Be honest and straightforward. "I am here by request of His Holiness to bring you documents and speak with you about providing services for the Papal Guard in the coming crusade. I am indeed Genoese, Your Excellency, and proud of it, but that is not something that will compromise my mission here."

"And what do you expect to gain from this mission—for yourself, that is."

How could a blind man look directly at you and see into your soul? Am I so transparent or is he that insightful? "In all honesty, Your Excellency, I am like any young man who seeks to better his lot through hard work. I would hope that my efforts will be rewarded with more assignments, perhaps a notarial position in the Holy See for the benefit of the church and my family."

"Come now, when this papal business is done you can take care of your family. You've seen what is on offer in our markets. There are goods to be had that can only be found here, unless you travel to the corners of the world."

"I have in fact traveled, Your Excellency, but I must confess that what I have seen in your markets astounds me. Let me attend to the business at hand, and then I hope to enjoy all that Venice has to offer."

He's smiling. I can hear the difference in his speech. The doge smiled back. "Well spoken, young man. I am glad His Holiness has sent us an experienced merchant as a legate instead of the usual pasty-faced functionaries or crooked churchmen. Now what good news do you bear in that satchel?"

Antonio had almost forgotten the leather bag at his side. *He must have heard the sound it made when I put it on the floor at my side.* He quickly opened it and took out a rolled manuscript. "Your Excellency, I bring His Holiness's blessings on your continued commerce with the infidels. His Holiness recognizes the unique situation of Venice in this. The church has faith that your trade will be of mutual benefit without aiding the infidels' efforts to destroy the Latin kingdoms."

"And what do you think of this trade, young man?"

"Well, sir . . . I believe that trade can bring peace, or at least accommodation, in the long run. It seems people are less willing to go to war if they have good commercial relations. And so many families depend on the trade—"

"Yes yes, but what do you think of this document? Genoa trades with the Syrian lands, so do the Pisans. Why should we want this document when every other trading power simply ignores the pope's prohibition?"

"I assume, Your Excellency, that Venice wishes to be honorable in its relation to the Holy See and abide by the command of the church in this matter. Given your historic role and prominence in the Syrian trade, I am sure that you wish to ensure its continued vitality."

"Your Genoese trade is harmless enough. But the Pisans supply iron to the port of Alexandria, where it is smelted into swords bearing inscriptions exhorting 'Death to Christians.' Should Venice and Genoa join together and prevent them from supplying the enemies of the church?"

"The Pisans are a problem for us all, to be sure, Your Excellency. As you are aware, we are currently at war with them." Rotundo had told Antonio that the doge was a diplomat in Constantinople when the Pisans ransacked and burned the Venetian quarter, brutally beating any Venetian trader they could find, then securing favorable trading rights from the corrupt and indolent Byzantine emperor. *The memory must burn fresh within him*, Antonio thought. "As a Genoese, I would be happy to see their nefarious trade cease. Our trade is minor in the Syrian lands. Much of what we buy comes through the hands of your own traders, at a reasonable markup. Your continued success in the Syrian trade only bodes well for ours. I am certain that all of Genoa would agree with me in this sentiment." *What am I doing? He already has me talking as a Genoese instead of the papal representative. It sounds like I am trying to negotiate a better trade deal between Venice and Genoa! I can't let him manipulate me so easily.*

The doge took the parchment and put it to one side. He cocked his head and asked Antonio what service Venice could provide the Holy See in this crusade.

"The church requires ships and crews sufficient for a thousand knights with mounts, livery, pages, and perhaps two thousand foot soldiers. His Holiness envisions a charter of eight months to a year."

"Has the Papal Guard expanded so? That is a lot of military for the church."

"I cannot say for certain, Your Excellency, but I believe that many of the knights are from the Lombard League cities. Florence, Milan, and others have responded to the call to crusade under the papal banner."

Dandolo thought for a moment. Even as doge he could not make a major commitment of Venetian resources and men without the approval of the council.

Antonio continued. "His Holiness would like to take delivery in Naples or perhaps Sicily, although the Papal Guard could also assemble here in Venice."

Not here. We do not want such a large force from Rome here, Dandolo thought. *This young man seems unaware that Markward's army has already taken Naples and is sailing toward Sicily. Who knows who will control the young king six months from now? We cannot chance our ships and crews being taken and ransomed by the Germans or getting into a war with them.* "I would suggest Bari or Taranto down the coast from here. Each has a large harbor and sufficient fields and taverns to quarter such a force. I am certain that our craftsmen can build the vessels timely, but it will be difficult to find enough good, local crew willing to be away for a year. What inducement do you offer the captains and crews?"

Antonio called upon all his internal resources to keep a calm voice. He knew what the pope had offered, but he thought he might as well try and get a better deal. "I have been instructed to offer five percent of the assessed value of any *spolia,* spoils lawfully taken by papal soldiers during the term of the charter."

Dandolo let the offer hang in the air for a few minutes, until he heard Antonio begin to squirm with discomfort. "Five percent? You will most likely need thirty large galleys for soldiers and foodstuffs, and another ten transports for the horses. That is roughly a thousand crew. Your knights would need a lot of spoils to make the commitment worthwhile for them. I suggest you pay the captains and crews a reasonable fee prior to departure and the promise of five percent spoils later. We can fold the fee into the total per man charge for the vessels."

"I believe His Holiness would be willing to raise the spoils to eight percent and not offer any upfront payment. We all know that sailors paid up front are less likely to show at the dock. Between the tavern and the hearth, the coin goes quickly and then they have nothing but a hard year ahead. Higher spoils might be more enticing."

The doge bristled. "The sailors of Venice are not your Genoese wharf rats! They are family men committed to the sea *and* La Serenissima. *Who* will support their families while they are away on your crusade? Their wives and children cannot survive on the prayers of Rome alone."

Antonio realized that he had gone too far.

"I did not mean to impugn the dignity of your fine sailors, Your Excellency. And you are correct. These good men need to provide for their families during the charter. I am certain that a reasonable upfront payment can be provided."

The doge seemed satisfied. "I must take counsel on this. We can discuss your proposal again on the morrow." He stood and made to leave. Then he stopped and turned to Antonio. "But tarry a moment. I would like to hear your thoughts on a certain matter."

Antonio was taken aback. *What is this?*

The doge continued. "We are visited this day by a delegation of French nobles. I believe they seek a similar arrangement with us. What should we do with them? We only have so many men and can only build so many ships."

Did Dandolo know he had been listening to the Frenchmen?

Did Rotundo or the innkeeper betray him to the doge? Was the doge testing him now to see where his sympathies lay? He had no allegiance to the French, yet they were on a crusader's mission as he was. *How much can I give him?* Antonio spoke cautiously.

"I did meet the French embassy briefly and did overhear them speaking of their mission. My French is not that good, but I believe I got the gist of it." *True for the most part.* "I can say that they seem honorable men. They seek ships and crew as well, that is true, and on a magnitude far greater than our request. Perhaps your shipwrights can accommodate the Holy See first and the French shortly thereafter."

"Do they have the funds to pay for their needs? Of course, His Holiness would have ample resources for a substantial down payment. He could mortgage the papal crown and jewels like his predecessor did to fund a crusade when I was a boy. But what of the French nobles?"

"I cannot be certain, Your Excellency. There did seem to be some question of funds for their own sustenance, but I cannot say whether that is a problem of poor planning or overspending on their travels here, or whether it represents a paucity of funds in the hands of their lords. I don't pretend to understand the ways of blood nobility." Antonio gritted his teeth and continued. "I am naught but a lowly merchant of Genoa."

<hr />

ROTUNDO WAS WAITING in the Piazza when Antonio emerged from the doge's palace. He saw the pensive look on Antonio's face. Antonio shared his conversation with the doge.

"I felt like a fish being slowly grilled by a master chef."

Rotundo brightened. "Then let me take you to a place I know in Castello, where they grill the best lagoon squid and sardines around! And the *barboni* and *stogetti*, ooh, no fish anywhere can beat their sweet white flesh." They walked along the Grand Canal toward Castello.

Antonio looked back to see the doge on the balcony again. *At least*

I've lost interest in meeting his great granddaughter. I wouldn't want that man as the patriarch of my family.

"Your Excellency, please come in. The Small Council is assembled, and we have news from Zara."

Dandolo turned toward the sound of Emilio's voice. *Ahh, all I wish is peace and quiet, yet so much is happening.* Inside his head he heard the soft reply. *Not yet, beloved, we have much to do. Your time of triumph and destiny is at hand. Look out toward me.* Dandolo turned back toward the sea. He quieted his mind. The lagoon was emptying her hidden currents into the sea, taking with her the sediment from the rivers that fed her. The sediment built up beyond Venice, creating a series of low barrier islands, *the lidi,* that protected Venice from the worst of the storms. The largest of these was simply named the Lido. "Bless you," Dandolo murmured aloud "You have wrapped us in your loving embrace." The hidden, shifting channels and shallows created by the sea around the islands also made navigating them nearly impossible—even for the most experienced Venetian fishermen. *The Lido will protect you,* the sea reassured him.

Emilio approached the doge. He had been his personal secretary for four years and knew that these moments on the balcony were internal in some unexplainable way. The doge always seemed to come back from the balcony refreshed and with new insights or strategies. "Please, sir," he repeated, "you only have a short time to discuss the pope's request with the Small Council before the French embassy arrives."

"Yes, yes." Dandolo turned and walked into the palace unaided. He was not concerned about the Small Council's reaction to the pope's request for ships and crews. They would quickly fashion a response that would be to every Venetian's benefit. The news from Zara would be another matter. The fortified town down the Dalmatian coast had once been a Venetian colony. A few years back Zara had won its freedom and now came under the protection of Emeric, the king of Hungary. For several years Zara-based pirates had been raiding Venetian merchant ships as they passed down the Dalmatian coast. The Venetians tried attacking the city but never succeeded in breaching its high walls or stopping the piracy. Emilio informed the doge that the king of Hungary had just taken the cross. That meant that his property, which included Zara, was now protected by the church. Dandolo was certain that Emeric was a false crusader who had no intention of joining the soldiers of Christ in the liberation of Jerusalem. He was just using the pledge of protection to counter Venice's growing aggression against the coastal city. He also thought that Emeric was eyeing the Brenner Pass, that low notch through the Alps that permitted Venice to import critical copper, iron, and silver ores from the German lands. *If he cuts off the Brenner Pass, we will be strangled from the north and assaulted from the south.* Dandolo had no time to consider a new strategy for dealing with Emeric and his intrigues. He heard a commotion on the plaza below and walked to the balcony. It was clear from the size of the crowd and the snippets of conversation that the French nobles had arrived.

Geoffroy de Villehardouin commanded the ferry to hold its place a stone's throw from the plaza bulkhead. He wanted the crowd on shore to gather and see them. The French were dressed in their white surcoats with huge red crosses sewn on the fronts. Their heads were covered in plumed, engraved helmets. They stood in the ferry as it approached the bulkhead and disembarked solemnly. They marched in two-by-two formation toward the doge's palace. Few in Venice had ever seen crusaders, certainly not clean and noble ones.

Several purple-robed patricians met the knights at the entrance to the doge's palace and ushered them into a waiting room. They could hear discussions in the nearby Small Council chamber but could not make out the words. They sat silently under the doleful eyes in portraits of earlier doges. After an hour they were brought into the chamber. There sat the small, frail doge, flanked by ten patricians. After brief introductions the doge asked what service Venice could offer these esteemed nobles of France.

Geoffroy stepped forward. "Your Excellencies, we come to you because of your great prowess on the sea. We wish you to help us in the cause of Christ to regain sacred Jerusalem from the infidels by providing us with ships for transport and battle. We present you these documents to demonstrate our authority." Geoffroy handed letters of introduction from the lords of France. These were reviewed by the council members and accepted. "We also have these." Geoffroy handed the letters carte blanc to Emilio.

Before Geoffroy could explain, the doge commanded Emilio to hand the documents over to him. He opened one rolled parchment and ran his hand over it from top to bottom, feeling the embossed seals at the bottom of the parchment. "These are sealed letters carte blanc. Your lords have given you full authority to negotiate and to accept terms on their behalf. You are invested with the same authority as if they themselves were here."

The knights were stunned that the blind doge could tell by feel what the parchments were. He was a learned man, indeed, and that withered body betrayed his enormous personal power and strength.

"Well do we know that of men uncrowned, your lords are the greatest," the doge continued. "They have put their faith in you and will maintain whatsoever you undertake. Now, tell us exactly what you require."

The knights went on to describe the size of the forces being mustered in Champagne and the surrounding lands. Walter of Gaudonville, the seneschal, read out a list of requirements. "Our forces will consist of four thousand, five hundred knights with horses, nine thousand squires and twenty thousand soldiers of foot. We require transport for all and supplies while on board and during the campaign expected to last nine months. We require galleys of war to accompany and protect the fleet, and to remain at anchor for the duration of the crusade."

The doge and council were surprised by the size of the projected force. There were a lot of murmurs among the council until the doge spoke. "Good knights, you ask a lot of us. Of course, it will take time to calculate fulfillment of your needs, which will cost us dearly in terms of manpower and material. We will work on a proposal to be presented in three days' time."

Geoffroy bowed slightly toward the doge, but Alard stepped in front of him and spoke insistently. "We understand you need time to calculate the number of ships and all that, but do you agree to support the crusade or not?" Geoffroy wanted to crack Alard across the face for the insolence, but he didn't want to show disunity or disrespect in front of the doge and the council.

He put his hand firmly on Alard's shoulder. "Please understand our anxiety over this, Your Excellencies. We have traveled all the way from France for the pure love of God and service to our lords. My companion only means to ask if you have the authority to commit to the Lord's cause."

The doge responded soothingly, though he burned at the insolence. "You are good and true men; of this we have no doubt. But you must understand that we have no lords here. In our commune of Venice we cannot commit to such an important endeavor without consulting the full council and even the people as a whole. Let us return to you with a proposal. If you agree we will present it for acceptance to the commune through the proper channels. Thank you for your time and passion in the name of Our Lord."

After the French took their leave, the doge canvassed the Small Council for their thoughts. Although they unanimously supported the crusade in principle, several of the council members voiced concern over the size of the endeavor, especially when added to the work to be done for the Papal Guard. The most vocal was patrician Mikiel, whose family had built trading vessels for two hundred years.

"Even a quick calculation tells me that we would have to commit our entire registry of boat builders exclusively to this endeavor. There would be no one left to build or repair our own merchant fleet. This is too much of a risk, unless there is a large reward at the end."

Moroni, whose trading House handled copper and iron ore shipments from Germany, felt the same. He feared that all the ores would be needed, and all the smelters dedicated merely to forging the fittings for this vast fleet. Someone piped in that even making thirty-five thousand wooden spoons for the French would be a challenge. More voices spoke up about the food for the horses and the crusaders. Venice was not an agricultural economy. Almost every Venetian trader abroad would have to dedicate the next year to purchasing foodstuffs to feed the huge army. There was not enough warehouse space in all of Venice to hold the sum of those provisions.

Dandolo felt he was losing the council. He spoke quickly. "Let us not fear what we do not know, good councilors. Go back to your houses and calculate the specifics. We must come together tomorrow and formulate a response to the pope's representative. Lesser men than you negotiate contracts like that every day on the Rialto. We must do the same for the French, although it will take more time and is more demanding. Then we shall take the French contract to the Great Council and hear their opinions. This is a great challenge and a great opportunity to serve God and Venice. Now go and prepare."

Antonio returned to the doge's palace the next morning. The old man stood on his balcony. The doge's assistant brought Antonio up to the office and handed him a parchment containing the Venetian offer. Antonio read the document and was relieved at the fairness of the upfront fees and the other terms. He told Emilio that he would take the parchment to Rome immediately for papal approval. As he turned to leave, he heard a thin voice from the balcony.

"We are similar, Venice and Genoa. Neither of us tills the soil. We both seek our livelihoods from the sea. Our food and our trade rely on the sea. We are not ruled by kings or priests but by men of vision and common sense. Let those rulers babble on about their religious convictions and whether Mary was a virgin or not. At the end of the day, it is we men of commerce who do all the work and make all the decisions that matter." The doge walked from the balcony into his office. "So how do I choose, Antonio, between a man's love of God and his ability to pay? How can we support these Frenchmen if they can only pay for our labors with their prayers? They are asking Venice to commit all we are and all we have to their cause, yet we both know they may not have the coin when the bill comes due." The old man rubbed his blank eyes. The news he received from Sicily this morning troubled him greatly. "I am tired, Antonio. What is your counsel in this?"

Antonio thought hard for a moment. "I think, Your Excellency, that sometimes a debtor is more powerfully in your grip than an ally by treaty."

The doge nodded slowly and smiled. "That is well said, my son. Thank you for that. I know that you are eager to be away to Rome with your parchment, but I wish for you to stay a bit. Tomorrow we take our proposal to the French, then to the people. You should watch our commune in action. If all goes well, we will celebrate tomorrow evening. I would like you to sit with me during the banquet."

Antonio knew he should rush back to Rome, but he could not resist the honoring he was receiving. He felt that fostering this relationship could lead to an alliance between Genoa and Venice. Together they would be an unstoppable force in Mediterranean trade, and House diCarlo would be in the vanguard.

"I am honored, Your Excellency. I have so much to learn and experience here in Venice."

"Yes," said the doge slowly and almost sadly, "there is much waiting for you."

AFTER A LIGHT midday meal of seafood soup, Enrico Dandolo called the waiting French nobles into his office. He had spent a long night with his staff and representatives of the shipping and mercantile sectors of Venice, hammering out the details of the offer he was about to make. The knights, ever dressed in their crusader surcoats, sat stoically but expectantly before the doge.

"You have told us your needs and here is what we can offer. We will build and man transports to carry four thousand, five hundred horses and nine thousand squires. We will build and man ships for four thousand, five hundred knights and twenty thousand soldiers of foot. All will be provisioned for nine months. You will pay us four marks per horse and two marks per man. You will muster and we shall embark from the port of Venice, to serve God and Christendom, wherever that may take us. The total sum for this contract will be ninety-four thousand marks."

Dear God, thought Geoffroy, *that's more than the annual treasury of all our blessed France!*

"We will also supply fifty armed galleys, without charge, for as long as our alliance lasts, on the condition that we receive half of all the conquests that we make, either by way of territory or money, either by land or at sea. Now please retire and consider our offer."

The knights went into an adjacent hall. They were stunned by the amount of the money. The seneschal tried to calm them.

"It is a huge amount, indeed. Yet on a per man basis, it is not unlike what the Genoese required of us in the last crusade."

"Make him a counteroffer," huffed Alard. "That's too much coin if we are giving away half of the spoils."

Geoffroy considered the arguments. They could go back to their lords empty-handed or with a deal. "Let's see if for dignity's sake we can knock down that price a bit."

They returned to the chamber and the doge agreed to drop the total price by 10 percent, provided the knights gave a good faith deposit of five thousand marks at the signing. *We are reduced to beggars,* thought Geoffroy. *We will have to borrow that sum on the Rialto, if anyone will lend to us.*

The Frenchmen agreed to the deal and the doge ordered the contract to be put in writing on the letters carte blanc. He cautioned that it still had to be approved by the Great Council later that day and by the entire Commune of Venice at a high mass the following day. The knights agreed to attend the mass and present their case to the people of Venice.

Later, Dandolo walked down to the hall of the Great Council. He heard the whispers of doges past on the walls, giving him advice, encouraging or warning him. He tried to block out the clamor as he thought of his strategy in the Great Council. There would be the usual complainers. They were easily silenced by offering lucrative tax collector or easy administrative work in the colonies to their wastrel sons. There were legitimate concerns, however. The French contract would be the largest financial undertaking in Venetian history. It would, in fact, demand a reorientation of the entire economy and workforce toward its fulfillment. The doge would have to convince everyone in the Great Council that they had a personal stake in the successful outcome of the contract and the ensuing crusade. He would appeal to their religious and their mercantile natures. If the crusade was a success, Jerusalem would return to Christian control thanks to the Venetians. Venice would be rich and powerful beyond imagination. If it failed, they might break even financially, but it could be at a cost of hundreds or thousands of Venetian lives—the lives of the sons of the Great Council. Dandolo would be torn apart in the street and thrown into the Grand Canal. *I have had a long and good life,* he thought. *It is worth the gamble.*

The doge entered the full hall. The loud buzz of a thousand conversations lowered immediately. Dandolo could hear his own footsteps as he mounted the dais to address the Great Council. He sensed a divided chamber. In his mind's eye he saw the chamber as a roiling and treacherous shoal in the lagoon, black clad arms waving about like the long seaweeds that ensnare oars and confound progress. He pushed his white sleeves up to his elbows.

"Patrician families of Venice, members of the Great Council, we come together at a turning point in our history. We are called by our God to rescue his holy land of Jerusalem from unclean infidel hands. He will reward our good works with bounty and territory. We will be praised and honored in this life and rewarded in the next—"

"Why should we risk our good trade relations with the Muslims to support this venture?" an old man thundered. "Richard of England with his vast armies couldn't retake Jerusalem. Old Frederick died trying too. We don't need to own Jerusalem to pray there or to make money there! Another crusade is madness, I say! Since Al-Adil consolidated control over most of the Syrian lands there has been relative peace and healthy trade. Not a single Venetian trader has been robbed, cheated, or molested by the infidels. Al-Adil makes overtures to treat with us even now. Why should we betray that and bring another round of destruction. For what?" A murmur of agreement went through the hall. Men began to stand and shout.

A grossly fat patrician from one of the newer families spoke loudly. "Agreed! Good men of Venice! We live by trade and by the sea. We benefit most from free and preferential access to markets across the known world. Venice has never held much territory. We seek no empire of lands. We receive all the benefits of empire without the burden of administration or maintenance of huge armies. Why should we throw our lot in with one side or another when we can have good commerce with all for little or no cost? This smells of a bad bargain."

He seeks to play the crowd for personal gain, Dandolo thought. *Like many of these men, he will swing with the tide.* A small voice rose in his ears. *Let them exhaust themselves, beloved. Ride out the storm.*

"Who will repair our trade galleys while all our shipwrights are busy building galleys and transports for the French?" another man pleaded.

"My sons can't walk away from their trading to scour the mountains and plains for grain for these crusaders. How do we feed our families if we have no income from trade for a year? We can't eat future promises of spoils and territory!"

The doge put up his hands to silence the hall. *If I cannot appeal to their love of God, I will appeal to their love of mammon.* "Think upon this. The coin the French pay will go directly to your families. It is less than we all make in our trades, but it will hold your families until the venture is done. Then, good men of Venice, the pot is sweetened by the spoils. Half of all conquests. Half of all territories. Half of all gold, jewels, carpets—everything that we and their soldiers can grab. Our wealth will only be limited by the strength of our arms to conquer and carry away the bounty we find. Afterward we will control the commerce from all lands captured. We will administer all trading in and out. And it will be your sons who will administer and tax the lands."

Patrician Morelli, one of the wealthiest men in Venice, stood to speak. "There is wealth to be had in the Syrian lands, although Jerusalem itself has been picked clean by the Latin kingdom and now Saladin and his brother Al-Adil. There is much value in the smaller coastal ports that sit astride those ancient trade routes." The patrician's eyes gleamed. "The real wealth of those infidels awaits in Cairo and Alexandria. Even the English King Richard said that the true key to Jerusalem lay in Cairo. I could support this unsettling venture if we went to Cairo instead of Jerusalem. In addition, if we attacked Alexandria and Cairo we could destroy the Pisan trade there. They supply war materials to the infidels. I am sure the pope would approve of such a move. We would have a monopoly in trade between those rich ports and Europe."

"A wise observation," noted Dandolo. "But the crusading knights would be wary of this approach. They have taken the cross to recapture Jerusalem, not to attack Cairo. They fight for the homeland of Our Lord and for their own salvation and will most likely not be swayed by the military strategy of choking off the supply lines of the Muslim armies. Of course, many are also moved by the wealth they hope to grab for themselves. We do have grounds to go to Alexandria and Cairo first since our contract states that in this crusade we serve God 'wherever that may take us.' I propose we do not share that fine point of distinction with the crusading masses. We only need tell their leaders. They are military men and will understand the strategy of attacking Cairo." He gave a sly smile. "More importantly, they will do anything at this point to get the contract signed and acted upon." The general hum of agreement around the room was interrupted by an exasperated younger trader whose family did well by the Muslim trade.

"But you will be attacking Al-Adil directly in his home of Cairo. We have good relations with him and are even now seeking trade preferences for those very ports. How will he react if we support a crusader attack on Cairo itself?"

Dandolo was waiting for this. *I will give you a lesson in diplomacy with the Arab leaders, young man.* "If Saladin was still the sultan, we could not do this. But Al-Adil is a man of more measured thought. He knows that kings and sultans come and go. He seeks good relations with all the remaining Latin kingdoms and with all trading partners. He knows we have to support the church in this, that we have no choice. After the dust has settled on this latest aggression, he will seek terms of peace. We will give him back most of the lands we conquer in exchange for granting Venice control of European trade. We set up our trading posts and colonies in Cairo, Alexandria, and beyond. We get rid of the Pisans. The Genoese are already subservient to us in the Syrian lands. Flood the lands with your sons and reap the rewards for your families and for Venice. We will create a grip on the throat of trade in the Mediterranean that will last for centuries. As long as Al-Adil and those who come after him receive their taxes and tributes and retain their luxuries, they will support the situation." He stopped for a moment and looked around the room as if he could see every man deep in thought. "I believe this is a very wise investment."

After another hour of debate there was sufficient agreement for Dandolo to declare he was ready to convene the Great Mass at the Basilica San Marco to seek the approval of the commune itself. Word was sent to ring the great bells of the Campile Tower and the basilica to announce the special mass, and to bring the French knights to the church. Within two hours the basilica and the plaza were overflowing with Venetians. Over ten thousand souls gathered and gossiped, waiting anxiously for the news from the doge. Dandolo sat in the first side pew of the great church, along with the most senior members of the Great Council. Geoffroy de Villehardouin and the other French knights sat in the first row facing the altar. The mass itself was straightforward and monotonous. To the anxious Venetians in the church and the plaza it was more a prelude to be tolerated than the profound service they usually experienced. Dandolo rose and walked directly to the altar as soon as the priest had finished. Not a sound was heard inside the church, and the silence rolled out into the plaza on a wave of quieting noises and gestures. The bright sunlight outside barely penetrated the thick, smoky incense haze that permeated the great church. What shafts of light did glimmer off the golden mosaics made the church seem like an underwater grotto. Dandolo felt the sea in the salty sweat of thousands of intent Venetians. He prayed aloud for guidance in this great calling and described the mission. The crowd was agitated, and the murmur began to rise. Dandolo raised his arms, and the crowd silenced immediately. He asked the French knights to present their case to the Commune of Venice itself, here, where church, sea, and people combined as one. They rose together, marched to the front of the altar, and turned to the sea of Venetian faces.

Geoffroy stepped forward into a shaft of light, his crimson cross blazing against the white of his surcoat. He cleared his throat and boomed his emotional message. "Good people of Venice! Our lords, who are the greatest and most powerful barons in all of France, have sent us to you. They beg you to take mercy on Jerusalem, which is enslaved by the infidel Turks, and for the love of God, beg you to help their expedition to avenge the honor of Jesus Christ. They have chosen you because there is no nation on earth as powerful at sea as yours, and they have ordered us to throw ourselves at your feet and not rise again until you have agreed to take pity on the Holy Land..." The old marshal intended to go on, but he was overwhelmed by emotion, exhaustion, and despair. He fell to his knees and began to cry, his wailing echoing throughout the cavernous church. Walter of Gaudonville dropped to his knees as well, as much from the pain in his wounded leg as the emotion. The two poets, Miles and Conon, grasped each other's hands and sank to the floor weeping. John of Friase was bewildered by the emotions yet was moved to tears by the sight of his comrades. Alard looked around at the wailing men. *Merde*, he thought, *better get on with it*. He sank to his knees and cried aloud with his hands clasped before him in supplication.

The emotional outburst rocked the souls of the Venetian onlookers. With a great swoon and a roar they started to shout, "We consent! We consent!" The chant reached out into the plaza, and the Commune of Venice spoke with one voice. Dandolo felt the consent of Venice like a warm embrace. He raised his arms in a gesture that seemed to surround the entirety of the crowd and shouted in a voice that came not from a frail old man, but from the sea itself.

"Behold, my good and pious people! Behold the honor that God has done us! France, the finest nation on earth, has scorned all others and asked our help and cooperation in undertaking a task of such magnitude as the deliverance of Our Lord!" He began to weep uncontrollably, as well. From the second row, Antonio and Rotundo looked on in amazement.

The celebration at the doge's palace that night was subdued. The French knights seemed exhausted as they made plans to borrow the needed down payment of five thousand marks at the Rialto the next day, and as they planned Geoffroy's and Walter's return to their lords while the others went to Pisa and Genoa to try and arrange more support for the crusade. The doge and councilmembers in attendance spoke in hushed tones throughout the evening. As the guests left the banquet hall, the doge asked Antonio to stay a while. Antonio felt a shock of pleasure at the invitation; he had apparently made quite an impression on the old doge. He chatted amiably with the few remaining guests until the hall was empty except for Antonio, the doge, and a few servants.

The doge turned toward Antonio with a grave look on his face. "You are under arrest."

Antonio stared at the doge with his mouth open. He shook his head to think clearly. "What have I done to offend you, sir?"

"Your brother is a Genoese spy and intriguer. We need to know how you are helping him."

"My brother? He is just a boy at home with our father. He spends his days in taverns and chasing skirts."

"He has been in Rome and Sicily with your uncle, the monk. And now he has fled to Constantinople. You know nothing of this?"

"I don't have an uncle who is a monk, Your Excellency. This must be some sort of prank. My brother has no head for intrigue. He can barely hold his own at the Troyes fair."

Dandolo sat quietly for a moment, wondering where the truth in this lay. Was Antonio sincere? His voice betrayed no tension, just fear and bewilderment. Was he overly clever? The intelligence that came to the doge this day spoke of the lad and the monk trying to heal the schism between Rome and Constantinople. That was not in the interest of Venice at all. Venice needed the tension between the two centers of Christianity to maintain its place in the middle. Was Antonio sent here to keep Venice in the dark while his brother sealed an alliance between Genoa or Rome and Constantinople?

"Your brother is on a mission for the church to bring Rome and Byzantium together. We have also been told that he is seeking the route to Presbyter John in the East. Or more likely the route to the spiceries."

"I swear, my lord, I know nothing of this. When I left home months ago my brother was mooning over some young Jewish girl. That was the extent of his passion for anything at all. And I have never heard of this Presbyter John or where he might abide, but I can assure you that my brother has never been east of Milan or south of Pisa. He wouldn't know how to find his nose if someone didn't punch it in a tavern every week. This cannot be right. As for me, Your Excellency, I have been here in the service of the church, nothing more. I have shared everything that you have asked of me, all I know about the French nobles, and all my thoughts about trade and the future of Genoa and Venice. No one could know me in Venice better than you. Please, sir, judge me yourself."

Enrico Dandolo rubbed his temples and exhaled slowly. This was a sad affair. He listened for her voice, but no sound came to him. He liked the young Genoese, yet if he was playing a double game then both he and his brother would suffer.

"Sleep this night in the dungeon below the palace. In the morning we shall see what we will do about this." Dandolo ordered two guards to escort Antonio to a cell in the damp lower dungeon. The young man protested but did not resist as they led him away.

There were no windows in the cell, so Antonio had no sense of the passage of time. All night he tried to think what Nicolo could possibly be involved in but could come to no conclusion. Would the doge think his claims of ignorance a mere shield? He was a papal emissary here in Venice, so he didn't think the doge would have him tortured, but he couldn't be sure. *What in the name of heaven was Nicolo up to?*

※

Antonio was shaken roughly by a guard at some point. He could not tell if it was the middle of the night or the early morning. He was led up the stairs to the third floor of the palace and through a doorway marked Magistrate. Inside he was pushed up another flight of stairs and into a small room with an eye slit on the far wall. He heard voices and looked through the slit. Below he could see three men sitting at a bench at one end of the room below. In the middle of the room a man was being forced to stand with ropes tied behind his back. At a sign from the men at the bench, the rope was hauled and the man was jerked off the floor. The man let out a sharp scream as he was lifted into the air by his hands behind his back. His arms bent unnaturally as the men at the benches asked him questions that Antonio could not interpret through the moans.

"You might as well tell the truth right away; it always comes out eventually."

Antonio turned to see a sad-faced Rotundo. He rushed to embrace his friend.

"But I know nothing at all," he pleaded. "I have no idea what my brother is up to, or if it even is my brother." He grabbed the monk's arm. "You must believe me, Romundo, you must." The monk put his hand over Antonio's.

"I do believe you, Antonio. But let's pray that the doge does too. Here, everyone confesses under torture. It is very effective. Oh, look, they are lowering the poor fellow. He must have admitted whatever they wanted him to."

"But that's not justice!" cried Antonio. "Torture is no guarantee of the truth! A man would say anything to end that treatment!"

"Next!" droned a voice from below. Antonio was hustled out of the room, followed by Rotundo. He was brought out to the middle of the interrogation room and had his hands trussed behind him. The men on the bench studied a parchment before them. Each wore a black, hooded robe. The one in the middle wore a shawl of sable over his shoulders. *He must be the magistrate*, Antonio thought. The man cleared his throat loudly.

"Antonio diCarlo, you have been charged with treason against the commune as a spy for Genoa. How do you answer?"

"I have done nothing, your honors. I am here as a representative of the pope to seek your support for the holy crusade, nothing more." Antonio noticed that along the side wall a man was threading the rope through a pulley and taking in the slack. "I was told by the doge last night that my brother is involved in some escapade in Sicily, but I know nothing of this. When I left Genoa on the holy mission my brother was away at the Troyes fair selling olive oil and buying wools." Antonio felt a jolt of fear as the rope tightened behind his back and inched upward. "Give me the chance to prove my innocence!" The pressure of the rope stopped at a nod from the man in the middle.

"How would you do that?" Antonio's mind raced for an answer.

"I will go to Constantinople and confront my brother, if it is him at all. I will find out what he is up to. If he is on some foolish mission, I will dissuade him or break his neck with my own two hands. In any event I will come back to Venice and report what I find to the doge."

"How can we guarantee that you will return and not escape with your brother back to the safety of Genoa?"

"You have the signed agreement with His Holiness for the ships and crews. Keep it until I return. Then hear my report and decide whether to honor the agreement or tear it up. My life and my family's future depend on that agreement. If you are satisfied with my report, let me take the agreement back to Rome and you will receive payment from the treasury. If you are not satisfied, well, I will be in your hands."

The men huddled and whispered to each other.

"We will suspend this inquiry for now. Leave for Constantinople immediately. Find your brother. Discover the truth of his mission. If in fact he is there to disrupt our trade with the East or to reunite the churches, dissuade him. Then come back here to receive your reward or your punishment. But remember this, Antonio diCarlo, the doge is counting on your integrity. It would be sad if the House of diCarlo were to lose both sons due to your betrayal." He scribbled on the parchment before him. "Next!"

CHAPTER 8

THE PISAN GALLEY

THE PISAN GALLEY was a large one. Fifty rowers to a side and three large masts. Besides the pilgrims, sheep, and other cargo, Nicolo watched as thirty Saracen archers practiced shooting arrows the length of the deck on the port side. This is no mere carrier of cargo, he thought, this is a full-blown war galley. The observation troubled him until he realized that all the maritime powers had mixed commercial fleets. The smaller, purely trading galleys like the *San Giorgio* and the *Minervi* were fine for short coastal runs, but these larger warships were essential to protect their cargo and crew offshore and between different countries.

The run from Palermo through the Strait of Messina and onward was peaceful. They sighted many smaller vessels flying the flags of Venice, Byzantium, Amalfi, and other maritime nations. But all of them steered clear of the lumbering Pisan war galley. During the first few days at sea, playing the fool suited Nicolo. Nobody seemed to expect anything of him, so he wandered the main deck every day listening to snippets of sailors' conversations and watching the pilgrims puke over the rail. Soon he was given simple chores that the sailors thought he could do, like cleaning the vomit off the rails, scrubbing the deck, and scouring the station off the bow where sailors and passengers went to relieve themselves. Although "cleaning the head" was disgusting and offended his sensitive nose, the task was made easier when the galley plunged into deep troughs between huge rollers in the open sea. This was also the only time Nicolo experienced total privacy on board. He could actually spend as much time hanging off the bow as he pleased, until someone needed the station. One early morning he sat straddling the head timber while several sailors gammed at the nearby foremast.

" . . .and I say we shoulda gotten a bigger share of the cargo. We coulda captured that galley and sold it instead of sinking her." Nicolo strained over the crashing bow wake to listen.

"Well, that was the captain's orders, so shut it. What would we have done with the damned Genoese on board? Better they drowned than we woulda had to slit their throats. I don't mind war, but murder is an affront to God."

"God? What does God have to do with it? If God was involved, do you think we woulda had to pay that high churchman his share?"

"That's the price for protection, brother. Anyway, we gotta unload all that cargo in Constantinople. Guess the captain was worried it woulda been identified in Palermo. What a waste of time dropping the hook there, eh? We didn't get rid of that stuff, and we didn't take on any new cargo. Barely a chance to have a drink and a grab at those dark whores in Palermo. Anyway, we better get back to work before the bosun catches us again. His mood's as dark as sin."

As the sailors walked aft Nicolo tried to piece their conversation together. Were they talking about the *San Giorgio*? That was the only Genoese galley lost this year. And who was the high churchman they talked about? He poked his head over the rail to see if he was alone.

"Hey you! What the hell are you doing there?" The bosun grabbed Nicolo's collar, yanked him over the rail and threw him to the deck. He stood over him with clenched fists the size of Parma hams. "You think that's your private office out there? Get astern and stone the deck!" The bosun kicked Nicolo in the ribs, rolling him down the deck. Nicolo got up and scrambled aft to the laughter of the sailors and the sympathetic looks of the pilgrims.

I need to see that cargo. If it came from the San Giorgio, I've got to tell someone when we get to Constantinople. I can't tell Mauro; he's got a big mouth and we'll both get thrown overboard if he talks. No, I have to keep this to myself until we land. And I have to keep smiling as I walk among these murderers every day. God protect me. Nicolo checked himself abruptly. He had never asked for God's protection before. *Huh, being around Brother Mauro is getting to me.* He grabbed the scrubbing stone and bucket and got to work on the deck. The pressure on his raw, blistered knees forced Nicolo to concentrate on the action of the stone in his hand. *I've got to keep this out of my mind completely.*

But Nicolo couldn't get the image of the drowning Genoese sailors out of his mind or forget the fact that his family could lose its House over the loss of the *San Giorgio*. Each day he watched the crewmen go about their business, trying to figure out where the cargo holds were and how he could find some excuse to access them. He figured that the goods from the *San Giorgio* must be nearest the deck, as the sailors had said they didn't take on new cargo in Palermo. He scrubbed and stoned the deck in a different area every morning. He even stoned the hatch grates so that he could see below. The sailors had never seen anyone do that and figured it was more foolishness from the imbecile nephew of the old monk.

"Hey, Admiral!" cried out the bosun one gray, wet morning. "Go below at the forward hatch and bring up some mops. This deck looks like a barn with all that chicken and sheep shit all over it. Move it!" He kicked Nicolo awake where he lay next to Mauro near the forward mast. Nicolo got up and ran to the open grate. He was halfway down the hatch when he realized that he had never been below and was finally getting his chance to search for the cargo. The mops stood at attention against a rack as he ran by. The upper cargo deck was broad and open, with crates stacked randomly and carelessly about him. Nicolo looked around quickly and saw that he was alone. There was not much light, but he could make out a few inscriptions on several of the crates. Ports, owners' names, weights. Nothing he recognized. He heard the bosun bellowing at some poor sailor and decided that he had done enough for one visit. He grabbed three mops and went back on deck.

✻

MAURO WAS PLEASED with himself. He had gained what the sailors called "sea legs" and didn't fall down while walking the deck anymore, nor did he throw up. The pilgrims on board were men of all ages and conditions. He felt sorry for them, as they seemed to have no other goal in life than to go to the Holy Land. He decided to offer a daily class in scripture to educate these poor men and to break the boredom of the long sail. Nicolo ignored these classes as he did the pilgrims, whom he thought ignorant and uncouth, but he was so bored that he relented and sat in on a meeting one afternoon. Mauro sat atop an overturned bucket while a dozen pilgrims squatted on the deck around him. When he saw Nicolo approach, he was delighted.

"Nicolo! Please join us. We are talking about loving one's neighbor. These good men are farmers from Germany. Most of them don't speak Latin but they seem content to bask in the words of scripture." Nicolo secretly wished he hadn't sat down but smiled pleasantly at the monk. He listened as Brother Mauro gently and patiently recited verses from the Bible and then explained what they meant. The farmers smiled and nodded. Nicolo realized that he was happy that the monk felt useful. After the class, Nicolo remained with Mauro.

"Tell me something," he whispered without moving his lips. "Why are these people going on pilgrimage? Do they think their souls will be cleansed or something?"

Mauro let out a long sigh. "Most are simple people who have immense fervor for Our Lord. They are sailing and marching all the way to the Holy Land for some unknown reward, but they feel they must go. Others seem to be going to have their sins forgiven or to grab something they can bring back home. Even a single gold ring or set of silver goblets could keep their family in food for a year." The monk paused a moment. "It is so sad, really. Look at how old and feeble some are. They will die on board this ship or while trying to walk to the Holy Land. Some of them are completely worn out already. They have little of their original passion, but they don't know what else to do. They cannot return so they go forward. All I can do is share some of the teachings of the church with these poor souls. It seems to lighten their burden."

Nicolo was about to make a disparaging comment about the stupidity of people, but he noticed that the monk's eyes had misted over. There was something about the older man's ability to have compassion for these people that touched Nicolo in a way he couldn't fathom. Competition and quick judgment were the ways of his world, not empathy and understanding. He held his tongue.

As DAYS TURNED into weeks and neared a month at sea, the crew's watchfulness over the passengers relaxed. Nicolo had made many trips down below and had scoured most of the upper cargo deck. He rose before dawn one morning to sneak below before the changing of the deck watch. He pushed back the grating slowly and lowered himself down to the deck below. He had not yet gone all the way aft on the cargo deck. He crawled over coils of tarred spare rigging and past extra spars and casks of water. This deep into the galley he could smell the bilge wafting between the timbers from two decks below. The rancid odor of spilled and spoiled oils mixed with the crap of sailors who didn't want to go up to the deck and the nauseous humors of bloated and burst dead rats made it difficult for Nicolo to breathe. The light heading aft grew dimmer as he approached a large tarp. Nicolo sniffed the air around the tarp. Mixed in with the salty moisture and acrid rat droppings he noticed a slight, pungent odor. He followed his nose to one side of the tarp. Was that the smell of cloves? He pulled back a corner of the tarp and squinted to try and see any writing. Toward the back of the covered crates he came upon squiggled lines that appeared to be Arabic. He tried to drag the corner of one crate around to take advantage of what little light there was. Besides the squiggled lines was the inscription '*San Giorgio*.' As Nicolo ran his finger across the name in disbelief the soft light disappeared. The bosun loomed behind Nicolo.

"What the hell are you doing here, boy?" Nicolo could not speak for fear of his accent. He just smiled stupidly at the brute of a man before him, as spittle drooled down the bosun's bushy, graying beard. "You tryin' to find a place to hide from me?" Suddenly, the menace in the bosun's voice faded. "Well, maybe we've been too hard on you. Guess it's time we gave you a promotion. Would you like that?" Nicolo didn't know what to do. The bosun was acting almost friendly, and Nicolo could see what appeared to be a smile on his face in the shadowy cargo area. "The captain told me he wants you to join the crew, so I am gonna perform the ceremony right here and you will be one of us." The bosun reached down and started to undo the drawstring of his trousers. "You are gonna be my personal cabin boy from now on. Come here, now, don't shy away." His huge hand shot out and grabbed Nicolo around the neck. The bosun seemed to growl as he pushed Nicolo down toward his crotch. Nicolo's nose was assaulted by the smell of stale sweat and piss. The young merchant felt a numbness coursing through his veins. If he spoke up it would be the death of him. If he remained silent, he would be brutalized. He started to faint.

"Oh! There you are!" came Brother Mauro's sweetest tone. "My boy, I told you to find the night soil bucket for me. It is in the front part of this room, not the back." He walked up to the bosun, ignoring the throbbing thing in the seamen's hand. "Come with me back on deck this instant. There is enough light now that I can use the front part of the boat. I no longer need the bucket. And thank you, dear Bosun, for helping me find my nephew. He can certainly be a . . . handful." The befuddled bosun let go of Nicolo's neck and turned away from the monk to cover himself.

Once on deck Nicolo squeezed Mauro's hand so tight that the monk grunted. He didn't let go of his hand until daybreak illuminated everything on deck and the usual morning routines were underway.

"I think you should stay close to me for the rest of this voyage, Nicolo, even if it means attending my classes."

"Port ho!" shouted the sailor in the bow. "Constantinople ahead!"

Mauro and Nicolo ran to the rail, along with most of the pilgrims well enough to stand. The bosun and several of the sailors started to push them back but got caught up as well in the magnificent sight ahead. Even though they were hours of sailing away from the port, the forty-foot walls that surrounded Constantinople were visible above the spindrift atop the waves. The golden dome of Hagia Sophia loomed beyond the walls, the only discernible feature of the city from that distance.

"It is so far away, yet so clear and beautiful. The dome glows like a beacon toward Heaven itself," Gustav, a Bavarian monk, said from behind Mauro. "It is the biggest dome in the known world. A tribute to the old Roman emperor's devotion to Our Lord."

"I . . . I . . . cannot believe its magnificence," Mauro stammered. He wanted to drop to his knees in supplication, but realized his head would be below the bulwark and he would not be able to see the cathedral.

"Yes, but is it a sin that it is under the control of the patriarch John Kamateros and his heretical followers?" the Bavarian grunted. "It belongs to us, the true faithful. Someday Byzantium must return to the fold."

"Amen," Mauro intoned.

"But it better happen soon," the Bavarian grunted. "The court of Constantinople is one of great sloth and luxury. Just as a decadent Rome was destroyed by my Hun ancestors, so too shall Byzantium and even Jerusalem be laid to waste."

Mauro was startled by the vehemence of the Bavarian. "By whom?"

"Gog and Magog, the evil ones. They have broken through the Gates of Alexander and their hordes will soon move west to destroy us all. They will ride upon horses, a great company, and a mighty army. 'Surely in that day there shall be a great shaking in the land of Israel.' The prophecy of Ezekiel is upon us." He turned and walked away from the rail, crossing himself and making gestures that Mauro didn't understand.

Nicolo looked quizzically at Mauro, who thought for a moment and whispered. "I don't remember much about Gog and Magog. In the Book of Revelation it is predicted that the hordes without number of Gog and Magog shall be let loose upon the world at the end of time by Satan." The monk shuddered. "They are supposed to be in the far North. I hope they are not where we are going."

The Pisan galley sailed toward the walls of Constantinople all that day. Mauro stood transfixed at the rail the whole time, staring at the great dome. Nicolo wandered the deck, picking up a stray piece of rope whipping or anything else that looked like trash, all the while listening to the sailors. By late afternoon the galley was close enough to the roads to furl the sails and engage the oarsmen to turn up into the Golden Horn and fight its powerful outward flow. They rowed past the Galatea Tower near the southern tip of the peninsula of Constantinople, where the huge chain hung that was pulled across the Golden Horn to shut off the harbors in case of invasion. It was dusk when they rowed past the first large anchorage, Prosphorion Harbor, where the Byzantine navy was moored.

"Look at those wrecks," a sailor sneered as he coiled a line and hung it on a pin rail. "Byzantium used to be the power in these waters, but their corruption and sloth has led to this. Great ships in total disrepair, and only twenty left out of the two hundred when I first sailed here ten years ago."

"Yeah," concurred another. "I hear the lord admiral pockets all the gold that's supposed to repair and maintain the fleet. I also hear that he sold most of the sails, anchors, and even spare nails. Guess he can get away with that since he's the empress's brother-in-law, eh?"

"Seems like they don't think they need a fleet anymore. After all, they hire the Venetians to protect their merchants in convoy and to carry their troops afield. That's why the damned Venetians have gotten their trade preferences back. They pay far less duty per ship than anyone. But we'll set them straight one of these days." He looked up at the three tall masts. "Aye, we'll put those Venetian ships to the bottom right next to that Genoese galley soon enough."

They rowed into Neorion Harbor and tied up to the head of the longest dock. Even at that late hour the docks were crowded with sailors, cargo-carrying merchants, customs agents, and Byzantine soldiers. Nicolo stared with amazement at the motley collection of races and outfits and strained at the babel of tongues that roiled the air.

A fat hand grabbed Nicolo's neck from behind. "See those soldiers, boy?" the bosun growled. "All made up pretty with their long hair and painted eyes. They are like women, these Byzantines, and I'm gonna pop a couple of them open tonight. Wanna join me, boy?" Nicolo smiled and bobbed his head. He slipped away from the bosun's grip and ran to the gangway to disembark at Mauro's side. He looked back to see the bosun leering his way and shuddered.

CHAPTER 9

CAIRO

THE HUGE BLACK banners flew everywhere, brooding above the heads of the massed troops like swirling, ominous thunderclouds. Al-Adil took comfort in the banners. For hundreds of years black banners had symbolized the solidarity of the various Sunni armies below them. As far as his eyes could see there were the small camel-skin tents of the ordinary soldiers. At the center of each group of soldiers a royal tent for the officers flew banners covered in Koranic inscriptions urging victory. He was proud to see Kurds, Arabs, even Persians united in arms against the Europeans, the "Franj" invaders. The troops wore the different colors and designs of their principalities. The Damascenes wore yellow, the Baghdadis olive, while his Egyptian soldiers wore white. Each formation shouted in unison the chant that reflected their passion in the fight ahead.

"Death to the Christians!" shouted the fanatical troops from Mosul. "Death to the Franj!" roared the soldiers of Damascus in response. *Death, death, death. Is that all that awaits us?* Al-Adil knew that the soldiers took the Koranic command literally. After all, that was their sole function as warriors. He was a religious man, of course, but in the Sunni tradition of his upbringing there was room for interpretation and the application of rational thought to a problem.

These crusades aren't about religion, he mused. *They are about power and glory wrapped in a mantle of faith.* Saladin knew that. He was a master at blending death and forgiveness, and appealing to faith, fear, and greed. Al-Adil aspired to follow his deceased older brother's path. *May his memory be a blessing.* But it was so difficult between the insanity of the Franj invaders, his soldiers' desire to protect their families, lands, and faith, and the scheming for power of many within his own dynasty. As he listened to the militant chants, he noted that the Damascus troops would never shout about the Christians. There were more Christians than Muslims in Damascus and there was no animosity between them. In the past, Christians had helped the Muslim rulers of Damascus against the Franj crusaders while many local Muslim leaders had sided with the Franj. Many times emirs and petty princes made alliances with the Franj against their own brothers or cousins in the incessant power struggles that haunted the lands of Islam. The wind shifted, causing black banners to beat against their neighbors until they all waved in the same direction again.

The loyalty of our commanders is as fickle as the breeze itself. As he rode in review past the troop formations, Al-Adil knew that the emirs and generals beneath the black banners were thinking of their own glories, their own fortunes, and of creating their own family dynasties. He did not fault them, for he'd done the same when he served under his brother. Saladin had risen up the ranks of the Seljuk Turks like so many other Kurdish fighters before him. He served under the great general Nur al-Din, the son of Zangi the conqueror, until the general's mysterious death. Saladin took it upon himself to be the protector of Nur al-Din's young son (who quickly died of poisoning) but eventually became sultan himself, uniting the Syrian lands from Baghdad to Cairo under his family Ayyubid dynasty. He ended the two-hundred-year Fatimid rule of Egypt, placing the former Shiite caliphate under the proper Sunni rule of Al-Nasir, the caliph in Baghdad. Saladin paid proper respect and dedicated daily prayers to the caliph, even though it was Saladin himself who was the ultimate power in the lives of the faithful. He defeated Richard Lionheart and many other Franj crusaders in battle and reconquered blessed Jerusalem.

Yet at the end of his life Saladin seemed to want no more of war. He sought to make alliances and peace with the few remaining Franj kingdoms, preferring commerce and taxation to conquest. This enraged many members of the *ulama*, the Muslim religious scholars who held that nothing short of a total cleansing of infidels from the holy lands would restore Islam and the caliphate to their rightful glory. *Death, death, death.*

Al-Adil was not afraid of war or death. He had fought the Franj at Acre, Ascalon, and the glorious Battle of Hattin. Sometimes the Franj were bested in battle, sometimes they murdered their own leaders and their armies dissolved. Sometimes Allah in his wisdom would take them away. How else could he understand the death of their King Frederick Barbarossa, who'd drowned while bathing in knee-deep water en route to Jerusalem at the head of a crusader army of thirty thousand? At the king's death his army simply turned around and went back to Europe. Al-Adil agreed with his brother's belief that the Franj would come and go like the tides, and ultimately give up their quest for territory in the lands of Islam. Better to trade with the Franj, allow them access to their holy places in Jerusalem and beyond, tax their commerce, and live in peace. He had even said yes to the incredible agreement between Saladin and Richard to marry Al-Adil to Richard's sister and make the young prince the king of Jerusalem! Of course, Saladin suspected it was just a ploy by Richard to gain Jerusalem through marriage instead of the sword. The plan fell apart when the sister refused to marry a Muslim and fled back to England. Al-Adil sometimes wondered what it would be like to marry and bed a fiery, educated, exotic Christian woman. Could such a plan truly end these interminable wars?

In truth, Al-Adil spent more time fighting the sons of Saladin than battling the Franj. It had taken eight years since the death of his brother for Al-Adil to wrest control of Cairo, Damascus, and smaller emirates from his many brothers and nephews. *The shroud may bring peace to the deceased,* he thought, *but it always brings chaos to those left behind. No matter what the wishes of the departed leader, power and greed quickly offer their solace and gifts of opportunity to the mourners.* He remembered well that as Saladin lay dying, his son Al-Malik demanded oaths of allegiance from the emirs of Syria assembled at the sultan's bedside. Yet all had demurred. As Al-Adil looked about the field, he saw many of the same men (or their sons) under those black banners. They wanted him dead and would pull their armies back at a critical time in the next battle to allow Al-Adil to be killed or captured. Some sought to create their own rule or restore Saladin's sons, but even more believed that only an Arab should be a sultan, never a Kurd like Al-Adil—even if he was a pious Sunni. *We will never push the Franj from our lands if we cannot aim all our lances toward them instead of constantly stabbing each other in the back,* he thought sadly. Al-Adil also knew that being the sultan of Egypt and the surrounding lands was a blessing and a curse. Of the sixteen sultans who had preceded him, only one had left the office alive. The others had been poisoned, tortured, crucified, dismembered, or simply beheaded by their fellow Muslims. *What fate awaits me?* he pondered. *Only Allah knows.*

"My lord!" Al-Adil's meditations were interrupted by the shout of an approaching rider. "We have urgent news from Sicily!"

Al-Adil read the proffered parchment in amazement. *Do these Franj ever cease their intrigues? The Persians should never have taught them how to play chess.* He turned to the other riders in his party.

"Call the council. Let us convene within the hour in the citadel."

※

THE COUNCIL ROOM in the sultan's palace was already full and buzzing by the time Al-Adil returned, refreshed, and changed clothes. He had exchanged the hot warrior's leather girdle for a loose and airy burnoose of silk with gold threading and brocaded collar and cuffs yet retained the white turban still covered with dust from the troop review. He sat on the sultan's throne instead of on the pillows that surrounded the long table below, where his council reclined. *I must always remind them who is in charge.* He called for Baha al-Din, Saladin's former personal secretary, to sit beside him. The old man shuffled across the room, kissed the sultan's hand, and sat in the chair next to the throne. Baha al-Din waved away the plate of dates and orange slices offered and struck a pose of authority. *He is not only wise counsel, but he also represents continuity and legitimacy,* Al-Adil thought. He looked about the council room, noting the holdovers from Saladin as well as his own advisers. He absently twisted the ruby signet ring that he had taken from Saladin's body, as Saladin had taken it from Nur al-Din before him. He stopped when he realized that several of the men in the room were staring at the ring with a powerful longing in their eyes.

"It appears the Franj are seeking to retake Jerusalem yet again. They are preparing another large army to invade our lands. We must attack their position at Tyre before they arrive." There was a murmur of agreement around the room. After more than a century of war there were only three Franj strongholds left in the Syrian lands. Tyre was the largest and most formidable. If Tyre fell, Tripoli to the north of Beirut would probably capitulate. That would leave distant Antioch, close to the borders of Byzantium. Neither Saladin nor his predecessor Nur al-Din attacked Antioch, as it would have enraged the emperors of Byzantium and needlessly opened another front in this unending war with the Franj. Besides, Antioch was such a blend of religions and cultures that it posed no threat to the caliphate. Although former Franj rulers of Antioch often attempted to take nearby Aleppo, most of the battles in Antioch took place among the ever-changing and scheming Franj themselves. Antioch was also one of the greatest trading cities in the world, a gateway to Europe for many of the spices and trade goods from the East. It was best left in peace.

"These Franj are like animals, beasts," Marwan, the son of the emir of Mosul intoned. "They know nothing but terror and death.

This is what comes of making treaties with brutes. The old sultan was too generous. He never pressed his advantage and always let the Franj leaders escape with their lives. When he won Acre, Ascalon, Jerusalem, Galilee, Samaria, and Gaza he let the Franj knights take their weapons and flee to Tyre. It is said that by his behavior it was Saladin himself who organized the defense of Tyre against his own army. His generosity will be the sword that kills my men at the gates of that fortress." The younger man glared at the sultan. His insides churned at the thought of this small, meek man at the head of the empire that had been cleverly stolen from Marwan's family by the duplicitous Saladin.

Al-Adil felt the sting of his words but showed no emotion. *He burns with the fire of youth and righteousness. He does not know that when you fight forever only the undertaker wins.* It was true that Saladin let many captured knights and lords go free after battle. He was not like the murderous blond giant Godfrey, who had killed seventy thousand Muslims, Christians, and Jews after he won Jerusalem, or even Richard, who had slain four thousand disarmed prisoners after he retook Acre. Saladin was known for his "chivalry," as the Franj called it. Saladin was a virtuous ruler, but also practical. He wanted to keep the Franj leadership intact so that he knew who he was dealing with after their defeat. Every time a new Franj leader replaced a dead one, all agreements were torn up and the Franj rampaged across the lands anew. Saladin also wisely wanted to keep the European merchants from fleeing those reconquered cities so that commerce and taxes would flow uninterrupted. Saladin knew that if he shook his sword at a Franj city, they would shower him with gold to go away. The Franj were not of the desert or the harsh lands, they didn't like their comfort threatened. Al-Adil agreed with his deceased brother's strategy. Even now he was negotiating with representatives of Venice to settle hundreds of merchants and their families into the recently liberated cities and ports and provide them special tax privileges. The more commerce the more people wanted peace. Al-Adil did not want to march on Tyre. It was too well defended and fortified. But the sultan was feeling the pressure to act from the assembled emirs. They wanted this symbol of Franj power—and of Saladin's weakness—destroyed. *We will march soon enough*, the sultan thought, *and set up a siege as Saladin had before. A few weeks of catapulted stones and sorties and we will wait for reasonable terms. We will take the city, or not, and everyone will go back to their families and their own lands. It will be at least a year before the Franj crusaders can mount another serious expedition against us.*

"Your advice is noted, Marwan, and your enthusiasm for our cause honored. Tyre will fall before these new Franj crusaders can organize and arrive. Yet you must recognize the difference between the Franj who have lived here now for generations and those who come anew. The older ones learn our ways and language. They show respect and act as good agents of trade. They are no threat. Some of them even convert to the true faith. It is the new ones who come with murder and pillage in their hearts. It is against them that we must fight."

"They all must die. None of them belong here. Their very presence is an affront to Islam. There will never be peace as long as one Franj survives in our lands."

Al-Adil broke away from Marwan's hot stare, looking around the room slowly and calming himself. *There will never be peace in our sacred lands as long as each side has its fanatics. It is time to change the subject.* "Yet I am mystified by this other piece of news. The pope of Rome has dispatched two emissaries to find a Christian king called Presbyter John somewhere in the East, beyond the Seljuk lands and beyond the trade routes. They expect to unite the forces of this king with those of Rome and create the largest army ever to invade us. I do not know of this king. Do any of you?"

Marwan shook his head dismissively. "There are no Christian kingdoms east of Persia. Trade from the East comes through Mosul, and the sword of Islam rules over all the lands to the great deserts. I know of no Christians living in the East."

No one spoke up after Marwan finished. In the silence, Al-Adil heard the quiet clicking of *subha*, prayer beads. He turned to the source of the sound, Baha al-Din. "Wise uncle, do you have anything to say?"

Old Baha al-Din finally said softly, "I know nothing of this kingdom of Presbyter John, but according to our historian Al-Masudi, there are many Nestorian Christian communities in al-Hind and beyond. I do remember that when I was a young man, the kings of Medes and Persia were defeated by a great army from the East, an unknown army of tens of thousands of horsemen that descended with the fury of a sandstorm. The leader of that army was a prince. His name was Jorchan, which could be John in the Latin, and he might have been a Nestorian."

Marwan sloughed off the vizier with a grunt. "Al-Masudi is a Shia heretic. He is not to be trusted. And the Nestorians are small in number. They cannot have a kingdom somewhere in the East beyond the light of Islam."

Baha al-Din kept looking at his beads. "Yet Al-Masudi, the great traveler and chronicler of our civilization is a respected adviser to our caliph. Would you question the caliph's wisdom, prince of Mosul? And there have been Christians, followers of their Apostle Thomas, including Nestorians, in Hind and even Sind for a millennium—long before our Prophet received his revelation."

A gray-haired emir spoke up. "I remember that great battle, as well. But it was the Seljuk prince Sanjar and one hundred thousand of his warriors who were slain, not the Persian kings. The victor was a Kor-Khan from Sind beyond the great deserts, not a Christian. The battle took place near Samarkand over sixty years ago. Even if the victor was this Presbyter John, he would be an old man now, beyond all our years. He is probably long dead."

Baha al-Din considered this. "Wisely noted, but 'Presbyter John' may be a title adopted by each king who ascends the throne, not the name of the man. This is the custom of Christian popes who take on a new name when they are chosen. New wine in old bottles. It is not unknown to us either. Many an emir renames himself after one of the sons or companions of the Prophet. And rebels too. How many newly minted Abu Bakrs are there now who have taken that name of our first caliph? The practice seems to legitimize the ruler in the eyes of his followers."

The old vizier turned toward the sultan. "Perhaps the Jewish physician will know of this Presbyter John. He is a very learned man. Since he left the service of Saladin, he has retired and writes his books of philosophy, uninvolved with the court."

The sultan felt the quiet disapproval in the old man's voice. Al-Adil had dismissed Maimonides after Saladin's death without a pension or any acknowledgment of the Jewish physician's years of service to the former sultan. Many felt it was an unnecessary slight to a well-respected scholar-physician, a Jew who had dedicated himself to study and who understood the *f'il-falsafa*, the philosophies of Islam, Christianity, and Judaism better than most scholars. Although the Shiites found Maimonides's writing heretical (and felt the same about Baha al-Din's prayer beads), the Sunni *ulama* ruled it conformed to the counsel of the Prophet's cousin Ibn Abbas to "take wisdom from whomever you may hear it."

"You are right, dear uncle. The wise Maimonides might be able to enlighten us about this eastern Christian king. Please visit the physician after we adjourn with my respect . . . and bring him a bag of gold dinars and some beautiful writing implements with my compliments. It is too long since his service to Saladin and his wisdom were acknowledged and rewarded." Al-Adil was pleased with the smile on Baha al-Din's face and the murmur of agreement throughout the room.

Only the troublesome Marwan seemed unsatisfied. He spoke in a haughty tone. "It is a sad day when we, the most powerful rulers of the land, must rely on heretics, Christians, and Jews for our intelligence."

The smile never left Baha al-Din's face as he spoke to Marwan. "And yet the Prophet himself received instruction from a Christian monk, a Nestorian, in fact."

"Regardless of what we know," the sultan continued, "the point is that these emissaries seek the priest king. We cannot take the chance that such a king and his armies await the command of the pope to strike us."

"There is more unsaid than said in this," Baha al-Din added. "The Christians of Rome and even Byzantium know nothing of Sind, Hind, and Zangi or the great eastern ocean we sail with every monsoon. Their Greek and Roman ancestors traded these same routes, but somehow these Christians lost memory of this centuries ago. That is why we have controlled the eastern trade routes since before the time of the Prophet. If we are to remain strong and expand the caliphate, we must prevent these emissaries from rediscovering this lost knowledge. They must not go beyond the Byzantine Empire. We must eliminate this threat immediately." Baha al-Din nodded to the sounds of assent throughout the room.

"How can we do anything while these men are in Sicily or the lands of Byzantium? They are beyond our jurisdiction," asked Al-Afdil, the *qadi* of Cairo. He had been the chief judge of administrative and legal matters for both Shiite and Sunni sultans and was the most practiced diplomat in the sultanate. Although Al-Afdil was retired, Al-Adil relied on his experienced counsel.

"It seems they are on the move to Constantinople now. If this Presbyter John awaits in the East, they will have to travel beyond Byzantium and through the lands of the Seljuk or the sultanate of Rum. That will most likely end the problem. But if they come south to Antioch or Edessa, they can travel past the worst of the Turks through Aleppo, Mosul, or even Baghdad itself and head east with the caravans. We must prepare for that." Al-Adil knew what he had to do, but he dreaded making the decision. Only one group could find these men and eliminate them anywhere they went. The Nizaris had been quiet for years. Few assassinations had been attributed to them recently. They lived in their fortresses from Persia to the coast of Syria practicing their perverse version of Shia Islam but were no longer the powerful political force they had been when Sinan, the Old Man of the Mountain, was alive. Al-Adil gazed toward Marwan. He would appoint him emissary to the Nizaris, the assassins. And if he didn't return, then perhaps two problems would be solved. "Prince Marwan, you will have the honor of eliminating these enemies before they reach this Presbyter John in the East. Ride in the morning for Masyaf Castle."

"Masyaf!" Marwan sputtered. "You would have me call on those madmen to do this? The Nizari assassins who tried to murder your brother Saladin twice when he besieged that same castle? They cannot be trusted. They have made alliance with the Franj and offered to become Christians to seek Franj protection against the faithful. Even the Shiites consider them *malahida*, heretics! They work in darkness and do not fight with honor." He turned to the assembled emirs for support. "These assassins stick their golden daggers into their victims, leave the weapons, and flee. It is a mockery of the honor of dispatching an enemy."

"Nevertheless, Marwan, they have the stealth and skill to find and approach the emissaries of the pope and eliminate them. It will be best if the disappearance of these men cannot be traced back to us. You must go to Masyaf Castle and make an offer to the Nizaris. We will pay them good gold for this assignment. And more importantly, if they succeed, we will allow them to practice their heresy unmolested within their Nizari communities. We would rather see them pray south toward Mecca than north toward Rome."

"But the Nizari assassins do not pray daily at all, and they do not follow sharia. They do not honor the caliph. They believe their imam is the supreme leader who knows some inner meaning of the Koran. The rules of the Prophet no longer guide their actions. That is *haram*! You blaspheme to call upon them!" The prince was furious. Not only was this meek sultan a usurper of Marwan's rightful succession, but he would allow this community of murderous heretics to thrive. Marwan rose from the cushions to a gasp from the room. The sultan sat unmoving. He put up one hand to still the gathering.

"You needn't be afraid, Marwan, prince of Mosul," the sultan taunted with feigned concern. "Sinan died years ago. Even though the Nizaris believe he will rise again when their Mahdi returns, I don't think he will jump out of his shrine at your visit." There was a ripple of laughter through the room. Marwan held his fury in check. He had brought this on himself by his arrogance and his open challenge to the sultan. This was not the time or the place for a challenge to Al-Adil. That would come in due course. He calmed himself and bowed in resignation.

"Do this honor, Prince Marwan," said the sultan soothingly, "then ride back to Aleppo and Mosul. Raise more troops and attack the Franj in Tripoli from the north. They will pull part of their army from Tyre to confront you, and we will be able to take Tyre. Then we will march north with your captains in the lead to join you in Tripoli and sweep the Franj out of our holy lands. As a reward for your bravery, we will expand your emirate from Mosul and Aleppo all the way to Beirut, all of us in obedience to Caliph Al-Nazir in Baghdad."

Marwan could find no fault with the plan. Leaving his eight hundred horsemen here meant eyes and ears on Al-Adil's movements. And when the time was right, perhaps at the walls of Tyre, his captains could dispatch the frail Al-Adil and unite Egypt and Syria together under the family of Zangi and Nur al-Din again. *My family. Our people have been in the shadow of the Turks and their Kurdish underlings for one hundred years. We must cleanse the land and restore our rightful Arab bloodline.*

"I will leave in the morning. It is a six-day ride to Jerusalem and another seven days beyond to Masyaf Castle. I pray for protection from bandits and Franj in those craggy hills that lead to the heretics' lair. Put your instructions and the offer in writing so that I may deliver it . . . my sultan." *May Allah protect me.*

"I will accompany the prince."

Al-Adil turned in surprise at the voice of Baha al-Din.

"I know what you are thinking, my sultan. I am strong enough to travel to Masyaf Castle. I was born in Hama, only a few hours' ride from the castle, and I would like to see my homeland one more time before I close my eyes for eternity. I miss the nuts and apricots of the Hama valley." Al-Adil understood the vizier's longing for home; he was not from this land either. He twirled his ring again, thinking of what value the old man could add to this mission. He smiled inwardly as the thought came to him.

Marwan was torn. He thought he would look like a coward if he asked the old man to go with him. Yet Baha al-Din knew the terrain and Marwan did not. Neither did he want to insult the old vizier by saying he did not want his company or his guidance. *Then again, if I take Baha al-Din with me, I remove one of Al-Adil's closest advisers and one pillar of his claim to authority. When the sultan is gone the old man will support me. What else can he do? He will kiss that ruby ring on my finger as he did when he took it off Saladin and passed it to Al-Adil.* He looked at the vizier and smiled. "I would be honored for your company and your wisdom in this, Baha al-Din. If our sultan desires you to accompany me, I will learn greatly under your tutelage in dealing with these Nizari heretics."

And he will watch for your mischief, thought the sultan.

THE JOURNEY UP the Syrian coast was pleasant enough, although they moved more slowly than Marwan would have liked. Between Baha al-Din needing to rest his back and having to piss it felt as if they stopped every hour. The countryside seemed quiet. The men of war sat in their fortresses preparing for the next war, and the people went about the routines of life. The air was thick with the sweet smell of ripe peaches and apricots. Bees drunk on the fermenting fallen fruit bounced off their heads occasionally. It was the time of the olive harvest in Palestine, and the roads were full of farmers bringing their harvest to the presses, as well as nomads moving their goats, camels, and sheep along the ridges and valleys. Baha al-Din stopped to observe the interplay between those who tilled the land and those who moved their animals through it.

"Look, Marwan! See how the cultivators and the nomads interact. They seem so different, yet they need each other."

Marwan turned in his saddle to look back at the vizier. "They fight over the same land. They keep their arms ready to defend themselves from each other."

Baha al-Din shook his head sadly. "You do not see, Marwan. They seem opposed because Allah has given them such different lives. But they provide each other with the things they need. The settled people need the hides and wool and meat the nomads have. The nomads need more food than their animals can provide, so they obtain dates, vegetables, and grains from the farmers. A wise ruler must understand the connection between the two and ensure each gets what he needs without upsetting the balance. This is the key to peace."

Marwan scoffed, turned, and rode on. *Why do men's passions for the struggle weaken when they age?* he wondered. *The old man babbles on about peace when we are in jihad. Saladin sought peace when he should have wet his sword with Franj blood. I pray I never become so feeble.* He flexed his hands on the reins, noticing how hard and defined his forearms were. *Control of the realm belongs to the young and the strong. I will restore the rightful bloodline and cleanse the land soon.*

The pair rode inland after Jerusalem. They avoided Damascus and Homs as well as the coast, traveling through the Beqaa valley and sticking to the secondary roads. They passed several fortresses held by Knights Templar, Hospitallers, and other Christian religious orders, like the massive Krac des Chevaliers that hung rugged and impenetrable off a steep cliff. Baha al-Din recited the histories of each, when it was built, how many times it had changed hands due to war or treachery. Yet at no fortress did a rider come out to challenge or molest them. *If only it could always be like this,* Baha al-Din sighed to himself. *There is so much beauty here, so much life.* He would have liked to share that thought with Marwan, but the young prince of Mosul glowered at him wherever he spoke. *His petulance and disdain will not serve him at court*, the old vizier thought. *No matter—I have my duty.*

They came to the fork in the road leading east to the city of Hama or west to Masyaf Castle. Baha al-Din was tempted to head east and remain in that sweet place of his birth until he died. He pushed the thought out of his mind, remembering his duty to his sultan. They turned west, directly into the blazing sunset. The pair spent the night at a small *madrassa* in Masyaf town, taking advantage of the hospitality schools like this offered travelers. As they sat in the courtyard sharing tea before retiring, Baha al-Din looked upward. An uncountable number of twinkling lights splashed across the night sky. He thought of the Persian fable his father had told him so long ago. Each star was a servant of Islam who found peace; the brightest ones were sultans, emirs, and the most faithful. He wondered how bright his star would shine.

Marwan and Baha al-Din left the *madrassa* at dawn. They crossed a wildflower-filled plain and reached the foot of the rocky escarpment leading up to the castle. There was no road ahead, only a path strewn with large boulders, deep ruts, and blind alleys. *We can only approach the castle on foot from here*, thought Marwan nervously.

"My legs will not carry me up that path, my prince," huffed the vizier. "I cannot go any further. You will have to meet the Nizaris alone. I will go back to the *madrassa* and await the results of your mission."

A hot arrow of fear struck Marwan's heart, but he refused to show it. Instead, he shrugged and thanked Baha al-Din for the companionship thus far. He turned and started walking up the path, leaving the old man alone with their horses. After almost an hour of climbing, crawling, and stumbling along the path, he stood up and dusted himself off. *No invader could assault this place easily. The defenders would pick them off one by one. Now I understand why Saladin failed to take the castle.* The path turned this way and that, and Marwan realized that every hundred feet or so he turned directly into the sun. *A brilliant design,* he thought, *no matter the time of day there is always a place that blinds the visitor. I will create a path like this before the palace in Mosul.*

He rounded a rocky point and came face to face with three masked men armed with crossbows. Two of the men grabbed Marwan's arms and began to take him forward. The third man followed behind, the crossbow bolt pushing against Marwan's back. They stopped before the gate of the castle. The walls of Masyaf were over fifty feet high. The castle followed the contour of the mountaintop, with ten or more archer towers built where the walls turned with the terrain. Masked men peered over the walls and out the arrow slits in the towers. The gates opened and they entered. They passed through a long entryway with dozens of murder holes cut into the stones on each side. Archers peered through the holes, arrows and bolts pointed at the prince. As they left the entryway Marwan was shocked to see beautiful gardens and a spring inside the castle walls. He had expected a military camp ready at any time for war. Many young men walked about, seemingly oblivious to Marwan's presence. They all wore silken shrouds, and their faces were uncovered and at peace. Marwan noticed that the faces bore such different features; high foreheads and long pointed noses mixed with square heads, blunt noses, flat faces, and slitted eyes. Red, blond, and black hair mingled with blue, green, and black eyes. *These Nizaris are not from one tribe or region,* he thought. *They come from every part of the realm and beyond. Many are probably freed or escaped slaves. How can such a community be cohesive? They can only be held together by fear or dark magic.* A kindly looking older man wearing the white turban and robes of court approached Marwan.

"We welcome you to our home, Prince Marwan of Mosul. I am Bahram, secretary to Sheikh Jalal. Please follow me and you will find refreshments and comfort awaiting you."

Marwan was wary. This was not what he expected—and how did they know who he was? They walked casually through a small grove of jasmine and oranges, the flowering trees filling the air with sweetness. Bahram motioned Marwan to follow him into a three-story tower and up a wide, winding stone staircase leading to a large room. The walls were decorated with beautiful tapestries depicting heroic battles and serene circles of learning. Thick Persian carpets covered the floor. At the far end of the room Marwan noticed a small writing table surrounded by pillows. A young turbaned man probably in his twenties looked up and smiled.

"Please, Marwan, prince of Mosul, join me. I am Jalal Hasan. I am the administrator of Masyaf, recently come from Alamut." The man stood and bowed slightly, beckoning Marwan to the pillows. "You must be hot and tired from your climb. I realize it is not an inviting path, but I am sure you can see the safety it offers our poor community. Bahram, please bring us jasmine tea." The secretary bowed and left the room. "Sit, sit, and please don't look so nervous. *Ahlan wa sahlan,* our home is your home." The men sat on pillows on opposite sides of the writing desk. The sheikh made no attempt to hide the parchments on the desk. "I am reading *Al Fatah,* 'The Brave Youth,' written by Caliph Al-Nazir concerning the new order he has established. He describes the noble and perfect man in submission to Islam, whose hospitality and generosity expands until he has nothing left of himself and becomes the pure servant. In one sense it seems the caliph has taken a lesson from the Franj orders. Isn't it a mystery how we can learn so much from one another, even our enemies? Of course, the Franj knighthoods are based on the fallacy of their faith and the greed of their adherents. This, however," Jalal tapped the pages three times, "is a masterpiece of thought and practice. I believe our grand master at Alamut, Muhammed, desires us to study, understand, and adopt these ways. I believe he wishes us to embrace the Sunni mantle under the Caliph Al-Nazir." He noticed the confused look on Marwan's face. "Don't be surprised, prince of Mosul. Are we not all the fallen children of the Prophet? Oh, I know that many believe we are murderers and heretics whose goal is to dominate the lands of Islam by sword or conversion. And there have been periods in our early history where each of those beliefs was true. But it is a different time, and we wish no more of war among the faithful." He looked ruefully into Marwan's eyes. "There are so many forces trying to destroy the true faith. We need to unite."

Marwan was completely disarmed by the sheikh. He seemed more a scribe than a military leader. He cleared his head of the words of the man before him, remembering that the Nizari had strange techniques of the mind as well as unequaled skills in individual combat. *They are consummate liars and manipulators. Their knives have ended the lives of so many leaders of the faithful over the years.* He needed to stay focused and not engage in philosophy or casual talk with this man. Their old leader, the feared Sinan, was dead. Judging by this weakling before him, Marwan thought their power must be broken. *A well-planned attack could take this castle*, he thought. *I must remember where the entrances are and look for weak spots in their defenses.*

"Your renunciation of past heresies would be welcome by the caliph, I am sure, but I am not here on matters of faith," Marwan said brusquely. "I am here to hire you to eliminate a serious threat to our lands." He handed the sealed parchment from Al-Adil over to the sheikh as Bahram returned with the jasmine tea and a plate of oranges and almonds. Marwan looked on nervously as Bahram poured the tea for the sheikh and his guest. *I am a powerful man. I am the prince of Mosul and the bloodline of Zangi and Nur al-Din. I am an emissary of the sultan, who is at peace with these Nizari. I have nothing to fear here. Ahlan wa sahlan.*

The sheikh read the document for a long time, pausing to tap his finger on it and close his eyes in thought now and again. He rolled the parchment and put it on the side of the writing desk, appearing to give it no more thought. "A serious threat to the realm, indeed. We accept your sultan's employ to eliminate this threat. Now, come, drink, and relax." The sheikh saw Marwan's hesitation and shook his head with a smile. "Really, Prince Marwan, you have nothing to fear here." He reached over and took Marwan's cup, raised it in salute to his guest and drank it down. Marwan thought for a moment. Then took up the sheikh's cup and did the same. The hot, sweet taste of the jasmine tea soothed his nerves. Sheikh Jalal put down his cup and asked Bahram to bring in five candidates for a mission. Soon the men filed in and stood at attention a few paces behind Marwan. The sheikh spread his open hands toward the men, looking at Marwan with a smile.

He looks like a merchant at the slave bazaar, Marwan sneered inwardly.

"Marwan, prince of Mosul. I will give you the honor of picking the *fidai*, the faithful one, for this mission. Please look them over and use your considered judgment to make the right choice."

What do I know of assassins? Marwan thought. *What an odd mismatch of young men. Well, I must decide. I will choose a man who looks like he can fight, but not one who looks too rough to pass close to an emissary of a ruler unnoticed. Who should I choose?*

Marwan stood up and walked past the line of men. They all had the pleasant airs of court pages or gardeners about them, not the battle-hardened expressions or stances of warriors. He stopped next to one of the men he had passed while coming through the gardens. The man with the flat face and slitted eyes. It was rare to see men like this in Syria. They belonged on the trade routes far to the north and east. Marwan put his face close to the man's to look at his eyes. He recoiled when he smelled a sickly-sweet odor on the man's breath. "Who is this man? Where is he from? Is he a slave?"

The sheikh brightened. "You are a wise judge of men, prince of Mosul. This man was indeed a slave. He was captured as a child by the Seljuk Turks from the nomadic Pechenegs and sold to a merchant from Edessa. They would have castrated him, as it is the only known manner of calming the wild Pechenegs. Fortunately, he escaped and found his way here, where he accepted Islam and the creed of Nizar. He is ready to enter the Garden of Paradise if the mission demands his life. In fact, I am sure he longs for it, don't you, Ashraf?"

The Nizari smiled broadly. "I am honored to strike the enemies of the imam. I pray for success and to be led into the Garden of Paradise swiftly."

"He has never been called upon for a mission such as this, but I am certain that he is ready. Ashraf, demonstrate the power of your loyalty and belief to our guest." Marwan stepped back from the man, expecting to see some display of martial prowess. The sheikh continued in that same gentle voice. "Leap from that window and enter the Garden of Paradise." Marwan was shocked. He looked back toward the man, but he was already running toward the window. He hurled himself headfirst into the air shouting *"Allahu Akbar!"* plunging downward and landing with a sickening thud. The other men stood motionless with placid looks on their faces. The sheikh put his hand on Marwan's shoulder and led him back to sit on the pillows. "You see, Prince Marwan, our belief is unshakable. It is more powerful than life itself. The Day of Judgment has arrived and those who accept the imam as the font of truth pass to Paradise right here, right now. Know the truth and there is no need for prayer or sharia. Those outer symbols are mere profanities for the unknowing. We who accept are in continuous union and are perfect. Thus, there is no death and nothing to fear. And for those who let go of this life in service such as Ashraf, delights beyond imagining await in the Garden of Paradise. He was the right choice for this mission."

How can a dead man fulfill the mission? These men are insane and dangerous. Their talk is all blaspheme. How can they believe this nonsense? But if they can do the work, that is all I care about. The sheikh can pick his own assassin. Let me say my peace and leave quickly. "I am impressed with your power over these men. Whoever you choose, I am certain he will succeed in murdering the emissaries of the infidels. Then you will get your reward right here in gold and freedom." Marwan could not keep the look of disgust off his face.

The sheikh chuckled and continued. "Oh, I have no power over them. They know the truth and have passed beyond the fears and troubles of this world. We Nizaris are the perfect men."

Marwan could not hold his tongue. "The perfect men! You are enemies of true Islam who hide in these castles and won't fight like men." The sheikh did not seem to take offense. *I insult him to his face and still he smiles. These men are cowards and weaklings. When I restore my bloodline, I will destroy every stone of this place.*

"I know you think of us as murderers without honor. But you must understand our point of view. We are a small nation of believers who live in a hostile world. We have no vast armies to confront the invaders—infidel and Muslim alike—who wash over our lands continuously seeking to destroy us. We have had to evolve a different strategy to survive. Why should we engage in the slaughter of thousands of innocents or even soldiers when with the slash of a blade we can defeat an army by cutting off the head of the snake who threatens us?"

"But you ally yourself with the Franj against Muslim rulers." Marwan could not help himself; his anger was rising again.

"The Franj are tools, just like the dagger and the shield. When we are threatened, we use the tools available. And we have never taken the life of a true believer, only those of misguided fools and drunkards who grab for power at the death of their lords and masters and attack us. You must know, prince of Mosul, leaders of our Muslim lands come and go. Some are tolerant, some fanatic, some seek peace and others war. There are no guarantees that the promise of one will be kept by the next. We must be eternally vigilant. We must kill our enemies and keep our word to our allies. We only seek to be left alone to study and practice our true Islamic faith." He held out his hands before him as if he were pleading to Marwan.

The prince flexed his forearms to control his anger. *It was a hard week in the saddle*, he thought. *I can't seem to close my fists fully.*

The sheikh continued. "Yes, we have assassinated many, from the sultans and generals who slaughter us to the local preachers who stir up a populace against us. Yet we are loyal to our allies, very loyal to our allies."

Marwan began to sweat as the sheikh intoned the names of victims in a prayer-like chant. *Why are my fingers so stiff?*

". . .Seljuk General Bursupi of Mosul, the Persian Said ibn Badi, qadi al-Khasab of Aleppo, the Seljuk sultan Daud, Caliph al-Rashid, Caliph al-Mustarshid, Caliph al-Amir, the crusader Richard's nephew in Acre, the crusader King Conrad in Tyre . . ."

My neck is stiff as well, and my shoulders.

The sheikh stopped his recitation. He sipped the remains of his tea and looked at Marwan. "We are loyal, prince of Mosul."

Why does he keep saying that?

"We fought to protect ourselves from the great Saladin when he attacked us here at Masyaf. We could not keep his armies beyond these walls forever. We tried to assassinate him twice before he decided that his life was more important than defeating us. We made a pact to protect and support each other from then on. He and his heirs would allow us to live in peace and we in turn would destroy any challenge to his bloodline. That is why we murdered your great-uncle Nur al-Din as he was preparing an army to attack Saladin. Power and betrayal; these are the ways of this world but not the way of faith." The sheikh picked up an orange and peeled it slowly with a gold-handled dagger.

Where did that knife come from? I can't feel my feet.

He offered a slice to Marwan, but only shrugged when the prince did not move a muscle in response. "We have remained loyal to Saladin and now his brother, Al-Adil. And who are you, Price Marwan of Mosul? You are the bloodline of sultan Ridwan of Aleppo, who massacred our people until we assassinated him. You are the bloodline of Ridwan's son Zangi and Zangi's son, Nur al-Din. Your grandfather, Sayyaf al-Din, was the emir of Mosul and brother of Nur al-Din. You wish desperately to restore the bloodline of Zangi and destroy that of Saladin and Al-Adil. We cannot permit this. Ridwan, Zangi, and Nur al-Din were our enemies. They attacked and destroyed our fortresses and villages. You as sultan would do the same, would you not? Saladin and Al-Adil have protected us. We are loyal to our allies,

Marwan, prince of Mosul." The sheikh stopped speaking and looked past Marwan with a smile. "Ah, faithful one, you have returned."

Marwan felt hot breath against his right ear. He smelled that sickly-sweet odor again. He could do nothing more than stare straight ahead as Ashraf, walking around the writing desk, took the dagger from the sheikh, bowed, and plunged the blade into the prince of Mosul's chest.

※

Baha al-Din sat in the garden of the madrassa, sipping jasmine tea. The man who approached him carried a red cloth. He had the slitted eyes of one from the northern mountains beyond the Seljuk lands. He stood before the old vizier and bowed, putting the red cloth on the table. Baha al-Din slowly unfolded the cloth. He nodded when he saw the bloodied, gold-handled dagger within. He looked up at the messenger sadly. "You have cut off the head of the snake. Please express to your master the sultan's gratitude. You have been loyal to your allies. The agreement between us shall continue. Go in peace." The man retrieved the cloth and its contents and left. Now I am going home. Baha al-Din rose from the table and stretched his sore back. He mounted his horse with some difficulty and headed east toward the rising sun and his beloved Hama.

CHAPTER 10

CONSTANTINOPLE

NICOLO AND MAURO walked to the base of the pier, turned, and stared along the docks. There were more than twenty piers, all choking with ships flying the banners of different nations. Nicolo's heart raced as he watched the activity. *I am on my own in the greatest port in the world.*

"Nicolo? Nicolo diConti?" a young man in a brightly colored tunic ran up laughing. "What are you doing in the city? You are supposed to be home waiting to grow hair between your legs! Are you here with Antonio?" Nicolo recognized Ludovici's older brother Giovanni. He embraced the Genoese merchant and introduced Mauro.

"I am accompanying my uncle, Brother Mauro, who wishes to study in the libraries and monasteries here."

Giovanni nodded at Mauro and looked at Nicolo curiously. "Well, any voyage offers possibilities. Let's see what awaits you here in *the city*."

"The city?"

Giovanni chuckled at the question. "Yeah, that's what the locals call Constantinople. They think it is the most magnificent city in the world, so they don't even call it by name. They call it 'the great city' or the 'queen of cities', but most just call it 'the city.' Their local name for it is 'Is-tan-buli.' It's pretty arrogant, but you get used to it. Anyway, we've got to get you settled in the Genoese quarter. It is the only safe place for us, and you know many of our fellows there." Giovanni jabbed his elbow into Nicolo's ribs. "Maybe we can arrange for you to lose your virginity, eh? Oh, sorry Father."

Nicolo looked past Giovanni's shoulder and gasped. Giovanni turned and laughed.

"What's the matter, Nicolo, never seen a Circassian beauty? They are the most exquisite women in the world. They live in the Circassus Mountains far to the north. The Turks raid their villages and grab the women and bring them here. They are sold as slaves to the Muslims and sometimes even to Europeans." Nicolo stared at the line of women as they passed by to be loaded onto a Venetian galley docked nearby. He walked toward them to get a better look, only to be whipped back by a huge man with skin of deepest ebony wearing balloon-legged pants and a turban. He stared at one of the women. She was tall and proud, with a lion's mane of black hair. Her fiery green eyes locked on Nicolo's for a moment and were instantly seared into his memory.

"Nicolo, come away! You want to lose your head the first day you are here?" Giovanni pulled at Nicolo's sleeve, putting some distance between the young merchant and the large guard. "She's probably already the property of some emir, judging by the looks of that guard. Lucky bastard."

Nicolo looked up the masthead to the flag of the ship where the women were being loaded. "Emir? But the women are headed to a Venetian ship."

"Yeah, the Venetians have a monopoly on transporting slaves from the city to the Syrian lands, regardless of who the buyers are."

"I have never seen slaves like this, only captured soldiers used as galley rowers. I never thought about women as slaves."

"Well, we don't have slaves in Genoa. But we do buy and sell them here in Constantinople, just like the Venetians and the Pisans. Every week there is an auction at the Vale of Tears, the women's slave auction house off the Meses. That's the main road through the city. I like to go and see the women. I saw that beauty there just last week. Her name is Jildana. Everybody was talking about her. They say even the emperor wanted to buy her, but the empress put her foot down. She is the real power in Constantinople. She's smart and fierce while he's a drunk and a wastrel." Giovanni cast a glance at the slave women and sighed. "They make for a good market, Nicolo, and you should think about getting your family involved. They don't rot at sea like food and grain. And if you go with the shipment as agent you can get away with a few pinches and grabs on the voyage without damaging the merchandise."

Nicolo was aghast at the suggestion but did not want to offend his first friend and contact in this strange port. "Slaves may work out well in this land, but can you imagine a beauty like that in one of our Great Houses? The wife would break the husband's nose the first time he sniffed in the woman's direction."

From behind the men the soft voice of Mauro purred. "So beautiful, so round. I must enter her, I must."

Nicolo and Giovanni turned in amazement. Mauro was staring through the big gate and up the street toward the giant dome of Hagia Sofia. The monk noticed the men staring at him.

"Nicolo, may we proceed to our lodgings? I am looking forward to something other than salted goat to eat and perhaps some soft hay to lie upon."

"Sway that cask over the side, you idiot! Not against the bulwarks! One more time and I swear I'll carlin' yer hatchway!" the bosun bellowed.

"Hey, Bosun, look over there. Isn't that the simpleton? What's he doin' talkin'?" The bosun called for the sailors to belay the cargo drop and looked toward the men on the dock.

"I'll be a son of a bitch! There's nothin' wrong with him. The bastard fooled us."

"Well, he's twitterin' like a bird to one of those Genoese dandies. You think he's Genoese?"

"Genoese? On my ship!" The bosun clenched his fists and let go a long, low growl. "Wait a minute. He was down in the cargo hold pokin' around. I thought he was just lost and lookin' for a good fotherin.' But now that I think of it, he was lookin' under the cargo canvas."

"You think he's some kinda spy tryin' to find the cargo from the *San Giorgio*?" The bosun rounded on the sailor and smacked him with the back of his hand.

"Never mention that name again!" he hissed. He grabbed the sailor by the ear and twisted hard. "Now I want you to follow that little bastard and the monk and find out what they're about. Get some of the boys to grab him, truss him up, and bring him back on board. I want him here tonight—and don't let anyone see you."

GIOVANNI LED THE men through the Gate of the Neorion at the end of the harbor and through the streets of Constantinople on the short walk to the Genoese quarter. Nicolo marveled at the polyglot of races, accents, and clothing they passed. Mauro looked up at the dozens of crosses that dotted the skyline above the many churches of Constantinople. The road out of the port divided the Genoese quarter on the left from the Pisan quarter on the right. Each of the quarters was surrounded by a stone wall higher than a man's head, with gates every hundred yards or so.

"Stay on this side of the road, Nicolo," warned Giovanni. "We are at war with Pisa, even though we mind our own business here. All it takes is a sideways glance and a mumbled insult to start a fight with the Pisans. The place is as ready to light up like dry kindling. If you have to go to the main market or if your uncle needs to visit some of the monasteries across the city, always take the long way. You may lose an hour, but you could gain a life."

The city walls and churches were massive stone buildings decorated with tile frescos and facings, but the inns, warehouses, churches, and other buildings in the merchants' quarters were functional wooden structures. After passing through a small park paved with a tile mosaic depicting some ancient battle scene, the men turned left through an open gate into a warren of squat, rough buildings.

"This inn is a little close to the Pisan quarters, but it is cheap and the food is good. It is safe enough but keep a weather eye out for Pisans and pickpockets just outside the gate—and never go out of the quarter alone after dark." Giovanni embraced Nicolo again and wished the men a good evening. He told them that the innkeeper was a retired Genoese merchant who had lived in Constantinople for decades and could direct them around the city where they needed to go.

Nicolo and Mauro entered the inn to find the owner asleep behind the counter. Nicolo shook the old man but failed to wake him.

"I hope this place is as safe as Giovanni says." Nicolo noticed a room board behind the old man on the wall and saw that the rooms on the second floor appeared to be empty. He led Mauro up the creaking stairs and pushed the first door open. "This looks good enough," he said as he looked around the sparse room. "Two hay mattresses and a window."

Mauro laid down on a mattress and promptly fell asleep. Nicolo shook his head at the sleeping monk and decided to find the book from Count Eugenio's library and look at Mauro's drawings and notes showing the way east. He rummaged through Mauro's small satchel until he found the package. Sitting back on his mattress he carefully undid the wrappings. He took out the volume entitled *The Book of Holy Places* and thumbed through it to find Mauro's notations. Nothing. He started at the beginning and worked his way methodically through the pages. Nothing again. Nicolo threw down the book and grabbed the sleeping monk's shoulder.

"Brother Mauro! Wake up! Where is the map? Where is the way east?" he shouted. Mauro woke drowsily.

"Why, it's all in the book. Xenophon's *Cyropaedia*."

"But this book is called *The Book of Holy Places*."

"Oh!" Mauro sat up, rubbed his eyes, and smiled. "It is a wonderful book. I had no idea of all the places where miracles have happened around our Christian world."

"But there is nothing in it. No writing, no maps. What happened?"

"Oh my," Mauro scratched his head. "The servants must have wrapped up the wrong book. I think I left them both out on the library table." Mauro looked down at his sandals.

"Well, do you remember the names of the places, the rivers and mountains we must pass on the way east?" Nicolo asked in desperation.

"They were such difficult names. I have never heard of them before. I can't remember any of them. I am sorry, truly sorry, Nicolo." Nicolo's head sank into his hands.

"Well, now we have nothing. How are we going to find our way east?"

Mauro thought for a moment. "There are so many monasteries here, maybe some of the monks will know. They are often great wanderers. Also, sometimes visitors stop at the monasteries to have a monk write a letter or report for them. Maybe we can find help there."

Nicolo groaned in despair. "The only monks I know besides you are illiterate drunks or perverts. That seems a slim reed to grasp." But he let go of his anger when he saw Mauro's misery. "Well, too late to worry about it now. At least you can enjoy your *Book of Holy Places*." The men lay back on their mattresses and stared at the ceiling until Mauro fell asleep.

Nicolo tossed restlessly on the bed and turned toward the window. It was a gray dusk. He looked over at the monk and listened to his steady, low snoring. *I've got to get out and have a look around. Maybe go back toward the docks before it gets too dark and return before Brother Mauro wakes up.* He slipped out of the room, down the stairs, and past the sleeping owner. As he walked down the main street Nicolo realized that he could get to the docks faster if he cut through the Pisan quarter. He peeked through one of the gates on the Pisan side of the road and saw the shimmer of water in the harbor at the far end of the street. There were no people on the narrow cobblestone street except for two men who turned into an alley further ahead, so he decided to chance it. He felt a wonderful sense of freedom walking through the streets alone and realized that he hadn't been away from Mauro or other people in over a month. He whistled as he strode down the street, thinking of what would be on offer in the local markets on the morrow. He noticed a lone monk in a dark brown hooded robe coming toward him and caught a sickly-sweet odor as he passed. *Cinnamon? Some strange fermented local fruit?* He let the thought pass as he continued toward the docks.

"He's comin'" whispered the man with the coiled rope in his hand. "Just let him pass, count to three and then you hit his head hard and I'll tie him up"

"We'll serve him up to the bosun right smartly, eh?"

"Shh!"

Nicolo was smiling as he walked past the alley on his left, thinking of green-eyed slave women serving him grapes in his large house overlooking Genoa's harbor.

"Wait another second—" A hand reached out and pulled back the sailor's head. A gold-handled knife slashed through the air and opened his throat. His bloody gurgle caught his partner's attention.

"What the—" As he turned towards the noise the knife flashed again, digging deep into the second man's stomach and arching upwards towards his heart. The sailor crumpled to the ground without another sound. The hooded monk cleaned the blade on the sailor's shirt, tucked it into his coarse brown sleeve, and receded silently into the alley.

николо and Mauro were just finishing a good Genoese stew of beef and vegetables, spiced with cumin and pepper (he had begged the innkeeper not to use garlic), when Giovanni ran into the small kitchen at the inn. He was out of breath and spoke quickly.

"Nicolo, you've got to stay away from the port today. Two Pisan sailors from that ship you came in on were found dead in an alley this morning not far from here. The word is spreading among the Pisans that some Genoese did it. It won't be safe to wander around until this thing blows over."

"Well, I certainly had nothing to do with it!"

"I'm not saying you did, Nicolo. These things happen around here all the time. But newcomers are always suspect. I don't think it's a problem for your uncle, but you should stay away from the docks. There are some good local markets by the Forum of Constantine that will keep you out of trouble for the day. And if you want," Giovanni said in a hushed voice so that Mauro could not hear, "I can take you to see the biggest, most beautiful women in the world. I know a place where they frolic naked all day. I'll wait for you outside."

After Giovanni left, Mauro sighed and turned to Nicolo.

"The world is so full of violence, especially, it seems, for sailors."

"Whoever they were, we sailed with them. It seems strange that two men we just spent the last month with are dead. I am only glad that we weren't involved. But I want to think about something else. I am going to the market today."

Mauro brightened. "Oh, Nicolo, could you find me some used parchment in the market? I didn't bring anything with me, and I will need to make notes for my work. I must go and meet the papal legates here to see how I may assist them in—"

"Yes, I know, Brother Mauro," Nicolo interrupted. "But I think you should be careful how you talk about that, remember?" The monk reddened.

"Oh, yes, well . . . I need to go to one of the monasteries and start my research then." He looked hopefully at Nicolo.

"Much better."

※

Giovanni and Nicolo walked with Mauro as far as the Auguosteion, the large square that marked the beginning of the Meses, the wide, ancient Roman way that fronted many of the city's oldest buildings and churches. Hagia Sophia loomed to their left. The monk stood spellbound before the six-hundred-year-old massive brick cathedral with its broad, dominating dome. He determined to visit soon but needed to get to his meeting with the papal legates at the Great Palace further down the Meses. The Genoese carried on past Hagia Sophia and the Brazen Gate, the domed entrance leading to the Great Palace. At the thunderous shout of a crowd ahead, Nicolo jerked to a stop.

"What is that noise?"

"Don't worry, Nicolo. That's just the crowd at the Hippodrome up ahead. I heard it can hold a hundred thousand people. Can you imagine, Nicolo? Four times as many people than are in all of Genoa can fit into that stadium. And that noise? It means there is some sort of ceremony going on. Maybe a chariot race, maybe the welcoming of some Russian or Bulgarian royalty. There's always some honoring or political marriage being arranged. The emperor is throwing gold around to pay off his friends and enemies every day. We could go there sometime. You can get a glimpse of the emperor and the empress and maybe her daughters. The youngest, Eudokia, is fiery and single. You could try your luck. But just know if you fail, you'll be castrated or have your eyes gouged out. They have a nasty way of treating people who disappoint them around here."

"I think I have had my fill of fiery women for a while, thank you. Aren't there any sweet, quiet young women I might pass my time with?"

"In Constantinople? Hah, not at all. This is a city known for its powerful women. Half the reason for the schism with Rome is that Byzantium was ruled by an empress who claimed the mantle of Holy

Roman empress. Can you imagine how upset the pope and those emasculated priests were at that? Even now, the emperor sits around drinking and fornicating and passing out gold trinkets while the empress makes the real decisions. No, no quiet women here."

They passed the women's slave market, where Nicolo entertained some fantasy and quickly felt the shame in doing so. In Genoa, women were not property and Nicolo remembered Esther's hard glare as she pounded into the young man the inherent dignity of women. *Women are like works of art*, she had told him, *you don't have to own them to appreciate them.* He remembered the slave on the dock. *Can eyes truly be so green or was it just a reflection off the water?*

Nicolo's reverie was cut short when they approached a tall pole guarded by two huge bearded blond warriors. He looked up to see a bruised, swollen head swarming with flies atop the pole. The men stared at the severed head for a moment until Giovanni pulled Nicolo away.

"That is the head of John Komnenos, or John the Fat as he was known. One of those noble families that keeps trying to regain the throne. Last month he raised the common people against the corruption of the other nobles, declaring himself emperor. He was crowned in Hagia Sophia while the patriarch hid in a cupboard. But he was so fat that he broke the Imperial Throne there. Guess he should have seen that as an omen. The mob seized most of the Great Palace and looted it, as usual."

Nicolo glanced back toward where they had left Mauro. "Should we have warned my uncle not to go to Hagia Sofia? He's not very worldly and can't take care of himself if there's trouble."

"Nah, things get back to normal quickly when these riots break out. Seems more entertainment for the commoners and a chance for some quick looting than a real challenge to the order here. Odd people. Anyway, the Varangian Guard swooped in and stopped the coup in a day. Those are two of the Varangian Guard right there. They're a mean lot of mercenaries from the Far North. Most of them are former "sea wolves." That's what they call the raiders from the Norse lands. Nothing but pirates, really, but they get richer and live longer by serving Byzantium instead of attacking it. They are the real military muscle that protects the emperor. The army has grown weak and effeminate and only gets paid occasionally, and then with debased gold coins specially minted by the emperor. Look at those Varangian Guards. Huge men with huge axes." Giovanni flexed his skinny arms and chuckled.

"That's really gruesome. How can you laugh at that?"

"I am only here for trade, Nicolo, not to get involved in their Byzantine treacheries. This is how it works here. The nobles are lazy and don't want to dirty their hands with trade. They let outsiders do all the trade and charge heavy customs duties to bring goods in and ship them out. Then the emperor shares out the duties among the nobility to keep them loyal. It is easy to get sucked in here, to be used by one noble or another for some unknown purpose. Look at John the Fat there. He and his friends were all executed. If I had been in bed with one of them, I'd be dead or blinded too. It is a sad fact that Our Lord put the greatest center of trade between East and West into the hands of this degenerate empire. Best to make your money and move on quickly."

"Why not go around them and find the source of these exotic goods, find out where the spices come from, for example."

Giovanni looked around nervously. "Don't even ask those questions in jest," he said in hushed tones. "We make good money here and don't need to try and make more at the risk of losing everything. All the trade goods in Constantinople come from somewhere in the East, but we can't go there. Only traders from those places or agents of Muslim leaders are allowed to transport them."

"So, if I was a sultan's agent I could travel those trade routes east?"

"Don't get any ideas, Nicolo. A real agent with the proper permissions might get through, but a pretender without language or the right papers? No way. And wipe that smirk off your face. Be careful how you talk to others around here. If anyone thinks you are trying to cut them out, they will cut you up and your empty head will be up there next to his." Giovanni gestured back toward the head on the pole. "Let's keep walking and change the subject."

A huge, odd tower covered with doors stood before them. Just as Nicolo began to ask Giovanni what it was, one of the doors sprang open and a life-sized figure of a Roman soldier lumbered out. A gong sounded eight times. Nicolo stared with his mouth agape.

"It's called the Horologion. It keeps the time all day long. Each door has a different bronze statue behind it. There is nothing like it anywhere in Europe."

"Does it run by a water wheel, like the timekeepers in the monasteries?"

"No, that's what is so amazing. It is nothing but a series of mechanical levers and wheels. I don't know how it works but it is truly a marvel, isn't it? I have heard that in the palace there is a tree full of golden birds that actually sing."

Many of the buildings along the Meses had rows of columns in front, creating colonnaded porticos that sheltered merchants spreading their wares on the marble sidewalks, and booth after booth of trade goods. Nicolo quickly picked up the pattern; silks in this area, jewelry in that one, swords, daggers, and shields further past. He strolled from booth to booth, eyeing the goods and making mental notes of where he would return. As he had little coin, he could not engage in banter and kept his arms crossed—a clear sign to the sellers that he was not buying. They came upon a booth selling old parchment sheets and Nicolo hailed the seller.

"Good morning! What have you in the way of used parchments this fine day?"

The seller turned to Nicolo and his eyes brightened. "Ah, a young scholar I see, and speaking such skilled Latin. I have the highest quality parchment from lambs in utero, soft and fine. Perfect for an oration or presenting a petition to the emperor." Giovanni chuckled and stepped back to watch Nicolo handle the seller.

Nicolo winced at the strong smell of garlic on the parchment seller's breath. *Why do they douse all their food in this garlic? How can they stand to be close to each other? Does it permeate the women's bodies as well? I pray this awful plant never comes to our sweet Genoa.* He took a deep breath beyond the range of the garlic and plunged into the transaction. "I see your wares are excellent, sir, and if it were for me, I would have nothing but the finest dead lamb guts you have on offer. Alas, the parchment is for a poor monk, and I am afraid that he would be embarrassed to possess such quality. It would violate his vows."

The seller grimaced, realizing he would have no sale of consequence out of this young stranger. *Not a single sale today,* he thought. *Oh well, better a copper than my cock in my hand again at the end of the day.* He smiled broadly at the potential buyer. "In that case, we have used parchment, recently scraped clean of past writings. Your impoverished friend could use either side for his meditations, although the scraped sides are a bit rough. Ten for a copper."

Nicolo looked at the roughened old parchment and shook his head. "A bargain, indeed. Yet I know that the poor monk has his own utensils for scraping parchments clean. In fact, it is part of his meditation to scrape while pondering the impermanence of what men create. I would not like to take away his good works. Do you have any used parchments with the writing intact?"

The seller shook his head in disgust. This pup would not line his pocket today. Better a small sale than none. "It is understandable that your poor friend would relish the opportunity to erase the works of the world. Lord knows they have not gotten us any closer to Heaven." He bent under his counter and grabbed a thick bundle of parchments. "These come from a monastery that houses useless pagan writings. Not easy to read the old Greek, but I am sure your poor friend will reach heights of ecstasy as he scrapes away the wicked words. Twenty for a copper and no returns if he doesn't want to touch the heathen utterances."

Nicolo paid the seller, and the Genovese wandered up the Meses.

"Not bad, Nicolo, your brother would be proud of you."

When will they stop comparing me to Antonio? "Haggling down an old man for used parchment is fun, but I need to make some real deals here. I have to go see the Knights Templar and exchange a note for my uncle. Can you help me find them?"

"The Templars? They'll cheat you blind. I heard they are charging forty percent to exchange notes from Rome."

"But they are the church's representatives, aren't they?"

"Maybe that's how they started out, but now the coin calls to them louder than the cross. Let me set you up with Kalomodius the Armenian. He's a minor noble who made a fortune gambling on long distance trade. He's as honest as a money changer gets and he only charges twenty percent. He also has a great nose for a bargain, so if he likes you, he may let you in on a deal that will make you back your twenty percent and then some." Giovanni smiled at the perplexed look on Nicolo's face. "I know it's a lot to take in all at once, but we'll take care of you. Now let's go see those giant beauties I told you about, just down the road there." Giovanni led Nicolo across the Forum of Constantine. In the center of the plaza stood a tall tower made of reddish marble.

"This is the Tower of Constantine. There used to be a great bronze statue of the old emperor on top, but it fell off and killed a bunch of citizens. That's why there is just that big cross up there now. These days the tower is used to punish traitors. They take them up there and throw them off. But don't worry, that's reserved for important criminals, not mere merchants. Ah, but look over there, Nicolo, have you ever seen such big, beautiful women? Didn't I tell you?" Nicolo looked past the tower to see several thirty-foot tall bronze statues of pagan goddesses scattered about the Forum. "That helmeted beauty is Pallas Athena, the old Greek goddess of wisdom. And that one is Aphrodite, goddess of love. She's my favorite. Over there is Hera, Zeus's wife." Nicolo looked perplexed. "Zeus was the leader of the old Greek gods. You have to learn this stuff if you are going to spend any time here. Even though these Greeks are Christians, or sort of Christians, they can't let go of those old gods. I think it helps them hold on to their crazy belief that they are the true successors to the Roman Empire and the true church. Can you imagine—Constantinople, not Rome?"

※

MAURO ENTERED THE hall of the Great Palace. Giovanni had told him that the emperor and his Imperial Court lived farther away, in the newer Blachernae Palace, so the older palace was used for administration, like customs and land records. Ever interested in new sources of revenue, the emperor was renting offices to diplomatic embassies also. A splendidly dressed guard told Mauro that the papal representative's office was on the second floor. Mauro moved slowly through the ancient, regal building. Everywhere he turned was evidence of past glories. Nude statues frowned as he averted his eyes from carved breasts and penises that seemed aimed his way. How does this bring glory to God? he wondered as he sped up his pace. The hallways were lined with silk tapestries depicting large battles with angels and saints blessing the soldiers from above. Mauro noticed that everyone he passed was elegantly dressed, and once again he became self-conscious of his poor clothing. He knocked on a large wooden door and was told to enter by a deep voice from within. As he stepped into the room, he immediately noticed the lush tapestries, marble statues, and golden vases along the walls. Two older men dressed in purple silk robes and bedecked with gold jewelry beckoned him to enter an inner chamber. The inner apartment seemed to Mauro to equal if not exceed the pope's own office in the Vatican. He presented a parchment of introduction from the pope to the men, who gazed at it with wide eyes. The taller of the two men smiled and bowed.

"Welcome to Constantinople, Brother Mauro. I am Lucius, papal legate, and this esteemed gentleman is Lorenzo, secretary to the mission. We are so excited that you have come. There is much to be done here. Many of the nobility are disenchanted with the emperor and his debauchery and heresy and are eager for reunification. Let us share with you the situation in detail, shall we?" Lorenzo offered Mauro wine in a golden cup, which the monk politely refused because of exhaustion from his long voyage. The legate and the secretary took their own wine and drank lustily. "There are many factions here. The patriarch is an intelligent man, and he has tried to converse with His Holiness on the matters of controversy between Rome and Constantinople. They have had a polite exchange of letters and views on everything from priestly marriage to the proper number of immersions for a baptism. But at the end of the day, the patriarch is stubborn, refusing to acknowledge Rome's primacy in matters of our faith. Then there is the emperor, Alexios III—"

"Not to be confused with Alexios II or Isaac II, who is Alexios III's brother but was deposed, blinded, and imprisoned by Alexios III," added Lorenzo.

"Yes, and Alexios III actually thinks he is the real Holy Roman emperor for some reason, even though we all know it is the pope who appoints the Holy Roman emperor. Are you following this, Brother Mauro?"

"Well, yes . . . Alexios III . . ."

"Right. Now Empress Euphrosyne, who comes from a long line of empresses, is also related to the patriarch. She is quite fond of the old gods of Rome and has a large following among the common people, who seem to have merged the old ways into their orthodox faith." Lucius looked directly at Mauro, who seemed confused. "I am telling you all this to demonstrate that the challenge of reunification is not simply a matter of theological argument. There is a heady brew of faith, power, politics, and more going on. That is why we have had to move slowly in these matters. We have worked hard to build confidence and trust between ourselves and all the relevant players here." His voice took on an urgency. "And now may be the perfect time for you to be here. Many of the aristocrats long for reunification, especially with the Muslims beating on the doors of the empire. The patriarch is sympathetic. Even the empress could be persuaded that reunification with Rome would serve her interests, provided she stop her pagan public rituals and pronouncements. She is crafty and has a nose for politics. I am sure she would figure out a way to keep her beliefs private in service to keeping her head."

"Your work here is critical. But I must say . . ." Lorenzo looked Mauro up and down, "if you are going to meet with important people in Constantinople and convince them of their errant ways, you must be better dressed. It is unfortunate and sinful, but these misguided people associate the outer garb with the inner strength. Your arguments will fall on deaf ears if you wear those rags to court."

"But I have no other clothes," Mauro stammered.

Lucius and Lorenzo looked at each other and shook their heads. "We will arrange for suitable clothing. For now, you are well advised to wear those rags and keep a low profile. When we have arranged for you to meet with the right people, we will make you presentable. Now go visit the monasteries and churches and talk casually to some of the priests and monks you meet. They are very willing to try to convince true Christians of the righteousness of the Eastern faith. If you listen with humility, you will learn all you need to know to prepare your arguments for reunification. Bless you for your work here."

※

AFTER MAURO LEFT the office, Lucius grimaced. Lorenzo toyed with his thick gold-braided necklace.

"Religion, religion, religion. That's all His Holiness ever talks about. Do you think he has any understanding of money and power at all?" Lorenzo threw his hands up in the air. "And can you believe His Holiness sent that ratty old monk? I imagine the pope thinks he is incorruptible. Do you think we've fallen out of favor in Rome, Lucius? I certainly hope not."

"Yes, Lorenzo, it looks as if we have run out of time. Our life of plenty is about to end now that the pope has sent this monk to push reunification forward. We can't delay anymore."

"It has been a wonderful three years, Lucius. But perhaps we can gain a little more time to tie up loose ends. I have a lot of property to sell and servants to dismiss." He dropped his voice. "And we need to get rid of all that gold, don't we?"

"Yes, Lorenzo, no more dribbling it out a little at a time. I am sure that Cardinal Orsini would be happy if we sent it all to him instead of these quarterly payments for giving us this office, but then we would probably never see any of it again. The emperor has been suspicious of us all along. He does tolerate us out of respect to our diplomatic office, though."

Lorenzo shuddered. "Not like his predecessor, who let the mob murder all the Latin priests they could find. I heard they even raped the legate. I have always been nervous about that gold. Why did we ever keep it? There are so many ways to get rich in Constantinople."

"The gold was going to be lost anyway. How were we to know that old German Henry the Holy Roman emperor was going to drop dead while we were in route to deliver the emperor's gold tribute?"

"Blaming the emperor's young nephew was a brilliant stroke, I must say. And now he is running around Europe looking for support to take the throne from his nasty uncle who usurped it from the boy's father and blinded the old man. You are a clever tactician, Lucius, although these fratricidal Byzantines do make it easy. Just pin the blame on the nearest disposable relative. Well, as someone once said, the Lord helps those who help themselves. Now what can we do to help ourselves out of this situation?"

"Let me think on it, Lorenzo. We need something to get the emperor's mind off us. That old monk might be the key. Have another cup of this Thracian wine. It is so much better than the swill from France and Sicily."

"I will hate to go back to that goat urine from the hills of Rome. And the weather here is so pleasant the year round."

"Isn't there an old story about a sacrificial lamb or a son or something like that, Lorenzo?"

"To be honest, Lucius, I have pretty much forgotten those tales. What were you thinking?"

MAURO STARED UP at the great dome ceiling inside Hagia Sophia. He had read about the church in The Book of Holy Places. The original dome had fallen in after three years; truly God's punishment for the arrogance of Emperor Justinian, who proclaimed that he had outdone Solomon's Temple. The dome must have been rebuilt with more humility, Mauro thought, for it had stood for over five hundred years. Huge gold-outlined angels surrounded by soft clouds stared back at him from the four cardinal directions. The interior of the great dome was upheld by a ring of huge columns, which Mauro had read were taken from pagan temples and placed in service to Our Lord. The incense of a thousand candles created a soft haze throughout the church. Deep, sonorous chanting from somewhere rose up and embraced him warmly. He moved to stand before a golden throne placed on a dais before the great altar. A hand gently touched his shoulder. Mauro emerged from his reverie and turned to look into large brown eyes embedded in the soft round face of an older cleric. He wore a tall, gold-embroidered hat and gold and red robes. His thick gray beard hung nearly to his waist.

Mauro's mouth dropped open. "Excuse me," he stammered, "I was so overwhelmed by the holiness of this place that I lost awareness. I hope that I have not intruded."

The patriarch smiled at the monk. "No, my friend. No seeker of wisdom is an intruder here. I am John Kamateros, patriarch of our Roman Orthodox Church. And who are you?"

Mauro took a deep breath to calm himself before answering. "I am Brother Mauro, teacher of logic and rhetoric at the university at

Bologna. I am seeking to deepen my insight into the mysteries of our faith, and perhaps help to heal the wounds that keep us divided during these troubled times. I had heard in Rome that you have corresponded with His Holiness in hopes of doing the same." *I want to be honest with the patriarch, but I have sworn not to tell him about my mission for the pope.*

The patriarch looked at Mauro sadly. "Alas, it is true, yet there is so much that clouds the vision. The wars of men, the lusts for power and wealth, all lead to the corruption of faith and good offices. All we can do is try to use our faith and our reason to bring light to counter the darkness." He looked up at the angels. "In this sanctuary we call upon both the inner and outer wisdom to aid us in our work."

"I am sorry, Your Holiness, I am not familiar with those terms."

"Come sit with me and we shall talk of these things." The patriarch smiled and put his hand on Mauro's arm, leading him through the crowd of visitors into a large office. The walls of the room were lined with shelves containing hundreds of bound manuscripts.

Mauro looked around the room and closed his eyes. He began to hear the whispers of conversation again, not from the monks and laypeople beyond the office, but from the volumes themselves.

The patriarch noticed the change in Mauro's demeanor, sensing that this man was not a typical Latin country monk. "Sit here, Brother Mauro. Make yourself comfortable and let the wisdom that surrounds you permeate your soul." Mauro sat in an overstuffed chair in front of the patriarch's large desk, closed his eyes, and felt the words washing over him. He came out of his reverie wondering if he had sat there a minute or an hour. The patriarch was observing him closely. "The inner wisdom is our Christian faith, supported by the writings of the church fathers and saints. The outer wisdom is that which we obtain from the ancients, from the early Greek and Roman philosophers and thinkers. In Rome, the outer wisdom is seen as pagan and wicked, uninformed by the miracle of Our Lord's time on this earth. But here we recognize the timelessness of the outer wisdom and seek to recover it and embrace it in service to our faith. We do not see a conflict, per se, between the inner and outer wisdom. I suspect that you do not either."

"I long to know the wisdom of the ancients. I have studied what I can find, yet there is so little material available. The works of Plato, Aristotle, Cicero, and so many other pagan writers have been banned by the church. Only fragments remain, lost in monasteries with abbots who have no idea what they contain. Much of what can be found in Bologna, Rome, and elsewhere in Europe comes through Al-Andalus. It has been translated from Greek to Arabic and then into Latin. It is so difficult to know what is authentic and what is obscured through the writings of the Arabs." Mauro had known the patriarch for less than an hour and he was already pouring his deepest—and most heretical—thoughts out to him. Yet he felt safe here, safer than in Bologna. Was this his true spiritual home? He shook the thought out of his head. *I must not be tempted away from the true faith so easily, even though these manuscripts call to me.*

The patriarch observed the deep longing in Brother Mauro's eyes. *The monk's beard is gray, yet I sense a childlike wonder and openness to learn. How rare in a monk these days, especially one from the Latin church.* "The fire for knowledge that burns in your soul reminds me of our great Saint Basil. Like you, Basil was a teacher of logic and applied that skill to his love of God. He searched for knowledge throughout Egypt and the Holy Land, exploring the outer wisdom. He took from it what was valuable and left behind what was not. Thus, he came to be known as *Ouranofantor*, 'the revealer of heavenly mysteries.' He was not afraid to apply reason and logic to those mysteries, in spite of opinions against such work." The patriarch turned to stare at the shelves behind his desk. He reached up and grabbed a small volume. "I would like you to read this. It is Saint Basil's essay 'On How Young Men Might Benefit from Pagan Literature.' It is a short work that argues for the importance of studying the ancient Greek philosophers. He wrote it at a time of great turmoil, when the Platonic academies that taught the outer wisdom were under fierce attack from the church. He was very brave. Look at this passage: *The true way of studying pagan authors: When they tell us the words and deeds of the good, let us follow their lessons; but when they tell us of evil, let us stop our ears.*

"You see, Brother Mauro, the truest spirit of the church is one of eclecticism and adaptation, not rigidity. We must learn and appropriate whatever is best in pagan thought and assimilate it as bees suck honey from poisonous plants, adapting it to our own pressing wants and necessities." He handed the small volume to the monk, who held its dried pages lovingly. Mauro turned a sheet carefully and read aloud with delight.

"*Let us gather up all the wise precepts of the pagans which may assist us on our way to eternity; store up knowledge for the future; open our ears to the maxims of reason and retain whatever tends to elevate the human mind.*" Mauro closed the volume and held it to his chest. He closed his eyes and breathed in its vibrant words and musty scent. He hadn't allowed himself to fully embrace the pope's permission to explore the ancients—he had experienced too much animosity in the church. But the words of Saint Basil reached through time to touch him, to open his heart and mind to the possibilities here. He opened his moist eyes to meet the glow of the patriarch's face.

"Thus we reconcile Athens with Jerusalem, Brother Mauro. We embrace the virtues and goodness that flow from Homer, Sophocles, Thucydides, Plato, and Aristotle, among so many others. Their struggles to understand the human condition are our struggles today, yet we have a way through the teachings of our Church that was not revealed in their time. We cannot condemn them for being born before the revelations of Our Lord." The patriarch put a hand gently on Mauro's shoulder. "There is much here for you to study. You can come to me any time you like, and feel free to browse this collection. But if you truly wish to dedicate yourself to the study of the outer wisdom, I will share something very special with you." The patriarch rose and walked to one of the shelves. He pulled down a thick parchment scroll, unrolled it on his desk and beckoned Mauro to look at the contents. "This is a list of all the outer wisdom manuscripts that remain in the monasteries here in Constantinople. Some have been here for centuries, many copied more recently by our monks. The list was originally prepared by Patriarch Photius over three hundred years ago and is updated when more manuscripts are found inside the monasteries or when they are saved from the plundering of the Turks throughout the realm of Byzantium and beyond. Last year, the Turks destroyed over a thousand ancient illuminated manuscripts of the inner and outer wisdom while rampaging through monasteries in Anatolia." The patriarch sighed, then turned back to Mauro and smiled again. "You are free to consult the list, find manuscripts of interest to you, and visit the monasteries where they are preserved. I will give you a letter permitting you to do so. There should be no impediments to a true seeker of wisdom."

"Thank you so much for your kindness, Your Holiness. Might I stay here this afternoon and look through the scroll? I am so eager to see what is available."

"Of course, good brother, you can stay right here in my office and use the large desk in the corner. I will have parchment and quill brought to you so that you might note where you want to go. Most of the monasteries and churches that house the manuscripts are within the old Roman wall around the city. They will be easy for you to find." The patriarch wearily rubbed his face with both of his hands. "It is unfortunate that many of the manuscripts are stolen and sold, which is against our law. Yet nobles who support certain monasteries are often given manuscripts in appreciation of their patronage. They either keep them in private libraries or sell them to Arab scholars for translation. It is ironic that the Muslims are keeping so much of our Greek and Roman heritage alive while at the same time besieging our empire and forcing captives to convert to Islam."

The patriarch fingered a decaying corner of the scroll. "Even the elements conspire to take our knowledge away. These old manuscripts deteriorate over time, especially in the dampness beneath the monasteries where they are stored. And though it is against the law to destroy a manuscript, unsavory monks and merchants still break them apart and sell them as used parchment. The sellers claim that they are the remains of manuscripts destroyed by time, which are legal to sell, but we know that is often a convenient cover for their nefarious behaviors."

※

Nicolo sat on the hay bed as the afternoon light began to fade. He was so excited to give the parchments to Mauro, as he felt he had not contributed anything to Mauro's part of their mission. When the old monk entered the room, Nicolo leaped up and held the parchments out.

"Look, Brother Mauro, I've brought you a gift!"

Mauro took the parchments in hand, turned them over and saw the writing on the undersides. His face turned ashen. Nicolo was bewildered.

"What's the matter? You wanted parchment, didn't you?"

Mauro sheepishly explained the situation with used parchments to Nicolo, trying not to deflate the young man's enthusiasm. Nicolo was totally lost by Mauro's explanation of inner and outer wisdom.

"Let me look over these parchments and make sure they are legal for us to own. I so greatly appreciate the gesture but don't want us to get into trouble." The monk began to read the texts, putting on one side of the bed parchments that were clearly old letters, proclamations, and ordinary correspondence in contemporary Latin and Greek. Three of the twenty parchments were in the old Greek. Mauro read them slowly, trying to gauge whether they were important philosophical texts or more mundane works. Two of them seemed like expositions on Aristotle with confusing allegorical references so popular with pagan rhetoricians, but they could have been letters between students and teachers. The third appeared to be a merchant's list of purchases in different ports, probably insignificant. Mauro didn't feel competent to judge the importance of the parchments. "These three I will take back to the patriarch for guidance. If you have stumbled upon a destroyer of outer wisdom, he will want to know about it. Why must these merchants interfere with the pursuit of knowledge just to make money?"

Although Nicolo understood it, he was disappointed and slightly angered by Mauro's reaction. He spoke sharply to Mauro.

"Don't be so naive, Uncle. All my life I have seen religion used to make money. The monasteries around Genoa are factories of prayer, and prayer has financial value. The rich and poor alike donate money to receive prayers in return. The priests have even started to sell forgiveness for sins. Religion is another form of commerce." Nicolo saw the hurt look on Mauro's face and felt awkward. "Look, I have only seen religion used to take advantage of people. I don't have your faith, and I don't have your understanding of these things. I don't know what's in those manuscripts, so I don't know why they are so important to you." Nicolo felt emotion growing in his chest. The words weren't making sense. He needed to get away. He wanted a drink and some Genoese companionship. "I don't mean to insult you, Uncle. I am going to the tavern and try to learn something about this place from the other Genoese merchants here."

Mauro didn't have time to react before Nicolo was out the door and down the stairs. He took a deep breath and tried to force Nicolo's words from his mind. He opened *The Book of Holy Places* and began to read, looking for sites that might be in or around Constantinople. Besides Hagia Sophia, the book told of the Church of the Holy Apostles, which held the heads of Saints Andrew, Luke, and Timothy in silver and gold reliquary urns, as well as the Pillar of Flagellation, to which Christ had been bound and whipped. The Seven Churches of Revelation—Ephesus (where the Virgin Mary lived her final days), Smyrna, Pergamum, Thyatira, Sardis, Philadelphia, and

Laodicea—were not far down the coast. There was Mount Ararat, where Noah had landed the Ark as the flood waters receded. So much holiness surrounded him! His faith was real and meaningful, regardless of how it was twisted by greedy monks and merchants or diminished by the absence of understanding. Mauro looked forward to the morrow, when he could begin exploring the nearest monasteries.

⁂

THE TAVERN WAS a squalid place; dirt floors and rough-hewn wooden benches in a building that looked ready to collapse or combust in an instant. But to Nicolo it was a vibrant reminder of home. He recognized so many of the young merchants there that night, and all of them welcomed him heartily. He was worried at first that they would question him too closely about what he was doing in Constantinople, but the men were mostly interested in stories of trade and women. Every time he started on a tale that might show him to be a seasoned trader or lover other men would jump in with their own outlandish exploits. Nicolo got a bit heated over this but soon relaxed into the familiar accents and faces. *Even without Antonio being here I am still the little brother in their eyes. Ahh, I am just glad for the company.*

"Hey Nicolo! What do you think of this Greek wine?" Nicolo looked up at the speaker. *Was that Robert the mason's brother Leonardo? He looks fatter than the last time I saw him.*

"I'd say it was a cross between tar and paint. I guess if you export this wine to Genoa and it doesn't sell, you could use it to hold your bricks together or repair the mole after a storm." The room exploded with laughter.

Leonardo looked offended. "Nah, nobody would export this dog piss. The real money here is in silks, carpets, grograms, and mohair— that's cloth spun of camel hair."

"You can stuff your hold with that itchy fabric and make fifty percent. I prefer gold and jewels," shouted Mauricio, the fair-haired son of a Great House. He looked at Leonardo and sniffed. "But if you don't have the coin to buy goods of value, I guess you must settle for camel hair and cheap wine." Leonardo leaped up and grabbed Mauricio's collar but was pulled back by Giovanni and two other Genoese.

"Save your fists for the Pisans," Giovanni said soothingly. "Nicolo says they were the ones who sank the *San Giorgio*. He says they have the cargo right here in Constantinople. Isn't that right, Nicolo?" All eyes turned toward Nicolo, who told the tale of his voyage on the Pisan galley without interruption. He sat back and enjoyed the looks of admiration mixed with concern his words elicited.

Mauricio stood and addressed the group. "If this is true, we are going to have to get those goods back. First, we have to find where they are. Giacomo, get your Armenian merchant friends to ask about purchasing some Syrian goods. They should be able to find the name of the shipowner and where his goods are stored."

"How do we get the cargo back?" Nicolo asked.

"We must wait for another riot. They happen here all the time. Some arsehole aristocrat seeks the throne and raises the mob. They march down the Meses, the old Roman road, to announce the usurper's coronation and imitate the old pagan rituals. The army fights back and the common folk go looting and burning. We usually keep our heads down during the riots, but they do provide good cover for a revenge raid and will muddy our tracks afterward."

"We should make it look like the Venetians did it," added Giovanni. "The Pisans poisoned the last emperor against those arrogant bastards and helped set the mob on them. It took years for the Venetians to return, but return they did. Constantinople is just too lucrative to ignore. Ever since Alexios III restored Venetian trade privileges and gave them a better customs rate than the Pisans, there has been a lot of bad blood between them. A few false pieces of evidence at the scene and they'll be at each other's throats in no time."

"But the Pisans are not stupid," Mauricio added. "If all we do is take the *San Giorgio* cargo, they will know what we are about. We might as well grab what other cargo and goods we can and burn down their quarter in the bargain. Then we need to take the goods directly onto our ships and sail them out immediately. It will look like we are just trying to save the ships from the fire. The sea swallows our footprints quickly, right friends?" He raised a flagon of wine. "To the honor of Genoa. To the memory of our fallen brothers!"

※

The royal treasurer leafed through a thick sheath of parchments and shook his head. He looked up at the emperor, who sat with one leg up on the arm of the golden throne on the dais in the council chamber, humming tunelessly and sipping from his golden cup.

"There is no way to avoid this, Basileus, the current customs receipts from trade will simply not allow us to continue to pay reparations to the Venetians. They press us daily."

Alexios didn't bother to look down at his treasurer but spoke to the air above his cup. "Why not lower their customs rate?"

"It is already lower than any other, and the Pisans are still outraged over the last time we lowered the Venetian's duties."

"Give the doge another title, then."

"He is already *protosebastos*, the first venerable one. We have nothing higher."

"Then make him *hyperprotosebastos*, damn it! That's above first venerable one."

Empress Euphrosyne looked dolefully at her husband. *This has gone on long enough.* She turned to Alexios and smiled sweetly. "Husband, the Venetians are slowly strangling us from within. They have gained the upper hand on all the other traders and are putting less and less into our treasury. Their navy has supplanted ours not only along our coast, but along the southern shores as well as the western."

"That would not be the case, my dear wife, if your brother-in-law, our good Lord Admiral Stryphnos, had not consistently usurped the funds meant to pay our sailors and keep our ships in fighting condition. His rapaciousness makes the rest of the nobility seem positively virtuous."

"We may all be guilty of the sin of gluttony, husband, but we must face the situation we are in." The empress turned to the treasurer. "What other financial catastrophes can you report today?"

The treasurer gulped and blinked at the empress, cleared his throat, and addressed the emperor. "There is the matter of the soldier's pay. The Varangian Guard will only accept Arab gold dinars, of which we have few, and there is talk of mutiny among the army."

The emperor shrugged. "Mint more coins, drop the gold content another five percent."

"I fear we have exhausted that avenue, Basileus."

"Then give the older soldiers more land outside the great walls. That has always kept them quiet and given us an experienced force along our boundary."

"Actually, Basileus, we have pretty much run out of land. We have allowed the nobles to acquire titles to most if not all the boundary land, and they have either thrown off the old soldiers or turned them into low-wage land tillers."

"Well, we have no choice but to plunder the tombs again." Alexios chuckled at the memory. "The last time we grabbed so much gold and so many old jewels from the Church of the Holy Sepulchre that we paid off the army and the nobles for what, two years or more?"

The empress bolted off her chair and rounded on Alexios. "Have the strains of this office driven you insane or is this who you truly are? A common grave robber and defiler of our great emperors for gold? What other madness are you capable of?"

The emperor looked at his consort through droopy eyelids, then hardened his glare. "Take another lover like Vatatses and you will find out," he said evenly.

The empress softened and sighed. She missed her lover, who had been strangled on her husband's orders. The emperor had no qualms about maiming or murdering anyone who crossed his path, and everyone, including the empress and their daughters, were no more than chess pieces to be used to improve his position on the board. She thought of her youngest daughter, Eudokia, so recently returned from the disastrous match he had made between her and the brutish Serbian king Stefan. The poor child had come back bruised, beaten, and raped, for what? A few months' respite from war with those barbarians?

She spoke soothingly. "Perhaps we do need to reconcile with Rome. They can hold the Venetians at bay and pay us a large tribute as the price of reconciliation. Our religious differences are not as important as the survival of the empire."

The emperor laughed hysterically. "Who is the mad one now? The religious squabbles are a mere mummer's play masking Rome's desire for our lands. How many times have we accommodated the crusades of Rome as they march through our empire and strip the countryside of food? Have you forgotten that Rome had agreed that as the price for our help and passage to conquer the holy lands, they would return to us our domains from Antioch to Jerusalem? But what did they do? They set up their own so-called Latin kingdoms on our lands. And who do those Latin kingdoms pay tribute to? Rome, not Constantinople." The emperor slammed his golden goblet to the floor "And in my exile did Rome come to my aid? No, it was Saladin who gave me comfort at his court. Rome doesn't know the difference between the Turks who ravage our countrysides and the Kurds and Arabs who trade and treaty with us. There are no sophisticated thinkers in Rome when it comes to the Muslims. No sense of diplomacy and trade, only armies and blood." He stood up and pointed to the wall-sized tapestry map of the empire behind him. "We don't need Rome; we need the Rus to the north. We need our Holy Church to bring God's light to those huge pagans and bring them into the fold. Even now they are beginning to quiet down under the influence of our Church at their new settlement, that mud hut trading post they call Moscow. And already they have proven their worth. Didn't they smash the Bulgars and the Cumins last year under our holy banner and bring those tribes to heel? If we bring in the Rus and the Slavs, Bulgars, Vlach, and Khazars, we will have a larger empire than Rome. We can roll back the Seljuk Turks across the Anatolia plains and regain our lands all the way to Armenia. Every port on the Black Sea will be ours again. No, my empress, we are not on our knees—we are on the verge of restored glory! *We* are the true heirs to the Holy Roman Empire, not those Latins in Rome! Reconcile with Rome? Never!"

Empress Euphrosyne knew better than to press her husband when he got into one of his rages. She also was aware that her first obligation was to her children and then to the citizens of Byzantium. She still worshipped the old gods, as did so many of the nobles and common people of the empire, and that worship was looked upon with tolerance by their Church. If there was reconciliation with Rome, her belief in omens and reliance on astrology and future telling would be seen as heresy by the fundamentalist priests who would inundate Constantinople. She would no longer be able to flagellate the old Greek statues in public to enhance her prophetic abilities. It would only be a matter of time before the Latin priests agitated among the people for a change of rulers. *No*, she thought, *I come from a long line of empresses and wish my daughters to continue that heritage. I am content without Rome as well. But where will Alexios find the gold to keep our family on the throne? Alas, that is his concern, not mine.* Once again, she realized that challenging her husband openly was a futile and fraught endeavor. Such was the way of powerful men. She would retreat to rule in the shadows. The empress smiled, bowed to her husband, and left the chamber followed by her train of attendants.

There was a long silence in the council chambers as the *logothetes* and functionaries waited for the emperor to calm himself and return to his throne. After Alexios had taken another goblet of wine and a few handfuls of raisins, order returned to the room. The treasurer bowed to the emperor.

"One other matter remains for today, Basileus."

"I feel like a mouse in front of a very large cat," Lorenzo whispered to Lucius as they sat on the marble bench, eyeing the immense Varangian guard outside the emperor's chamber. "Do you think he understands what we are saying to each other?" Lucius peeked past Lorenzo and watched the guard for the slightest movement or recognition.

"No, Lorenzo. The man has nothing inside his head besides sawdust and hard cider," he sniffed, "and none of those uncouth beasts speak Latin. I am more worried about the attendants coming in and out. Do you notice the harsh looks they give us? Their expression is usually a clue as to what treatment can be expected inside that room."

"Do you think the emperor will grill us again about the gold?" Lucius shot a look at Lorenzo.

"Shh! No. We asked for this meeting. He is probably just upset with that stewed prune of an empress hounding him about his sloth and drunkenness. We will delicately allude to the gold when the time is right. This is our chance to take the pressure off us, so let me do the talking when we go in."

"I hope the empress isn't in there. She gives me the shivers. She is so much cleverer than the emperor, and when she looks down on me from her throne it makes me feel as if I were hedge-born instead of an important diplomat. I don't think I could hold up under her glare."

The great wooden door swung open, and a purple-clad young man came smiling his way toward the legates. He bowed and indicated they should follow him into the chamber. The men passed the Varangian guard, motionless as a statue, and entered, the attendant closing the doors behind them.

Sawdust and hard cider, is it? the guard grumbled as he ground his teeth.

The emperor looked down at the legates. He waved away the servant and the tray of figs he carried, picking up the heavy gold wine goblet instead. He held the goblet high and admired it, turning his head slowly and theatrically toward the legates.

"Ah, the gold thieves have arrived. Here to confess?"

Lorenzo let out a little squeak and Lucius jabbed his side with an elbow.

"Basileus, oh highest sovereign, we are here to discuss the situation between our great church and yours. As you know we have diligently sought reconciliation over these past two years and—"

"You have sat on your fat asses and made a fortune in stolen gold, that's what you've done! I don't think you care at all about the conflict between our true church and our Latin brothers. I think you two are happy keeping things the way they are, so that you can stay here and spend my gold instead of crawling back to Rome in disgrace and going back to your country pulpits."

"If I may, AutoKrator, divinely appointed self-ruler, I have explained many times before that the gold was sent to Henry, may he rest in peace, before he died. We believe it was diverted in transit by your scheming, ungrateful nephew, who now roams the Venetian countryside trying to agitate for a return to the throne . . . which we, of course, do not endorse."

"So you say, so you say," groused the emperor. "As you know, our law states that no blind person may become emperor. I should have gouged my nephew's eyes out when I blinded my brother. It would have been the kind thing to do, as it relieves the pressure on them to try and regain the throne." The emperor stopped and considered his own words. "Pressure on the eyes relieves the pressure of politics. That's incredibly clever, don't you all think?" The bureaucrats guffawed while the legates forced a smile and a chuckle. The emperor looked down at them. "But you two seem to be living a rather rich life for church legates. How are you paying for all of it, eh?"

"Hyper Prophyrogennetos, Highest Purple Born, our Holy Father has been most generous with us, as he is so keenly aware of the importance of constantly improving our good relations with Constantinople, especially with the challenges to your southern, eastern, and northern borders."

"You are conveniently leaving out the challenge from the west, aren't you? Reunification under the papal banner? Never! I don't give a rat's ass about your errant theology, but I do care about your church taking rents and appointing clergy in the countryside. And stop using my titles whenever you speak. We will be here all day. Just call me Kyrios, which means 'my lord.'"

"Yes, Kyrios. Of course, our great institutions must live harmoniously side by side during these troubled times, and we can understand your financial concerns. We are also troubled by, shall we say, noise from within our camp for more than kindly reconciliation."

The emperor turned his gaze slowly toward Lucius. "What do you mean, legate?"

"There does seem to be a movement afoot to upset the careful balance we have struck during our time here. It pains us greatly to see this and puts us in an uncomfortable position, as we have been instructed to assist these forces in achieving their goals."

"Keep talking."

Lucius fidgeted, cleared his throat, and looked conspiratorially around the chamber. "I am conflicted about sharing this information with you, Kyrios, but it is critical to your successful rule that I do." He hesitated for effect, a cruel twinkle in his eyes. "In fact, my lord, I would say it is . . . worth its weight in gold . . ."

Nicolo squinted as the bright morning sun reflected off the cobblestones of the Meses. He wandered up the road as usual, noting the morning's offerings but didn't pay too much attention, as he was almost out of funds. He checked Giovanni's directions to the house of Kalomodius and turned left past the last colonnaded section of the street. He stopped for a moment, reflecting that this road went all the way to Rome and had been a major trading avenue for a thousand years. How many men and slaves did it take for the old Romans to build this? What treasures had passed this way? Was there ever a time when the road was peaceful all the way to Rome? His new path wound slowly upward toward the top of one of the many hills inside the walls of Constantinople where the nobles and wealthier traders had their huge houses. Each dwelling he passed was surrounded by a wall, but he could peek in through the gates under the dour scowls of the guards. He saw verdant gardens, tame animals, statuary in marble and bronze, and beautiful mosaic scenes of piousness or depravity. He came to a large stone villa midway up the hill and could hear the gurgle of a fountain inside the courtyard. The marble portico had mosaics of ships in the corners, connected by carved chains. Did that indicate connections between ships and ports or that the owner gained his wealth through the slave trade? Nicolo decided not to ask.

The guard took Nicolo's note from Giovanni and disappeared into the house. He returned shortly with a friendly demeanor and escorted Nicolo through the gate and lush garden and into the anteroom. Nicolo wandered the room admiring the ancient amphora, curious swords and shields and other objects he could not identify that adorned the room. A large door behind him opened and a short, round dark-haired man came forward to greet him. He placed both his hands on Nicolo's arms in a welcoming gesture, the gold and silver rings on each of his fingers adding to the pressure of his grip.

"*Pari egak*, my young friend. Welcome to my home. I have heard from my dear friend Giovanni that you are in some difficulty regarding funds and that I might be of assistance." Nicolo was taken aback by the man's friendly forwardness. "Come. Come, sit and have some wine. Let me see your document and we will consider what is to be done."

Nicolo soon realized that Kalomodius was a no-nonsense businessman. He was looking at Nicolo as if he were judging the ripeness of a melon in the market. The Armenian grabbed the parchment and read it quickly, grunting approval and returning it.

The younger man felt the need to establish himself in the older man's eyes. He spoke confidently. "It is a letter of credit. A new form of transaction where it is no longer necessary to carry large amounts of coin on long voyages. The Knights Templar have developed this, and I believe it will be the future of commerce."

The Armenian laughed loudly. "The Knights Templar? Young man, these documents have been used by our people and the Jews for centuries. It has taken a long time for the church to catch up with us, but then again, the system requires trust and faithfulness." Kalomodius stopped, thinking he was going far enough in this lesson. The boy needed an education, but who knows what he might report back to the church about Kalomodius? These were particularly dangerous times to make enemies.

"So, the church in Rome wants you to receive this money, but the Templars would take forty percent of it as a transaction fee. Well, that will certainly keep the Knights Templar in funds, but it doesn't do much for you, does it?" He watched the grimace on Nicolo's reddening face. "Look here, since this is a Church document, I can exchange this for you for twenty percent. I don't think you will do better elsewhere. You seem like a clever lad and Constantinople is a real snake pit. I will help you get your money."

Nicolo grasped Kalomodius's arms in appreciation. "Thank you, sir. I need these funds to keep my learned uncle and I in food and shelter during his pilgrimage." On a wild whim he added, "and what little else remains I would like to invest."

Kalomodius noted the young man's impetuousness.

"Ah, an opportunity to support a scholar! That is a good thing to do. Tell me what your uncle's interests are." Nicolo described what little of Mauro's rambling in philosophy he could remember, trying to sound like the names of old Greeks made some sense to him. Kalomodius listened carefully, nodding his head, pursing his lips, and twirling the rings on his fingers as Nicolo finished.

"I will have funds for you tomorrow in good gold. Venetian gold grosso, the best coins in the Mediterranean trade. None of those debased aspron trachy the emperor loves to toss about. Come in the afternoon. We can talk of all the fine things you can buy here. I may have something that will delight your uncle as well." The older merchant took a long look at Nicolo. "But listen to me, young man. What little you have will only serve you if you invest it wisely. Use your time in Constantinople to learn all you can about the trade here. Don't waste your days in the taverns like Giovanni and the other young men from your homeland. A smart young merchant can get enormously rich here if he is careful." He observed the light of desire kindled in his visitor's eyes. "Of course, he can also lose his eyes or his head if he offends those in power. That's no different anywhere in the world from my experience, but Constantinople is shockingly voracious. The whole city, no, the whole *empire* feeds off us, and the nobles can sniff out anything that might interfere with their ability to milk us to keep themselves in coin and finery. I have survived this long and prospered because I feed them well. But go now and return tomorrow afternoon. If you would like, come visit me every day and we will talk of trades and travel."

Nicolo left in high spirits. He determined to use every waking moment to meet traders and shopkeepers, find out where all the trade goods came from and what they were worth, and invest everything he could besides what he and Brother Mauro needed for sustenance. He walked the docks daily in the company of other Genoese traders. He questioned the sellers of silks, broadcloths, grograms, fillades, botanos, and gum dragon in the colonnades along the Meses. He began to think of trade in terms of flows and patterns, of seasons and climates, not as one-off transactions. He found out that the best relics came not from Constantinople, although the churches there were full of them, but from Antioch and other cities across the Holy Land. He would have to wait before investing in that lucrative market.

After several days he learned about the fur trade that brought beautiful white wolf and black bear pelts from the lands of the Rus to the north. He had met some of the Rus traders, huge, hard men who loved to drink and fight. Plied with an odd-burning liquor made from potatoes in one of their taverns, they told Nicolo of the difficulty of carrying the pelts down the Bosporus to Constantinople through the lands of the warlike Pechenegs, and how he wouldn't last a day north of the Theodosian Walls if he ventured north to try and buy furs on his own account. Nicolo shared these stories with Kalomodius during one afternoon as the men drank wine. The older man laughed heartily.

"It is true, Nicolo, and that is why we let them bring the furs in. You can double your money in the fur trade, but . . ." he leaned in and whispered, "the real money is in spices and jewels. Nothing in the world brings returns such as these do."

Spices and jewels. Nicolo's entire body ached at those words. Kalomodius noticed Nicolo's reaction. He poured more wine and began to question Nicolo closely about his family business, his experience in trade, and his ability to calculate with the Arab mathematics. The Armenian merchant sat back and looked at Nicolo with admiration.

"I have been here for almost twenty years, Nicolo, and I have never met anyone from Europe who could calculate like that. What a useful skill to have!" He toasted Nicolo and began pursing his lips again. He looked upward and closed his eyes, then nodded abruptly and looked straight at Nicolo. "I have made a decision, Nicolo. I have been thinking about changing how my House trades. I am tired of feeding these wolves in Constantinople. Perhaps it is time to go around them, sail my ships from Antioch directly to European ports, and avoid this place altogether."

"But aren't the seas between Antioch and Europe controlled by the Byzantine navy or the Venetians?"

Kalomodius snorted derisively. "The navy no longer exists. The ships are as rotten as the officers. The emperor has hired the Venetians to be a mercenary navy on his behalf. Those clever bastards have come back to Constantinople with a vengeance after their disgrace. But Venetians worship first and foremost at the altar of mammon, and they will look off leeward as we sail by, provided the right payments are made in advance." He twisted the rings on his left hand while staring at Nicolo. "I am getting too old to take on such a venture. I am thinking of forming partnerships with trading houses at each hailing port along the way from Antioch to Europe. My connections are solid in Cyprus and Crete. That allows our ships to sail the southern boundary of the empire and out to sea rather than skirting up the coast from Antioch to Constantinople. I am looking for partners in Sicily and perhaps Genoa. Would you like to be in on this, Nicolo? A direct trade from Antioch to Europe, and you could be the lead merchant for Genoa and maybe Rome, as well. I am only thinking out loud, Nicolo, and thinking dangerous thoughts at that. Take some time to consider this." Kalomodius thought about the bags of gold coins Nicolo had carted out of his house a few days earlier. "And to give you a chance to taste the fruits of success, I might consider allowing you to invest some of your gold into our next venture. We sail our ship *Lav Digin*—that means 'Good Wife' in Armenian—for Antioch in ten days. It will return with a full hold of nutmeg, cloves, cinnamon, pepper, and mace."

"I thought only the Venetians could sell spices."

Kalomodius winked and smiled. "True enough, but let's just say I have a subcontract from a Venetian firm to import a load for them. This will be the first shipment for this spice season, so the prices here will be the highest." He closed his eyes, inhaled deeply, and sighed. "But how much more the spices will be worth by the time they reach Rome. We need to cut out all these middlemen and grab that increase for ourselves."

"Are the spices grown around Antioch?" Nicolo asked gently.

"Oh no, Antioch is the Latin kingdom closest to the trade routes east. A mere one hundred miles away east of Antioch lies Aleppo, one of the great markets of the Muslims. That is where all the trade funnels in from the ancient routes. The Aleppians are the gatekeepers for all the spices and gems from the East."

"Why not go around Antioch and buy straight from Aleppo, or even beyond?"

"Ha! I like the way you think! But the Aleppians will only deal with Europeans through Antioch. They are links in a chain, nothing more. It is the same for Mosul regarding the Persian routes. All the commerce is controlled by the caliph in Baghdad. It is he and he alone who determines who will be allowed to trade within the entire realm of Islam, and his customs agents and tax collectors roam the souks and the ports making sure nobody violates the rules. We Armenians and the Jews, two peoples without countries, are allowed to transport goods for others throughout their realm and do minor trading on our own behalf, but no Europeans are allowed to trade directly within the Muslim lands. And since the sword of Islam hangs over increasing areas to the east, Europeans have less and less access. No, we must accept what is and make our money from Antioch toward the west."

Nicolo's blood was pumping furiously. He felt this was the opening he needed. He had to learn more.

"But why not go to the source of the spices? Why not make some deal to the east like you want to make to the west? You must know where the spices grow!"

Kalomodius leaned back and sipped his wine. "You must understand that the spices grow very far away to the east. Once there was a tribe of Jews, the Radhanites, I believe, who traded the entire length of the old routes from France to the lands of Hind and Sind at the eastern ends of the earth. But that was before the great flood of Islam northeastward. Now the Radhanites are barely a memory, and very few people have even heard of the kingdoms I just mentioned. I only know their names from hearing them as a child in Armenia. The old trade routes are now a series of cities stretching into the east, like a string of pearls. I think each segment is controlled by a tribe or small kingdom. Each trading post knows its immediate neighbor and passes on the goods at a markup. So nobody knows the entire route east, and nobody can get around the caliph's control."

"Have you ever heard of a Christian king in the east called Presbyter John?"

"Presbyter John? There was some talk of such a priest king years ago. His realm was in the East, past Armenia somewhere. He sent a letter to the patriarch or the emperor about a treaty or something. I don't recall anything coming of it. Why?"

"Nothing. I heard something at the tavern about this Presbyter John and spices."

"Well, spices come from the east and Presbyter John is somewhere in the east. That's the most I can tell you. Now, do you wish to invest in our spice shipment from Antioch?"

"Yes I do, but I need to think about it for another day or so. I need to calculate how much we will need while we are here and how much is left to invest. May I have some time?"

"It is wise to balance boldness with sobriety. Think it over, but I need an answer soon. I am making you this offer because I have had such great fortune here and I see in you the hungry young trader I once was. Besides, I like the Genoese. You are a friendly people, not like those scheming Venetians or the cutthroat Pisans." Kalomodius stood and began to walk Nicolo to the door. "If you would like, I can arrange for you to see our ships. We dock up the Golden Horn by the Blachernae Palace. It is a bit out of the way, but that is where the emperor has assigned the independent traders. Oh, before you go, let me show you something that might interest your uncle." He led Nicolo into a room off the back of the anteroom. It was full of old books and scrolls, and Nicolo was smacked by the smell of molding parchment. Kalomodius surveyed the room. "I am a student of history,

Nicolo. It is impossible for me to recreate the glory of Rome, but I have tried to capture the glory of their minds. These volumes hold their ancient knowledge and insight into the human condition. Truly learned men value the wisdom within these texts. I also act as agent for Muslim courtiers and rulers who wish to obtain these manuscripts for translation."

"I thought that was against the law."

Kalomodius winced. "No, no. I purchase them from the private libraries of the nobility. That is a little-known exemption some of the nobles managed to extract from the emperor over the objections of the patriarch. The nobles have no use for them but are always looking for coin and got the sale of these manuscripts exempted from taxes or duties. He ran a finger down the spine of one of the volumes, allowing himself a brief look of melancholy. I enjoy these works as long as I wish and then sell them on."

Nicolo suddenly saw the old manuscripts in a different light. "Let me understand. There is a market for these old manuscripts?"

"There is in the Syrian lands. Pagan literature is not appreciated in Rome and most authors are banned, so there are few who would buy these in Europe. If that ever changes, it could be a good but minor market." Kalomodius reached up and pulled a volume down. "This work of Euclid cost me four gold coins. I will sell it on for ten. That Plato up there is older, and I can get twenty gold coins for it. So three or four of these equals the salary of a midlevel *logothete*. Not the makings of a fortune, to be sure. To me, these manuscripts are enjoyable and a means of sweetening trade relationships with Muslim rulers, not a significant source of income." Kalomodius smiled as he took down another volume. "This commentary on Aristotle was written by the Byzantine princess Anna Comnena. It is well written and insightful, but the Muslims don't want works written by a woman. And this theology by Gregory of Nazianus is written in such a beautiful hand that some people want it as a work of art. Please let your uncle know he is welcome to visit my library anytime."

Nicolo thought about how Mauro spent each day searching out old manuscripts in the monasteries. *Maybe I should ask him what he is finding. If the church is letting him read all these pagan writings, they might be opening up a bit. There could be a market for these manuscripts back home after all, or I could help create one. What did the cardinal say? Help the church and help myself.*

MAURO ENTERED THE Great Palace with mixed emotions. He was overjoyed at the time he was spending at the various monasteries and churches around Constantinople. He saw so many relics but could not kiss them, as the monks in charge of the holy sites demanded payment. Nor could he even visit the most revered relics, because he couldn't pay the viewing fees or for an official guide. Thus, he did not see Christ's crown of thorns at the Chapel of the Holy Virgin of Pharos. He thought of asking Nicolo for a small amount of coin but felt guilty at the thought of using the money so selfishly when Nicolo was managing their small treasury so well. Still, through the kindness of the patriarch he was able to stand in Hagia Sophia next to the table used at the Last Supper. He considered Judas Iscariot, wondering how anyone could so horribly betray the innocent lamb—and for a mere thirty pieces of silver. Was the lesson that in a moment of weakness we can betray what we hold dearest? It was weakness, after all, as Judas cried later, throwing the coins back at the feet of the priests and hanging himself in despair. Mauro's rhetorical mind took another turn. Was it the power of money that tempted people into evil? Judas was a merchant. He was enraged when Mary Magdalene poured a container of expensive spikenard perfume on Jesus's feet. The fragrance could have been sold for three hundred copper pieces and the coins given to the poor. Was the betrayal an act of weakness or misplaced self-righteousness?

At the Church of the Pantocrator, Mauro knelt next to the red marble slab where Christ had been placed after his crucifixion (the stains from the Virgin Mary's tears were still visible). He felt the pain of the piercing nails in his palms and feet. He cried with joy at being able to experience his faith so acutely through these sacred objects.

Yet even without holding and praying over the many relics in Constantinople, the days melted into each other seamlessly as Mauro became lost in the great writings he found. It wasn't just the saints, theoreticians, and philosophers who moved Mauro. He skimmed through hundreds of letters and translations that detailed everything from how people thought to how they traveled, what they dreamed of and how they struggled to know God. As varied as they were, all the writings had one thing in common—they had all been silenced by Rome. Mauro wondered how a society could advance if it could not learn from the experiences and wisdom of its predecessors.

If delving into the lives and thoughts of earlier peoples was his sole reason to be in Constantinople, he thought he might never leave. However, Mauro was there for a greater purpose, and he didn't feel he was making progress on understanding the way toward reconciliation. He tried to talk to the monks at the monasteries but found that they were as narrow-minded and as limited in their education as their counterparts in Livorno. The patriarch was kind and immensely knowledgeable, but Mauro felt uncomfortable taking up too much of his time when there were so many other churchmen in Constantinople who were supposed to be willing to engage in the discussion of the differences between Rome and Constantinople. But where were they? He sought advice from the papal legates.

※

Lucius kept a sympathetic demeanor as Mauro shared his dilemma. Lorenzo repeatedly interrupted Mauro's lament with sighs and noises that would have sounded like chuckles if he didn't seem so moved emotionally. There was a long silence when Mauro finished. He waited for the legates to offer some advice or hope.

"To be honest, Brother Mauro, it seems that you are not working diligently enough at this. The citizens of Constantinople high and low born are near to wailing in the streets for reunification." Lucius stopped and looked sternly at Mauro, who seemed to shrink with misery. The legate relented, cast a glance at Lorenzo, and nodded imperceptibly.

Lorenzo cleared his throat and wiped his moist eyes. "Brother Mauro, we are touched by your efforts. It is obvious that you are not accustomed to seeking out men of influence. And quite frankly, monastic monks are not known for their erudition, as you are certainly aware. Lucius, what can we do for poor Brother Mauro?"

"Let me think, Lorenzo, let me think." Lucius paused, tapping his fingers on the rim of his wine goblet. "There is the disputation coming up."

Mauro brightened. "The disputation?"

"Yes, several times each year the emperor calls together the great thinkers of the realm to come to the Blachernae Palace to hear their views on matters of importance to the empire. It is attended by leading scholars, churchmen, nobles, and diplomats. The subjects vary depending on the state of the things, but it is not unusual for a portion of the disputation to be dedicated to religious matters. Lorenzo, do you think we could get good Brother Mauro invited to the disputation?"

"Well, it will take some doing. You know, Lucius, this is a very exclusive meeting, but I am confident we can convince the *logothetes* to allow us a guest this one time. You know what high esteem we are held in at court."

"The highest," Lucius offered.

Mauro was overjoyed at the suggestion. He clapped his hands and thanked the legates over and over again. "This is wonderful! I must go and prepare! Oh, and I know you will be excited to hear that I have found a way to reconcile the different number of baptismal immersions used here and in Rome. We must distinguish between

Aristotelian *essences* and Platonic *forms*. Do you think I should become familiar with the works of Boethius, or would they be more inclined to discuss—"

Lorenzo put up his hands. "Hold, Brother Mauro! As fascinating and important as your discoveries are, as a guest you will not be able to speak or otherwise participate. But you will hear the current state of things and be able to meet attendees afterward. You can make good contacts for your further investigations. I think you will get quite an education. Now, let us take care of the details." He looked the monk up and down and shook his head. "But we do need to get you those new clothes. Well, don't worry; we will have something special made for you. Yes, dear monk, we are as excited as you are to have you attend the disputation."

***

MAURO LEFT THE legates in high spirits. He sat on a marble bench outside the Great Palace to thumb through his parchments and determine where to go next to ready himself for the disputation. Even though he would not be speaking, he wanted to be as prepared as possible so that he could understand the arguments and follow up with the important thinkers he would meet. Mauro knew the key strategy to reconciliation would be to go beneath the surface of the issues of contention and find the underlying commonality in faith. Surely, reasonable minds could see that the differences were more about culture, style, and practice than deep substance. Should he go back to St. John Studion to continue reading how Boethius reconciled human happiness with the presence of evil? To Chora monastery beyond the Theodosian Wall, where a truly ancient papyrus collection of Roman thinkers like Varo of Atax, Cornelius Severus, Quintillian and others lay damp and molding?

As he sat with his face turned toward the sun soaking up the heat of midday, Mauro's mind drifted as it so often did to the wondrous places beyond Constantinople where miracles had occurred, great truths were revealed, and great martyrdoms suffered in pursuit of holiness. The patriarch had told him of an Iberian monk who lived in Saint Sergius monastery behind the Great Palace and the Hippodrome, down by the Harbor of Sophia. It was the only church in Constantinople reserved for Latin rites. Many Latin Christian voyagers on their way through Constantinople visited the monk, who would write down their travel tales for a fee. He was well schooled in the spiritual geography of the Bible, as well as the geographies of the ancients. If Mauro desired to find certain locations in *The Book of Holy Places*, this foreign monk would be helpful. The patriarch had told Mauro that the monk's name was Fra Joao, but he was known as "the Gray Monk."

"Ah," Mauro had pondered, "because gray symbolizes our predicament in this life, torn between the light of good and the darkness of evil?"

"I don't really know," the patriarch had replied. "I think it is because he only wears gray."

Saint Sergius sat on a rise overlooking the bright green sea. The building itself was run-down. Many of the marble facade pieces had fallen off or been removed, revealing patches of brick and mortar beneath. Mauro entered the forlorn monastery and found a monk dozing in the vestibule. When he asked where he might find Fra Joao, the sleepy monk merely waved a hand in the direction of a stone staircase that headed down into darkness. Mauro slowly shuffled his way down the stairs with one hand straight out and the other on the rough, damp wall. His eyes adjusted to the gloom, and he saw the glow of a single candle emanating from a small cell down the hall at the bottom of the stairway.

"Fra Joao?"

The seated monk was hunched over a parchment, scribbling furiously. At the call he turned toward Mauro. He was indeed dressed in a gray cassock. In the dim light Mauro noticed that his frizzy hair was gray as well, with a streak of white at each temple that looked like thunderbolts emanating from his head.

"Your Latin has an accent from Rome. I don't hear that often. Aristotle thought that accents can be a key to understanding the human condition . . ."

Mauro stared at the man before him as he prattled on, somehow tying together accents, Diogenes's search for an honest man and man's fall from grace. After what seemed like an eternity, Mauro realized that he needed to interrupt the monk to bring his mind back into the room. It felt rude, but at the same time Mauro often had to interrupt his students to bring them into the present.

"I understand you are from Iberia, al-Andaluz."

Fra Joao startled at the sound of the Arabic name. He blinked a few times as if to bring Mauro into focus and smiled. "Al-Andaluz. I haven't heard that name in years. Yes, I lived in Cordoba at the monastery of Santiago. I translated into Latin the Arabic translations of the great Greek writers." He stopped for a moment and frowned. "I felt I was making a contribution to knowledge. But I was attacked. Not by the Muslims. No, by the Christian lords of Navarre to the north. They tried to force the caliph to turn me over to them for the double heresy of translating the pagans and assisting Arab scholars. Fortunately, the caliph was a learned man. He told me it would be safer for me to pursue my work elsewhere. I took a ship to Sicily and ultimately came here." He looked around the dark cell. "It is not Cordoba, but it is safe and there are so many manuscripts here that I feel as if I am in Paradise. The original Hebrew and Persian for Paradise meant a park reserved for royalty, full of lush bushes and trees, quite unlike the dry areas around them. I don't think the early Hebrews could visualize Heaven so they called it a park, one that common people couldn't enter but could glimpse from outside."

There he goes again. "I am desirous of traveling to the holy sites described in this book. It recites the cities or valleys where the wondrous events occurred, but no more information than that. I was told you have knowledge of the geographies of the Holy Land and might offer guidance for my travels." Mauro handed the slim volume to Fra Joao. The monk held it close to his face for a minute.

"Ah, *The Book of Holy Places*. An important compendium, but you are right. It does not help you find the actual sites. Look here, for example." Joao flipped the volume open to a random page. "Here is a description of Gethsemane and a small illustration. Directly under it is another of Rachel's Tomb. It doesn't tell you that it takes eight hours to walk between the two, and that you must spend the night in between, as the road through Hebron can be dangerous for travelers."

"You seem to know so much about the holy places. Have you been to the Holy Land often?"

"No, I am much too timid to travel anymore. Like many a good Christian who cannot go to Jerusalem, I have traveled 'in my heart, not with my feet,' as Bernard of Clairveaux said. I study all the travel itineraries I can find, and I interview many of the pilgrims who pass through Constantinople on their way home. But here, let me show you my spiritual journey, my quest to touch the divine." Joao retrieved several candles from a nearby shelf, lit them and placed them in sconces along the side walls. Their combined light dispelled the darkness from the back of the cell, revealing an immense painting of angels, demons, strange creatures, and ancient cities connected by a whorl of lines and circles. Minute, long commentaries filled all available space on the wall. Mauro fell back at the sudden visual assault.

"Dear Mary! What is this?"

"This is my *mappaemundi*, my map of the world. Here is where I walk in the footsteps of Our Lord Jesus, fish in the Sea of Galilee, pray at the Second Temple and join Joshua at the battle of Jericho." Joao walked to the wall and placed both hands on it in reverence. He slid his hands to the right side of the map, touching a radiant sun with the face of Jesus imposed within it. "Mine is a map of spirit and matter. It begins in the east, where the sun rises and time begins. It is the location of the Garden of Eden, the Earthly Paradise. Look, see how Eden is on an island in the vast sea that circles the earth? See how it is protected by a ring of mountains and a wall of flames? The Earthly Paradise is located high in those mountains. That is how it remained unaffected by the flood. It is, of course, inaccessible because we are stained by original sin." Mauro approached the wall and touched the trees in the Garden of Eden. His fingers tingled as the candle shimmer made the flames surrounding the island dance and crackle. "And the four rivers that flow from Eden. See how they disappear under the earth and come up to feed the four great rivers of the world. Here, the Euphrates and the Tigris." Joao's fingers followed the illustrations on the wall. "And there the Ganges and the Nile."

"I do not know much of these rivers, but it is uplifting to know that their source is in the holiest of places."

"Yes, and the rivers create and surround one of the three continents where the sons of Noah settled, and the four great civilizations were born and crumbled." Joao followed the outline of each continent and pointed to tiny figures in various parts of the map. "Here are Sem, Cham, and Japhet in Asia, Africa, and Europe. But look at this." Joao took Mauro's arm and led him back a few steps from the wall. "See how spiritual time has unfolded on earth. It began in the east at sunrise and evolved westward. In Asia we can see the great wall built by Alexander to contain the giants Gog and Magog and their twelve tribes, who will break out at the end of time. And here is where Noah's Ark landed on Mount Ararat after the flood waters subsided. You see, Brother Mauro, man evolves increasingly aware of and closer to God as we travel west. There is Jerusalem at the center of my mappaemundi. It is where God judges man on earth. In the Holy Land the Son of God appeared, yet those lands are challenged and troubled. Why? Because we in Europe are geographically the final evolution from sin to repentance to redemption. Until we cleanse ourselves of the seven deadly sins, we will neither regain the Holy Land nor usher in the end times. That is why the earth ends here," Joao thrust a finger at the map, "at the Pillar of Hercules. It is the end of Europe and the last evolution of man, should we ever complete God's plan."

"I am in awe of your work, Fra Joao, but please help me understand something. I have seen other maps in the Vatican, although none as beautiful and complete as yours. But all the other maps show the east at the top of the map, where the sun rises. Isn't God's beauty and grace from above? Why does your map have the east on the right side?"

Joao came out of his reverie, blinked several times at Mauro and nodded. "Ah, that is where we cross from spiritual geography into the geography of place. You cannot find any of God's places of marvel and miracle that are illustrated on those maps in the Vatican. They are not meant for worldly travelers. The maps are meant for spiritual contemplation so, of course, we look up to God and we put creation above. Thus, east is above as well. But as a practical matter, if a traveler wants to go from Constantinople to Jerusalem or a merchant wishes to sail from here to Cairo, he will want to know the exact direction and distance. The ancients knew this well, and devised systems of measurement based on astronomical calculations. The mathematicians of Rome and Persia created a grid of lines called latitude and longitude to measure the earth and calculate distances. That allows a city or mountain to be located both by its relation to the north of the equator and the torrid zone and its relation to the east of Constantinople or Rome or Jerusalem. The system was formalized by Ptolemy, the archivist at the library of Alexandria before the fire destroyed all the great works there two hundred years after Our Savior. Ptolemy relied on the works of Eratosthenes and Strabo as well as some early Khorazmian geographers. He listed the eighty thousand known place names in the world, the entire Greek *oikoumene*, or *ecumene* as the Romans called it, along with their longitude and latitude. All this knowledge was lost during the dark times and is only now becoming available again as more manuscripts are discovered and more Arabic translations brought to Latin. Look at my mappaemundi closely. I have added the work of Ptolemy to the spiritual map, but his mathematics requires that east be on the right and north be on top. Like Ptolemy, I supplement the earlier geographers with pilgrims' and travelers' accounts."

"Does the church approve of moving Eden from the top of the map?" Mauro asked gingerly.

Fra Joao shrugged. "Here in this cell under Saint Sergius I am unknown to Rome and tolerated by the patriarch, so the issue never comes up. But there is a conundrum, isn't there?" He looked back at the wall. "The divine is just beyond the edge of our knowledge and we are always seeking its grace. Yet the more we learn of the earth and the more we fill in the blank spaces the further away we push the divine. Are we falling away from the heavenly realms by measuring the material world? I don't know, certainly not intentionally. Maybe that is why our church condemns curiosity and limits our inquiries to the natural philosophies."

Mauro walked back to the map. It was so filled with names, images, and minute details that he could barely read the entries. He was excited to find Mount Sinai and Pisgah, Joseph's barns, the Valley of Jehoshaphat, and so many of the holy sites around Jerusalem and throughout the Holy Land. He was delighted when Joao said he would give him detailed directions to several of the places in Mauro's book. In return, Joao asked if Mauro would visit on his way back and give him even more details for his map. Mauro readily agreed and returned to examining the map. He felt he could spend all day and night in the small cell with Fra Joao listening to his tales of spiritual geography. He was growing more and more fond of Constantinople, where he felt he could learn, read, even teach in a place that seemed to have a genuine respect for seekers of knowledge. Yet he knew he had to move on at some point, and he reminded himself that he would have the chance to examine so many different faiths, to meet so many fallen men if he ever got beyond this frontier of God's evolving plan. As his finger wandered from Jerusalem toward the east and the north, Mauro began to find small figures with grotesque shapes, men with eyes in their stomachs, large women warriors above the name "Amazonas," giant birds carrying away pleading men and other disquieting oddities. In the middle of these figures Mauro noticed a castle encompassing the words "Ionnes Presbyter."

"Fra Joao! Look here! Is this the land of Presbyter John? What do you know of him?"

Fra Joao approached the wall and squinted at the minute detail on the map. "Ah, the Christian king in the East. Constantinople was full of rumors years ago about Presbyter John. His emissary, a bishop from Syria, came here delivering a letter describing his realm and his desire to be of service in the wars with the Muslims."

"Yes, yes," Mauro cried out. "I have read the letter!"

"Ah, you may have read the original Latin. But thereafter many dissimilar copies of the letter circulated in different languages—Greek, French, and Hebrew, two others in Latin—each claiming to be the original, and each more full of wonder than the last. It is very confusing. I have added the most important features of each iteration of the letter to my map. Some of the letters described his wealth, much of it from the gems and gold found in his rivers. Some told in detail about the size of his empire, the structure of his administration and huge armies. Several mentioned wondrous things, like the oculus Presbyter John keeps on top of a tower where he can see anywhere in the world, or the fountain of youth that keeps Presbyter John eternally young. He carries a scepter covered by the largest emeralds in the world, all from his rivers."

Mauro was confused by the additional letters. No one had mentioned them in Rome. "Fra Joao, I would like to read those other letters. Can you help me find them?"

"Certainly. I will make you a list of the monasteries here in Constantinople where they can be found. My favorite French version tells of the many frightening creatures that live in his forests. Those are the images you see on the map."

Mauro was unnerved by the sight of the ungodly creatures. "Are those abominations still alive or are they from the spiritual past?"

"It is difficult to say. I have never met anyone who has been to the lands of Presbyter John. I only hear tales from travelers who have heard them from others. There are two types of monsters written about in the Presbyter John letters and many are mentioned in early Greek and Roman histories and travels. There are these disfigured men that you see here." Joao pointed to the man with one eye in the middle of his face, another with a giant horn, and a third with only one large foot. "These men may be fallen angels or represent peoples who have not yet heard the Word of God. Their physical ugliness symbolizes their fallen state. If they are human, the sons of Adam, they must be rational and mortal and thus worthy of salvation. The other monsters are not human. There are centaurs and satyrs, giant birds, salamanders that can withstand fire, serpents with the head of a bird and a stare that kills. They are the creatures of Satan let loose from the Garden or raised in a tortured Hell. Perhaps Presbyter John sought to reclaim their souls."

"And what of those women warriors, the Amazonas? Who are they?"

"Presbyter John tells us that they are a tribe of fierce women who guard the boundary between civilization in the west and chaos in the east. Apparently, they only meet with men of neighboring tribes once a year for procreation. If the child is female, she is taken in and trained as a warrior. If a male, it is either returned to the father or eaten by the Amazonas, depending on which letter you read."

Mauro remembered the large woman on the dock when they arrived in port. "Fra Joao, I think I have seen an Amazona right here in Constantinople. She was a slave on her way to the Syrian lands. Could that be?"

Joao thought for a moment. "It is possible. The Muslims raid the lands in the east for slaves and gold. They could have captured an Amazona and brought her back as a prize."

Mauro was excited at the first real evidence that he and Nicolo were on the right path to the realm of Presbyter John.

Joao stepped away from the wall and motioned for Mauro to sit next to him on the hay bedding in the corner of his cell. "But other letters mention nothing of the Amazonas or the giant birds. I have seen many missives from kings, bishops, and sultans. These royal letters often exaggerate the wealth or the dominions of sovereigns to make them appear mighty or invincible. Powerful rulers have been known throughout history to use false information to confuse their enemies. I suspect that some of the descriptions of those creatures are meant to keep potential invaders away, or safeguard special trading routes. Does Presbyter John live between the realms of spirit and matter, like the Earthly Paradise, called forth by prayer and unleashed by God's grace during times of deep trouble for Christianity? Or is he here now, somewhere out there among the ungodly? Can there be a living Christian king in the East? How much is truth, how much is exaggeration and how much is the pure imagination of the letter writers cannot be known except by someone who goes to that realm."

"But how can there be a Christian kingdom in the Far East if God's plan evolved westward as you say? Isn't the Far East just the land of those fallen men and monsters?"

Joao thought for a moment. "It is true. The East is a heathen realm. That is precisely why the Apostle Thomas, the one who doubted Jesus, went east toward the Indias after the Resurrection to spread the Word and convert the heathens. It could be that Presbyter John is a descendant of Saint Thomas. There are many stories of Nestorian communities in the East. They would be the heirs to St. Thomas, still surviving and doing the Lord's work among the heathens there."

"Yes! That must be it! The letter I read states that in Presbyter John's kingdom lies the Patriarchy of Saint Thomas!" Mauro placed his hands before him in contemplation. When he was finished with his work in Constantinople he was supposed to go forth and find this Presbyter John. Now the Lord had delivered him a way to do just that, if his courage didn't fail. He took a deep breath. He went back to the wall and traced a route from Constantinople straight toward the realm of Presbyter John.

Joao noticed him and laughed. "There are no straight lines for travelers. Ptolemy's lines are for measurement. They do not take into account the great seas of sand and mountains that block the eastern passages, nor the Seljuk Turks who would slit the throat of any Christian traveling east of Byzantium."

Mauro turned to Joao and grabbed his hands. "Would it be possible to make a map that could show me the way to the land of Presbyter John?"

Fra Joao looked at his mappaemundi and thought for a minute. "I can draw you a map that will show the cities, the mountain passes, and trade routes. Years ago, you could have traveled the coast of the Black Sea to Trebizond. But from there the Seljuks rule. I can take you to Antioch and then on to Aleppo and Baghdad, northeast over the Persian Royal Road and east past the old Roman province of Scythia. That much I know with certainty. Beyond that is only speculation and hearsay. Even Ptolemy's longitudes and latitudes are uncertain in those distant lands. Presbyter John's kingdom is not on Ptolemy's great list. But my map cannot fill your nostrils with the smell of desiccated camels close to the torrid zone or illustrate the distress of your stomach over the strange fruits of the East. It cannot show you how to escape from an angry crowd in a market or where to go when the boatman won't take you across the river. And it won't help you if, God forbid," he stuck his finger on the wall near the castle of Presbyter John, "the cannibals or giant birds of prey find you there." Joao relented when he saw the terror on Mauro's face. "Well, my friend, we all have our quests. I pray that whatever you are trying to do brings you spiritual satisfaction in this world . . . or the next."

Mauro was both agitated and energized when he returned to the inn. He was excited about the disputation but couldn't get the Amazonas, fallen men, giant birds, and cannibals out of his mind. He felt some comfort that Nicolo would be heading their expedition. Nicolo was an experienced traveler. Nicolo would purchase the passages and lead them through dangerous places. Until that point Mauro felt he hadn't contributed at all to the ultimate mission of finding Presbyter John. In fact, he had made such a mess out of the plan to take the book out of Count Eugenio's library that he had actually set them back. Meeting Joao had given him the chance to redeem himself. He determined to tell Nicolo immediately and return to Fra Joao with the merchant.

He entered their room to find Nicolo on his bed, surrounded by papers and a package. Mauro greeted him pleasantly but was met with a grunt. He tried to engage him in small talk, but Nicolo cut him off abruptly.

"I am sorry, Uncle, but I am trying to concentrate. I have been learning so much about the trade goods around here, but I can't get the traders to give me the names of the towns they get their goods from. This city is surrounded by enemies and rough terrain. I know we can't go north because of the Rus. We can't go east because of the Seljuks. It seems our only choice is to go to Antioch and maybe Aleppo after that." Nicolo caught himself. "That is, on our way to find Presbyter John."

Mauro suppressed a giggle. "Perhaps the monks in the monasteries can help us. Some of them receive pilgrims and travelers and write down their stories. They are known as repositories of—"

"Look, Uncle, I don't mean to be rude, but I am sure that the merchants here know a lot more than pilgrims and monks. I just need more time to gather information." Nicolo was getting frustrated with his failure to get more out of the other traders in Constantinople. He wanted to make a deal with Kalomodius and move on to Antioch.

"But I have actually met the most interesting monk—"

"That's wonderful, it really is, Uncle, but I need to figure this out on my own." Nicolo looked down at the package on his bed. "Oh, by the way, this came for you while we were out today." Mauro's curiosity displaced the slight, and he took the package from Nicolo and opened it. He pulled out a long white silk robe with purple collar and sleeves.

Nicolo looked up in amazement. "That's quite a robe. Are you going to see the emperor?" he said jokingly.

"Actually, yes." Mauro noticed a letter still in the package, next to a new pair of sandals. He opened it and read aloud. "*Dear Brother Mauro. We have obtained permission from His Excellency, the emperor, for your attendance at the disputation to take place in Blachernae Palace on Thursday afternoon hence at two o'clock. This robe is appropriate attire for the gathering. Be well rested, as it will be a long day and evening for everyone. We are greatly anticipating your attendance. Sincerely, Lucius Severus, papal legate.*" He put the letter down and held up the robe. "I am not comfortable with this robe. It is very ostentatious."

"Well, you have two days to get used to it. Besides, I think it makes you look distinguished, like a cardinal or a bishop." Mauro looked at Nicolo to see if he was making fun of him but couldn't detect a sign of it on his face. "If you are going to an event at the palace, you need to dress the part. It is a sign of respect at court. And it sounds like this is the opportunity you were hoping for, right?"

"Yes, of course you are right. I am very excited about this. I will meet so many learned men and hear arguments about all the major issues at court, including the conflicts with Rome."

Nicolo moved his papers aside, stood up, and stretched. "Well, I am very excited for you, too, Uncle. I think I will go to the tavern and celebrate your good luck. Will you join me just this one time?"

"No thank you, Nicolo. I need to study and organize the arguments again. I must be able to understand everything that is going on, even if I cannot participate."

Nicolo nodded and sighed, feigning disappointment. *Thank the Lord he didn't call my bluff. Away to the tavern!*

NICOLO HAD BEEN begging off the nose game until tonight. There were just too many unfamiliar spices, fruits, and drugs traded through Constantinople. He didn't like to play a game he couldn't win and didn't want to spend his money foolishly when Kalomodius's rich venture awaited him. But tonight the Genoese traders were so insistent and cheerful. After a month in Constantinople, he felt confident that he would at least keep his losses to a minimum and at the same time reinforce his friendships with the Genoese community that had taught him so much here. At first he couldn't tell a yusdrome from a mitigale or a lodero from a batman, but with their support he could translate any of them into drams, ounces, and gallons faster than the other merchants. A night of drinks and brotherly embarrassment was small coin for how far he had come under their tutelage.

He easily handled the more usual spices, and barely stumbled on the saffron, anise, and ginger so common here yet barely known at home. He bought a few rounds for confusing the peaches and the apricots, and not even guessing at some of the drugs. His head was swirling and the noise in the tavern was deafening. Then, yet another cloth passed into his hands. The crowd quieted as he brought it to his nose. It had a musky smell. Was it the cumin seed that he had just learned about? It wasn't a fruit. It wasn't sweet like cinnamon, but it was slightly pungent, like a mild clove. There was a roughness to the smell, a vague hint of tar, like ship's rigging. Why was it so familiar? He was certain he knew that smell. It came to him like a thunderbolt. He whipped off the blindfold to gape at the figure before him.

"Antonio!" Nicolo and his older brother embraced as the traders cheered them on. "What are you doing here? You are supposed to be in Venice!" Giovanni jumped into the embrace, his wine-reddened eyes shedding a tear.

"It's so beautiful to see you together. I wish my little brother was here." Giovanni belched and laughed. "Antonio, you would be so proud of your little brother. He is gorging himself on bargains here. He's a smart lad. You better watch out or he'll take over your House soon!"

Antonio cocked an eye at his brother. "Yes, he has a lot of secret talents."

Giovanni looked from Antonio's stone face to Nicolo's. He raised his eyebrows and turned to the crowd. "Brothers! Let us give these men a chance to reunite in private. I am sure they have much to share." The Genoese went back to their tables and their tales.

Nicolo held Antonio at arm's length. His joy at seeing his older brother suddenly tempered. "But wait. What *are* you doing in Constantinople?"

"In truth, Brother, I was sent to find out what you are up to. I had just finished a deal with the doge in Venice to supply ships and more for the coming crusade—a deal that would have meant a fortune for our family. Yet I was accused of being a spy and nearly tortured because my brother was wandering abroad trying to unite Rome and Constantinople. I told my jailers that it couldn't be so." He gave Nicolo the hard stare that always crumbled the younger man's defenses. "So tell me, Nicolo, what are *you* doing here?"

How could they know this? Nicolo steeled himself and returned Antonio's stare without flinching. "I . . . am the companion for an old monk who is seeking to study at the great monasteries here."

"Oh, yes, our *uncle*."

"Father arranged it," Nicolo pleaded, trying to hide his growing panic. "Brother Mauro is actually a cousin to the pope. If that was known, he would be kidnapped and ransomed by every prince along the route." Nicolo marveled at how easily the creative lie came to his lips. He felt some satisfaction at deceiving his brother and relaxed a bit. "I am simply guiding him along the way. You know how these churchmen are, Brother. He would get lost at the first crossroads." He smiled at Antonio, who retained a skeptical look. "And yes, he is interested in those church arguments and wants to understand them better, but that's pretty harmless." *I cannot let Antonio goad me into telling him anything else.* "I mean, he is just trying to help his family, right?"

Antonio stared hard at his younger brother. *The little bastard is hiding something from me.* "Nicolo, if I am successful in Venice, I will be made a notary at the Vatican. Our family will get contracts and connections for generations. Whatever you and the monk are doing is interfering with what I am trying to accomplish for all of us. You need to go back to Genoa immediately. I can get you on the next boat."

"I made a promise to Father and a vow to the pope that I would help Brother Mauro. I can't go back to Genoa just yet. I need to stay here with the monk."

"So being a religious hero is more important than wealth and power for your family," scoffed Antonio. "Saint Nicolo! Maybe the church will make a relic of your head, and we can honor it in the new cathedral in Genoa." Antonio saw the flush of anger or embarrassment on Nicolo's face and changed tack. He had always been able to cow Nicolo by being angry, then gentle. "When your monk is finished with his studies here, will you return to Genoa? I need to know, Nicolo. I need to go back to the doge and tell him this. If you are lying to me, I will probably be tortured, and you will be killed by the Venetians. How would that help our family?"

Nicolo felt sick. He finally had the chance to make something of himself—on his own. Yet here was Antonio, trying to hold him back again. He needed to sort this all out. He needed to see how long Mauro would take to finish his work. Was Mauro even concentrating on that, or was he spending all his time reading those damned old manuscripts? He needed to close the deal with Kalomodius and invest in the spice shipment. Even if he never found the source of the spices, he could make a fortune working with the Armenian. He didn't really care anymore if he found Presbyter John, but a trip to Antioch could be lucrative. He just needed time.

"Look, Brother, I know you are doing a great thing for the family, but so am I. I am sure that Brother Mauro will be finished soon. Let me go back to the inn, talk to the monk, and see how much time he needs. In the meantime, I am doing a little trading here that will make us good coin. I just need a few more days, that's all." He knew that Antonio softened when he deferred to him. "Then I promise we will leave."

※

Mauro sat on the polished marble bench between Lucius and Lorenzo in the top row of the seating that formed a large semicircle before the emperor's throne at the Blachernae Palace. Everywhere he looked the men wore robes of purple or purple, black, and white. He forgot his self-consciousness at his new clothing and listened as the legates pointed out the important men of the empire who were participating in the disputation. They pointed out nobles like Choniates, the historian and Laskaris, the general, who sat close to the emperor in seats of honor. Mauro thought he would see the patriarch or some of the more learned men of the church in the audience, but the legates didn't identify any.

All day long men were coming in and out of the emperor's chamber, arguing gently or shouting their point of view until the emperor dismissed them with a gift of gold, a robe, or an insult. Three Hesychast monks from Mount Athos talked of meditating on one spot at the base of their stomach and concentrating on their breath as a new, proven way to unite with God. They were ridiculed as "navel gazers" and pelted with figs by the emperor as they hurried out of the chamber. There was a debate between an astronomer and a mathematician regarding the influence of celestial spheres on human behavior. The emperor's fool sat by his side making sly comments and rude gestures and being quite the snoutband, although Mauro noticed that the fool was rather insightful beneath his raucous behavior. The audience was largely quiet during the debates, shouting assent at each of the emperor's verdicts. Two wealthy nobles argued the impact of debasing currency on the position of Byzantium in world trade. The emperor rewarded one with a bag of debased gold coins to good-humored laughter and the other with a bag of copper coins. Young men walked the steps between rows of visitors offering wine, fruit, or small pieces of roasted meat to keep the guests refreshed during the long day. Jugglers and acrobats entertained the assembly between debates. A pair of academics debated whether Greek was losing its primacy to Latin throughout the realm due to the recent surge in immigration of Western merchants and craftsmen. A fistfight nearly broke out when the argument deteriorated into whether allowing too many noncitizen craftsmen and unskilled workers was taking away work from the local population and driving down wages.

Mauro became drowsy during the long and mostly confusing debates. He had hoped for something more relevant to his mission but was grateful for the opportunity to hear intelligent arguments at least. He jolted awake when he heard the voice of a page announce the next disputation.

"Our lord, our emperor, next wishes to hear arguments as to which is the true seat of our Christian faith—Constantinople or Rome? We invite the representative of our holy church to join us." The crowd cheered as the fool reappeared from behind the emperor's throne dressed in an overly long gold-embroidered gown. His face was covered with the usual fool's paint, but he wore a beard that reached to the ground. He turned to the emperor and bowed, making a long farting sound toward the audience that drew howls of laughter.

"And from Rome, we present Pope Guilty the Hundredth! He's not so Innocent, is he?" Mauro was aghast at the rude spectacle of a dwarf with a tall conical hat strutting onto the floor. He looked to Lucius and Lorenzo, who seemed in shock as well.

"Don't be too alarmed, dear Brother Mauro," Lucius whispered. "The emperor has an odd sense of humor. He is just entertaining his guests and breaking up this long day. This will pass quickly, I am sure."

The fool and the dwarf squared off in front of the smiling emperor, dug their feet at the floor and circled round like a pair of wrestlers at a fair.

"I am Orthodox! I am the true church!" shouted the fool. He ran up and kicked the dwarf in his shin. The dwarf grabbed his leg and hopped around to general laughter and cheers.

"I am Catholic! That means universal! I am the true church!" yelled the dwarf as he ran up to the fool and knocked him on the head with a wooden scepter that appeared out of nowhere. The two grappled and rolled on the ground, grunting and yelling obscenities at each other.

"Your priests marry women! They love carnality over God!" the Roman dwarf cried.

"Ha!" replied the Byzantine fool. "Your priests prefer boys and farm animals because they live an unnatural life!" He grabbed the dwarf's crotch, which elicited a scream. "See? You don't even have the tools of the trade down there!"

"STOP!" shouted the emperor as he stood up. "This is boring and not getting us anywhere. I wish to hear about the topic at hand, not watch a brawl. You, Pope Guilty, obviously do not understand the subtleties of these issues. There must be someone here who can do better at representing Rome." He turned and scanned the audience. "Ah, yes. The papal legates. Isn't it your job to present the position of Rome to this court? Why don't you come down here and defend your faith?" Lucius shook in his seat and Lorenzo put his head between his shoulders as if to disappear. "What say you?"

"Your Most Purple," squeaked Lucius, "we are administrators, not debaters. We would not want to dishonor your court with weak arguments."

"What about your guest, then?" The emperor looked squarely at Mauro. "I hear that he is quite the scholar and has been spending his days in our monasteries. Surely you can represent the position of our brothers in Rome? Come here and participate in the disputation. Come down now!"

Lucius turned to Mauro and pleaded quietly. "You must go, Brother Mauro. The emperor commands it. Go down and defend the true faith. This is the chance we have been waiting for."

"But I have no authority to represent Rome. I am only here to lend support to those in Constantinople who wish to see reunification."

"My goodness, Brother Mauro, you are being called to defend the faith. Just go do it!" Lucius shoved Mauro toward the aisle, where a waiting page took his arm and guided him down to the floor before the emperor.

"And I see you wear the royal purple. How dare you! That color is reserved for our nobility." The emperor took a deep swig of wine and smiled warmly at the monk. "If you perform your duties here today, I will forgive the slight and allow you to wear it again, and even afford you the title of *hyperpriap*."

"That means 'big prick!'" shouted the fool. "Looking around this room I'd say you'll be in good company."

The emperor frowned at the fool. "I said hyper*prioph*, fool. High purple. Regardless, you there, monk! Put on your pope's hat and resume the disputation. And this time, Patriarch, no squeezing balls to make a point. I want respectful debate." Mauro looked up toward Lucius and Lorenzo, but they were no longer in their seats. "Put it on, sir, or we will relieve you of your purple robe and send you into the street naked."

The dwarf took off his hat and bowed as he passed it to Mauro. "Thank you, brother. If I had lost the argument, I would be shorter than I am by a head, I'm afraid. Good luck!" The monk put the hat on, thinking that this was a sort of martyrdom for his faith, although it was merely embarrassing, not death or a piercing of flesh. He bowed slightly to the emperor and turned to face the fool.

"To begin, noble sirs, Rome is the heir to Saint Peter. Saint Peter was martyred and buried in Rome. His spiritual power resides in the Vatican, which was built atop his remains. Thus—"

"That's nothing!" interrupted the fool. "Our Emperor Constantine was the first Christian emperor and created the Holy Roman Empire. So we are even. One saint for one emperor. There are five great patriarchs in our Christian world. Only one is in Europe. Yours. The other four are here in the East. There is Jerusalem, Antioch, Constantinople, and Alexandria. We beat you four to one! And in the past, questions of faith were decided by councils of bishops from all the patriarchs." The fool turned to the audience and waved his hands in a flourish. "I ask you, my friends, why should Rome have the only say in these matters now? It is a pure grab for earthly power, that's all. Besides, we have thousands of relics and lots of saints buried here. The power of the Holy Spirit is much stronger in Constantinople." He bowed. The crowd applauded politely, and the emperor nodded.

"That's enough of that," said the emperor as he reached for another glass of wine. "What is your opinion of the *filioque* clause?"

"Your Highness," Mauro began, "the church—"

"You mean the *Rome* church," interrupted the fool.

"Well, yes, the church in Rome believes that the Holy Spirit emanates from the Father through his son, the filioque, Jesus Christ, as is manifest on earth."

"And who gave you the right to change the Nicene Creed that we recite every day? The Holy Spirit emanates from God. End of story." The fool juggled three oranges as he spoke.

Mauro took a deep breath to regain his composure. "Our understanding of the holy mysteries evolves. Of course, the ultimate source of holiness is the Lord, but once his son was born, the procession of spirit came to earth through him. But let me suggest that many of the arguments between Rome and Constantinople are matters of form, not substance. If we consider Aristotelian—"

A loud fart echoed through the chamber, interrupting Mauro. The fool shook his finger at the monk. "These arguments mask your intention to plunder our wealth on earth for your supposedly holy pursuits . . ."

The next hour was excruciating for Mauro. The use of unleavened bread in the Eucharist, clerical marriage, whether the wine turned to actual blood, the number of immersions in a proper baptism—Mauro tried to lay out each issue logically and rationally, even though he found himself doubting some of his own arguments. He tried to calm himself and not lose track of his arguments by silently repeating the words of Isaiah: *No weapon forged against you will prevail, and you will refute every tongue that accuses you.*

Yet the fool was relentless and surprisingly well educated on the issues. Each time Mauro sought to clarify a philosophical point or put a matter into the context of ecclesiastical culture versus theological belief, the fool interrupted with an argument that to Mauro seemed beside the point or turned the issue into a commentary on the political or social dynamics that underlie it. Mauro had no knowledge of these things. He was relieved when the emperor called a halt to the proceedings.

"I have had enough of these religious squabbles. Fool, you continue to amaze me. I should make you our ambassador to Rome. Pope Guilty, you have not convinced me that there is any religious authority that commands the obeisance of Constantinople to Rome or why we should change any of our practices to conform to those of Rome. Ordinarily, I would throw you in a dark cell to ponder your sins. Or worse, force you to marry one of my daughters. And you, a country monk, wearing the royal purple? You mock us, sir."

"But it was never my intention to—"

"Enough! Since you seem the real fool here, I will be magnanimous and neither imprison you nor grind glass into your eyes. However, you no longer have permission to address the emperor. In fact, I decree that you are banned from the Empire immediately." The emperor took a draft of wine and waved a hand limply at Mauro. "Leave now. Oh, and don't forget to give the hat back to the dwarf."

Mauro reeled in disbelief. He turned and wobbled shakily out of the chamber to a mountainous wave of cruel laughter and jeers. The monk's heart was pounding, and he felt faint. He reached out to the wall as his knees gave way and was grabbed by Lucius.

"Oh, Brother Mauro, that was horrible. The emperor was so cruel to treat you like that. We couldn't bear to watch him do that to you, so we left the room to spare you the embarrassment." Lorenzo came around the corner whistling, with two cups of wine and a plate of figs.

"Oh!" Lorenzo cried in surprise. He quickly recovered. "Here, Brother Mauro, I brought you something to drink and eat. You must be so exhausted after that humiliation." Mauro waved away the cup and plate. Lorenzo took a sip from one cup and handed the other to Lucius. "Well, waste not, want not." He popped a fig into his mouth and spoke through his chewing. "So where are you going to go now that you are banned from the entire Empire? Back to Rome, I suppose, although His Holiness will probably be very upset with the mess you made here."

Mauro shook the fog from his head rapidly and stared at the legates. "Mess? All I did was try to defend the positions of our Church."

"Yes, but you failed, didn't you?" Lucius said sharply. "Look at the position you have put us all in now. It will take a lot of gold to calm the emperor down and maintain our positions here for the church. Where will we ever find that? "

"Search me," mumbled Lorenzo with a suppressed chuckle.

"Honestly, Brother Mauro, I thought you were more skilled in these matters. Well, you can keep the robe as a symbol of our generosity, but you had best leave Constantinople immediately before you get us all into more trouble."

Mauro staggered away. Pages and administrators shook their heads or turned as he passed. The legates watched the monk leave the palace.

"It is so sad to see the innocent martyred," Lucius sighed. "The world is such a brutal place." They looked at each other and raised their cups.

"Nicely done, Lucius."

"Now, now, Lorenzo. It was a joint effort. And worth a lot more than thirty pieces of silver, wouldn't you agree?"

Mauro was deeply troubled as he wandered back toward the inn alone in the dark night. He went over and over in his mind what happened at the palace. He was not prepared for that kind of debate. It didn't abide by the known rules of logic and rhetoric. It wasn't at all focused on the real issues and their underlying dynamics—or was it? What was the value of faith if men who professed it didn't live by it? As he passed the many churches of Constantinople, Mauro realized that he was more comfortable in the libraries and the monasteries amid the voices of the past, speaking in dead languages than he was arguing in the present with its hidden motives and competing interests. He had done nothing to further the faith since leaving the cocoon of the university in Bologna. He wasn't feeling doubt about his faith, but he was seeing how the beautiful truths of Christianity were manipulated and used by men to justify their power and position on earth. Maybe it was a mistake to bring faith into the world as a sword to wield against kings. They only seem to pervert its purity for their own selfish ends. Perhaps the older view of man was correct; nothing the church could do on this earthly plane could help. God's grace was preordained. But that was not the pope's belief, and he was infallible. Wasn't he? Yes, of course he was.

The legates were right. Mauro had failed the church. The monk looked down at his fancy silk robe with despair. Where was his humility? What hubris to believe that he could argue with the great minds of the world when he couldn't even best a fool! He prayed that as he and Nicolo continued into distant lands, he could learn things about other faiths that could be of service to the church to redeem himself. He prayed that with the map from Fra Joao they could find Presbyter John and that Mauro could enlist the Christian king to come west with his armies under the banner of Rome. But what if Presbyter John was like the emperor, more interested in drink than dogma? If Mauro couldn't argue past a Byzantine fool, how could he convince an unknown foreign sovereign of the truth of the church and the need to come to its aid?

※

Back at the inn Mauro tore off the purple robe. Standing naked in the room, he held up the robe and thought about what it meant: wealth and power in this world with little thought of the next. It wasn't just the humiliation of the night that grieved Mauro so profoundly. It was the feeling that what he did simply didn't matter, that all his study, his thinking, his actions were of little consequence in a world that was so ignorant yet so full of potential for spiritual healing. He took a deep, calming breath, using the technique of breathing to join with God described by the Hesychast monks at the disposition. It didn't work—his mind was too clouded by despair and confusion. The monk threw the silk robe back to the floor. Render unto Caesar that which is Caesar's. He put on his rough wool robe and sat heavily on the mattress. He thumbed through The Book of Holy Places but couldn't concentrate. He lay back and tried to think of soothing prayers or sayings, but his mind kept returning to his failures on this mission. He had made a hash of getting the information Nicolo wanted in Sicily. He didn't feel he'd made any impact on little King Frederick, who was probably in the hands of an enemy of the church. Although Mauro had selfishly learned a lot in the monasteries of Constantinople, he had failed to promote reunification and was now banned from the entire Byzantine Empire.

Nicolo entered the room intent on grabbing the box of gold he had sequestered for investing in the spice shipment. He had to get to Kalomodius tonight, before it was too late to invest. He saw Mauro lying on his mattress looking miserable.

"Uncle! You look awful! What happened to you?" Nicolo regretted the words as soon as they escaped his mouth. Mauro launched into a long monologue about the disputation. Nicolo stood listening with a mask of sympathy, but inside he was desperate to leave the inn. Finally, Mauro finished his tale. He looked up at Nicolo with a face twisted in anguish.

"The emperor said I must leave immediately. What should we do now?"

"Then we have to leave and that's that. We don't want to end up in an imperial dungeon." Nicolo saw all his plans for making a fortune in Constantinople falling apart. First, Antonio had shown up and tried to get Nicolo to leave. Now the emperor had banished Brother Mauro. "Look, Uncle, I need to see some people tonight and make arrangements to get us out of here. It will take me a few hours. I am sure we will be safe if we leave in the morning."

"I will go to Saint Sergius and spend the night in contemplation. Perhaps the monk there can guide—"

"Yeah, well, we'd better hurry. The Varangian Guards could be on their way to collect us right now. I will walk with you as far as Hagia Sophia and meet you back here in the morning ready to leave. I don't know exactly where we're going or how, but leave that to me."

"Thank you, Nicolo. You are so selfless. You always think of our mission first. I am so grateful to be in your hands."

※

THE BOSUN EASILY tied up the old inn owner and carried him into the storeroom. He spied several bottles of the local alcohol ouzo on the shelf, grabbed them, and headed to the entryway.

"All clear?" he grumbled to the mate.

"Aye, Bosun. Nobody in sight."

"Good. Let's get up there and see what we can find."

The two men climbed the stairs and pushed in the door. They surveyed the room, entered, and closed the door behind them. The bosun broke off a bottle top against the wall and took a deep draft. The fiery *ouzo* burned but felt good. The men sat down on the mattresses and finished both bottles quickly. The mate spied a small box in the corner and opened it. The shine of gold illuminated his face.

"Look, Bosun! The Imperial Treasury!" The bosun stepped over to the box and smiled.

"Well, well. Seems our idiot struck it rich here. That should cover the cost of the voyage. But we'll just keep this our secret, right?" He looked over and saw the purple robe in the corner. "And look here! A fine robe for me to wear to the hanging when we get 'em back on board." He slipped the robe over his head and put on the new sandals that he found nearby. "Pretty rich gear for a monk."

They rummaged through the parchments that Mauro had bundled up next to the mattress, as well as the small bags the men carried containing clothes and a small book.

"Nothing else here. Well, we might as well enjoy the comforts of this fine inn while we wait for them to come back. Go below and grab any bottles you find. Kick the old innkeeper for good measure, the Genoese bastard."

The Pisans drank several bottles of *ouzo* until they passed out on the mattresses. From the alley below, a brown-hooded monk watched the candlelight slowly die in the second-floor room.

※

NICOLO WALKED QUICKLY up the Meses toward the house of Kalomodius after leaving Mauro, clutching the small box of gold. It was Thursday, and the Armenian had said that the *Lav Digin* was sailing on the Friday morning tide. He prayed it was not too late to invest. As he started up the last hill toward the merchant's house, he heard the boisterous sounds of a crowd approaching. Nicolo moved off the road into the shadow of the villa walls as people ran past him down the hill. Soon the trickle coming his way grew to a mob. He couldn't understand the common Greek they were shouting. A phalanx of Varangian Guards moved in the center of the mob. At first, Nicolo thought the mob was attacking the guards, but when the soldiers passed, he realized the crowd was actually cheering them on. He grabbed a well-dressed spectator and asked what was going on. The man pointed to the middle of the soldiers and shouted cheerfully.

"They arrested the Armenian! The emperor's going to make him pay for what he did!"

Nicolo looked deep inside the crowd and saw Kalomodius trussed up and being led away by the soldiers. He gripped his box closely and shouted to his neighbor.

"What did he do?"

"What else?" the man laughed. "He got rich without giving enough of it to the emperor!"

Nicolo ran into the tavern. He saw Antonio and Mauricio playing cards.

"The Varangians arrested the Armenian Kalomodius!"

Mauricio put down his cards. "Excellent! He's very popular with the craftsmen. That means there will be a riot tonight when they try to free him." He turned to the crowd at the tavern. "Fellow Genoese! Tonight is the time for justice for our lost brothers! Let's get that cargo back and burn the Pisans out of the city!"

Nicolo grabbed Mauricio's arm. "Wait! What about Kalomodius?"

Mauricio gave Nicolo a curious look. "Who cares about the Armenian? He's not one of us." He shook his arm free of Nicolo's grip and shouted to the assembled merchants. "Who is with me?"

The young men poured out of the tavern with shouts of "For Genoa!" and "Vengeance!" When the tavern was nearly empty Antonio suggested he and several of the other Genoese walk Nicolo back to the inn, as the streets were not going to be safe that night. Nicolo bridled at the offer.

"I am not a child anymore, Antonio. I don't need your protection." Antonio smiled at Nicolo. Giovanni and Leonardo laughed and shook their heads, commenting about little brothers.

"No, Brother, you are not. But we should stick together tonight for all our sakes. For the sake of our family. Think on it, Nicolo. A lot of people will be talking about you keeping company with Kalomodius. If someone at court thinks you are dealing with him, they may smell coin in it and send the Varangians after you next." He looked down at the box Nicolo clutched. "And we need to make sure you hide the evidence."

THE FOUR GENOESE hurried to the inn as the sounds of breaking glass, shouts, and laughter increasingly surrounded them. Nicolo wondered where the innkeeper was as they ran up the stairs. They opened the door to Nicolo's room and walked in carrying candles. In the dim light Nicolo saw two men sleeping on their mattresses. One was a bearded man in a silk purple robe, and Nicolo thought it strange that Mauro had returned so early. He walked over to the sleeping monk and jostled his shoulder. He pulled back his hand. It was wet with blood.

"Brother Mauro!" But when Nicolo turned the monk over, he saw the bosun's face. Giovanni put his candle by the face of the other man.

"Hey! This guy is one of the Pisans!" he shouted.

Antonio reached down beside the body and took hold of a gold-handled dagger. He grabbed Nicolo's arm roughly and shoved the dagger close to Nicolo's face. "What the hell is going on here, Brother? Why are there two dead Pisan sailors in your room?"

Nicolo was stunned. He could only stammer that he didn't know. Antonio pressed on.

"You've been hiding something from me all along, and there's no more time for games. What are you really doing in Constantinople?

Tell me now!" Nicolo could never stand up to his brother's wrath, and now seemed the time to tell Antonio at least something.

"You were right, Brother. The monk is here on the orders of the pope to help reunify Rome and Constantinople. I am his guide."

"You little shit!" Antonio exploded. "The doge was right all along. And you were willing to get me tortured so that you could do this? What do you get out of it? What does the family get out of it?"

"Well, it doesn't matter anymore. The monk failed and we have to leave. So you can tell your Venetian masters that you succeeded in stopping us. You can tell them I was only the guide. I didn't have any other role in this."

Antonio saw the look of dejection on his brother's face. "Let's just get you and your monk out of here safely. We will drag these bodies over to the Pisan side of the wall. No one will see. Whoever killed these men obviously thought they were you and the monk. That's in our favor. We can get you on one of our boats back to Genoa tonight. But we better hurry since half the waterfront will be on fire before morning."

"I can't go back to Genoa. Brother Mauro and I are not done with our work yet."

"Jesus Christ, what more is there?"

"We need to go east, to try and find Presbyter John. Brother Mauro is supposed to enlist him to fight in the crusades to recapture Jerusalem."

Antonio stepped back and appraised his younger brother. He felt a growing pride under his anger as Nicolo told more of the story. He also felt anxiety about his brother's crazy mission.

"You are full of surprises, Nicolo. But nobody has ever found that king and returned alive to tell about it. What makes you think you can succeed?"

Nicolo's eyes blazed. "I am a lot smarter than you give me credit for, Antonio. I have just been in your shadow for so long that you and Father never saw it. I am not going back to Genoa. I am going to board Kalomodius's ship to Antioch tomorrow and then figure out my way east." The men glared at each other until Antonio sighed and put his hands on his brother's shoulders.

"Oh my little brother. I can understand why you are doing this mad thing." He hugged Nicolo hard. "Well, since you are already dead you might as well stay dead. Get on board that Armenian ship under new names right away. We will spread the word that you and the monk were killed tonight." He looked at the bloody dagger. "Somebody is already doing that anyway, I suppose." He turned to the other Genoese, who stood staring at the brothers in bewilderment. "Giovanni, head to Saint Bacchus and bring the monk to the Armenian docks. Take the long way behind the Hippodrome and the palace so you won't be seen. Take his bag and papers with you. Leonardo, run back and get some of the others to drag these Pisans out of here." Giovanni gathered up Mauro's belongings and the two men ran out of the inn. Antonio waited until it was quiet.

"All right, Nicolo, we are alone. There must be more. I understand that you will be a hero if you pull this off, but this new crusade will probably succeed without Presbyter John. I was there when the French knights committed their forces in Venice and the Venetians rallied to the cause. So you don't have to risk your life looking for this Eastern king. Please, just go home."

"I will not."

"Why, Nicolo? Tell me what this is really about. What have they promised you in Rome that is worth all of this?" Nicolo churned inside. He was torn between keeping the secret and his desire to brag and show up his brother. But Antonio was so persistent.

"I was promised that our family will be the exclusive importer of any new trade goods I find that are not being directly imported into Rome or Genoa. There are a lot of things I have found already. I am learning all about the patterns of trade here and think I can go around Byzantium and import directly home. I know that many goods can be found in Antioch. As I search for Presbyter John, I will find more new goods. But Brother Mauro doesn't know about this. It is a private deal between me and the church."

Antonio was shocked. He sat down on the mattress, pushing aside the corpse of the Pisan sailor. "You are searching for the source of the spices, aren't you?"

Nicolo hesitated, then looked straight into Antonio's eyes. "Yes, Brother, I am."

"You don't need to do this, Nicolo. The doge has already promised me that our family will be the exclusive spice importer to Genoa. We don't have to risk our lives for more than that."

"It's always about *you*, *your* deal, *your* future. What about *me*, Antonio? You are willing to settle for the crumbs off the doge's plate. I am not. I am seeking the *source*. We can have all the control, all the money, all the power. That's what I can offer our family."

"Well, my little brother has truly grown up. If you make it back at all, you probably won't be home for well over a year. By that time the old doge will probably be dead. In the meantime, I will make good money for the family." He held Nicolo closely again. "I doubt we will ever see each other again, little brother, but if we do, I will build you a new room."

Nicolo's eyes twinkled and he laughed.

"We *will* see each other again, big brother. And when we do, I will build us a new house!"

THE DOCK WORKERS and sailors were busy loading the ships by the Stone Bridge. The noise from the riot in the lower part of the city seemed far away. Only the glow from the fires gave a hint of the damage being done. Mauro and Nicolo approached a foreman and asked which ship was headed to Antioch in the morning. Nicolo was careful not to mention Kalomodius's name. The foreman motioned to the *Lav Digin*, a beamy two-masted vessel that seemed to pull at its dock lines in anticipation. They approached the *Lav Digin* and hailed her master. He was a squat, thickset man with long black ringlets of hair. Nicolo had passed him while leaving Kalomodius's house a week earlier. The master looked anxiously around the dock, then nodded in recognition.

"*Inch beses*, friend. We wish to book passage to Antioch, payment up front in good gold." Nicolo took a handful of gold coins from a small pouch.

The master smiled. "I know those coins, Master Nicolo. You two are welcome aboard. We must sail immediately, before the Varangians or the mobs seize our vessel. And we must race to Antioch before news of the arrest of Kalomodius reaches there." He looked over Nicolo's shoulder toward the burning city. He shrugged. "Although Kalomodius will probably be released before we clear the Golden Horn."

Nicolo was confused by the master's nonchalance. "How is that? I saw the Varangians nearly drag him down the Meses."

"This is just another squeeze by the nobility or maybe the emperor himself. They want to grab some of his wealth or punish him for insolence."

"But what about all the goods in his house? His gold and silver?"

"Kalomodius is too smart to leave much of value where the mob can find it. As to the goods and the statuary and those old manuscripts he loves? They're already gone by now. The mob is pretty efficient. They know they need to get in and get out quickly, before the victim's fortune changes. Many a man is held just long enough for his house to be looted."

Nicolo thought about the manuscripts. As if he was reading Nicolo's mind, the master continued.

"The manuscripts will be resold to the nobles for a few coppers each, or maybe torn up and sold as spare parchment or padding for shipping delicate goods. In any event, they are gone. Now go below and our bosun will find you quarters."

"Thank you, Captain." Nicolo lowered his voice. "But from now on I am Matteo, and this is . . ."

"Brother John" Mauro stated simply, using the Latin for Joao.

※

IN THE MIDDLE of the night the crew slipped the dock lines and the *Lav Digin* moved with the current quietly down the Golden Horn. Nicolo and Mauro stood at the rail as they glided past the Pisan and Genoese docks. The fires were burning out of control in the Pisan quarters and the harbor was crowded with ships trying to avoid the conflagration. Nicolo saw Genoese flags at the mastheads of some of the ships in the flickering half-light of the fire's reflection off the water. He wondered which one carried the recaptured cargo of the *San Giorgio*.

At least I accomplished something good here, he thought soberly. They were headed to Antioch, a fortified Latin kingdom that hung like a barnacle on the coast of a hostile and unknown Muslim empire. He had a sour feeling in his stomach as he realized he knew nothing of the port, nothing of the people, and nothing of the way east from there. He looked over at Mauro, who seemed equally glum. Antonio's words haunted him. They probably didn't need to find Presbyter John for the crusaders to take back Jerusalem. Antonio was going to bring wealth and power to the family. So Nicolo was putting his life and Brother Mauro's life at risk for what? His pride and the desire to gain more money than Antonio? He was using Mauro and his mission for the pope to get to the East for his own gain—and the gain of that crooked cardinal. The old monk trusted him to lead them onward, but Nicolo had been betraying him every step of the way, and now didn't even know where to go.

Down in their cramped cabin, a small oil lantern provided a smoky, dull light. Nicolo propped himself up onto one arm and looked over at Mauro. He had to tell Mauro the truth: they were sailing blind, and he had nothing to offer. He sat up and stared at the monk, who lay in his bunk reading a parchment, as always.

"Brother Mauro, I need to tell you that once we get to Antioch I am totally lost. I didn't have enough time in Constantinople to find a path east. The merchants wouldn't tell me what they knew or simply didn't know anything. I know that I have let you down." Mauro remained on his bunk staring at the parchment. "That means I don't know the way to the lands of Presbyter John. Brother Mauro?"

The monk never took his eyes off the parchment. "Excuse me, you mean Brother John."

"Uh, yes, Brother John."

"Much better." Mauro sat up and looked at Nicolo. "I think after Antioch we might go to Aleppo and then on to Baghdad. From there we must take the old Royal Persian Road to the northeast. That should lead us to the old trade routes." He turned the parchment over, revealing an intricate map. "Look, it is right here."

Nicolo took the map and stared at it for a long time. A small image of a castle stood out among the confusing whorl of lines, drawings, and text. "Ionnes Presbyter." When he looked up, Mauro was smiling broadly. Nicolo realized that he had underestimated Mauro all along, never giving the older man credit for his intelligence and resourcefulness. He would not make that mistake again. He determined to be more attentive and open with the monk, although, of course, he would not reveal his mission to find the source of the spices. They would have six weeks together in that cramped cabin until they reached the Latin kingdom of Antioch. Six weeks to dig deeply into the dense scrawl of the map, considering the wonders of Hind, Sind, and the strange creatures that lurked along the way thither. He felt certain that with this map they would be able to find the kingdom of Presbyter John. He put down the map and looked at the monk with newfound respect.

"Uncle, you truly amaze me."

CHAPTER 11

KARAKORUM

AS THE LAST pulses of life ebbed from William the Physician's shattered body, he sensed the long torture was finally over.

"I pray none will follow me."

His mind didn't register the words mumbled out of a toothless mouth, but the scribes dutifully noted them. They threw powder on their yak skin parchments to set the ink and tapped on the door for Captain Yerzengh. The old horse soldier grunted and ran from the cells to the palace in the light rain. He slipped off his muddy leather boots and donned the clean, soft felt slippers required when entering the abode of his master.

"The cup has been emptied, my lord," Captain Yerzengh whispered as he bent low before the Great Khan. "All that can be gathered has been collected. The work of the scribes is done."

Temujin sniffed the air around his subordinate. Horse sweat mixed with human exertion and fear. He missed those raw odors as he sat in this new palace, surrounded by flowers and perfumed women. Horses meant action, conquest, and the building of an empire. Yet time at the palace was necessary in his new role as Genghis, the Great Khan, the man who pulled together by sheer force of will and arms the disparate tribes of Mongol warriors. It had been twelve cycles of the moon since the European physician William had wandered half-starved into his domain, seeking Presbyter John, the Christian king in the East, on behalf of some potentate in the West—a king called pope. His appearance coincided with the Khan's thoughts of moving west, to conquer the lands beyond the Middle Desert, where the Muslims and Christians held sway. New lands, rich lands. Under the deft hands of the torturers, William provided all the information he knew regarding the society he came from. The scribes recorded everything, from the structures of their armies and their chains of command in civil matters to their religion, their roads, and their architecture. He provided maps of their territories and of their minds. Maps that would be the key to the future invasion of the West.

The Khan moved away from the huge bronze brazier that took the chill off the morning air. His thoughts flew toward a distant, muddy practice field, where he heard men laugh as they rode under the bellies of their horses, shooting arrows at prisoners tied to stakes. *The Christians' slow, steel-covered armies described by William cannot resist ours.* He shook his great head and glanced back at the two rows of military, political, and spiritual advisers who flanked the soft leather cushions he sat on while in morning council. The smoke from the brazier mixed with the light streaming in from the openings in the tile roof, creating a path for all thoughts between heaven and earth.

The Great Khan found many beliefs among the conquered peoples, including Buddhists, Taoists, Muslims, and spirit callers. Christian monks had wandered the grasslands and mountains of the Mongol's world for hundreds of years, converting a few princes and many women in the various clans. The religion was particularly appealing to old men like Togrul, the Ong Khan of the Keraits, who feared the silence of approaching death and was enticed by the Christian promise of a paradise beyond the Eternal Blue Sky. The monks were poor, solitary men who depicted a religion of peace that had neither great armies nor worldly ambitions.

But the Christian kingdom of Rome described by William was different. It was wealthy beyond measure. It controlled massive lands for grazing and agriculture and mines for iron, copper, and silver. William's Christian religion was unlike that of the monks, as well. It seemed complex and foolish to the Khan. *Too many myths, rules, and set prayers. God does not live inside a book or the four walls of some building of stone, no matter how tall and ornate. Even a child knows the Eternal Blue Sky that stretches in all directions is the source of life. Beneath it, the power of the earth, wind, and seas are in a constant motion that any strong soul can harness with the proper intention.* Genghis Khan knew many rituals to call down the favor of the Eternal Blue Sky or simply to acknowledge a man's place under it. His people often borrowed rituals from conquered lands, just as they plundered goods. They kept the rituals that made sense and discarded those that did not. There was nothing he had heard about William's Christian rites that offered anything to him. The weakness of the Christians, it seemed, was their inflexibility and their blind credulity. *It was all centered in Rome. Kill the king called pope and his advisers, level Rome, and the Christians would understand that the Great Khan was the true messenger of god, the Eternal Blue Sky, not that man who had died, came to life again, and disappeared. Then they would follow the Khan and become another conquered people in his growing empire.* It had been five hundred years since the Mongols' ancestors called the Huns, the People of the Sun, had invaded Europe and plundered Rome. They had settled in those lands and disappeared into the cultures of the conquered. *This time it will be different.*

"Bury him with honors according to the rituals he described. Sprinkle mare's milk around his body for his soul's flight. Then convene the Khurultai council. This pope is desperate to join forces with Presbyter John. He will send other emissaries, and we must be ready to receive them." The Khan reached for the letter that William had carried with him all the way from Rome. It was a letter from Presbyter John to the pope flaunting his wealth, his armies, and his desire to aid Rome in the battle for the lands they called "Holy." He closed his massive fists on the parchment, crushing the Christian king's boasts and the Europeans' foolish dreams.

Coming Soon

THE EMERALD SCEPTER

BOOK TWO OF THE EMISSARIES

Printed in Great Britain
by Amazon